Lily Monadjemi was born in Iran. She was educated in England and the United States. She holds a degree in Social Welfare and an M.A. in Educational Psychology. Her previous books have been successfully published in Australia and the U.K. and are entitled *Blood & Carnations* and *A Matter of Survival*.

THE MULBERRY TREE

This is for those who suffer from the consequences of sexual abuse.

Lily Monadjemi

THE MULBERRY TREE

REDARROW
BOOKS

A CIP catalogue record for this title is
available from the British Library.

ISBN 9781844330232

*RedArrow Books is an imprint of
Austin & Macauley Publishers Ltd.*

First Published in 2012

RedArrow Books
CGC-33-01, 25 Canada Square
Canary Wharf, London E14 5LQ

The paper used in this product is grown in sustainable forests

**This book is entirely a work of fiction. All the characters and events
are imaginary creations of the author. Apart from President Ahmadi
Nejad and Mr. Mousavi, any resemblance between these fictional
characters and actual persons, living or dead, is purely coincidental.**

Printed & Bound in Great Britain

The problem of sexual abuse is prevalent in all societies and has never been dealt with effectively – if that is at all possible. Due to the social stigma attached to 'rape', particularly in traditional societies, the victims suffer silently, allowing their internal turmoil to traumatise their lives.

I personally know two victims who have taken me into their confidence. This story reflects their pains, and had it not been for the love and understanding of those who mattered to them, they would have lived in misery for the rest of their lives.

I would like to thank Doctor C. Azimi, a prominent professor of pysychology, for reading the manuscript and checking the accuracy of my statements. My thanks also go to my dear friends Sousan Majidi, Farhad Diba and my husband for their valuable time and helpful suggestions.

Dear Reader, please think of me as Shahrzad, the story-teller. Be my Sultan Harun Al-Rashid, close your eyes and let me take your imagination to à land filled with mysteries.

Chapter 1

A small town by the Caspian Sea – 2nd May 2009

May is a delightful month to be by the Caspian coast. The air is pleasantly cool, the sea breeze tinged with the scent of orange blossoms and the earth beneath a lace of shed pinkie petals that shine like precious pearls. These aromatic gifts of nature soon will be gathered and turned into a delicious jam natives call 'Bahar Narenj'. Spring roses and various bulbs are in bloom competing with the wild flowers that grow relentlessly where the soil is fertile. The majestic Damavand Peak is still snow-capped but the rest of the Alborz range is a vibrant tapestry of wild plants – even thistles are verdant. Within sporadic mountain folds, waterfalls rush in haste to join the various murky rivers that feed the sea – their noise soothing to the soul.

This year, being an election year, Khanum had decided to come to Iran in May rather than as usual in July. Her water-front villa, where she stays when in Iran, is claimed by many as the most gracious residence in the area – an area now occupied by enterprising investors who, earlier had purchased their properties cheaply from one Foundation or another, responsible for confiscations from the original owners who allegedly had been deemed 'corrupters on earth', or were Jewish or Bahai! The income of these lucrative foundations, even today, finds its way into the coffers of the Revolutionary Guard Corps (RGC), the members of which have taken up influential positions in almost all of the important sectors of society.

Khanum, unlike her neighbours, comes from the 'one thousand' ruling clans of the Imperial era – persecuted during and after the 1979 Revolution. This property had also been confiscated and had it not been for her persistent appeals to various committees and influential clerics, it would have been devoured like everything else her parental family had owned in Iran.

Khanum had two sisters who had emigrated to the States before the political troubles surfaced in Iran. After the death of their parents when she offered to buy their shares of this inherited estate and all the problems that went with it, they smiled at lady luck.

During the heat of the Revolution, the local Komiteh being informed of the death of the owners had the property appropriated for the Foundation of the Emmam giving the new claimants one year to present themselves to the Foundation, prove themselves innocent of possible charges, pay Khoms a compulsory religious fife plus certain accumulated monthly expenditure in lieu of the Foundation's maintenance of the property, before they could regain their deeds.

Bureaucratic work in Iran has always been strenuous. Unnecessary obstacles have to be overcome through relationships and under-the-table gifts. Over time, it has become worse – without paying every individual whose signature is required, nothing can be achieved.

It took Khanum much hassle and expense to regain the ownership of the pride of her life – this precious souvenir of the past, when her family was intact, Iran prosperous and the majority of the people content. Against all advice, she commissioned a famous architect and together they managed to come up with a unique plan that gave every room both views of the Alborz mountains in the south and the sea in the north with a very high void that wound up to a pointed dome encased by clear windows through which the moon could be seen making its round.

The Caspian is a polluted sea. The rivers that run into it carry the sewage waste of the adjacent towns and villages and only God knows what the neighbouring countries feed into it. Before the disintegration of the USSR the Caspian shore belonged to only two countries. Now the new independent states have become partners in the ownership of the coast, the waterway and its fisheries. On the Iranian side, for unknown reasons, the sea level has risen so high that, to preserve the land not already under water, most costal property owners have had to construct massive dams.

Within the last twenty years, most beaches have disappeared and swimming in some areas has become next to impossible. Besides, for women to swim clothed was something that did not appeal to Khanum. Therefore she built a huge indoor heated pool, a fully equipped gym and a sauna. She loved swimming and sunbathing. That is why she only visited the property during the summer months when she could spread her bamboo mat on the lawn and then follow the sun around to bake her body bronze. She loved the sun and it seemed to love her back, for its rays never harmed the purity of her olive skin – only tanned it and made her even more beautiful than she was. People who knew her joked about her persisting beauty and called her a female Dorian Grey.

It had been such a long time since she had stayed at her villa in the spring that she had forgotten how stunning her garden had now become. She was enchanted to see that her various citrus and other fruit trees were exotically in bloom and the two triangular flowerbeds that bordered the main building's impressive entrance, packed with tulips, tuberoses, narcissus and violets in orderly rows. She noticed that, amongst this perfection, some wild poppies had decided to impose their own order and guessed Mohammad had found them so pretty that he had let them be – even if he stood to be reprimanded by his pedantic mistress. She smiled at his audacity and admired his judgement. She observed, with joyous surprise, that just before the gravel path that ran in front of the entrance several mature jasmine

17

bushes had spread their branches like yellow umbrellas. She could not recall having ever seen them dressed in any other colour than green. However she remembered well how beautiful were the four huge majestic magnolia trees she called the Four Sisters, when in flower exuding their sweet scent particularly at night. They guarded the front of the huge guest house in which no one had as yet lived and probably would never live while the house belonged to this twice-widowed barren woman who loved her country so much, in spite of all the hardship she had endured.

The place she loved to use most in this house was the wide veranda that ran across the northern side of the white-washed building. It faced an expansive weed-free lawn that led to tightly boxed rose beds behind which ran a wide pebble path constructed to absorb the salty splashes that poured in through the wire fence when the waves went wild. No concrete construction was visible behind the old tall ferns, cypresses, magnolias, mimosas and evergreen creepers, particularly the honeysuckles and white jasmines that had conquered the length and the breadth of the surrounding walls. Around the lawn were more flower beds with roses in tiny buds, irises in bloom and parsley sown to avoid weeds. Separating the lawn from the veranda was a wide crowded stretch of large hydrangea beds that remained colourful throughout summer. On the left of the garden was another tight, neatly-trimmed box hedge from among which stood a huge mulberry tree like a sore thumb. Khanum tried to avoid looking at it, for it gave her the creeps and goose pimples. In fact she hated it, but more than hating the tree, she detested hurting, and for her cutting the tree meant inflicting pain on a living entity – so to her annoyance the tree stood erect and provided the domestics and their friends with plenty of juicy, sweet white berries.

It was carrying a tray of this fruit that Shahri entered the veranda. She was dressed in her usual long, black cotton skirt, cotton pullover, and a white polyester scarf tied in the back of her long hennaed hair, in the twisted turban like-style women of the north wear their head covers. She found Khanum dressed in a white silk kaftan, resembling an angel, sitting very composed behind her computer staring at its blue screen thinking the nostalgic thoughts that manoeuvred in her mind when in this paradise. She did not hear the maid enter.

Shahri, as was her habit, whispered "Ya Allah", which means 'in the name of God', a polite way to announce one's presence.

Jerked out of her trance Khanum turned up her large black eyes and saw the tray that was being put in front of her on the large opaque glass dining table. Dismay spread over her pleasant countenance and her stomach churned with disgust. She pinched her shapely nose, and through her tinted spectacles glared into the round, glittering, grey eyes of Shahri, and sharply gesturing with her hand said, "Take this away. You know I never eat mulberries."

"But why Khanum – they are full of vitamins. And this year, God be praised, there are large and as sweet as honey."

"Yes they are nutritious, but they make me sick – so never again bring mulberries for me. You eat them," she paused, and then with a kind smile that intended to rectify the unnecessary harshness in her voice added, "In moderation Shahri. They are fattening and you do not want to put any more weight on. If you are not careful, one of these days Mohammad will take another wife!"

Habitually amiable Shahri smiled, lifted her arched thinly plucked eyebrows and replied, "He will never find anyone better than me."

"No, I assume not. You are pretty, much younger and a very good cook," Khanum said in a teasing tone. Then added, "You are right. He cannot find anyone better than you."

With a smile still tilting on her radiant round face, Shahri nodded her agreement, thanked her mistress for the compliment, picked up the tray to leave when Khanum asked, "Where is Nargess? I am waiting for her to come and resume her English lesson."

"She hasn't returned from school yet. Today she had religious studies and Agha, God bless his soul, has offered to spend a bit more time helping her so that she can pass her exam with a good mark."

Suspicious of all men, a morbid current ran through Khanum's mind. An eyebrow raised she enquired, "How come a man is teaching the girls?"

"He is a clergyman. Men of God are fathers to our girls."

"Let us hope so. Your daughter is a smart young lady and does not need extra help. I wish your son was as studious."

"I know what you mean, Khanum, but Taghi is good at gardening. He is a great help to his father."

"If you stop him from being hooked to your television set, he might do better at school."

"I swear by God and hope to die if I lie – I turn the television off when he is in the room."

Khanum threw her a bemused glance and forged a frown. "I do not want you to die; so don't lie to me Shahri. What I say is for the good of your son. Follow my advice, you won't regret it. Taghi is a bit slow and needs to spend a lot more time studying than his sister."

Tired of being lectured, Shahri announced her obedience with a loud, "Chashm Khanum", then asked if she should bring tea.

"That is a very good idea. Make sure it is still hot when it arrives."

Glad to get away, the maid, swinging her large bottom

20

left the veranda for her quarters of which she was very proud and in which she felt safe and content. She loved her open kitchen and modern shower room which she kept immaculately clean. When the new building went up, to Mohammad's delight, the domestic quarter was also renovated and fitted with all the modern electrical appliances that took Shahri almost six months to get used to and now she couldn't do without.

The house had two kitchens, one for the domestics and one in the main building, and as brewing a tasty tea takes time and requires patience and Khanum had neither, Shahri was in charge – and her tea was indeed strong and aromatic.

Iranians are very pedantic about the quality, taste and colour of their tea – to serve an insipid colourless tea is a sign of the hostess being undomesticated. Khanum did not care much for tea but nevertheless, in her house, everything had to be made to perfection.

Alone again, she turned her computer on and began to check her emails.

Suddenly the telecom sounded. She rose, crossed the open kitchen to the dining area, the winter room that boasted of a huge fireplace, and then the entrance hall brightly lit by shafts of sun pouring in through a pair of south-facing windows, splashing over the travertine floor and bouncing back like fire tongues.

"Yes?"

"Khanum, Agha Ali is here," Shahri informed her.

Khanum glanced at her watch and, amused, said, "He is on time for once! Let him in."

Hearing the sound of Ali's car rambling down the gravelled drive way she opened the huge oak-door and stepped out to welcome her steward in charge of the running of her affairs here.

Ali was an honest young man with a head on his narrow shoulders. To be clever and honest in Iran had become quite

21

a rarity so Khanum valued his service and was very careful not to offend him in any way.

Son of a gardener, he had put himself through university and had become a successful building contractor. Khanum trusted him so much that she had opened a joint bank account with him and left enough money in the account for the estate's annual expenditure and more. Ali was her eyes and ears and, because he was so popular and trustworthy, he knew everything that happened along the extensive coast and he also knew who was on the take and how much the solution of each obstacle cost. So in his briefcase bundles of cash took more space than anything else.

A devotee, he did all the shopping for Khanum so that she did not have to venture out of the house. Outside was a world foreign to her – there, he knew she felt like a fish out of water – that is how drastically attitudes and behaviour had changed since the Revolution – but inside time had stood still. Within her four walls she felt happy and relaxed. Her vegetables and herbs came from a huge well-planned kitchen garden, her fruit what the garden seasonally offered and her eggs from the chickens that sauntered around and provided ample manure for Mohammad to throw in the garden refuse pit for use in the spring.

Ali, as thin as Mahatma Gandhi, dressed in his usual jeans and a crisp white shirt, smiling broadly stretched his long bony hand to greet Khanum – something not done with a female in the Islamic Republic. Khanum ignored the gesture; put her arm around his erect shoulders as though he was her son and guided him to the veranda – followed by Shahri and her tea tray. Somewhere from behind the bushes Mohammad emerged with his wheelbarrow overflowing with weeds and cuttings – his wide black pants muddy and his shirt wet with sweat.

"Mohammad come and have tea with us." Khanum called out.

Another skeleton of a man, he smiled at his egalitarian mistress and pronouncing his 'Ya Allah', climbed the sparkling travertine steps, walked to the table and stood waiting to be asked to sit. He loved his tea – and Shahri made sure he drank plenty.

"You may sit down, Mohammad." Khanum commanded before asking Shahri to bring the plate of cookies that was always on the kitchen's green granite top waiting for visitors. She enjoyed hosting the town's folk who paid her genuine respect. They knew her well. They knew that she was not a parvenu and that was very important to her. In spite of her Western education, she was very traditional and traditional people believe in "respect" and "respectability".

Ali took his usual place next to Khanum facing the sparkling blue sea that joined the horizon, becoming one with the spotless sky. Comfortably settled in his seat, he looked at her with glittering eyes, gave her a proud smile and said, "Khanum, today I have interesting news for you."

"Why have you not shaved today?" Khanum asked, her tone teasing, her meaning taunting. She hated looking at spiky hair on men who could look clean and tidy otherwise. She had read the Koran both in English and Persian and nowhere had she read that Muslim men must grow beards, nor had she read that they had to shave – so she had concluded the task was a matter of choice. People always did things to please the authorities and this was one of them, she assumed albeit distastefully.

Ali, aware of her preference, offered his excuse, "I did not have time this morning, besides a little black bristle on the face opens many doors!"

Khanum smiled at his presence of mind and teased, "I knew you were conniving – but not this much! Ok, tell us your news."

Mohammad lifted a saucer with its tea glass from the tray and placed it in front of their guest. Ali was not a great eater but he too loved his tea and biscuits.

"Mohammad, offer Ali Khan some cookies."

"Chashm, Khanum."

As Mohammad made a move to serve, Ali motioned him to stay put, stretched across the table, took two jam cookies, fitted one over the other on the side of his saucer and then took two sugar cubes and gently dropped them into his tea glass. While stirring the tea with a teaspoon he took a deep breath through his long straight nose and began, "Yesterday they put the Mayor of Kelarabad in a large empty rice sack and carried him away."

Khanum's curious eyes widened. Surprised by the absurdity of the information she asked, "Who and why?"

"The men from the Ministry of Information; who else?"

"Ya them!" she exclaimed her tone sarcastic.

"The Mayor, like most mayors, was on the "take". However being young and naïve he was living off his money and throwing his weight around. People began to whisper, particularly when the Municipality accepted the plan for the new hotel within a week. These things usually take months. If you remember we had to go to our Municipality twenty times before our permit was granted."

Recalling the ordeals she had been through, Khanum shook her head several times before saying, "I will never forget how hard we had to work and the thousands of toomans I had to pay to that good for nothing clerk, Agha Ahmadi'. She stopped, sipped at her tea before it got cold and then asked, "Well, did they catch him red-handed?"

"Yes Khanum and how! I have it first-hand from his assistant who is married to my second cousin by marriage."

Ali stopped, took a bite from his biscuit, washed it down with hurried sips of tea and then resumed, "A few weeks ago, a man who, apparently, had recently purchased the water-front land on the right side of the hotel had gone to the Municipality to apply for a home building permit. There he had been told he couldn't build on waterfront land unless it was for commercial purposes. Disappointed, he had demanded to see the Mayor himself. After many days of waiting in the corridor, he had managed to have a private audience during which, after a long testing dialogue, he had been told his case had to be referred to the Town's Council which, jointly with the Mayor, would decide whether they could grant him the permit or not. Then he was told to return on the following Saturday. During the second meeting he was made to understand that the permit would cost him ten Samand cars. The guy had expressed his inability to provide the cars but had assured the Mayor he could give fifty million toomans, the sum equivalent to the market value of ten Samands. They had shaken hands on the deal and he was told to return the following Wednesday. Yesterday being Wednesday they met in the Mayor's office; the applicant gave the Mayor a suitcase full of cash in return for his signed building permit. As soon as he left the Municipality, the Secret Service men who must have been watching him, went inside and straight to the Mayor's office, seized the cash case, handcuffed the baffled man, shoved him into a large rice sack which they carried out and fitted in the back of a van and drove him to the town's prison where they lodged him in an isolated cell. I have heard so far he has confessed to having received ten billion toomans in bribes."

"This is incredible!" Khanum exclaimed while fiddling with the biscuit crumbs on her plate.

Mohammad who had finished his tea and biscuit shook his head, exhaled a heavy sigh and wistfully said, more to himself than to his audience,

"God curse them all. I cannot put meat in front of my children, even once a month, while there is so much money in the hands of corrupt people."

Khanum, always on guard in front of the domestics,

interrupted,

"Well it seems the government has stepped up its battle against corruption."

No one made a comment. Then Ali turned to Mohammad and asked if he had already collected his Saham-e-Edalat (Justice Shares) which this year had been handed out two months before its due date – the eve of Norooz, (the Iranian New Year day). Surprised Mohammad asked him what Saham-e-Edalat was. Ali cleared his throat and explained, "Saham-e-Edalat are shares issued by the government to distribute part of the oil revenue amongst the people, particularly the poor and the retirees. Each adult is entitled to one million toomans (1000 dollars) worth of the shares which are unredeemable for two years and give an annual dividend of eight percent paid before Norooz. They are first sent to the needy, those on Social Insurance and the retirees." He paused, threw a glance at Khanum to judge her reaction. Her attentive eyes caught his and thrilled him – her opinion mattered to him a lot. Satisfied, he took a sharp bite from his second cookie, closed his eyes to enjoy its taste and without wanting to wash it away with a sip of tea he looked at Mohammad and said, "You qualify, so take all of your family's identity cards to the Saham-e-Edalat bureau at the local council's office and for each card receive eighty thousand toomans."

A broad smile brightened Mohammad's stern face, revealing three missing front teeth. He thanked Ali profusely and asked permission to leave in the morning to chase his shares.

Khanum granted him consent, thought for a long time, and then turned to Ali. "This is an excellent endearing ploy especially during an election year – good way of buying votes – my God he is clever!" she exclaimed, banging the table with her fist – deeply agitated by the political connivance.

Ali pursed his thin lips, shook his balding head, and said, "The share-offering started last year and it took ten months before people received their due dividends. This year's order from the Ministry of the Interior to the banks was to start payment two months before Norooz and the speed with which the order was carried out was incredible. This delighted the needy and made them grateful to the President."

Khanum shook her head and replied, "Of course it would delight them. Our President is very clever. He has already started his election campaigning."

Both men let out a loud wistful sigh and Ali, shaking his index finger in the air, exclaimed, "No matter what he does, this year there will be a change of government. No one is building any more, our youth are unemployed, and hardworking people like Mohammad cannot put meat in front of their families."

Khanum, knowing that Ali only thought about his pocket, gave him a long meaningful look and said, "Let us pray for what is best for Iran to happen enshallah."

"Enshallah" had become the most used word in conversations, for people had no choice but put their hope in God – the only saviour they could count on.

"Khanum do you have any orders for me?"

"Yes Ali. Please buy me a lamb to sacrifice on Thursday evening so that Mohammad can put meat in front of his family." Khanum diverted her teasing gaze at Mohammad who went crimson in the face.

Too embarrassed to stay, he rose, murmured, "I have a lot to do before it gets dark," and walked down the stairs towards his wheelbarrow.

"Khanum salam," Taghi said appearing from the right side of the building, with the legs of his pants unevenly folded up, holding a running hose. He had come to wash the floor and the steps that led to the gravel path and the lawn.

His face was as calm as ever and his smile as innocent as his mind.

"Salam Taghi. How was school today?"

"Khanum you wouldn't believe it if I told you. I was chosen from among twenty of my classmates to be honoured with the title of Basiji!"

The smile froze on her radiant face and Ali's joint brows knitted tight.

"Congratulations." Khanum forced herself to say. Then she turned to Mohammad who was about to push his wheelbarrow towards the pit at the end of the garden and commanded, "Come and see me when you finish your chore." The stern tone worried the gardener. He responded with a loud, "Chashm Khanum," and began pushing his heavy load towards its target.

Suddenly a deafening noise broke out from above and all eyes turned towards the three helicopters flying side by side, their shadows gliding over the silver waves.

"Khanum, Khanum, these choppers belong to the President. We were told he was coming to visit our Province to hear the people's grievances and relieve the poor from their poverty," Taghi shouted in his cracked, effeminate voice, pointing to the helicopters with the hand that held the jetting hose. Suddenly a heavy rain fell over the table and Khanum's head. Bemused at the boy's enthusiasm, maintaining her calm she said, "That is wonderful. Now, please direct the hose towards the grass before we are all soaked."

"I am so very sorry, Khanum," a panicked Taghi cried out, dropping the hose and rushing inside to fetch a towel. The hose coiled around itself like a scared boa before resting its nozzle towards the open glass door of the kitchen. Ali jumped off his seat, grabbed the hose and pulling it hard threw it down from the edge of the veranda onto the ground below. Just then Taghi returned, towel in hand, profusely apologising.

Khanum shaking away the water from her kaftans, took the towel from him, dried her hair and face, threw the towel on the table; then ordered him to quickly finish his errand and run back to his room to study.

Then resuming a grave air, she guided Ali to the summer room which was encased by wall-to-wall glass windows exposing an extensive view of the garden and the sea melting into the horizon.

"I will change later. Let us sit here and wait for Mohammad. I don't think he knows what his son is in for – becoming a Basiji! All I need is to have a spy in my house!"

Ali, hesitatingly scratched his head, fidgeted in his seat and said,

"Khanum be careful of what you say. These days you never know whom you can trust. He might be one himself."

"I don't think so. He has too many mouths to feed to think of dedicating his life to a "cause" he would never understand. Look he is coming now."

By the door Mohammad kicked off his wet flip-flops, wiped his moist feet on the mat, walked in and stood still – his heart thumping with anxiety.

"Close the door and come and sit down," Khanum ordered in such a stern tone that made Mohammad's tanned face turn pale. They all knew how harsh she could become.

"Why did you not tell us Taghi has become a Basiji?" Ali asked looking straight at the anxiety-ridden man's face.

"I did not think much of it, Agha Ali?"

"Do you know what it means to be a Basiji?" Khanum interrupted.

"All I know is that it is an honour to become one."

Khanum shook her head in denial.

"Basijis are a paramilitary force with total dedication to the regime. They are dedicated to fundamentalist values and trained to obey orders without question. Those orders might entail wrapping a bomb around their waists to blow themselves up killing the alleged enemies of the regime. Do you want such a thing happen to your son?" asked Khanum leaning across the coffee table towards the gardener whose eyes were down-cast and his thin cracked fingers so intertwined that his white knuckles seemed about to protrude out. A few moments of heavy silence dragged on before Mohammad, eager to save his job, lifted his head up, looked intently into Khanum's questioning eyes and said, "Thank you for educating me. I shall do something so that he himself tears up that certificate they have given him."

A heavy burden lifted from her shoulders, Khanum relaxed her posture and released a heavy sigh of relief.

"That is what I wanted to hear from you, but do it in a gentle diplomatic way and be careful. You never know what they ask these kids to do. And from now on, I don't want Taghi to enter the villa or be around while I am swimming or sunbathing."

"Chashm Khanum."

Ali also relieved asked, "Can you slaughter the lamb or shall I commission a butcher?"

"I can do it myself."

"Ali I don't want you to bring the lamb here. Please have it slaughtered in the grounds of your local mosque, bring Mohammad's share to him and give the rest to the poor."

"Chashm, Khanum," Ali said, rising to leave.

Khanum walked him to his car, then turned to Mohammad and said, "Be careful with your son. He is gullible and naïve. He needs love, attention and constant supervision."

"God be thanked that you are our patroness."

"Go now and cut me a bunch of tuberoses. I have nothing that smells good in the house. What a pity that the white jasmines are not out yet."

"Chashm, Khanum. The jasmines come out early summer."

Left alone Khanum turned to her computer. It was dead. Frustrated she rose and turned the light on. It was dead. No electricity again.

"And we don't need nuclear power! I like this to happen in a Western home – everyday – no electricity – no TV, no fridge, no heater – nothing – in a country with seventy million people!" Khanum sighed before walking to the indoor swimming room, unzipping her Kaftan and diving into the pool.

Chapter 2

The same evening

She was standing on the edge of her dam, lost in the sweet melancholy of dusk, a cool breeze brushing her long curly hair away from her tranquil face as she enjoyed the rhythm of the waves teasing the sloping stone barrier. She had already seen the sun gracefully retire, leaving the sky all pink from its passage, dabbed with gold dust; and from below her feet to eternity the Caspian without a wrinkle, without a shiver, smooth, still shining under the dying light, seemed an enormous sheet of polished metal. She turned her gaze at the moon-lit sky thinking of the past and the way things had changed – at the same time changing her from a frightened insecure child to what she had become.

She loved the dusk – for her it signified an end that would lead to a new beginning – like the course her life had taken so far.

Nature had a captivating effect on her. Here – alone – with only its trophies as her companions she felt happy. Very happy – but never carefree! The events of her life had made her intensely socially conscious. In this wide world, where her two sisters were as good as dead to her, she had no one except God. He was her friend and protector. To please him she not only gave of her money but of herself to worthy causes. For her altruistic love was part and parcel of being a conscientious human being. The more evil she saw in the world the more convinced she became there was a purpose to life. So she lived trying to find and fulfil that purpose.

Suddenly the breeze became gusty, a passing cloud momentarily hid the moon and the sea disappeared in the grip of darkness. Folding her arms in front of her chest to warm herself, she dashed back to the villa, locked all the doors from inside, made herself a vodka lime, spread some hummus she had made herself on a piece of fresh Barbari bread, put her plate on a colourfully hand-crafted wooden tray and went to the TV room to watch the Voice of America. She liked to hear what the Opposition had to say – of course, all wishful thinking she thought! Nothing could destabilize the Islamic Republic and its champions. They had already established their roots deep and spread their tentacles long and wide. With the backing of dedicated Revolutionary Guards and a devoted Basiji force to silence opposition, plus the regular handouts to the poor by the Bureau of the Emmam and the President himself, they were well in control of the country. Yet Khanum refused to give up hope. The voice in her head kept whispering perhaps and only perhaps in the coming election the vote of the people would be counted correctly and a moderately liberal president would be elected. After all, the candidates were all handpicked by The Council of The Guardians, and were from within the system so there would be no reason for dishonest counting – as it had been since the Pahlavi reign.

Half an hour into the program the electricity went off again. It was good that the moon had come out of hiding. Its shafts glowed through the glass that encircled the dome of the void romantically illuminating the space directly below it. Khanum went to the kitchen where on a shelf stood her several oil burner lamps and candelabras. She swore at whoever was responsible for this miserable state, nervously lit one of the oil burners and took it up to her bedroom. There she lit two candles in wooden candelabra which had a permanent place on her desk and together with the oil burner placed on the bedside table, gave enough light enabling her to solve puzzles in bed – when there was nothing else to do.

Grumbling under her breath she carried one of the

candelabras to her bathroom, put it on the vanity top, took a shower, put her white cotton night-dress on and heard Mohammad, presumably holding his torch lock the security shutters from the outside.

It was only half past eight and the evening was too young to draw the curtains and retire to bed. So she took the oil lamp, stepped onto the balcony of her bedroom, pulled out one of the six white plastic chairs that were around a large rectangular matching table, sat down gazing at the sea that changed hue as the waves left their fluffy, white foam on the barriers and rushed back. The moon had moved away and now was on the other side but the sky, profoundly blue, was dotted with silver stars. She could see the twinkling lights of the shore that stretched out on both sides of her balcony. Memories returned. She closed her eyes and let her imagination take her to the good times – when life seemed secure and everlasting – when Iran was hers and when no one had died yet and then suddenly the garden lights blinked on and she remembered she had left the TV and the lights on downstairs. She put her dressing gown on and walked down the stairs to turn everything off when she heard Shahri's screams. She dashed to the entrance door, unlocked it, and ran to the domestic quarters. Screams were becoming louder and louder as she approached their residence. Now Taghi's cry of Baba Baba could be heard too. She climbed the few steps to the porch, opened the door and saw Shahri gripping Mohammad's raised right arm that was waving a butcher's knife – his face an ugly mask of hate. In front of him humped Nargess her long skirt tucked beneath her narrow bottom, her face covered by her tiny hands, softly crying. Taghi was holding his father's other arm and repeating: "Baba Baba."

Shocked Khanum screamed, "What has happened? Mohammad drop the knife. Have you gone insane man? Have you?"

No one uttered a word. Mohammad wiggling aimlessly tried to free his arms from the tight grips of his wife and son. Foamed saliva oozed out from the right corner of his twitching mouth. Suddenly he let the knife drop, freed his arms with a quick twist, knelt down, covered his face with his large hands and began to howl, his thin shoulders shaking like tremors of an earthquake. Khanum knelt by him, put her arms around his quivering back, and waited for him to pour out his anguish. Shahri, tears running down her colourless face bent down, took the knife, disappeared behind the kitchen partition and returned with a glass of fridge water. She knelt on the floor, stroked her husband's grey hair and whispered: "Drink this, Agha."

Mohammad lifted his head up, threw her a quick pathetic glance, took the glass, drank all its content, and handed it back to her. Then with his chapped fingers he wiped his tears and his nose, dried his hand on his trousers without a single word. His eyes were open but saw nothing except the dark catacomb of shame in which he was buried.

Khanum waited in silence. She had already guessed what might have happened to the girl. She felt faint and then nauseated. She rose, stepped out, bent towards the pavement and allowed a surge of bitter sour bile spur out, burning her throat and tongue. She squatted on the tiled porch, as lifeless as a statue. Shocked, her mind felt numbed.

The moon was still shining but had lost its glory. Zombie-like she rose, ambled to the hose tap, nervously detached the hose, turned the tap on and washed her face. The cold water calmed her a little. She wiped her face with the edge of her dressing gown's loose sleeve and walked back to the gloomy room in which only the sound of sadness could be heard. She sat on the floor by the foursome and waited. The grief was too profound to break.

Khanum, turned her questioning eyes to the father, then the mother and then the girl who had stopped crying but kept her head immersed in the folds of her bony arms that rested on her knees.

"Nargess, go and take a shower and change," Khanum ordered in a kind but firm tone. The girl instantly rose, sniffed her nose several times and sauntered towards the corridor that led to their shower room.

"Mohammad, may I have a private word with Nargess please?" Mohammad furrowed his thick greying eye brows, spat on the carpet with disgust and waving his hand in the air said, "My Nargess is dead. This slut is not my daughter. I will kill her for the shame she has brought to my name." Khanum felt his pain, gently patted his back and said, "Mohammad one doesn't punish a victim, one punishes the criminal."

"Khanum is right. Enshallah Khanum will find a way to wipe away our shame – trust her. She knows how to deal with everything. This is what you have been telling me all the time. So believe in it yourself," Shahri uttered in a soothing yet emphatic tone. In her own way, as illiterate as she was, she always came out with the right statement at the right time.

"She doesn't bear Khanum's name. It is my name she has stained."

"What is more important to you, your name or your daughter?"

Burst out Khanum losing her patience.

"My honour – a man without honour is less than a stray dog."

"Yes honour is important. An honourable man is a good man. A good man is patient and forgiving. A murderer is not an honourable man but a coward – are you a coward?"

Mohammad, traumatized and overwhelmed became irritated by Khanum's logical statements which he always had to listen to and abide by. For the first time in years of service he snapped back, "Khanum you have a way with

36

words – words and words. For once please stop giving advice and be a human being rather than an iceberg."

The outburst hurt the woman whose intentions had always been benign. Yet she let it pass.

"At the moment you are highly emotional, Mohammad. I am going to take Nargess to sleep in the villa with me. You rest and get your calm back. Tomorrow when we are all in charge of our faculties we can talk again and together we will find a solution – a sane one to our problem – remember – as long as you live under my roof, your problem is also mine."

Lost for words, Mohammad covered his face and began to weep again.

At that moment Nargess returned. Khanum rose took her hand and together they walked to the villa.

Inside, Khanum turned the electrical kettle on, from the tea container, took two chamomile tea bags, dropped them in a porcelain tea pot which she placed on a try with two tea glasses and the biscuit dish. The kettle forcefully jetting out its steam turned itself off. She poured the boiling water into the tea pot, took the tray and walked to the sitting room. Mute, shamefaced and pensive the girl followed her like a prisoner going to the inquisition chamber.

"Come here and sit next to me, Nargess joon."

She obeyed, shivering in spite of the pleasant room temperature. Khanum gently pulled her towards herself, wrapped her arms around her, stroked her scarved head that was resting on her chest and kissed it several times. Time reverted decades back – another girl – another cry – another self-detestation.

The clock ticked away.

The girl stopped trembling.

Khanum unfolded her arms and looked into her red swollen eyes with compassion and understanding.

"Can you tell me what happened – everything – from

the beginning to the end?"

"I am ashamed."

"You can only be ashamed if you have done something wrong. Have you?"

"Yes Khanum. I am guilty of vanity."

"Vanity! What does that mean?"

"I wanted to be distinguished from among my classmates – that is why I let myself be fooled."

What maturity in a teenager. Khanum thought with admiration.

"Tell me who fooled you, dear."

Nargess recalling the man's contorted face inflicting pain on her began to shiver again.

Khanum allowed her time.

The waves had gone mad now and their howl was breaking the silence of the room. Nargess pushed the memory away, swallowed the lump in her throat, looked through the window at the endless darkness and whispered, "God curse his soul – Agha Abolfazl." Her hand shaking Khanum poured the tea spilling some on the saucer. She put the pot down, took a biscuit and put it on a plate which she placed in front of the girl. She pulled a tissue from its box and handing it to her softly ordered, "Wipe the saucer and the bottom of your tea glass."

The girl did as requested.

"Drink the tea, it will calm you."

Nargess, pulled a new tissue from the box, with it wiped her face, blew her straight rather long nose inherited from her father into it and automatically shoved the crumbled moist tissues under her sleeve. Slowly she took the tea glass, drank its content and devoured the biscuit – like a hungry beggar. Khanum put two more biscuits on the plate. She ate those too – hunger or nerves or perhaps both Khanum surmised.

Energized the girl released a sigh of satisfaction, feeling

38

a bit at ease she fixed her eyes on the floor travertine and began fidgeting with the end of her sleeve. "I am waiting, Nargess."

"Yesterday Agha told me he wants to take a few of us to Emmamzadeh Asghar's shrine and let us experience heaven – this had to be kept a secret as he did not want the other students to think he has favourites. I couldn't quite understand what he meant. So I asked him how can one experience heaven while alive. He told me to trust him and if I wanted to do well in my exam and get twenty out of twenty I had to abide by his rules. This afternoon, he asked four of us to get into his car. I was glad to have company. Then I noticed he dropped each one of the others by their homes as he often did and I was the only one being taken to the Emmamzadeh. I asked him why he was not taking the others. He said I was the only true believer so only I had to experience heaven. He parked the car in the parking of the shrine's ground, took a picnic rug from the boot of his car, and asked me to follow him. I thought we would be going inside the shrine. But he walked towards the forest that surrounds the shrine. We walked deep into the woods and reached an expansion by which ran a brook. He spread the rug on the grass, asked me to sit down. I did. He went to the brook, took his shoes and socks off, made an ablution, found a stone, returned, and put the stone on the rug and facing Mecca performed his afternoon prayer – a very short one. Then he took his turban and cloak off, sat by me, put his arms around me and pulled me to him kissing my face and lips whispering he was purifying me for my entrance to heaven. Then he went wild, he nailed me down with one hand and with his other hand he untied the rope of his pantaloon which slipped down his legs and I saw his large 'thing' protrude out. Suddenly I realized what was happening to me. I tried to rise but his hand glued me to the ground. Then furiously he pulled my pants down, climbed over me and tried to force himself into me. Kicking and twisting I fought as hard as I could but he was too strong for me. With his hand and 'thing' he inflicted so much pain on me that I lost consciousness and next I knew he opened the car door and pushed me out by our gate whispering if I uttered a word about what had happened I would meet with eternal fire of hell here on earth. The strange thing was that he was crying all the time that he was abusing me. Khanum, I swear to the life of my parents this is the honest truth."

Nargess paused and noticed she had torn the fabric of her sleeve. Bewildered, she raised her sad eyes to Khanum who had been looking at the bruises around her mouth, eyes, cheek, hands and neck.

"You must have put out a good fight against that brute."

"If I had, he wouldn't have been able to disgrace me Khanum joon."

"You couldn't possibly win against a beast, my child."

Khanum pulled the girl to her chest, patted her shoulders gently and whispered: "I will make him pay for this. I will make him pay."

"God! I have brought shame to my family. I am as worthless as an ant," Nargess exclaimed her eyes wide with exasperation.

"No, no, no. You must not think that way my child. You have done nothing to be ashamed of. You have been victimized and that is all there is to it. Believe me, worth of a woman – a human being does not depend on her virginity. The idea is a démodé cultural bullshit. Being lecherous is sinful; being unfaithful is sinful but being raped is not the same. Rape is a sexual assault that physically and mentally traumatizes the victim. You are an innocent victim of a criminal act. You must not allow yourself to feel guilty or ashamed. You have done nothing wrong. I can have the virginity problem fixed with ease. Just promise me and yourself stop feeling dirty."

The girl, like a statue of gloom looked at Khanum with lethargic eyes without hearing a word of what she was saying. Her mouth agape she slowly turned her eyes to the darkness into which Caspian had melted. How does she know I feel dirty? She asked herself before collapsing sideway on the sofa. The recall had exhausted her endurance. Khanum gently pulled her towards herself and then lifted her up and slowly carried her to the downstairs' bedroom. There she laid her on the bed, took her shoes off, and covered her with the neatly folded duvet that lay on the edge of the bed. Tenderly she pushed away a smudged string of hair from over her closed eyes, lightly kissed her narrow forehead and left the room, letting the door remain open in case the girl woke up with a nightmare. She returned to the sofa and noticed a wide blood stain where the girl had sat.

"The bastard has done that too. Crying while raping? What kind of a creep is this one?" Mumbling to herself she aimed for her bedroom. There she sat on her bed holding her head that was about to burst with tension. A few minutes passed without the pain subsiding. Now she couldn't even open her eyes. Slowly she rose, with one hand holding her head, eyes half closed, walked to the medicine cabinet in the bathroom, took a painkiller and a sleeping pill which she swallowed with the help of water from the tap. She splashed her face with handfuls of cold water, took several deep breaths, slipped her dressing gown off, hung it on the door peg, returned to her bedroom and crept into bed muttering incoherent sentences – that perhaps meant something to her – and only her.

Chapter 3

A weekend in the spring of 1951 – Niavaran

Mashhadi Mosayeb, the old hunch-backed gatekeeper was sitting on a chair as old as himself, placed on the narrow porch of his comfortable lodging, patiently minding the open gate. It was unsafe to leave the gate open nowadays with the well-diggers roaming around instead of working the wells that supposedly irrigated the estate – it seemed they were always clogged with something or other – very unusual for such deep wells. His guess was that the diggers did not do a good job so that they could remain employed. There were three robberies only last month. Mashhadi Mosayeb himself had caught one thief with a mount of rice dangling from inside the large pockets of his dirty black pantaloon, slithering out through the closed door of the provision room which an ass had left unlocked! Wiggling to free himself, the crook had cried and begged not to be handed over to the gendarmerie or Bagher Khan whose ferocious temper was known by all. Mosayeb's kind heart had taken pity on him but not before a few sharp slaps landing on his pock-marked face and telling him how lucky he had been for not having been caught by Bagher Khan who would have cut him into pieces like the weekly lamb he slaughtered to feed the household. The thief, shamed faced had returned the rice to its sac, kissed Mosayeb's hand and ran out of the gate never to return.

Recently age had eroded Mosayeb's zests and made him lethargic. He no longer found energy to accompany his Master in his hunting expeditions, afternoon walks and other pleasurable outings. His considerate Master had excused him without, even, the lifting of an eyebrow.

Physically inactive, now, he found joy in reminiscing

while smoking his faranghi (foreign) pipe brought for him by the Master from Paris instead of his old chopogh, the Iranian equivalent. He loved holding his pipe like his Master, with faranghi elegance and showing it off to the rest of the household. The possession of such a luxury increased his stature in front of the rest of the staff. Every morning after breakfast, weather permitting, he would place his flimsy wooden chair on his porch, face the gate, tilt his head to the side, raise a brow, lit his pipe and let his mind roam back to his youth. His favourite memory was of the day the shah had spotted him amongst the cuttings in his father's wheelbarrow, with only his tiny head protruding out of the green pile, staring at the shah wide eyed. The old shah had approached the wheelbarrow and with the tip of his cane had lifted his chin up and asked, "Lad do you know who I am?"

"Of course your Majesty. You are the Pivot of the Universe."

The shah's thick eye brows had risen in surprise at such appropriate response from such a young boy. Shaking his head, he had praised the child's intelligence and ordered his gardener to take him to the anadroon (the women's quarter) of his widowed sister to become his nephew's live-in playmate. Thrilled by the luck that had landed on his lap, his father, the palace's chief gardener, had dropped on his knees and kissed the tip of the shah's shoe. That same afternoon washed and dressed properly with his straight black hair combed and parted on the side, his father had walked him to the andaroon. At the gate he had lifted him up, kissed him and whispered into his ear, "Never look back. God has been very kind to you. Be worthy of his kindness."

Too young to comprehend, he had wrapped his thin arms around his father's hairy thick tanned neck and began to weep. The fat, smartly attired eunuch who was at the gate to take deliverance of him had gently unhooked him from his father's folds and put him down. Then he had taken out from his paisley embroidered long coat pocket a small sack of gold coins, tucked it into his father's calico vest pocket before taking his hand and guiding him inside a new world that soon became his. There, he was taken to the shah's nephew Abdullah Mirza, two years his junior. At first with curious eyes, the two had stood appraising one another. Mosayeb had found the young Master as tall as himself, as thin as himself but regally dressed, not like him in loose calico pantaloon and a coarse white cotton shirt – his only garb daily washed and smoothed out by his mother's large palms. The Master's smile had assured him of being approved of. Suddenly he had remembered he had not bowed to the royal entity. So he had placed his right arm on his chest and bent so deep that he had lost his balance and capsized. The Master, laughing from the heart, had offered him his delicate hand. Purple with embarrassment he had grabbed the hand and risen. That hand was still being held by him. In time they had become so close that he was allowed to sleep on the floor of the Master's bedroom and be taught by his private tutor until the Master was sent to study at Saint Cyr Military Academy in France. However, before leaving he had made his mother promise to make Mosayeb, who was excellent with numbers, her steward. Mosayeb had worked diligently, proved efficient, honest and above all loyal. And when the Master returned, married and moved to his own house which he named Golestan, after the palace in which he was born, Mosayeb was asked to choose a chore. To everyone's astonishment he decided to become the gate keeper. To justify his choice to the Master he had said the position would give him ample time to read the Koran, Ferdousy's Shahnameh (The King's letters) and Hafez's Robayat, (the book of poems).

No one could say no to that request.

Mosayeb took his responsibility seriously particularly today when they expected the entire family to come and stay for the weekend. He had to keep the gate open until the last car entered the property which meant another hour or two. He had heard there was trouble in Teheran. The cursed nonbeliever communist Tudeh members were again stirring things up. But he was confident with Mossadegh as the Prime Minister the troubles would never reach his gate at Niavaran. All the same, to seek God's protection he quickly whispered a Safe Guard prayer in Arabic the words of which he did not understand and blew the verses out in the direction of the green gate. Assured that the heavenly magic of the words would take evils away from his gate, he took out his pipe from its black leather case, gently shook out the stale tobacco remnants in the saucer that was acting as his ashtray, filled the pipe with tobacco from a black suede pouch and lit it with the Master's old gold Cartier lighter. Then, feeling assured of being aided by the Almighty in his vigilance, he rested his feet on his flimsy little folding table and relaxed to enjoy his treat.

The hooting of Ali Khan's white Chevrolet interrupted Mosayeb's tranquillity. He jumped off his chair, placed his pipe on the ashtray, and with his hand beckoned the driver in. Then he politely saluted Ali Khan who was regally seated next to his driver and behind him on the back seat, his wife Aziz Bano, the Master's generous daughter whom he liked very much. When the car passed through the gate, he threw a venomous glance at the back of the driver who was to share his room for the weekend and made a mental note to complain to the Master when he saw him next. He did not want any intruders in his small domain, in case they pinched his pipe, or his gold lighter or God forbid both.

Abdullah Mirza, tall, handsome and European chic was among the few nobles who had acquired western attitude, habits and manners. Highly educated, he spoke fluent

45

French and Russian. His behaviour was so gentle and his judgements so sound that he was respected by his peers and subordinates. His wife, Shokat Bano, loved him dearly, and patiently tolerated his extra-marital activities – all reported to her by Mosayeb who disapproved of his Master's adultery especially when married to a saint like his Khanum. There was a rumour amongst the staff that Mosayeb was in love with the Mistress. But on the other hand who was not.

In total control of her domestic affairs, Shokat Bano with an effervescent smile, and a hand ready to give, had eyes and ears everywhere. Wisely accepting that men are lecherous by nature and content that all of her husband's affairs were conducted with maximum discretion, she had turned her attention to his finer qualities. Considerate and respectful, he never took a single financial step without consulting with her and he made sure she never lacked anything. She was wealthy in her own right, however according to Islamic law what she had was hers while he was responsible for all expenditures. For him she was an ideal mother, a hospitable hostess and extremely dignified and humorous individual. She made him laugh even at times of trouble. Her great charm and wisdom compensated for her plain, yet appealing looks.

As was the custom of the day, all their children had been weaned by a wet nurse but they grew up under the strict supervision of their mother. Shokat Bano had been confined ten times, only four infants had survived the prevalent childhood diseases that were claiming thousands of lives each year. Penicillin had just found its way to the pharmacies.

A music lover, Shokat Bano had commissioned Maestro Javad Maroofi to teach her two daughters the piano and Mahjoubi, the violin.

The lady of Golestan was down to earth, observant, and

basically a good human being. She was so perceptive to the needs of others that she always offered help before being asked. That was why Farhad Mirza, her financially despondent brother, and her oldest daughter and her husband lived with her, in their own separate quarters set at a corner of her huge estate in which spring water ran through skilfully designed waterways. In those days piped water had not, as yet, reached Niavaran.

Shokat Bano did not like her resident son-in-law because she knew he was pimping for her husband. Those days it was fashionable for men of means to visit Khadijeh Khanum's establishment. She was the most famous Madam of Teheran and her ladies, mostly Georgian and Armenian, were known for their beauty and skill.

Like all the other prudent ladies of Teheran, Shokat Bano turned a blind eye to the regular male Wednesday-night outings. In fact she was glad of it since it reduced the sudden pregnancies of female domestics.

The occupants of Golestan intermingled at will and habitually lunched at the large dining room of the main mansion.

There were several children of different ages roving around during the holidays and driving the Master crazy. They were allowed in his presence only when he had nothing better to occupy his time than set the youngsters against each other and enjoy their fights. But Shokat Bano genuinely enjoyed having children around her. She believed their energy and exuberance elevated her spirit. Amongst her five grandchildren her favourite was Lalleh, tall for her age of eight, extremely curious, dignified and wise. Because of this last quality she was called Khanum (Lady), and not the customary Lalleh Khanum (Miss Lalleh). Khanum by itself is the title by which the most respected females of the family are addressed and referred to.

Lalleh's parents lived in Teheran but since she loved

swimming and her grandparents had a huge swimming pool, she spent the weekends and summer holidays at Niavaran. Shokat Bano loved the little girl's independence, sense of humour and vivaciousness which she assumed the girl had inherited from her. It was a joy to pamper Lalleh and teach her how to be a real lady – both in manners and in heart. Khanum, a quick learner, was her pet and she Khanum's idol. Thus every Thursday afternoon, when schools closed at noon for the weekend, her chauffeur, Haji Agha, would drive the Cadillac, to Khanum's door, pick her up and bring her to Golestan where she had her own room and a wardrobe accommodating her clothes, books and puzzle magazines. She was a prodigious reader and fast crossword solver. Unlike other kids she did not read the cartoon magazines with Batman stories which she found boring. Her favourite author was Tolstoy and she had already gone through half of 'War and Peace' dreaming to become Natasha to a Pierre.

At Golestan, there were several domestics of all ages and skills. Most were married and had children. So there were plenty of playmates to keep Khanum occupied particularly when her grandparents entertained and that was often. Children played no part in the lives of the adults. The wet nurses who had remained with the family took care of the new energetic generation, albeit reluctantly.

To the great annoyance of Mosayeb, the Master wished to keep Golestan's gate open to all, particularly famous musicians and singers who stayed for days during summer months and entertained the household free of a fee. Unfortunately some of the aristocrats, after the fall of the old dynasty had turned to opium. Technically they blamed their addiction on Reza Khan who had forced Ahmad Shah's abdication and caused the collapse of their dynasty. Almost none of the Qajar royals could bring themselves to refer to him as the shah. To them he had remained Reza

Khan even now that he was dead and his young son was ruling the country.

Ali Khan, Khanum's father – was not of royal blood, yet more dignified than all the aristocrats around him. He blamed the addiction not on Reza Shah of whom he thought highly but on lack of will-power and laziness. Ali Khan, a very tall and handsome man, came from an established family with huge land holdings on the periphery of the capital. But that did not stop him from working hard and improving the living standard of his family. He believed the man's worth did not depend on his ancestry but on his achievements in and contribution to society. He hardly ever sat on the opium mat that was spread on the carpet at the right corner of the Hoz Khaneh, (the pond hall) where the addicts indulged in self-destruction. Even Agha Abdullah Mirza sometimes part-took in the indulgence, with a puff or two. He did this not because he liked opium. He, too, detested it. He smoked only when the pain killers could not sooth the throbbing pain in his chest.

As much as he hated opium, Abdullah Mirza loved red wine. It reminded him of his youth, Paris and the cafés at St. Germaine. To make his own wine he had commissioned an Armenian wine maker to teach Mosayeb the art. A keen learner, Mosayeb had accomplished learning the skill quickly whilst the Master turned the basement into a French-style cellar something rare in Iran of those days. There, he had Mosayeb put two small stools and a converted oak wine barrel as table, for the two of them, like brothers, to sit around and taste wine while amusing themselves recalling the secrets that had remained theirs alone. The one story they both cherished was of the way the shah's prettiest wife had lured them to her private chamber, (under the watchful eyes of the heavily bribed chief eunuch) and allowed them to share her bed till the crack of dawn. She was the best they ever had – so hungry and so willing!

Neither could blame her. The shah was old and ill, she only fourteen and vibrant. Abdullah Mirza believed that Mosayeb had fallen in love with the woman and that was why he had never married. Of course Mosayeb always denied the fact but nonetheless it gave them pleasure to dispute it.

The family's favourite pastime was playing cards, backgammon or chess which often terminated in angry disputes and later resumed with a vengeance. Only a few male members of the family worked for a living. The others lived on the Master's generosity. He owned several villages all over the country and was a liberal and humane landlord respected by his employees. Consequently his stewards and peasants did not steal from him as much as they could and provided him with enough provision for Golestan and income for his regular trips to Paris and the South of France. No rice, tea, date, saffron or citrus fruit was ever purchased. They arrived from different villages at various times of the year, even when there was a draught.

Golestan means flower garden. However, this Golestan was not only cultivated with varieties of annuals and perennials that decorated the beds around the rectangular lawn, but also with herbs, vegetables, shrubs and fruit trees in the perfect order necessary for the existing methods of irrigation. There were orchards of apples, pears, pomegranates, quinces, plums, and medlars. Walnut, hazelnut and mulberry trees grew at will. The gardeners had orders not to remove them as the household loved fresh walnuts and mulberries. Khanum was a mulberry lover. An agile child she used to climb the trees like a monkey, sit on a sturdy branch, eat the fruits, and once about to burst see-saw on the branch to shed the remainder of its ripe berries onto the table cloth she habitually laid on the ground so that she could take the sweetest and the juiciest to her grandmother.

Everybody knew of Khanum's passion for the fruit including her uncle, Abbass Mirza, a handsome middle-aged man trusted and liked by all, except the Mistress of the house. His father-in-law swore on his head and all mothers trusted their children with him. Often he was spotted disappearing into the thickness of an orchard with one or two children following him like poppies. Khanum was the only child who did not like him. There was something about the way he leered at her that made her uncomfortable. She did not dare mention it to her grandmother who would have never understood what she meant by the 'wickedness flashing out of his eyes.' Her mother never paid much attention to her and her two sisters were boarding at a finishing school near Geneva. At home, she felt desperately lonely. Sometimes she even missed the beatings her sisters used to inflict upon her. Her only friend was her father.

Ali Khan loved Lalleh dearly and was proud of his little studious and undemanding daughter. In spite of being the only child at home, she never complained of being bored. He had observed that she always busied herself with constructive chores and was very observant and caring. He thought she would make a good medical practitioner. So he decided to send her to England when she finished her primary school. Ali Khan did not approve of having her spend so much time at Golestan with all those lechers around but he could never bring himself to deny her the pleasure of being with her grandmother whom he knew loved her very much.

This Thursday which had fallen on the birthday of the Prophet, the entire family had been invited to spend the weekend at Golestan and celebrate the occasion together.

It was three in the afternoon when the last car passed through the gate. An exuberant Mosayeb locked it and hurried to join the rest of the staff in the pantry.

The inside was bustling with joyous noises of talk and

laughter. Delkesh, a young singer reclined on one of the four chaise lounges placed on each side of the blue pond in the Hoz Khaneh, was drinking tea and from the corner of her eyes watching Farhad Mirza. Maroofi seated behind the grand piano, his fingers lightly touching the keyboard patiently waiting for his host to order him to commence. To the aggravation of the elders, the children were running around playing hide and seek behind the sofas. The Master, annoyed by the disorder in the room, turned to Fatimeh Sadat, the senior housekeeper who stood behind her Mistress, and ordered, "Sadat take the brats out of here and keep them entertained." The maid responded with a heavy "Chashm Agha". Terribly disappointed for having to forfeit being present in the same room as her favourite singer, she frowned and began hastily hurling her wards out into the garden.

Khanum, assuming that Grandma would allow her to remain inside, ran to her and with her large black eyes pleaded her request. Shokat Bano who had never acted contrary to the will of her Agha (lord) threw him a questioning glance. He nodded in negation. She softly padded the bony back of her little pet, kissed her black head, promised her a few pieces of Belgian chocolates and sent her off to join the others.

Outside in the garden nature seemed in a celebratory mood. The air was pleasantly cool, a fresh spring breeze was fluttering the new born leaves making them catch the rays of the mild sun and sparkle like large emeralds. Chirping birds were playing hide and seek in the midst of quivering branches and bees buzzed over roses that had just opened up their pink lips. From the inside the melodious sound of Maroofi's piano escaped out to overwhelm nature's own music.

Fatimeh Sadat sat cross-legged on the recently mowed lawn with the boisterous children encircled around her.

They all knew the story she was about to tell them – in fact the only one she knew – of the most famous Persian heroes amongst them, Rostam and Sohrab, as told by poet Ferdousy in his Shahnameh, the sole epic poem ever written that contains not one single Arabic word in its entire content. The intent of the masterpiece was to impress upon the Arab conqueror, the magnitude of Iranian history.

(During the Arab conquest of Iran, a large number of Arabic words found their way into Farsi, the language of the Iranians).

Today it was the tenth time Fatimeh Sadat was recounting the tale; yet her listeners were glued to the grass, to hear how Rostam fights and kills Sohrab, only to realize that he has killed his own son. The tragic end always produced tears in the children's eyes and turned Fatimeh Sadat's voice husky with grief.

Inside now Delkash was singing to the rhythmic tune of Maroofi's piano, her soft, enchanting voice drifting out of the open windows and enthralling those who heard it, specially the well-diggers, who upon recognizing the voice, had dropped their ropes and shovels, sat on the edge of their respective wells swinging their legs and heads to the tempo of the music. Ecstatic, they murmured the well-known song in unison with the singer – an experience none of them would ever forget. Inside even the ageing Farhad Mirza was humming her tune. The rumour had it that he was having an affair with her and that was why she frequented the house without expecting to be paid. Nevertheless Shokat Bano regularly gave her a few Pahlavi gold coins before she parted.

Farhad Mirza with his trimmed moustache was still very handsome and his twinkling large black eyes had not lost their bewitching power. He had remained generous in spite of being on a monthly allowance from his sister. It was his excessive generosity that had reduced him to his present dire state. He was such a polite and caring gentleman that one could not but love and respect him. Delkesh, voluptuous and sexy, could not do better than become friend of such lovely gentleman – even though he was almost forty years her senior. To be associated with the old aristocracy and sing at Golestan was an honour for a young and upcoming singer – with a hot reputation. Later Delkesh became one of the most cherished singers of Iran.

Servants, honoured to see Delkesh in person, kept serving tea and later red wine. They heard her voice daily, from the radio the Master had given to Bagher Khan, the head cook. But seeing her perform in person was altogether something else. If told, no one would ever believe them that they had seen Delkesh in real life and listened to her live.

Farhad Mirza, in company with the other male guests was sitting cross-legged on the floor around an ornamental charcoal burner busy reciting poetry and swearing at the British who were to blame for all the miseries of the world – particularly Iran's. Delkesh's voice and the smell of opium had lifted his spirit out of its usual dire state and had brought a charming smile to his dark purple lips. Shaking his head to the rhythm of the music he bent slightly towards the burner, picked up the tongue that lay on the tray beneath it, searched for a crimson charcoal, found it, shook the ash from the glittering piece and then put it on the opium morsel he had pushed inside the hole of the pipe. He closed his eyes, took the pipe to his mouth and began puffing in deeply, and then slowly exhaling the smoke out of his pursed mouth and nostrils. Gently he passed the pipe to Ali Khan next to him. Ali Khan threw him a demeaning glance and, twitching his nose in disgust, took the pipe and passed it to Abbass Mirza.

The pipe circulated till the participants dropped into a hazy trance. Delkesh stopped singing and began drinking her tea but Maroofi continued to play the Golden Dreams followed by Shiella, his two most recent compositions that were to become eternal.

Chapter 4

May 2009

Mohammad's first chore of the morning was to unlock the villa's safety shutters and turn the swimming pool filter on. It was seven in the morning, Khanum was already in her bathing suit by the pool and he had not showed up yet. Under normal circumstances, she would have been very cross with him but not today. Besides, the water was only two days old and chlorinated. Slowly she climbed the aluminium ladder down and commenced her fifty laps that would be followed by half an hour of aqua-aerobics.

At sixty-seven she was as fit as a fiddle. Her slender, muscular figure was the envy of those of her friends who had become floppy in figure and expressionless in their lifted faces. Her motto was: "remain fit and age gracefully."

Highly disciplined, she followed a strict rule of conduct – at times severe enough to arouse criticism from friends and foes. Fortunately she did not pay much attention to what people said behind her back. She believed that dwelling on negatives poisons the blood. She loved life too much to make it bitter over petty things.

Now, almost breathless, she climbed up the ladder, took her shower, put on her robe, and hung her bathing suit and towel on the clothes peg of the shower room until Mohammad's unlocking would allow her to step onto the veranda. She could open the entrance door, but she did not want to make a detour of the building while she could step out into the veranda from the swimming area and hang the bathing suit and the towel on the mobile laundry rails that usually stood in a discreet sunny corner nearby. Exhilarated by the exercise, she went to the kitchen, prepared her breakfast tray of instant Nescafé and a piece of pastry. She put her tray on the kitchen table and went to check on Nargess.

The girl was fast sleep. She returned to the kitchen, picked up her tray, climbed the stairs to her bedroom, where she usually had her breakfast.

It was a bright day, the sky cloudless and the dews on the grass shimmered like large diamonds. The sea was calm, like a sheet of silver and the gentle breeze that wafted in through the criss-cross of the green safety grills was tinged with the smell of wet earth. Today she took no joy in the heaven that stretched in her view. Her mind was too agitated. So much was at stake – one wrong word, one wrong move could jeopardise everything. She too, like everybody in Iran, was scared of the faceless 'they'– the watching, monitoring 'they'. She wanted to avoid them at all costs – because she loved Iran and admired the new generation of the Iranians – they were the children she had never had. One wrong move and she would be finished. No one would ever believe her that in her entire tumultuous life, she had remained apolitical. She was just an Iranian in love with her country and wanted to be buried under the same earth that covered her loved ones. She simply could not afford to get involved with the "system."

Contemplating, she went through her breakfast without really tasting anything and then hurried to the intercom and pressed the staff room's number. No one responded. Not unusual – Shahri was lazy, Taghi slept in his own room and Mohammad was always busy with early morning irrigation. But he had not as yet been to the front which he usually came to first. That worried her. She grabbed her dressing gown and putting it on dashed down the stairs to the entrance door which she hastily unlocked and hurried to the domestic quarters the door of which was surprisingly enough closed. Annoyed and apprehensive she knocked furiously. A good few minutes later Shahri, eyes puffy, opened the door and was about to apologize when Khanum asked for Mohammad.

"He is still sleep Khanum."

"Still sleep? That is unlike him. Did he take anything last night?"

"I think he took a few opium pills."

"Opium pills?"

"Yes. Saeed the Afghan sells them. He says they reduce pain and are helpful when one cannot sleep."

Khanum ran to the adjoining bedroom, and saw Mohammad's colourless face visible from under the fold of the blanket, his lips slightly apart and purple. She immediately put her head on his chest. She had to concentrate hard before she could hear any beats. She put her hand on his forehead and found it cold. She ran to the phone lodged on a vinyl covered mantelpiece and dialled Ali's mobile number.

He answered.

"Ali it is urgent. Please hurry here at once." She put the receiver down, returned to Mohammad and began slapping him on the face.

Shahri screamed her objections. "I am doing this to revive him." Khanum retorted with anger.

"Revive him!" Shahri exclaimed filled with anxiety.

"Yes revive him. Opium kills. Go and get some iced water."

Bewildered and completely lost, the woman ran to her fridge, opened its door with a shaky hand, and extracted a water pitcher and brought it to Khanum.

"Throw the water over his face."

"It will give him pneumonia." Shahri's eyes were wide with fear.

"Do it." Biting her lower lip with doubts Shahri hesitated and then holding the pitcher with both hands splashed the icy liquid over her husband's face.

The water saturated the bedding but he did not move.

Clenching her teeth, Khanum bent over him and resumed her slapping.

Taghi woken by the noise, unkempt and puffy-eyed burst into the room, seeing his father being slapped, started screaming.

"Shut up, Taghi," Shahri yelled.

Helpless he covered his face with his hands and began to cry.

"Taghi calm down. I am only trying to wake your father up."

The boy frightened beyond his wits continued to howl – nothing of what was happening around him, made sense.

"Please be calm son... please," Khanum begged in an exasperated tone. She gave up slapping him, sat on the edge of Mohammad's bed, pulled out his hand from under the wet blanket and held it tight – as though to stop life escaping from the tip of his dirty, chapped fingers. In her heart she was begging God's help. Life and death came from him. But she did not want anyone to die under her roof – not if she could help it. So she started whispering all the prayers Sadat had taught her.

Half an hour passed in a hushed silence. Only God knew what each person in that room was thinking. Then they heard honking of Ali's car. Taghi rushed to open the gate. A few minutes later the two stepped inside – one looking frightened the other bewildered.

Khanum took Ali's arm and guided him outside, away from Taghi's hearing range. There quickly she summarized the events of the past twelve hours. Ali was so shocked that he kept repeating Allah Akbar. Khanum led him back to the room, showed him the patient and said, "We must take him to the hospital at Babolsar."

"Yes and we must hurry Khanum," he replied and then turned to Shahri. "Come and give me a hand."

Taghi ran to his mother's side and together they lifted Mohammad and carried him to the car, the door of which had been opened by Khanum. Once they fitted him inside Shahri noticed he was shoeless. She ran back, picked up his sandals from the porch, returned, knelt on the gravel and gently fitted them on his dangling feet.

"Shahri can I borrow your chador please." The woman took it off and handed it to her. Khanum spread it over her head.

"Thank you Shahri, after breakfast go to the villa and wait for Nargess to wake up. Be kind to her, not a word about her father until we return."

"Chashm, Khanum."

"Taghi, you stay home and help your mother today."

"Chashm, Khanum."

Having finalized her wishes, Khanum took the front seat, turned to Ali and remarked, "For once the chador has become useful."

He looked at her dressing gown protruding from between the folds of the chador and nodded his agreement with an unfelt smile.

In the hospital, fortunately not as crowded as usual, Mohammad was rushed to the emergency ward. No questions were asked. Opium intoxication was common in Iran. After fifteen minutes of impatient wait, Mohammad's stretcher was rushed into the operating room where they cleansed his intestine of the poison, and rushed him back to be taken home as there was not one single bed available. His doctor came to Khanum and said, "He is very lucky to be alive, the silly man. I only recently rehabilitated him from opium addiction and am surprised why he has again taken the drug – enough to kill an elephant. It did not kill him because his body seems to be immune to the toxin."

That was why he couldn't put meat on his family's plates, the stupid man. Khanum surmised with anger. She stretched her arm to shake the doctor's hand and then remembered that was not done. "Agha Doctor, thank you for saving his life. I never knew he took opium and promise you he will not touch it again."

The doctor shook his head in denial.

"Khanum Aziz, once an addict, always an addict."

"No, doctor, I will make sure he stays away from it while working for me. That I promise you."

On the way back home Khanum asked Ali to drive to Saeed's house which was three doors from Golestan. (In memory of her grandparents she had named her home Golestan.)

"Why Khanum?"

"I have a few words to say to that bastard."

"He is dangerous and your words will have no effect on him. He is legal."

"Legal or not I know what to tell him."

Ali slowed the car, turned his left signal light on, and waited for a gap in the traffic flow to allow him to cross the busy highway. Several minutes later he turned left and parked the car on the drive-way of the villa, frantically blowing his horn. A few minutes later the gate slid open, Saeed, protruded his head out and with his shrewd narrow black eyes scrutinized the car and its passengers. Recognizing them, a broad smile appeared on his handsome face. Quickly he stepped out and walked to Khanum to ingratiate himself to her. Hitherto Khanum had been very generous to him and his wife. His patron, a rich industrialist from Isfehan hardly ever stayed at his villa. Saeed, though only twenty-one, did everything he could, legal or illegal, to earn enough money to one day return to Herat – his home town. Two years ago he had brought his fifteen years old wife to Iran and locked her up in the studio that was his quarters. She was not allowed to go out and visit the neighbours nor show her face to any male stranger.

Withering away in loneliness, without any family or friends she had threatened to drown herself in the sea, if he didn't take her back home. Knowing that she was pregnant, for the sake of his child and not her, he had taken her back and upon his return had turned his studio into an opium den – he was clever enough never to touch the drug himself. He knew that Khanum and Ali were amongst the few who knew what he was up to.

Khanum, her eyes wide with hate, turned her window down, protruded her head out and in a voice flamed in fury said, "Saeed, look at the back seat and see what your merchandize has done to my gardener. If I ever catch you near my villa or anyone who works for me I shall call your employer and tell him what you are up to. I will also call the Town's Council as well as the Mayor. I am sure you already know opium smugglers are daily hanged by the dozen. I am also sure you do not want your little baby girl to be orphaned before she has had a chance to see her father."

Saeed's face became darker than it was but he said nothing. He just glared at her with his piercing eyes, in his heart wishing her dead.

"Did you hear me, you dirty dog?"

Wordless, nodding his head, he turned his back to the car, walked inside and banged the gate shut.

Ali starting the engine said, "Khanum do you know why he has become so daring?"

"No."

"His married master brings his girl friends here and the Afghan knows this. So in a way they have made a deal!"

"Madness – this is all madness," Khanum, totally exasperated, murmured; her eyes on the speeding cars.

They heard Mohammad moan. She turned her head and saw that a bit of colour had returned to his cheeks but his eyes were still closed. She released a sigh of relief and sent heaven a loud prayer of praise.

They arrived home and found Taghi standing by the gate. He was silent and his facial expression expectant. Quickly he opened the gate and stood aside. Then he came forward and gave Ali a helping hand. The two gently carried Mohammad inside and tucked him in bed. He opened his eyes for a few seconds and then shut them again – tears slithering out from the corners of his eyelids. The world was going around and around in his painful head and his heart was tight with grief.

Khanum walked Ali to his car and then returned to the room where she ordered Shahri to find Mohammad's opium pills and give them to her. Shahri ran to the kitchen, searched the tins she knew belonged to Mohammad and returned with a little match box that contained several dark-brown unevenly loafed pills. Khanum took the box, returned to Shahri her chador and walked to the villa thinking of how wide-spread opium addiction had become in Iran. Only the other day Ali had told her if one rubs his nose three times at Noshahr's main shopping mall, a pusher will appear asking what is needed – opium, heroin, cocaine or crack – all this in spite of the seriously vigilant anti-drug force of which Iran is very proud.

Inside the villa, she found Nargess cross-legged sitting on the floor, facing the garden, her mind totally numbed staring at an empty void. Hearing the slight screech of the door; she blinked several times before she could find her orientation. She turned her head and seeing Khanum enter, slowly rose to greet her. Attempt at movements had become hard for her.

"Are you better now dear?"

The girl bit her lower lip, kept her eyes on the floor and instead of responding asked "how is my father Khanum joon?"

"He is alive. How are you my dear?"

"I wish I was dead!"

"That is a silly thing to say. I told you last night, you are not to blame for what has happened. It could have happened to my daughter if I had one! So stop this nonsense. I will take you to a doctor in Teheran he will fix you up. Now go home, take care of your father and don't show your face at school until I tell you."

The girl, with her head down, shoulders stooped reached to take her hand to kiss. Khanum withdrew it and folded her arms around her thin frame. She kissed her cold colourless forehead and whispered, "Enshallah, all will be well again. Have faith in God and don't look back, dear."

Chapter 5

A spring day in l951 – Niavaran

Abbass Mirza, and his wife, Tooran, lived in a small house, unfortunately not far enough from the mansion. The noise of their constant quarrels always gave Shokat Bano goose pimples and disturbed the peace of the other inhabitants. She often wondered how her daughter could have such a vulgar tongue – she was lucky to have a husband at all. In spite of his few faults, Abbass Mirza was from the rank of nobility and very handsome. Many beautiful women craved his companionship and bed. Shokat Bano was realistic enough to know he was with Tooran only for financial security but people's patience had a limit and she prayed his would never reaches its end – at least while she was still alive. It was fortunate that they were childless. In the family's opinion this was why he pampered other people's children. Mohsen, the lanky, teenage son of Bagher Khan followed him like a puppy, and recently he was showing interest in the twelve-year-old timid Parviz, his own nephew whose parents were overseas and had left the boy in his care. Parviz and Khanum were good mates and played well together. This early afternoon, in the company of the other children they had gathered by the poolside waiting for Abbass Mirza to come and take them to his library where they were to view his military objects of which he was very proud and had told them so much about.

Abbass Mirza, an army general during Ahmad Shah's reign, was sacked by Reza Shah who had manipulated the Parliament to ask for the Qajar Shah's abdication. Wealthy and financially careless, he had occupied himself with gambling and blown away his handsome inheritance at various private poker games. His in-laws, to save face, had taken him under their patronage and thus had saved their obese and at times obnoxious daughter's marriage.

Tall and slender he had a well-trimmed moustache and a pair of large black eyes with a notorious glitter. His features were delicate and his straight black hair plentiful and shiny. His manner was immaculate and he dressed elegantly. He had a way with words – he could charm a snake out of its hole. Some of the children loved him, some tried to avoid him and many ran away even from his shadow.

Lunch had finished already and Abbass Mirza, who never took a siesta, left the main building for his place of rendezvous, whistling a happy tune. His father-in-law's red wine had lifted his spirit up and he was looking forward to what waited for him. As soon as the children saw him they ran towards him with excited greetings and then, like a tamed herd, followed him to his cosy study where they sat on the floor, cross-legged facing the wall which was adorned with various intimidating weapons. The awesomeness of the objects in their view purged their earlier excitement and delved them into an eerie silence. The other walls were lined with tidy rows of hard cover books in Farsi and French. In the absence of any constructive occupation, he had become an avid reader. Having graduated from Saint Cyr Military Academy he was fluent in French and had acquired the French taste for life's pleasures, especially those of a carnal nature.

Feeling imperious within his private domain he stood erect by his mementoes. The wall showcased a sword with a bejewelled handle, daggers of different sizes, rifles and various pistols he had inherited from his father. He turned his eyes around, fixed them on Parviz for a second and then, as though lecturing to his army officers, explained the use of each device and in which battle he had used it – in fact, unlike his father, he had never fought a battle in his life. And then he pointed to the largest dagger on the wall, redirected his gaze at Parviz and said, "With this I used to cut wagging tongues."

The boy's posture stiffened and his face lost its colour.

"Dear uncle, what is a wagging tongue?"

Forever curious, Khanum asked smiling coquettishly.

Abbass Mirza gave her a tender gaze, smiled and said, "A tongue that divulges secrets, my pretty angel."

Suddenly a hush fell in the room as each child tried to gauge the meaning of the statement and if, God forbidden, it applied to him or her. Khanum did not comprehend what he meant but in order not to seem stupid in front of the others, especially Parviz, she nodded her understanding with a pensive expression mapped on her round face.

Having made his point, whistling a happy tune again, he turned his back to his collection and went to his writing desk, drew out a drawer from which he extracted three bars of chocolate. The sight of the bars evaporated the children's fear. They quickly rose and gathered around the desk like flies wheezing over an open jar of quince jam.

Slowly Abbass Mirza unwrapped and broke the bars into square pieces which he distributed amongst the children with a double square going to Khanum.

A happy smile lit her face and she gave him loud thanks. He bent down and kissed her rosy cheek. She blushed, grabbed Parviz's hand with a tight grip – as though needing some kind of protection. Parviz moved closer to her as though there was indeed a need for his help.

"Now, children, leave and not a word to anyone as where you have been. Tooran Khanum won't like to hear that you have been messing up my study. She will give you a good spanking if she hears you have set foot in this house without her permission."

A commotion stirred. The youngsters timidly nodded their pledge and busied themselves deciding what to do next when Abbass Mirza turned to Khanum and said, "Mohsen here and I are going to pick some mulberries for your aunt would you like to come with us."

A "yes" was being formed on her round lips when Parviz squeezed her hand hard and hastily said, "I will give you my share of chocolate if you come and play with me instead."

The girl hesitated for a second, threw a quick glance at her uncle. He was holding Mohsen's arm. Disliking the aura surrounding the two she found herself saying, "No thank you uncle, I would rather have Parviz's chocolate."

It was almost four in the afternoon. No one was out except Bagher Khan. Infuriated, he was pacing up and down, in front of the main kitchen, waiting for his son whose responsibility was to clean the rice from mice droppings and dregs and clean the fresh herbs used in khoreshts (stews). Recently the boy was late almost every afternoon. That made Bagher late for dinner. What was he up to when everyone else was having their siesta? Bagher kept asking himself and eventually, in the absence of any rational explanation, his anger turned into exasperation. Unable to maintain his calm he increased the speed of his pace while under his breath swearing at his son. Then he saw him protrude out from amongst the blackberry bushes followed by Abbass Mirza. Seeing his father the boy ran up towards the kitchen and as soon as he reached him a sharp slap landed on his cheek. "Why are you late again, you bastard? Do you want to get me sacked – do you?"

Another slap landed on the boy's other cheek.

Mohsen, his lips quivering from pain and his eyes flushing with defiance replied, "I was just helping Abbass Mirza pick mulberries for Tooran Khanum."

"No one goes mulberry picking at this hour of the afternoon. All the snakes are out and their sting kills – you know that better than anyone else. One almost killed you last month."

Bagher, his face contorted with rage, paused and then unable to sooth his fury he grabbed hold of his son's earlobe twisted it as hard as he could and yelled: "If you are ever late again I will strangle you with my own hands."

The boy twisted himself out of his father's grip, ran to the kitchen where he squatted in front of the large rice tray. Seething with resentment, he began horridly fingering out the black droppings. Suddenly he saw a mouse cross the open front door. Displacing his burning fume onto the animal he took off his sandal and threw it at the disappearing rodent.

Bagher regretting his brutality, moderated his tone, and said, "When you finish the spinach chopping, go to the alchemist at Tajrish and buy me a sack of rat-poison. They are everywhere – not even the cats can exterminate them."

The boy threw a hateful glance at his father.

"I have no money."

Bagher dipped his large hand in his pocket, drew out a five toomans note and threw it on the rice.

"Buy yourself an ice cream too."

Ice cream was Mohsen's favourite treat. Quickly he picked up the note, shoved it into his shirt pocket, increased his search pace, had the rice inspected and then within an hour, looking like an Agha (a gentleman) he stood at the bus station for Tajrish.

Bagher adored his son and had high hopes for him. It distressed him to see that he was not as conscientious at work as he, himself. Mohsen could do no better than replace him as the head cook at Golestan, when he retired. The Mistress was wonderful to them. She would find him a nice wife and allow them to live under her roof until their dying days. He was getting old and weary and wished Mohsen would show more interest in cooking, take over and let him have some peace. He had been working since he could remember his name, helping his father sow rice seeds. And then, when he was a bit older and could follow orders, his father had brought him to Golestan and left him there to be fed nutritious food, learn a skill and the manner of city folks.

No one knew Bagher's exact age. He certainly didn't look old. He was a pleasant looking man – well built, tall, strong and in spite of his ferocious temper always composed. He adored his kind Mistress who had saved him, many times, from his supervisor, the old cook's cruel tongue and sharp slaps and heavy kicks. Thank God he had died soon after Bagher had been recognized as a good cook. Once on an adequate salary the Mistress having noticed his fascination for Kobra, the new maid, had suggested to him to wed her. Delighted he married the girl and found great happiness in her arms. His mission in life was to please Shokat Bano. He was proud that the Mistress liked his tasty cooking and treated him like an Agha. He was eternally grateful to her for buying his Kobra a grave at Mesgarabad cemetery. She had died of tuberculosis.

Ever so kind to Mohsen, the Mistress had used her influence to get him into the best Government school in the neighbourhood and to his astonishment had commissioned a private tutor to help him with the subjects he was failing – and they were plenty. No mistress was as kind and thoughtful as his and he simply adored her.

Bagher Khan was chief of the domestic staff excluding Mashhadi Mosayeb who was not considered a servant. Bagher loved Mosayeb and looked upon him as a surrogate father for he had taught him how to please the Mistress. He had told him, 'If you please the Mistress, the Master will look after you well.' He had listened to his advice and profited well. So to return the favour, Mosayeb was fed well and his food was served in the same porcelain dishes as were sent to the main building. The rest ate out of copper vessels.

Being honest beyond belief, Bagher had the only key to the storage room. The Mistress trusted him and at times sought his counsel. In fact in a very special way they were friends.

It was Shokat Bano's habit to personally supervise the dishing out of the meals. There was a wooden chair in the kitchen on which she sat and ordered Bagher what and how much to dish out for each household. From the Master's to the gardeners' meal came from this kitchen and it took almost an hour before all was done. The amount of meat portion in each dish was indicative of the Mistress's cordiality towards that recipient. After the Master, her brother faired best.

Outside the western horizon was crimson red, the sky was clear and a narrow crescent of the moon twinkled its appearance. The air had become cooler and a mild breeze aided the fanning of the chicken kebab skews on the charcoal burner. Bagher Khan, anxious about why Mohsen had not returned after three hours of absence, was nervously fanning and turning the skews for equal cooking. In spite of the cool air beads of sweat had gathered on his broad forehead and his gaze often went to the sky in search of heavenly assistance. He always saw God, up above, never down on earth. Suddenly he spotted the narrow moon crescent which meant it was the first night of the lunar month. He kept his eyes closed and ordered Ahmad, his apprentice nephew who was in the kitchen minding the steaming of the rice, to bring him his Koran, always stationed on the kitchen mantle piece next to his prayer mat. Ahmad, a large boy of sixteen, picked the holy book up, kissed it before taking it to his uncle. Bagher Khan, first opened the book, then opened his eyes and read the verses. Feeling as light as a feather, he kissed the Koran and handed it over to his nephew waiting to return the holy book to its place. It is believed that once the moon crescent is gazed at and then that gaze falls on something propitious, the month will bring prosperity and, if it falls on an ominous object or unpleasant looking person, the month will be dreadful. Bagher in his excitement had not noticed that before his eyes fell on the verses of the Koran they had passed over a dead ant squashed between the pages of the holy book.

Ahmad was an orphan living with his uncle. The boy was conscientious, obedient, and rather slow, but loved cooking. He knew exactly what was expected of him in the kitchen and he did his best which was good enough for his uncle. He had already arranged the rice trays and khoresht containers in their proper orders so that Bagher Khan knew for which household he was dishing out. The lunch was served in the main dining room but dinners went to individual quarters.

As the Mistress, followed by Fatimeh Sadat, entered for the usual ritual the two rose and stood up until she took her seat and then they squatted to dish out the rice from its huge copper vessel that the two had removed from the cooker and placed on the kitchen's brick floor. Inside was hot and the man and the boy were perspiring heavily. Shokat Bano was fanning herself with the Spanish fan she had bought in Barcelona.

"Ahmad I don't need you here, go out and mind the kebab," ordered Bagher Khan and then threw a pleading glance at his patroness, There was something in that glance that made Shokat Bano turn to Fatimeh Sadat, her shadow, and ask her to go and fetch her spectacles which she had left on her bed.

Alone, Bagher Khan looked up at his Mistress and she saw fear in his anxious grey eyes. She always detected his moods. Her countenance tense with concern, she asked, "What is bothering you Agha Bagher? Has there been a theft that you want to report?"

Bagher, withdrew a handkerchief from his pant's

pocket, wiped away his wet face, shoved the cloth back, threw her a sad look and said, "No Mistress, there has been no theft. It is Mohsen I am worried about."

"What has he been up to that has upset you so much?"

"Mistress, his behaviour has changed. He has become insolent and careless. He is always late for his chores and when I ask him the reason he offers ridiculous excuses and I do not like to see him hang around Agha Abbass Mirza so much. This afternoon I saw them together at four o'clock. He was late by one hour. When I asked him what he was doing with the Mirza he told me they were picking mulberries for Tooran Khanum – but they were not carrying anything with them. So what were they doing Khanum joon, what?"

"I have no idea. Perhaps they had already left their basket on the veranda of his house. Bagher, Abbass Mirza is a kind man. Perhaps he is paying Mohsen for his chores and that is why the boy follows him," Shokat Bano said and then furrowing her brows added, "I too have noticed their proximity."

"If he is paid why then is he always asking me for money?"

"Your son is a shrewd boy. Perhaps he is not telling you of his earning on the side, in case you stop his pocket money? Does he have a Money tin?"

"Yes he does."

"Open it and find out. Do not worry so much. Mohsen is just a young boy and at certain ages all boys become naughty – and then they mature and make life easy for their parents. Now call Ahamd to come and help you with the dishing out. The rice will get cold."

"I have to find out what he is up to."

"OK, there is nothing wrong for wanting to regain your peace of mind. But be very discreet – he is just a boy – a lovely boy."

Food dishes had already been dispersed when Mohsen arrived with his sack of rat poison and a newspaper wrapped bundle. He handed the sack to his father and was taking the parcel to their shared room when Bagher asked what it contained.

"A shirt."

"A new shirt? The Mistress just gave you three of the Master's foreign made shirts. What do you need any more shirts for son, and besides where did you get the money to buy a new shirt? Did you lie when you told me you had no money?'

"I did not lie to you father when I said I had no grocery money. We went through the expenditure account only last night and I accounted for every rial you had given me. Regarding the Master's shirts they are a bit too big for me and I bought this with the pocket money I had saved."

"Let me see what you have bought for yourself." Bagher nodded to the bundle controlling his urge to grab and tear up the wrapping.

The boy smiled, pride oozing out of his large black eyes that sometimes became grey, slowly unwrapped his white shirt, took the end of each shoulder by his fingers and shaking it smooth said, "Just like the one Parviz wears."

"Dear, you don't want to compete with Parviz Khan."

"Why not father? Are we not children of the same God?"

"Yes we are but remember whose physical son you are."

"Do you mean that makes a difference in the eyes of God?"

"It shouldn't but in the eyes of men you are the son of a cook and Parviz Khan is the son of a noble man."

"Then there is no justice on earth."

Colour drained from the cook's usually healthy cheeks. He cursed the devil that was diverting his son from the right path and said, "Don't be too hasty child. God gives us life and religion gives us a direction to the right path – what we make out of these gifts is up to us. A man feeding on bread and cheese can be happier than a man eating pheasant kebab. How do you know that you might not die a happier man than Parviz Khan?"

Having finished his sermon Bagher looked up at the white kitchen ceiling and through it to heaven and prayed, "Enshallah both you and Parviz Khan reach the end of your road grateful for your fates."

Mohsen threw his father a contemptuous glance before saying 'enshallah'. Then he went to their room, carefully folded and placed his shirt in a small suit case that served him as a dresser. Pleased with himself, he took his towel and went to the shower room that all the servants shared. There he washed himself from the sins of the afternoon so that he could pray to the God he did not believe in – just to please his silly father. He did not know why but he continued to do so.

Chapter 6

May 2009

It was one in the afternoon. Khanum had already performed her noon prayer and was preparing her spicy Bloody Mary when Shahri, lunch tray in hand, whispered her 'Ya Allah', kicked off her pink plastic sandals and stepped in. The smell of her saffron rice and Lamb Khoresht teased Khanum's nostrils and watered her dry mouth. She smiled and told the maid to put the tray on the kitchen bar table. Outside was a bit chilly and the cloudy sky promised a wet afternoon which, under normal circumstances, would have made Mohammad happy. One could take a longer siesta when the sky was overcast especially after a heavy meal like the inviting one sitting on Shahri's tray. Khanum was hungry. She had not had a proper meal since that awful evening.

Shahri obeyed her Mistress and then with her hands free adjusted her white scarf that had slipped off her head, pulled the end of her polyester pullover down over her skirt to hide her bulging tummy of which she had become conscious by her Mistress's teasing remarks. Pulling out the high chair to sit on, Khanum asked after Mohammad's health and was told that he could now sit up in bed and drink tea. "Thank God for that." Khanum responded with a sigh of relief.

Shahri knew how to turn events to her advantage except when dealing with her patroness. However, even with that knowledge she did not stop trying. Her world revolved around her family, her chickens and the gardens' edibles. Much younger than her step-children, through kindness and sagacity she had won their respect and thus had become a matriarch in her own right. Respect in Iran is and has always been an imperative norm within the family structure and the larger society. Those who enjoy it feel extremely secure and in return feel extremely responsible.

Now from her drawn face, Khanum guessed that she was worried – obviously about her daughter's future. In a closed society, an abused girl has no future except prostitution if not death!

Usually, after delivering Khanum's lunch tray Shahri hurried home to feed Mohammad, her Agha, but today she lingered on. Khanum assumed she must have something in mind – something that worried her.

"What is it Shahri?"

"Khanum I think Mohammad is determined to kill Nargess."

"Has he said anything since he gained consciousness?"

"No, but I see murder in his eyes when he looks at her."

"Have any of your step-children been here?"

"Yes my two step-sons. They both know what has happened but I made them swear on the Koran not to tell their wives."

"Good girl. After lunch I want to rest a bit. When I wake up I will call you to bring Nargess and Taghi here to help you clean the house. I want to catch Mohammad alone for a private talk, and whatever you do, do not let Taghi go to school until the dust settles."

"Chashm Khanum – enshallah God gives you a long life."

"I don't want a long life. Pray for a happy life. Go now and let me enjoy my meal before it gets cold."

Shadow of a smile crossed the maid's plump lips and the frown on her forehead faded away. She set the table, took her empty tray and quietly disappeared.

After her siesta, Khanum rang for the cleaning team. When broom and duster in hand they arrived, she walked to Mohammad's quarters. There she found him sitting cross-legged on the floor watching the news on his satellite television. Seeing his Mistress he moved to rise. Khanum's hand motioned him to remain seated. She went to the television, switched it off and sat by him. Distressed, he offered his salam and remained silent. His face was pale, a vain on his temple was throbbing hard and his long fingers fidgeted with the fold of his black polyester pantaloons. Some grey chest hair protruded from the slit of his white shirt that was missing two buttons. He looked beaten.

"Are you feeling better now?"

"No, Khanum. I wish you had let me die!"

"Do not talk nonsense. I am glad you are alive not only because I still have a good gardener but that your family has a breadwinner. Now stop being stupid and listen to me. At the moment we have two very serious problems to deal with – your perpetual addiction and Nargess's state of mind."

The man lifted his head, threw a surprised glance at Khanum and said,

"I hope Nargess dies."

"Don't talk rubbish. Your addiction is as shameful as what has happened to her. Let us hope that you will never again touch opium."

Khanum paused, knitted her tidy eyebrows, pointed her manicured index finger at him and threatened "if you ever touch opium again Ali will terminate your contract immediately." She stopped, fixed her gaze on the speechless man whose pointed jaw was trembling and felt sorry for him. A fly wheezed near his long nose. Infuriated, his hand jerked up, missing the insect landed on his own cheek with a hard whack. It felt so good that he kept slapping himself harder and harder until Khanum caught his hand in the air and forcefully nailed it down. She waited for him to calm down.

"Mohammad I know what you are going through. It is hard isn't it?"

Nodding his head he mumbled a heavy "yes".

"Can you imagine what Nargess is going through?"

77

No response.

"Mohammad the privilege of being a parent is the ability to love unconditionally. You love your daughter because she is your flesh and blood. She is part of you and you part of her. What has happened to her has happened to you. That is why you are so ashamed. Without knowing you are sharing her pain. Show her the compassion, the love and understanding that you feel for her. That will enable her to respect herself again. Think reasonably man. What has happened to your daughter could have happened to anyone's daughter. You cannot condemn that innocent child for having been victim of another's lust. You must accept what has happened as a misfortune and try to help her. Be supportive instead of being accusative. The wise of the world will think of you as a selfish man if you do not bring yourself to acknowledge her innocence and relieve her from the feeling of shame and self-hate that is consuming her."

Khanum paused to control the tears that were moistening her eyes. She took couple of deep breaths and then continued.

"I know you are a practising Muslim. This might be God testing to see if you mean what you pledge in terms of forgiveness. Show God that your prayers are not false, that you are a true believer and that you are capable of being unselfish. Perform your allocated role in the testing arena of the universe – then see if the God you worship is worthy of your adoration. Rest assured he will not fail you, my man. My life testifies to that."

A deep silence fell in the room. The sound of her words was soul-soothing but the wisdom hidden in the crux of those words was too complex for Mohammad's agitated mind to comprehend. His eyes were still fixed on the whizzing fly that eventually found a little hole in the window's mosquito screen and flew out.

Mohammad slowly turned his moist eyes to Khanum,

swallowed the lump that had suddenly began choking him, waited a few seconds more and then in a hardly audible voice said, "It is hard – very hard. But she must have done something – something to provoke him to do what he did."

"A lecher does not need any provocation. He must have been planning this when he started spending time with her after school hours."

"God curse his soul and the soul of his father." Mohammad whispered to himself.

"I have made an appointment with a plastic surgeon in Teheran for next week. I am going to take Nargess to his clinic where he will sew her up so tight that no husband will notice the difference. When we return from Teheran you will call your sons and tell them that I had taken Nargess to a doctor to examine her virginity and, thank God, no penetration has taken place from the front. Do you understand what I mean?"

"I only understand that you want me to lie."

"Don't make me angry man. You have lied to me a thousand times before – lie once more, then stop and beg God to forgive you."

Mohammad's grey colour turned blood red. He covered his face with both hands and began to weep loudly.

"It is alright to cry. It will cleanse your mind and relieve your heart from sadness." She patted him on the shoulder, and then moved to rise.

He removed his hands from his wet puffed-up face, looked Khanum straight in the eyes and begged, "Through your grace please my Mistress forgive me. Please."

She knew why he asked for forgiveness – all the oranges that he had sold without telling her and the ten percent he had added up to the grocery expenditure. Aware as how expensive life had become in Iran she had made allowance for his dalliances by ignoring the pilfering.

Giving him a meaningful smile she said: "Mohammad

who am I to pass judgment on you? Ask the all knowing, ever present God for forgiveness. I am a creature just like you, also needing plenty of forgiveness from the Almighty."

"You and I Khanum are not birds of the same feather?"

"True you and I are not birds of the same feather but we are children of the same God, born in the same way – the difference lies in the way we use our intellect, our judgments and the decisions we make. Now, my brother, I expect you to make the right decision both regarding opium and the operation on your daughter and not a word to any one especially Taghi."

"Chashm Khanum". Mohammad said rising with Khanum.

At the door, he took her soft hand and kissed it several times loudly asking God to grant her whatever she wished in life and to keep his family living forever under her shadow.

In the villa, Khanum consulted her telephone directory and having found the home number of the town's Mayor she dialled it. Office hours were till five in the afternoon and she knew she would find the Mayor at home now. He had been on her pay roll for a long time. The Mayor himself picked up the phone and Khanum invited him to come and take tea with her. They were neighbours and he loved her garden, enjoyed her interesting company and her expensive European gifts.

Half an hour later, Shahri leading the Mayor in his one size too big black suit knocked at the open front door. Khanum who was filling the pastry dish with the Mayor's favourites invited the guest in and asked Shahri to bring tea.

The Mayor was a thin, short, pleasant looking man with greying hair and moustache. He was no more than forty years of age but like most men of the post-revolution Iran, looked old, thwarted and tired. He was married and had four girls none of whom had as yet married. So he had many mouths to feed on the meagre salary of a bureaucrat. That was why he was on the take – like most those on a government salary. But in comparison to other local bureaucrats he was a fair man and Khanum liked him very much. In spite of his moustache, unshaved face and round collarless, buttoned up white shirt of the fundamentalists, he was a staunch critic of the government.

Shahri arrived with her tea tray, placed it on the coffee table in the summer room where Khanum and the Mayor were sitting and busied herself in the Kitchen area to eavesdrop. Somehow she had sensed the Mayor's presence was related to her family's problem.

The Mayor, his eyes roaming around the interior's elegant open space eventually turned to the garden and fidgeting in his seat said, "Khanum you have the most beautiful garden in the whole of the Caspian area."

"Thank you, Agha Mayor. It is your eyes that see the garden so beautiful. It is just that I love flowers and no one else in this area plants flowers. They all go for trees and shrubs. Now would you like sugar in your tea?"

"Two spoons please." Khanum quickly sweetened his tea and then asked,

"What about a piece of your favourite cream-puffs?"

"That would be lovely. You always spoil me, Khanum joon."

She smiled, took the pastry tongue and with it placed two cream puffs on his dessert plate – porcelain from Limoges. Then, relaxing on her seat she replied, "Well, I probably am as old as your mother. So I can spoil you! I remember your father well. He used to manage the rice fields of my father's friend, Mr. Salary."

"My father passed away last winter, Khanum joon," the Mayor whispered, giving his face the expected mournful expression of a bereaved.

"God forgive his sins and take him to heaven."

"Thank you, Khanum joon."

Mayor withdrew a clean white handkerchief from his coat pocket and wiped away his not yet formed tears.

"Agha Mayor, I am going to tell you something which I want you to pledge on the spirit of your father not to divulge to a single soul."

Khanum's tone forewarned of a serious matter. The Mayor straightened his thin narrow shoulders, stopped fidgeting, placed his hands one on the top of the other on his knees, fixed his dark, anticipating eyes on her and vouched to keep his lips sealed.

In order for Shahri not to hear anything, Khanum moved closer to the man and whispering, detailed the events of the past two days.

Frustrated Shahri slipped out from the kitchen door.

The Mayor, his frame rigid with tension, listened with his mouth agape, sweat beads glowing on his frowned forehead. The story was so incredible that he could not trust his ears – wondering how a man of God could be capable of such an act – such satanic transgression – of course he could be a fraud – there are many of them around. To be or pretend to be a mullah had become a prestigious and lucrative profession. "Damn man's insatiable desire for taboo," he murmured – and then for a second visualized one of his daughters being victimized and shivered. To erase the thought from his mind he took a third cream puff and consumed it fast. It would be a terribly difficult task to remove the man from the town, because no one would believe the story. That was why Khanum had not been to the authorities. The police, even if they had believed her, would not have dared to lift a finger against the mullah, and the Town Council to save face, would have blamed the girl for provocative behaviour. 'Mashallah, Khanum is a clever woman', he thought, unconsciously shaking his head.

Few moments passed in silence. The two drank their by

now lukewarm tea and the Mayor finished all the pastries in the serving dish before saying, "Khanum give me time to investigate the background of this man. I promise you I will start work tonight. I cannot believe that he is a true man of God. He is relatively new in town. He might be a fraud – a dangerous one and in the worst possible place. I have to get him out of the school. But how, I have to figure that out. As it is, we cannot bring any charges against him because his aba (robe) is his protection!"

"Agha Mayor, if you bring this animal to justice you will buy heaven for yourself."

"Enshallah. Khanum I know, like me, you are also a good Muslim. We respect our faith too much to allow people like this dog to disgrace it. Enshallah, God will help us to bring him to justice."

"Enshallah. So I can count on your help Agha Mayor?"

"Yes Khanum, I shall call you when I have news. Now may I have a stroll in the garden? Mashallah (God be praised) I can see you have lots of mulberries this year."

"Come let's walk to the tree and you eat as much as you want and I shall ask Mohammad to shake the tree tomorrow and bring a tray for your family."

"They would love it, Khanum Joon."

Outside the clouds had disappeared and the sky was as blue as the sea. Most of the roses had opened up revealing their true colours and exuding their aroma. A cool breeze was tossing the narcissus that had overwhelmed their beds. The lawn was moist and the creepers had extended their climbs. A lonely empty dinghy was swinging on the water. A fish smuggler must have had attached his net beneath it and had left it there to do his job for him. Shilat was the government's official fishery and only its members could fish. But the natives broke the rule and fished to feed their family and sell to the neighbours. The jewel of the Caspian next to sturgeon is Mahi Sefid (white fish). It is often fried to accompany herbed rice, a favourite of all Iranians and a specialty of the cuisine of the Northern provinces. Khanum was not a fish eater but she could eat Mahi Sefid every day. Instead of having Shahri deep fry it, she had brought a fish steamer from London in which her fish was steamed without any oil. Of course Shahri frowned upon steamed cooking and thought the expensive fish was being wasted in insipidity.

Standing under the tree, the Mayor ate all he could of the sweet, ripe mulberries while Khanum stood away, her back to the tree, waiting for him to become satiated.

Chapter 7

Niavaran – April 1951

It was a pleasant late spring afternoon – a bit on the cool side. The grownups and supposedly the children were taking their siesta while Khanum, having sneaked out of her room, was waiting for Parviz. Slightly nervy she was sitting on the tiled edge of the pool, her feet immersed in the cold water, thinking about her grandfather's illness. Earlier that morning, resting in bed with pillows piled behind his back he had looked pale and listless. When he was sick not even a fly dared to enter the room without permission – except for Parviz who was his favourite. Once or twice her grandmother had asked her to come and massage her arthritic legs. At the end of each session she had sent her off with a hug and a kiss. Her Grandma, ridden with arthritis, found comfort in having her legs and back massaged. The real masseuse was Fatimeh Sadat. She was never thanked and was lucky to get out of the room without being reprimanded for not having performed zealously enough. Fortunately Sadat was blessed with a strong ego. Used to her Mistress' reprimands, she hardly ever heard them.

Traditionally servants were treated badly but Abdullah Mirza and Shokat Bano were more considerate than other employers – and very generous.

Most of the servants at Golestan came from the Master's different villages. Bagher was in charge of teaching the new employees proper Farsi as they each only spoke the dialect of their respective Provinces. Then according to their fortés they were put under a skilled senior with a meagre salary that increased in accordance with capability and progress. Those lazy or insubordinate were hastily returned to their villages.

It was not unusual for the servants to marry among themselves. In such cases a wedding was arranged and the Mistress gave a small dowry to the bride and an adequate salary increase to the groom. Only married couples had their own rooms near the kitchen. The boys slept in a huge corridor that connected the kitchen to Bagher's moderately large chamber and the girls shared space with Fatimeh Sadat next to the villa's pantry. But humans know how to satisfy their desires and it wasn't rare that under the cover of the night lovers crept out, found a secluded corner and took their pleasures. Fatimeh Sadat in her vigilance kept count of each girl's time of the month and if one was late, a report was made to the Mistress, followed by investigations and a quick wedding that saved the honour of the culprits. Thus domestic affairs ran smoothly with thorough respect for and understanding of human needs.

The air was getting cold for a swim and Khanum's patience had run out. Something must have happened to Parviz to miss his swim which he loved, she thought and was about to rise when she saw a carefree Mohsen rush out of his room and run down the slope towards the orchard. Then she saw Bagher Khan creep out of the kitchen, carefully look around, and then take Mohsen's route. He seemed cautious not to be seen. His steps were firm but noiseless and his pace slow as though spying on someone or something. She stood, motionless, until he disappeared from her sight. Confused she dried her legs with her yellow towel and then wrapped the towel around her tiny waist, fitted her sandals on and hurried back inside. Terribly bothered by the way Bagher had behaved she sensed something was amiss and if so, Grandma had to know. She went to her little room which was next to the master bedroom, changed, hung her wet gear on the balustrade of her room's balcony, returned; then quietly lay on her bed reading 'War and Peace' until she heard her grandmother ring for the afternoon tea. She put the book on the bedside table, rose, smoothed her eiderdown, brushed her skirt smooth and then knocked and entered her grandparent's bedroom. Shokat Bano was lying on her bed which faced her husband's. They liked to face each other rather than sleep side-by-side. That position made conversation easier and more enjoyable. Television had not arrived in Teheran as yet and small talk was the couple's pastime. Their bedroom was very large and very bright. Two large south-facing French windows exposed the manicured garden and the turquoise pond with its forever-hopping fountain. All houses in Iran face south, towards the Ghebleh or Mecca. This automatically allows for bright, sunny rooms that sometimes are so cosy one finds it difficult to leave their delicious warmth. Such was the atmosphere of this bedroom and it was here that often family members gathered rather than the formal sitting room or the cold Hoz Khaneh.

Ailing Abdullah Mirza had not left his bed for days and it was too early for the others to come for a visit. Khanum found her bored grandmother receptive to her tale which at the end upset her greatly. The girl, relieved by having rallied the information, kissed the wrinkled hand she was holding, threw a fearful glance at her grandfather whose face was hidden behind his newspaper and dashed out to find what had detained Parviz. She found him forlorn, sitting alone, on a step of the veranda one side of his face swollen and bruised. Giving herself an air of annoyance she sat next to him and asked, "What happened to your face? Did you have a fight with anyone?"

"I fell on my face."

"Oh that is why you kept me waiting by the pool?"

"Yes, sorry about that."

"Ok. I forgive you," she said light-heartedly and taking his hand said, "Let's go and see if the sour plums have ripened?" He pulled his hand away and frowning said, "I shall never go near the orchards again."

"Why? Did you find any snakes there?"

"No, but I will never go there again, at least not alone."

"Well with me you won't be alone."

"Not now, and I want to ask you a favour."

"And you think I will oblige when you are so moody with me?"

"Yes, because you are my friend and cousin." There was something in his aura that worried Khanum.

"Ok, what do you want me to do?"

"Can you ask your Grandma to let me sleep on the floor of your room from now on?"

"Are you an ass? No one will allow a boy to sleep in a girl's room!"

Realizing how stupid his request had been, Parviz bit his lower lip hard.

Khanum looked at him with troubled eyes and said, "I think there is something wrong and you are not willing to tell me."

"No there is nothing wrong."

"There is and you do not want to tell me."

"No."

"Ok, then I think you should ask my grandfather to allow you sleep on the floor by his bed. He will never say no to you. We all know you are his favourite!"

"I cannot do that. He will ask me why and I cannot…"

"You cannot what?" Khanum asked her curiosity inflamed.

Parviz threw her a weary glance, slowly rose and without a word limped away a hand on his buttocks, leaving behind a lingering air of mystery. Khanum found Parviz's behaviour strange. He had fallen on his face, yet it seemed his bottom was in pain. What could have happened to him? She wondered with deep concern. Suddenly a surge of fear flamed inside her and made her anxious for the wellbeing of her forever-timid friend. She had to do something for him, but what? Perhaps his uncle, Abbass Mirza, would help once he saw his swollen face – after all he was living in his house and was his charge. The thought evaporated her anxiety. She breathed easy and once more carefree she rose, stretched her arms up, sent a short thanks to God, returned to her room and resumed her reading. She loved Pierre and definitely wanted him to marry Natasha.

In the other corner of the garden, hidden between two blackberry bushes, Bagher, face crimson, seething with fury was watching his son and Abbass Mirza in action; their humph and heaves, axing his soul apart, making his head throb with ache and his stomach churn with revulsion. His heart was beating so hard that he wished it would break its cage, pop out and end his wretched life. The revulsion, the shame, the repulsiveness of the intimacy in his view, made him feel like a wolf craving for flesh. He stood still, somehow unable to move, unable to utter a word, unable to strangle both of them with his own hands – then and there. He saw Abbass Mirza withdraw, bend and kiss Mohsen's round, firm buttocks. He heard his son moan with pleasure. Utterly disgusted the world became a wavering darkness and when sight returned to his vision he saw Abbass Mirza place money into Mohsen's open palm and whistling his usual tune walk away. Mohsen, feeling the delicious texture of the notes in his hand lingered on a bit longer. Then he shoved them in his pants pocket and smiling hip-hopped towards the kitchen. Bagher stood still, his legs immobilized, his mind stoned and his senses dead. Suddenly as though earth's gravity had pulled him down he fell on the dried mud, hitting his nose on a rock. He let out a muffled cry of desperation and, heaving hard, began to weep like a father who has just lost his son to a savage death. He remained coiled on the ground until Huppy the watch dog, untimely on the loose, began licking the nape of his neck.

With the edge of his elbow he fiercely nudged the dog away, slowly uncoiled, crept up, took couple of deep breaths and, with trembling hands, shook the dust off his black trousers and then withdrew a handkerchief from his pocket, wiped off the nosebleed from his chin and neck, held his nose tight to stop further bleeding and, dragging his feet, managed to reach the mouth of the spring near the turquoise pond. The dog followed his master wagging his tail nervously. Bagher squatted by the spring, cupped his shaky palms, dipped them in and began splashing his face with the icy water. Then he shifted his head backward to stop his nose bleed. Huppy dared to inch closer. Bagher now calmed a bit, patted the dog gently, washed his face again, performed his ablution and lumbered to the kitchen where he picked up his prayer mat from the mantelpiece, went to his room, spread the mat on the threadbare Kilim and began to pray.

For three days Bagher could not utter a single word, as though he had lost the power of speech. Wordless he bowed to the Mistress, did not look at his son at all and did all the chores by himself. He did not want either Mohsen or Ahmad near him. Mohsen was delighted, Ahmad confused and the Mistress alarmed. She guessed whatever had induced the muteness in him concerned his son. Using her charm she tried to extract something out of Mohsen to no avail and then she decided to corner Bagher when alone. To this end, one mid-morning she walked to the kitchen garden where she was sure to find him picking the herbs he needed for the forthcoming meal. There he was busy pulling spring onions out when his mistress wished him good morning. Her loud greeting shook him out of his dark thoughts with a sudden jerk. He bowed and stood still.

"Your herb garden is flourishing, Bagher Khan."

For a while he stood mute and then trying hard he managed to stutter, "Yes Mis... tress, than... ks to good weather a... nd cow manure."

"And your green fingers"

Bagher remained mute.

"Dear man, I know something is bothering you. Please take me into your confidence and allow me to help you."

Touched by the concern in her tone and ready to explode, tears welled in his large gloomy eyes. He let go of the spring onion bunch, covered his face with his muddy, smelly palms and began to wail like a child. Shokat Bano, forgot her rank, put her arms around his round muscular shoulders and drew him to herself. He was so much taller than her. She gently patted his back and whispered, "Dear, nothing can ever be so bad to induce such anguish. Allow me into your confidence and let me help you son; remember I am your friend as well." The tenderness and compassion in her tone appeased Bagher's injured soul. He gently detached himself, took her hand and kissed it several times.

"Let us go to the pergola and talk," the Mistress commanded.

Huppy, chained to the Master's favourite pear tree, began to bark. None of the two paid any attention to the poor frustrated dog. He was unchained at dusk to catch thieves. At dawn he was chained back to safeguard the pear tree – even when there was no fruit.

In silence, Bagher one step behind his Mistress, walked on the paved path that passed by the swimming pool and led to the pergola that stood erect, like a bouquet of yellow roses. Creeper tea roses had invaded its entire structure, hanging like a lace curtain over its entrance. Inside, a wooden bench circled the cool enclosure. They sat face-to-face. The Mistress relaxed her tense shoulders, crossed her chubby legs, put her hands one on the top of the other on her knee, and fixed her large kind and perplexed eyes on her tormented, twitching companion. At first he could not bring himself to utter a word. He kept shaking his head back and forth, side to side, clenching and unclenching his fists, scratching his round hairy chin until eventually he found enough courage to verbalize the inferno that was burning his entity, allowing its flames to catch the sense of decency in the old lady, making her face blush with anger and her forehead saturate with beads of perspiration. Astound by the gravity of the event she could not utter a word for a long while. Only her tight facial muscles and the throbbing of her temple's veins told of the rage inside her. Thoughts raced in her aching head. It was shocking to learn that the man, who owed them his livelihood, could stain their family honour, fail his wife and take advantage of the innocent – how many of them – only God knew.

The silence in the pergola was thick with perplexed emotions. Suddenly a chicken dared to enter searching for morsels. Its intrusion broke their thread of thought. The Mistress lifted her head up and shook it in bewilderment.

"Shocking – had I not heard it from you I would have not believed a word."

Bagher kept his head down and, fidgeting with his fingers, said,

"This evil man has diverted my son from the right path. He has stolen my honour." Then he lifted his face up, looked into her sad eyes and continued, "Khanum a man without honour is as worthless as an ant. I cannot forgive either of them – nor myself."

He paused to swallow his grief and then begged, "Your ladyship has always been understanding and kind. Will you allow me vengeance?"

The hungry chicken, twitting its disappointment, left to search elsewhere.

A deep pensive silence fell again and then was disturbed by the buzz of a daring wasp. Bagher rose and with his large hands chased the excited insect out. He returned to his seat and waited for a response.

Shokat Bano's mind was agitated – Abbass – how many of them had he dishonoured – how many? She visualized the innocent faces of Khanum and Parviz and all the other children roaming around – who next – she thought. The menace had to be dealt with immediately, but how?

What about Tooran? And the Master who would never believe any of this – there was no use getting him involved. If not killed by the shock he would protect the bastard. Only Bagher could help without getting the family involved – perhaps an accident – perhaps. Her mind was too disturbed to think further than 'perhaps'.

She straightened her shoulders that had hunched, took a deep breath and said, "This lecher has brought disgrace to both of our families – his action is so vile that I cannot tell anyone, both for your sake and my own daughter's. So I leave it to you to decide how best justice can be served. Son, do as your conscience dictates."

Bagher's eyes regained a bit of light and shadow of a smile crossed his dry, chapped lips.

"I have one request to make and I expect you to fulfil it."

"Khanum your request is my command."

"You must never let your son know that you know what he has been up to. Never allow the respect between you and him rupture, find him a wife and marry him off."

She stopped, thought for a moment and then added.

"Zahra would make a good wife. She is an honest girl, pleasant to look at and a good ironer. I will give her a sufficient dowry for Mohsen to open a grocery story. We have a room on the street-facing wall. We can close it from the garden side and open it to the outside. It will make a good size grocery shop for him."

Deeply touched, Bagher left his seat and fell on his knees kissing her shoes. She gently patted his shoulder and whispered, "Get up and let's go. We have a lot of work to do."

"Yes my Khanum – a lot"

One week later Bagher Khan humbly asked the Master for permission to take Zahra for his son. The permission was promptly granted with a set bride price of one thousand toomans and a dowry in cash of the same amount. The wedding day was set for the following Thursday.

Zahra, only fourteen was orphaned at the age of seven when her uncle had brought her to Golestan. Tall for her age, she was pretty with two large black eyes and bushy eyebrows. Her skin was the colour of olive and a bit hairy. There was a twinkle in her large eyes that stole everyone's heart and the smile never left her rosy round lips above which lay a thin stretch of fluffy hair. The Mistress was very fond of her and believed she had a funny face which brought her luck. For this reason, every morning, she and not Fatimeh Sadat served her breakfast.

Amongst all the house boys Zahra liked Mohsen best. She found him attractive, poised and dignified. She could not wait to make him a good wife – at nights she dreamt of him and during days she gave him one or two cookies the Mistress usually left for her on the tea tray. But nothing she did seemed to please him. That hurt her. To divert the 'evil eye' of those jealous of her luck every evening when praying she asked God to open his heart to her and bring a smile to his lips – for her and not only for Agha Abbass Mirza.

People love weddings and those days when the only entertainment was listening to radio, it was a treat one embraced with excitement. So at Golestan participation in the preparations was total – that is with the exception of the Master who was seriously ill. And when he was ill the Mistress's world became gloomy. However, the new event was her doing and she had to partake and make sure all went according to plan.

Fatimeh Sadat, an expert tailor, was put in charge of the wedding dress, and the other servants were delegated tasks in accordance to their skills and capabilities. The atmosphere that had recently turned dire brightened and everyone found joy in being constructively occupied by performing tasks that pleased God and Bagher Khan. The man was the happiest of them all. Together with Ahmad and Mohsen, whose absences had become rare, were baking the various pastries needed for the Sofreh Aghd. This Sofreh had to be filled with everything that symbolized happiness, prosperity and fertility. The Mistress had already given Zahra a pair of candelabra, a small gilded mirror and an ancient volume of the Koran for the Sofreh – symbols of light, reflection and holy guidance. Eggs were being painted on by those artistic and the rest was left in the capable hands of Bagher.

The weather was warming and the mulberries were drying out and falling down. Every siesta time, Khanum tiptoed out of her bedroom, ran to the trees and scavenged the area below the branches, gathering the good ones and piling them up in her bamboo basket meant for her Grandma and then she would climb up a tree, sit on a sturdy branch and eat the dried ones which were deliciously sweet and crunchy.

That afternoon she was comfortably lodged on a thick branch with her legs dangling down, happily absorbed in her pleasure when Abbass Mirza crept out from behind the apple trees flipping up and down one of his daggers, its blade catching the sun's rays and dazzling like a fire tongue. His gaze fixed on the girl's bare legs he tried to attract her attention – without success. When near enough he grabbed one of her legs with his left hand and began shaking it. Frightened out of her wits she let out a cry, almost choked on the mulberry in her mouth and, coughing it out, fastened her grip on the branch staring at him with panic-stricken eyes. He smiled at her with lust.

She recognized the glare she disliked so much. A shiver passed through her tense body. "Uncle you frightened me."

"You must never be frightened of me. I am your friend and I love playing with you," he said while letting go of the girl's legs and returning his dagger to its case attached to his leather belt. Then he moved closer to the tree, grabbed Khanum's legs again and now began lustfully caressing them. She let out a cry.

"Don't be scared, little girl. I have come to play with you – a play that will give you lots and lots of pleasure. Just slide a bit further down for me, dear, and relax."

She did as told.

"Come down a bit more."

She slid further down until her legs were touching his neck. He fitted his face between her legs, sniffed the mild odour that exuded from her and felt even more excited.

"Come let me see what you are hiding between those white legs." Suddenly she felt terrified and then she remembered Parviz saying to her that he would never go alone to the orchards. Helpless, her eyes roamed around hoping to find the gardener or one of his aides and then they fell on the dagger case. Recalling its function she began to tremble hard. She became conscious of his hard breathing and contorted face. He seemed like a monster ready to devour her. She let out another cry. Suddenly with one hand he hooked her to the branch and with the other pulled her white pants down and threw them away. Then, swiftly, he lifted her up and placed her on his shoulders, his tongue finding its way to her private part. The girl kept screaming and screaming. Panting with excitement, he put her down and, pointing to his dagger, motioned her to be silent. Her cry froze in her throat and she began to shiver ceaselessly. He swiftly unbuttoned his trousers and pulled out his erected organ from the slit of his under pants and began to masturbate until a spray of creamy sperm jetted out landing on the girl's basket of mulberries. She cried a loud "no, no, no." He slapped her on the face. She held her aching cheek with her tiny hand, threw a horrified glance at the soiled basket; feeling nauseated she kicked it empty, and ran away as fast as she could towards the house suddenly finding herself within the strong folds of Bagher's arms. Struggling to free herself she began to cry hysterically. He lifted her up, held her tight, gently stroked her shoulder, kissed her black hair and patiently let her release her fright. In her ears he kept murmuring, "You are safe with me, God be praised you are safe, my little Khanum." Then he put her down, knelt to her height and said, "Khanum joon I saw everything. Thank God the worst has not been done to you. Do not ever again come to this part of the garden alone. He is here all the time, I have been watching him."

He stopped, looked deep into the girl's frightened eyes and whispered, "Not a word to anyone. This will be our secret. Ok, my daughter?"

The devastated girl without any comprehension looked at him with wide, moist eyes, her chest heaving ceaselessly, her mind trying to figure out what had happened to her. Then she asked, "What do you mean Bagher Khan? He put his tongue in me. He has made me dirty – very dirty. Fatimeh Sadat told me if any one touches you there the virginity blood will break. This means I have lost my honour. My father will kill me – honest to God he will kill me."

She began wailing and punching at her chest with all her might.

Bagher grabbed her hand and gently shaking it said, "No, no. Fatimeh Sadat is wrong. Child, believe me virginity is not lost that easy. Trust me and say not one word even to Fatimeh Sadat. I promise your honour is intact and if you want it to remain intact avoid your uncle and never come to this part of the garden alone. Run in, have a bath and try to forget the whole incident."

He let her hand go. She threw him an uncertain glance, caught his kind eyes, turned and ran to the house where she gave herself a long shower rubbing her vagina with soap until it began to burn. She stepped out of the shower still holding her vagina – protecting it even from her own sight. Quickly she dressed and ran to her bedroom. There she took her Koran, cuddled it and, rocking back and forth, began weeping again until exhaustion took over and blissfully she fell asleep. A few hours later, Fatimeh Sadat burst into the room and found her cuddling the Koran like a teddy bear, fast asleep. Gently tapping on her shoulder she woke her up. Not knowing where she was, the girl stared at her, conscious of tears welling up in her eyes. "What is wrong Khanum?" Sadat asked, deeply concerned. "Nothing Sadat, I have a bad headache – just that."

"You are hungry, that is why. Dinner is on the table and if you do not hurry it will get cold." She was not hungry at all, but not to raise any suspicions she rose, kissed her Koran and respectfully placed it on its holder sitting on the table next to her bed.

"Go, Sadat, I will be there in a minute."

When Sadat left she knelt by her bed, put her head on its edge and began to recite the verses of the Koran she knew by heart and then begged God to kill her before her shame became a public knowledge.

Chicken kebab with bread and fresh herbs was for dinner. Her grandparents had already dished their share and her plate was ready for her. She picked it up, sat on the comfortable chair facing the television (just arrived in Iran), forced down two small breast pieces while watching Delkesh's new show. Fortunately her grandparents were too absorbed in the program to notice her lack of appetite. Otherwise a stream of questions would have ensued, followed by a sharp reprimand. Then Fatimeh Sadat appeared with a large tray of mulberries for dessert. The sight of the fruit brought a sudden surge of bile to her mouth and she threw up her dinner with spasms that wouldn't stop. Frightened, Fatimeh Sadat put the tray on the floor, ran to the bathroom, and returned with a towel with which she gently wiped the girl's colourless mouth, and then the mess on the carpet.

The Mistress rushed to her grandchild frowning, turned to the maid and gave her a penetrating stare. "You idiot, you should have washed them better. The girl must have seen a worm stuck to a mulberry. Take the tray and throw away the infested lot."

Fatimeh Sadat knitted her thin eyebrows, hung the soiled towel over her arm, picked the tray up and walking out of the room whispered, "Allah Akbar."

"Grandma, I don't feel well, may I return to bed."

"Yes love. Tomorrow you feel better."

The girl, still giddy, limped to the bathroom, brushed her teeth, washed her face and then retired to bed. The next morning she woke to a very busy day. No one had time to notice either her pallor or her frequent visits to the toilet where she kept washing herself sore.

The Mistress's dalak (the bath masseur) had been summoned to prepare the bride for the nuptial night at the ancient bathhouse. Golestan had four modern bathrooms with white bath tubs and showers but the Persian style bath house was also maintained and used. It was beautiful with its blue tiled walls and seats, white floor tiles and hot and cold marble ponds. The garden's spring provided the water for both ponds through a sophisticated canal system which also was responsible for the garden's irrigation jointly with the water from the three existing wells. The Master who loved the tradition of being washed and scrubbed by a dalak in the bath house had even installed an oil burner in the drying room – something very rare. For him bathing in the traditional way every Thursday evening, in the company of his close friends, was a cherished social gathering which he hardly ever missed. Abdullah Mirza did not like change and within the security of his four walls had managed to preserve the lifestyle of his predecessors who hated to break with old customs and values. To his chagrin, the Pahlavi Shah was introducing change practically every month. Reza Khan, and after him Mohammad Reza, were upstarts planted on the Peacock throne by the British whose aim was to subjugate Iran and steal its oil – everything evil in Iran was their fault. The sensitivity to British interference in the internal affairs of Iran was such that even draughts were considered a result of British conspiracy. The saying was that if the British Prime Minister farted at Westminster the shah would smell it at his Palace of Marbles.

Since Abdullah Mirza's illness, the bath house had not been used; consequently its walls had moulded and it smelled of damp. Bagher had already visited the place and together with Ahmad using bleach and baking soda, had scrubbed the tiles shiny; placed goblets and jars of fruit cordials on the tiled seats and a large dish of fresh green almonds and sour plums picked from the garden – spring's delicious offerings.

The festive ceremony of preparing the body of the bride for the groom is an ancient ritual to which traditional family and friends look forward to. Usually the Mistress only attended the Aghad, the actual marriage ceremony, but for Zahra she wanted to be present at all the events. Bagher had spread a small mat on the tiled bench on which her ladyship was sitting and watching the dalak's expert hand remove Zahra's body hair, with the honey wax that had replaced the usual string method. When she reached the pubic hair the girl's cry of pain brought a momentary hush to the misty room. The dalak took a spoon full of corn flour, dusted it over the sore skin, then continued to inflict more pain until Zahra's gate to heaven became spotless pink ready to give and receive pleasure. Once her facial hair was removed and her eyebrows plucked she was dipped into the warm water of the first pond. Her hair wet, the dalak washed it with an olive soap, combed the foams out, and dipped her in water several times until no soap suds came out from midst of the comb teeth. Then she was rinsed in the cold pond. Clean and glowing with happiness Zahra, shyly covering her private part and breasts with her hands, climbed out to be dried and massaged with almond oil and be sprayed with rose water. Finally she was left to rest. The pause gave the spectators repose to chat while enjoying the refreshments laid out for them. Only one little being sat silent trying to control the tears that sparkled in her beautiful, almond-shaped black eyes. No one noticed her, not even her Grandma.

Suddenly the door of the bath house opened and in floated the joyous sound of Marzieh the washer woman's tambourine followed by Fatimeh Sadat proudly carrying on both arms the white wedding gown she had sewn and embroidered with her own hands. Pride exuded from her sparkling amber eyes. She stood erect by her Mistress, bowed deep and then presented the dress to her ladyship for inspection, in her heart praying for praise. Shokat Bano knitted her thin brows, per habit wetted her lips and began examining the seams and the embroidery as carefully as if the dress was stitched for her and then she slowly lifted her head up, smiling her satisfaction, took out a gold Pahlavi coin from her purse that sat on her lap and gave it to the maid. Fatimeh Sadat was so overwhelmed by the generosity, particularly in view of the others, that she forgave all her Mistress's previous rebukes and loved her forever. Then smiling triumphantly, she took the gown to the bride and patiently dressed and coiffed her with a neatly

101

pleated white lace that fell over her pink face. The girl rose and gracefully walked around the room for the guests to appraise her. Their approving head shakes and smiles soothed her nerves and brought a shy smile to her rouged lips. Once the round ended, she posed in front of her Mistress who, taking her hand for help, rose, kissed her forehead, took her arm and left the bath house to Marzieh and the music of her tambourine.

Khanum, dolled up in a white taffeta short dress also tailored by Fatimeh Sadat, was reading her book when her mother entered her room. The girl threw the book onto the floor, jumped up and ran to the open arms of a brightly smiling Aziz Bano and began to cry. Surprised Aziz Bano kissed her face and in a tender voice asked, "Azizam what is wrong?"

"I missed you Mamman joon, I missed you."

"That is a silly thing to do, my love," her mother said over the tiny head that rested on her flat stomach.

"Let us go and wash your face and if you really want, you can return home after the wedding."

Khanum shook her head, grabbed her soft hand and held it tight – in its warmth she found reassurance.

Aziz Bano wore a black and white suit made by the city's most famous couture. She always dressed elegantly and smelled deliciously. It was her belief that wives must never take their husbands for granted. In a way she was a better wife to her husband than a mother to her children – but her good nature endeared her to all, even her often neglected daughters. Calmly she led Khanum to the bathroom, washed her face with warm water, and opened the Nivea cream jar that sat on the vanity shelf, dipped her finger in, drew a small portion out and gently rubbed it on her skin and lips. Then she combed her hair, tidied her fringe, kissed her shiny face and gently patting her back sent her off to join the other children. Alone in the bathroom, she carefully examined her own reflection in the mirror, tidied her curls and then left for the crowded Hoz Khaneh where the boisterous guests and several baskets of flowers were waiting for the bride.

There, Aziz Bano, smiling and nodding to salutations, went to sit by her sister. Tooran, whose big bottom had occupied most of the sofa, threw a resentful glance at her, nudged slightly to one side and furrowing her pencil thin eyebrows in an expression of annoyance, turned her back and engaged in conversation with Farhad Mirza standing by her, eyeing the young girls serving tea and soft drinks. Aziz Bano, shaking her head at her sister's rudeness squeezed in between her and the sofa's cushioned arm with a smile that hid her annoyance.

Tooran was a sombre looking woman, grossly over-sized, short and badly dressed. She was one of those to whom the world owed much – never satisfied and always resentful of those with a smile, specially her younger sister. Malicious, she delighted in belittling others. She took special joy in demeaning Ali Khan's background which, she thought was not as colourful as her husband's. Her imagination often played tricks on her perception of reality. This had become worse since her husband had decided to leave their four-poster bed for an uncomfortable bunk placed in his study where he could amuse himself with porno pictures; no one knew where he had acquired them from. Her objection had caused a great row ending in humiliation. Unhappy in marriage, her tongue had become even more venomous especially towards her sister and her little brat of a daughter. Aziz Bano never graced her remarks with a response. She was blessed with a forgiving nature. She believed bearing grudge and being nasty poisoned the soul while forgiving nourished it. The relationship being such they sat with their backs to each other and made conversation with others until the local minstrel commenced playing the joyous Yar Mobarak Bad, (the wedding song) announcing the arrival of the bridal entourage. Fatimeh Sadat, the surrogate mother that she had been to Zahra, dressed in a long simple light blue satin dress with a matching scarf, entered from the main entrance gracefully leading the bride to the white lace-covered stools placed facing the Sofreh Aghd and Mecca. A few minutes after the bride, the groom walked in, dressed in a black suit, white shirt and a new tie – all made for him by the Master's Armenian tailor except the French tie. His long straight black hair was oiled and combed back. He held himself erect and graceful – more graceful than some of the nobles present. He was followed by his father, Ahmad and Parviz who appeared thinner and sicklier than ever. The groom sat next to his bride. Bagher, who, from the corner of his eye was watching Abbass Mirza, saw the mocking wink he threw at Mohsen. The bastard was standing behind his wife's chair playing with her curls. A dreadful pain squeezed his heart and made him cringe. He threw a quick glance at his Mistress. She seemed too absorbed in her own thoughts to notice anything at all. The anxiety-ridden lady impatiently waited for the event to end. She knew her husband was suffering and it was out of chivalry that he had left his bed to honour the ceremony with his presence. She wanted him back resting in bed – the sooner the better. A feeling of premonition had been nagging at her ever since the morning. She had tried to obliterate it without success.

Bagher swallowed his indignation, stepped aside to make room for the mullah upon whose hand laid an open volume of the holy book from which he was about to read the verses that were to bless the union. Aziz Bano on one side and Marzieh the laundress on the other, held the corners of a white lace stretched over the head of the couple, on which two sugar canes were being rubbed against one another by Nasrin the wife of Hussain Agha the gardener. Those engaged in this ancient act have to be happily married, as it is believed their luck inoculates. No divorcee is allowed in the room, during the Aghd ceremony. The sugar dust that settles on the head and the shoulders of the couple supposedly blesses the union.

When the recital finished, sugar candies mixed with copper coins were thrown over the head of the couple by an ecstatic Fatimeh Sadat. Zahra for her was the daughter she never had.

Mohsen, with a false smile titillating on his round lips turned to Zahra and reluctantly lifted the white lace from her face. The beauty in his view took his breath away. An unconscious exclamation of surprise escaped his lips and his heart missed several beats. She looked absolutely stunning. Her black eyes were much larger now that her eye brows were plucked thin and her hairless skin was deliciously soft and creamy. And above all, her voluptuous rosy lips, slightly apart in a shy smile had become utterly irresistible. He could kiss them forever. Overwhelmed, he looked deep into her eyes that shone with love. His heart melted. She felt it and broadened her smile. He took her hand and squeezed it hard. Feeling his desire, her heart almost burst with joy.

The Mistress whose eyes were fixed on the couple saw the glitter of passion in Mohsen's eyes. A broad smile of satisfaction brightened her hitherto grave countenance. She caught Bagher's happy eyes and gave him a triumphant wink.

Chapter 8

The same evening – Niavaran April 1951

Dusk had cast its grey wings over the horizon when the cheerfully boisterous domestic cadre left the villa for Bagher's domain where a delicious dinner awaited them. The children so far behaving properly, found the Aghd area – to their delight unattended by any grownups. Thrilled by the opportunity they playfully attacked the pastries and untouched sugar candies mounted in ornamental dishes. The assault was so untamed that not only did it crush dishes but also led to a fight that attracted the attention of Ali Khan passing by. Frowning, he threw a thrashing look at each and every one of them except his own daughter, angrily shouted his reprimand, got hold of the nearest boy who happened to be the gardener's son, slapped him on the face before harshly ordering them all to return to their living quarters. Disappointed their fun was so quickly disrupted, whispering their objections, they left a pale Khanum alone. Embarrassed by her father's outburst and cruelty, she threw him a contemptible glance and ran after the boy who had been slapped, grabbed his arm and apologized for her father's unreasonableness. He looked at her with kind eyes and said, "It is Ok. One of us servant boys had to be blamed and I happened to be the nearest to him." Khanum noticed the glimmer of tears in the boy's eyes. Her heart tight with sympathy, she stretched up to his height and gave him a big kiss. The boy smiled at her kindly and ran to where the dinner was being served.

As the noble mob dispersed, the Hoz Khaneh, left in a messy state, became empty and bleak. Some of the guests returned home, a few went to Abbass Mirza's house and a couple of addicts headed for Farhad Mirza's apartment to smoke opium. Khanum headed to the pantry where Fatimeh Sadat had just dished out the Master's barley soup, and was squeezing lemon juice on it. To have an excuse to enter the forbidden bedchamber, Khanum, begging with her large eyes, began to hassle the maid to let her take in the tray. Exhausted by the chores and excitement of the day, Fatimeh Sadat relented with a sigh of relief. She handed over the silver tray cautioning the girl to walk very slowly so as not to spill the contents and get her into trouble. Pleased, Khanum gave her arm a big kiss, took the tray from her and watching each step, careful to avoid the chairs and the cushions that were strewn around she walked at a snail's pace towards the bedroom.

Abdullah Mirza, having signed the marriage contract, as the guardian of the orphan Zahra, had immediately retired to the solitude of his room to rest in peace. The long illness had evaporated his vigour, rendering him impatient and lethargic. He had no appetite for food or socializing. His handsome face had sunken deep; his forever trimmed moustache, eyebrows and hair turned peppery and his colour jaundiced. There were two large black rings around his dull, hollow eyes. Ruffled and unshaved, was the countenance that had captured and hurt so many hearts – and agitated was the mind that lately had become guilt ridden.

Lying in bed his eyes followed his wife's every move; not wishing to let her out of his sight, he begged her to stay in the room and whisper to him the stories that had made them laugh. Shokat Bano, herself, sensing a dismal gnawing at the pit of her heart, did not want to miss one single moment of his company. She loved him with every fibre of her entity and thus was so sensitive to his desires that she could read his mind immediately. She had noticed the recent glow of tenderness in his eyes and read in their depth the plea for forgiveness which she knew he was too proud to ask. It did not matter to her at all, for it was not in her nature to bear grudge against anyone let alone her beloved. Tonight, with all the merriment that had surrounded her she had felt miserable. Throughout the ceremony, sitting by him, she had sensed his pain and listlessness. She knew of no more medicine to give him. The only thing she could do was to relieve him from the mental pain guilt bestows. So when he changed and retired to bed and asked her to remain in the room, she sat on the edge of his bed, took his hand to her lips, kissed it several times, told him the stories she knew he wanted to hear and at the end said, "My love, thank you for being such a good husband. You have been the pillar of my strength, the light of my sight and the love of my life. If I have ever displeased you in anyway, I beg you to forgive me."

Touched by the extraordinary nobility of her soul, his throat tightened and the pain in his chest intensified. He closed his eyes, breathed heavily for a while and then took her hand, kissed it, put it on his heart and murmured "thank you for these kind words and thank you for your absolution. No lucky man has ever had a better wife than I. Now I fear death no more. I shall die a happy man. Thank you my angel- thank you my Khanum."

Deeply touched, she gently squeezed his bony cold hand, bent and stole a quick kiss from his cold forehead and whispered, "You made me who I am. My Agha, your love brought the best out of me. Thank you Azizam thank you."

Brimming with an unprecedented feeling of love mixed with gratitude he embraced her tightly. Their body and soul joint in the power of love – they felt united and in that unity all mêlées were forgiven and forgotten. Her head on his chest, she heard his heart beat a little too fast and felt the heavy rhythm of his breathing. She inhaled the smell of his sick body, still pleasant; brushed her face against the visible white hair of his chest before kissing it. In a state of blissfulness she lifted up her head, looked at his tranquil face still handsome and noticed he had fallen asleep.

Gently she tidied up his cover and tiptoed to her own bed and laid on it, closed her eyes and let her mind travel through time, to when they were young and life seemed endless.

Half an hour later the door crept open and Aziz Bano came in. The room was very stuffy so she left the door open. No one dared to open a window in case Agha caught a chill. She quietly walked to her mother's bed. The old woman recognized her perfume and opened her eyes.

"Your father is sleeping, sit here, on this chair near me." Pointing to the chair Shokat Bano whispered in a loving tone.

Aziz Bano, tiptoed to her father's bed, tidied his cover that had become slightly skewed, switched on his bed lamp, turned the room's light off and returned to the seat by her mother's bed. The two began chatting about the happenings of the evening and the cutting tongue of Tooran that had impelled Abbass Mirza to run to his quarters before the two-tier creamed cake was cut. Their voices were low and their elongated silhouettes moved on the facing wall like sinister images in a black and while thriller movie.

A soft click-clack on the marble tiles became audible. It interrupted their conversation. They both turned their heads towards the door to hush the entrant when they saw Khanum, her head half visible from behind the silver tray step in. The little girl hit by the room's gloom halted – not knowing what to do.

To wake up her husband Shokat Bano softly called his name.

Aziz Bano took the tray from her daughter with a loving smile, carried it to her father and whispered, "Agha, your soup will get cold."

No response.

She put the tray on the bedside table and began lightly shaking his legs. Agha did not move. Brows knitted into a deep frown she gently took his hand and searched for his pulse. There was none. She put her face by his nose and felt no breath. She hesitated, turned to her mother with wide, frightened eyes a woeful cry escaping her mouth. She dropped on her knees; put her head on the edge of the bed crying. Shokat Bano jumped off the bed and ran to her husband. Unbelieving, she rested her head on his heart and listened for a sign of life, then she too knelt by the bed and began to weep.

Khanum stood there mortified, not daring even to dart a glance towards the dead. Terrified she ran to the pantry, grabbed Fatimeh Sadat's hand and stuttering incoherently, pulled her off the ground, towards the bedroom. Bewildered by the pallor of the girl's face the maid followed her and once inside hastened to the deathbed, whispered a couple of Allah Akbars, turned towards the door, took the little girl's hand and pulling her behind her rushed out of the room. Accustomed to finding dead corpses amongst the old servants, she immediately picked up the telephone in her pantry and informed those living within the compound of the incident. Then she ran to Mosayeb's room.

One by one, Abbass Mirza, Tooran Khanum, Farhad Mirza blissfully sober and Dr. Nafisi the family doctor who was a close neighbour arrived. Ali Khan amongst others had returned home. The doctor, examined the corpse, asked several questions from Shokat Bano, pondered for a little before diagnosing a heart attack as the cause of death. He knew Agha had been suffering from Angina.

In the main guest room a mattress covered by a white sheet was placed by a tearful Mosayeb on the floor, facing the Ghebleh. The men carried the Master out of the bedroom and laid him on this mattress and then covered him with a white sheet. The same mullah who had performed the

Aghad ceremony sat on the floor, above the head of the deceased and began reciting verses from his Koran to bless the departed's soul. Mosayeb, trembling with grief sat at the feet of his beloved Master crying like a helpless orphan. The recitation continued until dawn when a tent was erected by the spring, under which Mosayeb gently and lovingly washed his Master's body, sprinkled it with rose water, kissed its hands several times before shrouding it in a white cloth consecrated by the Master himself at the shrine of Emmam Hussain in Karbala. He was with him when he had bought two shrouds from the city's Bazaar, one for himself and one for him. That was thirty years ago. How time flies away! The gardener's son wondered before stealing a kiss from his Master's forehead. During his lifetime he would have never dared to kiss him on the face – always on his hand – the hand that had been his support in life. At that miserable moment, Mosayeb asked God for his end. Every morning he had opened his eyes with joy, because he knew he would see his Master, even though lately bedridden and exchange a few intimate words with him – those words nourished his soul and made him happy. His passing away took joy out of his solitary life. He hoped, perhaps, if all that they say was true and there was another world, he was sure he could serve his Master there too. Mosayeb had never been a praying type but from that day on he became a conscientious Moslem, hoping God would forgive his sins and grant him his last wish.

The widow's grief was profound yet controlled. Her husband had been the pillar of her strength and because of him she had bloomed into the beautiful flower that she was. She had married him at the age of sixteen when he was just twenty one. Fifty years of blissful living was enough to bring her on her knees and thank God. In her strength she had reasoned that everyone has a predestined birth day and a death day and she counted herself among the lucky ones to have enjoyed fifty years with a man like her husband. Now she had to make do without him, that was the will of Allah, hard but tolerable because she was fortunate enough to be surrounded by people who were good human beings except one.

News travelled fast. By nine in the morning the house was teeming with relatives and friends attired in black, come to pay their last respects. The washing ceremony had taken place after the morning prayers. The neatly shrouded body was now ready to be taken to the family mausoleum. At eleven o'clock the corpse resting on Ali Khan, Abbass Mirza, Farhad Mirza and Mosayeb's shoulders was carried to the hearse. The entire party except for the children and the servants left for the mausoleum in Emmamzadeh Abdullah. Mosayb sat in the hearse by his Master – wooing him and praying for his salvation.

The official mourning lasted seven days during which the house was filled with genuine mourners and those that come out of respect for an ancient luminary at whose generous table they had frequently dined – and his two sons returned to bury their illustrious father. Their French wives had remained in Paris.

On the evening of the seventh day, when Delkesh and Maroofi had ended the ceremony with a heartbreaking performance of their own improvisation, the Hoz Khaneh and its veranda were hastily cleared of the hired chairs and tables so that the venue be prepared for the reading of the will next morning. Shokat Bano was so impressed by the devotion the two musicians had revealed for her husband that she gave them her everlasting gratitude by kissing their faces and giving them ten gold coins each – a fortune at the time.

Morning arrived dark and gloomy as though the sky was also in mourning. Females of the household clad in black and men black arm banded, all sombre and silent gathered at the Hoz Khaneh which had already lost its soul. Once the seats where all taken up, Farhad Mirza, being the eldest member of the family, his chest tight with grief, holding the paper close to his myopic eyes with trembling hands, stood up and in a voice quivering with emotion read the will. Every sentence he uttered made a pair of lips move in prayer for the salvation of the generous man who had been thoughtful to the end.

Mosayeb was to reside in the house, in full comfort and respect until his dying day and then be buried next to his Master and friend. Fatimeh Sadat was left five thousand toomans and Bagher a large piece of land in Fumen, his home village. The rest of the senior staff members were to be given a thousand toomans each.

Seething with resentment, Tooran kept shaking her head to the injustice her father had inflicted upon his children by his generosity to the staff – something unheard of in Iran. Shokat Bano guessing what was going on in her head kept throwing her indignant glances. Aziz Bano, mourning loss of a wonderful father was silently crying and her two arrogant brothers, faces serious, postures upright, were planning as how to spend the great fortune that had come to them.

Khanum, downcast by the grave atmosphere of the assembly was sitting on the edge of the turquoise pond focussed on the playfulness of the five gold fish somersaulting under the sprouting fountain when she saw Abbass Mirza's reflection wave on the blue water that was shimmering under the light of the chandelier. She began to tremble and her thigh muscles stiffened tight as though protecting her untouchable zone against further hazard.

"Little girl, did you enjoy the game we played under the mulberry tree?"

Contemplating, Khanum kept her eyes focused on the ugly hovering reflection without saying anything. Then she

113

looked up and in his eyes detected the same notorious detestable sparkle that used to frighten her – but no longer. She tightened the muscles of her face, narrowed her eyes, threw him a murderous glance, quickly got to her feet; summoned all her courage and spat on the revolting satanic face that she prayed never to see again. Then she hurried to her mother and sat by her side.

After the dreadful event that had shaken the girl out of her wits, to impede further abuse, her ego created in her a defensive audacity too aggressive for her age. The survival urge awakened in her a sixth sense which she followed diligently. Her everlasting smile, together with her trust in people having been lost, she began to take preventive measures against possible mishaps. Her first step was to discard her skirts in favour of trousers.

Initially the strange change in her behaviour had surprised both her mother and grandmother. Then in the absence of any comprehensible reason they had looked upon it as a sign of early maturity. In a world that men ruled supreme, it was better to be strong and independent than weak and vulnerable – so their hope for a secure future for her had increased.

Sadly, neither had even perceived an inkling of the fume and fear that was boiling inside her and craftily hidden beneath the calm seriousness of her demeanour. It hardly ever burst out, but when it did, it became an inferno. That also had surprised them. But in those days parents led their own lives and left the nurturing of their children to the nannies and servants – at least that was what was current at Golestan.

Khanum left for her home five weeks later. Before leaving she went to the kitchen where she found Bagher bent over a huge carcass of a sacrificed lamb he intended to chop up for the coming Kharji ceremony during which the recipients were to pray for the salvation of the Master.

114

Kharji is food donation to the needy; often given in remembrance of a death day.

Khanum gently tapped on the cook's back. He lifted his head up and saw her smiling. "I have come to say goodbye, Bagher Khan, and thank you for being my friend."

Bagher wiped his blood stained hands on his dirty white apron, lifted her up, kissed her tiny head, put her down and said, "I shall miss you my little Khanum Khanuma (lady of ladies)."

"Me, you too," she said before running back to the car in which her mother was waiting for her. Bagher's eyes followed her to the vehicle from where Aziz Bano was waving at him. He returned the wave with a shy smile in his heart sending them a Safe Guard prayer.

Death of the Master had its consequences for those living in the compound which was to be subdivided. Farhad Mirza was left land and enough funds to build his own house. Abbass Mirza could now live off his wife instead of his father-in-law. She, like the rest of his children, had become very wealthy.

Bagher, longing for retirement decided to take his family back home. His decision was respected by his Mistress under the condition that he remained until she moved into the house that was going to be built for her.

Bagher had always thought he would live under the shadow of his beloved Mistress until his dying day but events of the recent past had turned his paradise into hell. Every time he closed his eyes the memories of that dreadful scene haunted him. The bastard had not only stained his honour but had robbed him of peace of mind. The existence of that sinner had become an affront to his concept of justice and Bagher believed it was his duty to become the sword of justice – but how? It was this 'how' that was bothering him day and night.

The Kharji's menu consisted of rice with khoresht-e-sabzie (a delicious aromatic vegetable stew with diced lamb). Usually the mullah of the local mosque is asked to let his congregation know of the date of the Kharji and the address in which it is taking place.

On the afternoon of the eve of the Master's chelah (fortieth death-day) the needy of Niavaran queued up, pot in hand, by the closed gate of the compound to wait their turn for Bagher Khan to dish out their share and hear their prayer for the deceased. This was the only meal not supervised by the Mistress and Bagher was in charge of all distributions.

Bagher, Mohsen and Ahmad had been at work since the crack of dawn. The kitchen was hot, crowded with several extra hands busy preparing the various herbs to be used in the khoresht. Trays and utensils were scattered on the kitchen floor and a population of excited mice and cockroaches were feasting on the scraps and crumps strewn everywhere. Even with all doors and windows open the heat given off by the two huge charcoal cookers on which the khoresht and the rice were being boiled was unbearable. Droplets of perspiration trickled down the faces of all participants, making them irritable and impatient. Bagher turned to the gigantic pan of rice that required two people to lift. He wanted to take it to the sink to drain the water in which the rice was boiling through the huge strainer already in place. Mohsen gave him a hand and the two lifted the heavy container up and slowly walked towards the sink when Bagher stepped on a mouse slipped and almost fell with the pan tilting towards the floor and spilling some of its sizzling water on the floor bricks. Had it not been for Ahmad's timely grab of his arm and Mohsen's steady grip on the pan's other handle Bagher would have capsized and burnt himself and those standing by him. He sent a loud curse, steadied himself, drained the rice, put oil, saffron and yogurt mixed with a little water on the bottom of the pan, returned the drained rice into the container and together with Mohsen they placed it over the cooker, wrapped its huge lid with a large dish cloth, fitted it on the pan and let the rice simmer until the bottom became crusty. The mouse incident gave Bagher an idea for which God had to be praised. He had been planning and deplanning for a long time and now he knew exactly what had to be done. Ahmad standing behind his uncle heard him whisper a "Khodaya Shokret," thanks be to God. The boy assumed the prayer was because God had saved him from falling and spoiling the rice. His respect for his uncle increased and when he was asked to go and fetch the rat poison, he ran towards the provision room which today was left unlocked.

Once everything was prepared to the chef's satisfaction he took his prayer mat and retired to his room. After his prayer he sent Mohsen to the Mistress to ask her if Tooran Khanum was dining with her tonight. After her bereavement, Shokat Bano had asked her daughter, and she alone, to dine with her at night. This naturally had annoyed Tooran and delighted her husband.

Mohsen returned assuring his father that the Mistress would be dining with Tooran Khanum and that he should send food only for Abbass Mirza.

A few days after his wedding, love stricken and guilt-ridden, Mohsen had confessed his sin to his father and had begged his forgiveness. Bagher, had hugged him, kissed his forehead and urged him to ask for forgiveness from God. Sodomy is forbidden in Islam. Mohsen, in return, made a vow to become a deserving human being and not harm or hurt a living soul again – even a rat.

Once the meal was ready Bagher dished out the portions that were to be distributed within the compound. He chose Mohsen to deliver Abbass Mirza's share. But for the first time he put a cover on the dish so that Mohsen could not nick the tah-dig, the thick rice crust he liked so much.

Mohsen found the mission strange. Since his wedding,

his father had not asked him to deliver anything to that house. It also surprised him to find the dish tightly covered. He had noticed that Mirza's tray was the only tray always delivered unceremoniously exposed to air – like those sent to the servants' quarters. Knowing his father, he had guessed this was his means of insulting the man he knew he detested, whose sole ally had died, and was cunning enough not to bother his mother- in -law with any complaints about Bagher Khan.

Mohsen had changed since his confession. As though a heavy burden had been lifted from his shoulders he felt light, clean and very friendly – even to the timid Parviz who had always been subject of his envy and resentment. Upon the return of his parents from Europe, Parviz had returned home and no one had heard from him ever since.

On the other side of the garden, Mashhadi Mosayeb, desperately missing his Master, waited for the evening Azan. Nothing gave him joy anymore. Forlorn, he often sat on his old chair, smoking his pipe and watching the gate, even when it was closed – as though waiting for an arrival. Shokat Bano believed he was waiting for Ezrael, the angel of death – which did arrive two weeks later, at night when he was sleep – just like his Master.

At the sound of the Moaz's first Allah Akbar wafting through his radio, Mosayeb, rose and ambled to the gate. He unlocked and opened it wide to the waiting, tin-pot in hand crowd, mostly the well-diggers he knew so well. Like always pushing and pulling each other they rushed in to be the recipient of the best meat pieces in the khoresht.

"Don't rush. There is enough to feed an army." He shouted at the unruly mob before returning to his seat.

Out of respect for, or fear of the old man the entrants improved their behaviour. They formed a line; each saluted him politely before hastening his pace towards the well-known kitchen. Proudly holding his pipe, Mosayeb

118

responded with a light head nod, a meritless wink or a quick hand wave.

The two enormous containers, steaming and exuding mouth watering aroma had been removed from the kitchen and placed outside. When the head of the line reached the kitchen front, Ahmad began serving the rice and Bagher the khoresth. In order not to be later, labelled as 'unfair', they both had to pay careful attention to the amount of rice and number of meat chunks they dished out in each vessel – regardless of its size. Gossip spread fast after a Kharji event.

Bagher changed into a clean white shirt and well-pressed black trousers seemed very happy and talkative. From his aura emanated the confidence of a man in control of his and everybody else's destiny. He cordially chatted with the recipients, asked after their welfare and made small talk, something he hardly ever did. Ahmad was enchanted to see his uncle in such an amicable mood.

From above, a full moon lit the earth with its golden glow and a canopy of silver stars twinkled at the contented crowd politely waiting their turn and willingly murmuring their prayers. A pleasantly cool evening breeze consecrated by the current power of prayer gently rustled the branches of the cypresses that lined the path to the kitchen – on its way to reach Abdullah Mirza waiting in the other dimension of life for this last worldly blessing.

The bright night was indeed as magnificent as the generous deed being undertaken in remembrance of a man loved by all. The participants seemed to be enjoying the mouth-watering smell of delicious food that they would share with their families who at home were impatiently waiting for the treat. Under the country's dire economic situation, not many could afford to buy rice let alone meat.

At home, Abbass Mirza, vodka glass in hand stretched comfortably on a sofa that faced the television set. He was watching Delkesh's show when he heard the door bell ring.

Without taking his eyes from the singer's big swinging bosoms he called out that the door was unlocked. Mohsen heard him. He opened the door, stepped in and coughed his arrival. Abbass Mirza recognized the sound, put his glass on the table and shaking his head with delight, rose to greet the lad. Mohsen, his handsome face set in seriousness, murmured a quick greeting, put the meal tray on the dining table in the adjoining room and turned to leave when Abbass Mirza cuddled him from behind and began to rub himself against his back and steal lustful kisses from the nape of his long neck. A feeling of unprecedented disgust engulfed the boy; he summoned all his energy in his hands, and like a wild beast grabbed the man's arms and uncoiled them from around his waist. Then he turned, threw the flabbergasted Mirza a hateful glance and spat on his face.

"Bisharaf," (Ignoble) Mohsen shouted before running towards the open door and out into the garden.

Shaken by the assault, it took the Mirza couple of minutes to collect himself. He withdrew a handkerchief from the pocket of his trousers and wiped the spit off his face. Astonished by the boy's changed behaviour that he instantly attributed to his being married, he shrugged his shoulders and thinking that the boy had become a passé anyway, lifted and carried his tray to the sitting room. Delkesh was still singing. He placed the tray on the coffee table, removed the copper lid from his plate of rice and khoresht-e-sabzie. To his delight it was steaming hot. Forgetting the obligatory prayer before eating a Kharji, he dined with appetite, and washed the rice down with vodka. After a few minutes, a dreadful spasm erupted inside him. He let out a cry and held his stomach with both hands. Beads of cold perspiration formed on his furrowed forehead. Then another, even more excruciating spasm attacked. Twitching with pain he began to vomit blood. His body started to convulse so violently that he collapsed face down on the carpet squashed between the sofa and the coffee table. Gradually the trembling subsided.

An hour later, Tooran Khanum walked into the corridor surprised and annoyed at the door being left unlocked. She heard the voice of the newsreader coming from the sitting room. "Agha I am back," she announced coquettishly. His non-responsiveness irritated her. Gritting her teeth she hurried to the sitting room intending to coax him for having left the door unlocked when she saw him curved face down between the sofa and the coffee table. 'He is drunk again.' she thought with disgust. Reluctantly she bent to shake him out of his stupor when she saw the blood vomit on the carpet. She pushed the table away with her leg, knelt down and gently lifted his stiff head up. A cry of horror escaped her throat when she saw his purple, blood smudged face, his mouth agape and his open eyes bulging out of their sockets. Dropping on the floor she began to scream, pull her hair out and beat at her chest. No one could hear her – realizing that, she rose and ran out of the house to the main villa and hysterically pushed on the bell button and repeatedly banged on the door. A grumbling Fatimeh Sadat, her hair out of the cover, opened the door to the frantic woman whose wails brought the rest of the household into the Hoz Khaneh and then to where the deceased laid. There, in the absence of any sober male member (Farhad Mirza was zonked) Bagher took charge. He forbade anyone to touch the body until the arrival of Dr. Nafisi already summoned by Fatimeh Sadat and then ordered Mohsen to take the dinner tray away and give to Ahmad to wash the dishes, with the rest of the crockery he was cleaning in the main kitchen.

Shokat Bano knelt on the floor next to her daughter and tried to calm her anguish with kind words, soft kisses and promise of companionship. Tooran, a pathetic sight squatting by Mirza was gently stroking his hair crying softly and cursing herself for having been so nasty to him – the gentleman that he had been, so handsome and so calm. Why had she been so vile – why? And how could she ever forget him? Who could ever replace him in her life? Who and who and who? Horrified at the thought of having to live alone, she increased the vehemence of her cry and started beating her head with both hands. Those present felt her sorrow deeply. Her mother, embarrassed at her unseemly behaviour particularly in front of the domestics, grabbed her hands, held and kissed them before whispering, "Azizam, please try to control yourself."

Fatimeh Sadat ran out of the room to the main building and some minutes later returned with a tray of camomile tea which she placed on the coffee table.

Shokat Bano turned her face to her maid, threw her an appreciative glance, picked up a cup and in the kindest tone said, "Tooran joon drink this, it will calm you."

Without raising her head, like a stubborn child, with her elbow she nudged the cup away. It capsized on its saucer with most of its hot content spilling over the carpet missing the lady's skin. Crimson with embarrassment, she uttered an 'Allah Akbar.'

Fatimeh Sadat, threw the widow a contemptuous glance before taking the saucer from the stretched hand of her Mistress careful not to let anymore tea spill down.

No one dared to talk. Bagher unable to look at the corpse any longer left the room for Mosayeb's Quarters.

Half an hour wasted in silence. Then Bagher's voice came in from the corridor. He was talking to the doctor just let in by Mosayeb. The three entered the room looking befittingly sombre. All eyes turned to the doctor. Almost in unison they greeted him with their 'salam doctor joon'. The doctor acknowledged their greeting with a brief head nod and spotting the corpse knelt by it. Tooran's sad eyes fixed on him. In them he read implore for the impossible. For once he felt for her.

"Tooran Khanum, please allow me to examine Mirza." She made a move to rise, but couldn't. The cramp in her legs was too painful. The doctor gave her a hand. She was very heavy. After the second attempt she managed to rise. He slowly led her to the armchair on which she dropped almost breathless. Then he returned to the corpse, lifted its head up, and one look at the purple facial skin and the blood vomit made him ask for what he had eaten. Shokat Bano threw Bagher a meaningful glance. Their eyes met for the briefest of seconds. Unable to hide his guilt he lowered his and began describing for the doctor the ingredients of the meal fed to almost sixty people. The doctor saw the empty vodka bottle and the almost empty glass by it. He took the glass to his nose, sniffed it. Pure vodka! He shook his head in regret and diagnosed alcohol poisoning as the cause of death. He was privy to everyone's health problems in the family and he knew well how much Mirza drank. So he was not surprised to find him alcohol poisoned.

"Do we have to call the police and have an autopsy doctor?"

Shokat Bano asked in a troubled voice.

"Why would we need the police, Khanum? I shall sign the death certificate myself. He ate the same meal as everyone else, cooked by Bagher Khan and brought to him by Mohsen. The food could not have been rotten and no one here is the Mirza's enemy to murder him. I am sure it is alcohol poisoning – prevalent amongst alcoholics – we all know how much Mirza liked his vodka."

Everyone nodded their acquiescence and no one noticed Shokat Bano's sigh of relief – except Bagher.

The next morning Bagher found himself summoned to the Hoz Khaneh. For the first time in his life he felt an attack of anxiety hit him hard. He took off his apron and threw it on the Mistress's kitchen chair, washed his hand with soap, brushed his hair with his hand and rushed to test his Mistress's fairness. He found her sitting alone, deep in thought, dressed in full black of mourning, now for two. With a nod of her head she invited him in and with her hand pointed to the chair near her sofa. He bowed and walked to the seat. Fatimeh Sadat appeared from her pantry and was immediately motioned out by the Mistress. The two friends sat face-to-face. A fragranced breeze was whiffing through the open windows teasing the sun shafts that were splashing on the marble tiles giving the interior a surrealistic ambiance. The fountain was jetting high, splashing down over the goldfish playing their usual game. The Hoz Khaneh, the place of the family's merrymakings, now mirthlessly glittered with light – a blinding, spiritless light.

Shokat Bano gave Bagher a serene smile, fixed her kind eyes on his pale and anxiety ridden face and said, "I called you here to tell you that it might take much longer than I thought to finish my house and it is not fair to expect you to stay here that long when I know you are longing to retire home and begin a new life. In spite of the fact that I be losing a trustworthy friend I want you to leave as soon as you are ready."

She paused, picked up the envelope that was on her lap and handed it to him. "Here is a cheque for ten thousand toomans to help with the building of the house I know you are planning to construct on your land. It is just to say thank you for all you have done for the family and me."

Bagher, whose face was now wet with tears, took the envelope, set it aside and then went on his knees, grabbed his Mistress's legs and sobbing begged her forgiveness. Gently she pushed him away and then with fingers lifted his chin up, gazed deep into his imploring eyes and said, "There is nothing to forgive. Man is the architect of his own destiny – always remember that. We all deserve what we get. You are a fair and good human being – I am very fond of you

124

and if ever you need anything you must remember that you have a mother in me. Now go and get going."

Bagher looked deep into the eyes that shown with affection for him and loved them more than ever. However, as his station in life required he had to obey her order and this was an 'order' and not release from a promise. So he picked up his envelope, rose, wiped his nose with his sleeve dropped his head for a second and shyly asked, "May I be impertinent enough to ask for a picture of you and the Master Khanum joon?" Smiling a very sad smile, Shokat Bano rose, slowly walked to her bed room and returned with a silver frame that held a family photo. She handed it to Bagher and then gave him a warm hug before sending him off.

Bagher stayed and cooked until the mourning ceremonies of Abbass Mirza ended and then together with his son and daughter-in-law left for Fumen.

Ahmad replaced him as the principal cook.

Chapter 9

Niavaran – a few years later

A year after the division of Golestan, Shokat Bano settled into her new, comparatively modest house. Well-water ran through a large swimming pool and was cleverly channelled out for irrigation. She was lucky in that one of Golestan's deep wells had fallen in her land lot. God be thanked, there was talk that soon pipe water would reach Niavaran. However, no one ever trusted the municipalities to actually undertake any projects that improved the living standard of the inhabitants in the area under their jurisdiction. The Mayors danced to the tunes of the rich and created ridiculous difficulties for the less privileged. Happily the Mayor of Niavaran liked Shokat Bano and regularly visited her home for a glass of cold coca cola just arrived in Iran, fresh fruit and the neighbourhood gossip. The old lady enjoyed having visitors. Now that she was left with only Tooran, Fatimeh Sadat, Ahmad the cook and Hussain Agha the gardener she felt lonely. The other servants had returned to their villages or had found occupation elsewhere. Farhad Mirza was living in his own house lost to opium. Aziz Bano was living in Teheran and the rest were in Europe either studying or jet setting. At the beginning it was hard, but Shokat Bano was blessed with a cheerful nature and saw beauty and purpose in almost everything. Soon she adjusted to her new life and began taking delight in its offerings.

Her family members and those who had bought land from them had also built their own villas; however most of them had rented their properties to the foreigners who had come to invest or work in Iran. Authorized by the municipality (for which a handsome bribe had been paid) a road was constructed in the middle of the old garden leading to Saltanat Abad Street, the main thoroughfare that connected to the old Shemiran Road and eventually the city centre. This road was named Golestan. Two narrow brooks had to be constructed on each side of this road. The street brooks were necessary for irrigation before piped water reached Shemiran. Each neighbourhood had a Mirab or water-chief responsible for fair division of water rushing through these conduits. Each water recipient had to construct a canal connected to the side of the brook. This opening was closed off with a cap and was opened at the due time by the gardener or the farmer under the cautious eyes of the Mirab who returned to close it off. Water theft was common as the Mirab couldn't possibly stop it. The sources of this liquid gold were the local springs and 'Ghanats', underground canals through which subterranean water ran and resurfaced at random. The allocated time share of the water depended on the area to be irrigated for agricultural purposes. However as the city was sprawling towards the north, agricultural land was being turned into residential for which there was no water allowance. Thus the Mirabs made a small fortune by letting water run into the gardens of rich owners without wells.

To decorate Golestan Avenue, Hussain Agha designed a narrow flower bed on the edge of each brook in which he planted a neat row of young plane trees. Hussain Agha was not only a very good gardener but also a socially conscious individual. He knew the drivers in Teheran were careless so he hoped his trees would eventually create a protective fence for pedestrians and the students who often, book in hand, sat under the shade of street trees to study for their final exams.

So life went on. The old died and babies were born.

Hitherto, the political problems had intensified. An escape from an attempted assassination by a young member of the Tudeh Party had changed the young shah from a playboy into a monarch aspiring to introduce revolutionary social and economic reforms. His progressive steps and subsequent success in crushing the communists impressed President Truman enough to grant Iran a considerable financial aid to be spent on developments.

At the same time Prime Minister Mossadegh, a seasoned politician and a devout nationalist, turned his attention to addressing the problem of the country's oil and stirring up violent attacks against the British. Chairman of the National Front, a party with only nine members, he succeeded in imposing the law which nationalized Iranian oil. The nationalization infuriated the British Government enough to send paratroopers to Cyprus, amass troops she had based in Iraq on the Iranian border, and ask the International Court of Justice at the Hague to appoint an arbiter in the oil dispute and impose an economic blockade on Iran. In retaliation Mossadegh appealed to the United Nations. In response to his appeal the Security Council voted to look into Britain's complaint against Iran.

A week later, in New York, the Prime Minister influenced the Security Council to postpone examination of Britain's request until the International Court came to a decision regarding the issue.

Back in Iran, to manage financial problems, Mossadegh floated a loan of two billion rials and started printing money. Inflation soared, but the people supported and stood by him. In an attempt to solve the country's political problems, the Prime Minister asked the newly re-elected Parliament for six months of absolute power. This request was granted. He also asked for the portfolio of war minister, but the shah refused to oblige. Mossadegh resigned. Riots broke out. The Majlis voted for Mossadegh's reinstatement. He became war minister, took over the crown's budget and exiled many of the shah's meddlesome family members.

Tension confused a divided nation. Rumours began to circulate that Mossadegh was selling the country to the Communists. The Tudeh Party was beginning to resurface – and nothing scared the average Iranian more than the threat of communism.

Mossadegh's popularity began to wane. An adverse wind of fortune made Churchill Prime Minister of England and General Eisenhower the American president. The two war-mates decided to do away with the old politician.

On July 6th 1953 Kermit Roosevelt, a CIA operative entered Iran to tackle the Mossadegh nuisance and reinstate the shah's power. Only three people knew of the plot: the shah, General Zahedi, and his son Ardeshir. The initial plan was for the shah to issue a decree to remove Mossadegh and replace him with Zahedi.

On August 10th the shah and his queen left Teheran for a short holiday at Kalardacht in the mountains. Colonel Nematollah Nassiri, commander of the Imperial Guard, was to deliver the dismissal decree to Mossadegh. The information leaked out. Early the next morning, Mossadegh went on radio and broadcasted the news of the unsuccessful coup d'état against his government. The entire press attacked the shah, pronouncing him 'the foreign puppet'. At Kalardachte, the royal couple panicked and hurried to Ramsar where the king's aircraft was waiting for them. They flew to Rome.

Back in Teheran, the conspirators, who had been lying low, were regrouping, biding their time for the right moment to set their second plot into motion. Conspiracy was in the air and the atmosphere was dense with anticipated trouble. People respected Mossadegh, but feared the Tudeh who had resurfaced fully. They were also accustomed to having a shah. Monarchy was part of their culture, part of their heritage but their monarch had left them at the mercy of Providence.

During those history-making August days everyone was restless, unhappy, anxious, indecisive and above all tired. Then on a boiling hot day a political volcano erupted in Avenue Istambul and its force turned Iran's chance of becoming a democracy to ash.

It started with small groups of men, shouting 'Long live the shah!' tucking ten rial notes bearing the sovereign's portrait under the windshield wipers of cars as they passed by. People, cautiously at first, then boldly, began to cluster around them stretching out their hands for a bill. Gradually the crowd turned wild waving the notes around, shouting, 'Long live the shah! Long live the shah!' All the streets converging on Parliament Square filled with masses of moving black heads and outstretched arms waving the notes. Mossadagh supporters mixing with the demonstrators began snatching the notes and tearing them up. But they were outnumbered. A heavy fight broke out, as a tank carrying a smiling and waving Zahedi appeared slithering through the mass hysteria. Now the collaborators shouted, 'Long live Zahedi!' and 'God protect the shah!'

In Rome the fugitive sovereign heard their cries and safety guaranteed by CIA, returned to reign – with what seemed at the time, an iron fist.

A few days later Mossadegh was arrested, his house looted and ransacked. Soon Iran's oil flowed again, as did further American aid. A heavy crackdown on the Tudeh drove the activists underground. Confidence returned to the Bazaar, the trade pulse of the country. Commercial activities began to thrive and Iran commenced a hasty run towards westernization. Everything Western was emulated. The wealthy began to send their children to European schools and take overseas vacations. One such person was Khanum. She was taken to England and enrolled at an English boarding school. The separation was hard for the girl, only eleven, yet to spare her parents the usual parting pains; she hid her fear of loneliness beneath her usual timid smile. Ali Khan consoled himself by believing that the step was to guarantee his daughter a secure future. Once eavesdropping on the grownups, Khanum had heard her father say to a friend, "Wealth can be lost but never a good education". An insightful child she had immediately discerned the wisdom of the statement and made scholastic achievement her primary goal.

St. Peter's Private School for girls had five Houses in which the boarders were lodged. Khanum was left in the care of a middle-aged spinster House Mistress, with a chip on her fat curved shoulders, a mocking smile on her moderately pleasant face, a cutting tongue and an unnatural devotion to a fat ugly cat which Khanum, as the only foreigner in her House had to feed. Miss Nicholson, as her name was, had a penchant for unreasonable punishment implemented most severely on those who did not take her Chemistry course. That included the new foreigner.

At first Khanum's inability to speak English rescued her from understanding the Mistress's catty remarks but her ability to learn fast destroyed her immunity and exposed her to Miss Nicholson's stings that at times were sharper than that of an asp's. Nevertheless she persevered.

Time passed agonizingly slowly.

Alone in the midst of strangers, her inner turmoil intensified. At times she found herself terribly confused and terrified and when anxiety attacks flared up she lost her power of concentration affecting her learning ability. Often she had to read a page several times before comprehending its content. That worried her immensely. Then one day when her world became too sinister she found herself at the school's infirmary supervised by a Scottish nurse who had been kind to her when sick. In the homely corpulent Matron's convivial company she found enough courage to divulge her secret and ask to be examined. Appalled by the

131

story, the Matron fed her a cup of hot tea and a piece of Scottish shortbread before asking her to take her pants off, lie on the bed and spread her legs wide apart. Flushed with embarrassment she did as told. The nurse consoling the girl with kind words put her surgical gloves on and set to work. After a few minutes of careful vaginal examination, delighted, she confirmed that Khanum was still as pure as the Virgin herself. The news brought tears of happiness to Khanum's eyes and she began to laugh and cry at the same time. She jumped off the bed and gave a tight and loving hug to the delighted Matron whose plump cheeks flushed with joy.

However the next Miss Nicholson venomous reprimand shattered the girl's fragile confidence and returned the awful doubts to her aching head. The thought of having been touched 'that way' became more haunting, taunting and reprehensible than ever. Irrational convictions and self-blame resurfaced again and again. It was she who had brought the abuse upon herself. Had she not been glutinous, had she been obedient and not a spoilt brat nothing of the kind could have ever happened to her. Thus inferiority complex became firmly implanted in her mind leading to a compulsive desire for self assertion. At times she became unnecessarily aggressive and snappy. Those who knew her wondered at the duplicity of her character.

Through immense effort Khanum finished school with eight Ordinary Level and three Advance Level certificates which allowed her entrance to any good university had she been permitted to apply? But further education was not on her mother's' agenda for her. She had to return home and marry.

The gift for her excellent A-Level results was a summer holiday at Cannes – where she joined her parents at the end of her last school term.

Aziz Bano had not seen her daughter for two years. She

was delightfully surprised to find her so beautiful and elegant. Her greatest ambition in life was to have this daughter married off to a decent worthy man – like her other son-in-laws who were from good families, highly educated and handsome. Several names raced through her agile mind; she examined their credentials meticulously and then concluded only a few were worthy enough to be enlisted and discreetly pursued. To impress upon her daughter the virtues of her candidates she craftily introduced the question of marriage albeit so regularly that both Ali Khan and Khanum became fed up and politely asked her to stop her serenades. Marriage was far from her mind. At first she reasoned with her mother and, when that failed, she began to argue with her. They disputed and disputed until they began to hate each other. Ali Khan knew they were as obstinate as one another so he decided to step in, make amends and save the holiday from a bitter end.

One early afternoon, fresh from his siesta he summoned his wife and daughter for a talk. At first both refused and then when he raised his voice which rarely happened they yielded. Sulking like children and avoiding each other's eyes they presented themselves from different corners of the large suite and took their seats on the balcony that overlooked the calm water of the Mediterranean. The length and breadth of the beach was colourfully crowded with people sunbathing and having fun. Boats of all sizes and sorts floated around and a few speed boats roared away with water-skis savagely cutting the waves leaving behind a stretch of fluffy line.

Pretending to be angry, Ali Khan scolded them for their silliness and accused them to be spoiling their expensive holiday. Feeling guilty neither responded; each avoided his eyes and occasionally vented a short sigh. Ali Khan mellowed his tone, addressed his daughter and rationally justified her mother's concern for her future which naturally was out of love. Then, he turned to his wife and told her the time when parents chose mates for their children had expired and the reason why he had sent his daughter overseas to become educated was that she could learn to decide for herself. Carefully avoiding his wife's angry stare, he carried on to provide logical reasons for his decision to give Khanum permission to apply for further education. This unexpected turn of events induced a deep frown on Aziz Bano's already tight forehead and a charming smile on Khanum's glowing face.

To regain his wife's favour, he took out from his cream coloured linen jacket pocket a beautifully wrapped small box and offered it to her.

"What is this for?" Aziz Bano asked in a hurt and mocking tone, her frown intact.

"This is a little gift to thank you for being such a good mother. It is from your daughter and not me."

Surprised by the invention, Khanum, threw her father a probing glance. He returned it with a teasing wink.

Aziz Bano, her air still sombre, unwrapped and opened the red Cartier box. There she found the huge emerald ring she had been eyeing on the jeweller's display window at the Casino ever since that first night of their arrival in Cannes. Her frown disappeared; her eyes began to sparkle like fire flames and her tight lips unbolted into an ecstatic smile. Ali Khan giggled like a child who has been given the treat of his life. Khanum rose and went to her mother, apologized for having been belligerent and bent to kiss her when Aziz Bano's arms wrapped around her shapely shoulders. They embraced, whispered endearing words and kissed their differences away.

Ali Khan, content that the rest of their holiday would pass pleasantly, rose and went to change for the Casino hoping to win back the cost of the ring. Khanum, who guessed his intention gave him a loving smile. "Baba thank you and good luck tonight."

"Darling, you are my luck. Did you know that ever since you were born when I touched copper it turned gold?"

"I cannot believe that, Baba joon. But thank you for the compliment," Khanum said, hugging her father with all the love in her.

It was during this holiday that they heard that Queen Farah, the shah's third wife, had given birth to a son – the heir Mohammad Reza Shah had been so eagerly waiting for. He was named Reza after his grandfather, the founder of their dynasty.

Khanum, to the delight of her father, was accepted at Cambridge University where she studied Psychology and graduated with an honours degree. Now, even the shah's brothers were not good enough for her – that is in her mother's opinion who proudly hugged her one sultry July evening at the crowded Mehrabad airport.

The new chauffeur pushed Khanum's packed trolley to a white Mercedes Benz around which a few admirers were exchanging opinions. When they realized the owners had arrived, they voiced their praise and dispersed.

Giggling, Ali Khan asked his daughter, "Do you like this car?"

"It is beautiful Baba."

"It is yours – our gift for your graduation."

Seething with excitement, Khanum hugged and kissed each parent several times. She had never dreamt of owning a car let alone her favourite. Now she had to learn how to drive.

On their way home, Aziz Bano was as talkative as ever and Ali Khan mutely enjoyed his daughter's delicious fragrance. She always smelled of Jasmine that was why he had the gardener plant a shrub just outside his bedroom window. During springs and summers the scent wafted through the open window teasing his nostrils and reviving in him fond memories of his beloved Lalleh. Now she was back – at home – near him – what joy! He was not a superstitious man but he truly believed Lalleh was born with a lucky star because, ever since her birth, his touch had indeed turned copper into gold.

Usually it took thirty five minutes from Mehrabad airport to Niavaran. But tonight the traffic was heavier than usual. It provided Aziz Bano ample time to tell her daughter about a vernacular mullah named Khomeini whose fiery sermons had initiated an anti-government uprising that fortunately had been smashed and the agitator exiled to Iraq. Iran was on the road to becoming an industrial state like those in Europe all due to Shahanshah's wisdom and international standing.

Khanum patiently listened to her mother's unending reports while longing for a hot bath and her comfortable bed. She detested politics and thought of all politicians as self-serving ambitious individuals who often changed sides as easily as they changed neck ties.

As the driver turned into Golestan Avenue, Khanum passed her grandmother's new house and smiled. Tomorrow morning she would visit her, kiss her face, sit on her bed and massage her legs the way she used to do years ago. She loved her so much.

At the gate of the new villa, the driver beeped a couple of times before Gholam Reza, the gardener, opened the gate and the car drove into the huge, manicured garden that was surrounded by young fruit trees of all kinds, two huge weeping willows and fortunately no mulberry trees. An inviting blue swimming pool lit to the shade of aquamarine, was twinkling its glamour. A new maid rushed to the car, welcomed the Master's daughter and lifted one of the lighter suitcases; pulling it behind her she climbed the stairs to the tiled veranda and Khanum's bedroom that opened to it. The driver brought in the rest. Aziz Bano gave Khanum a grand tour of the house before they sat to dine.

Khanum, jet lagged and exhausted, retired to bed earlier than the others. In spite of her fatigue she felt light and happy. It was good to be back and a joy to be able to inhale the familiar aroma of a Persian garden breezing through the open window and hear the sounds of frogs and the cicadas that broke the stillness of the cool night. And, above all, her parents slept next door. She had missed them so much – and this beautiful dream house had its own swimming pool. What joy!

Early in the morning she dived into the pool for her usual fifty laps; refreshed and cool, dressed in a white T-shirt and jeans, she had half a melon for breakfast and walked to her grandmother's house. Their happiness was beyond measure and their talk non-stop only interrupted by Fatimeh Sadat's tea offerings and her ceaseless utterances of Mashallah (God be praised) in admiration of her extraordinary beauty and grace.

Khanum, sitting on the edge of the bed holding her hand was delighted to find her physically aged but little. She surmised it was her vibrant spirit and active mind that had kept her looking young for her age – of course no one really knew how old she was because at the time of her birth it had not been compulsory to register for a birth certificate. She noticed from her smiles that her teeth were her own and that her silver hair was still thick and shiny. Only the inevitable force of gravity had deepened the lines on her broad forehead and around her drooping mouth. It seemed her arthritic joints had reduced her mobility leading to weight gain that had in fact increased her grace. Khanum, listening to her tales, realized she still smiled at the travesties and unpredictabilites of life. Having heard about all present in Iran save her aunt she asked, "Granny how is aunty Tooran?"

Shokat Bano threw her a surprised glance and realized

her mother had not given her the bad news. "She left us azizam a year ago – I miss her so much – even her gossips and malicious tongue – but I think God in his compassion took her away to spare her from much pain. Cancer had spread to her lungs – why one would never know – no one in our family has ever had that disease."

The old lady paused to swallow her grief and then continued, "You know, Lalleh joon, death is not an end but beginning of another life. Thus the dead should not be mourned but remembered with fondness and you, my dear, must never ever mourn me when I go. You must rejoice in the fact that I will be joining my beloved Agha – there – wherever that may be."

"I am sure it will be heaven, Granny."

"I am not so sure child. I pray for salvation every day." She sighed and then added, "I have done things in my life that I am not proud of! But it is all in the hands of God and the God I worship is a forgiving one."

The sadness Khanum saw mapped on her grandmother's face distressed her deeply.

What could this kindest of women have done that had given her such feeling of remorse? She wondered before saying, "Granny you have done so much good in your life that one or two mistakes will count for nothing. Allah is wise and he judges per circumstance and that is why it comes in the Koran 'it is better to leave vengeance to Allah.' I think this verse is to remind us of the forgiveness that Allah wants his creatures to exercise."

"Child, with all the years spent amongst the Christians I never thought you still remembered your religion."

"Granny I went through so many doubts that I had to take several religious courses at university to find my path. That is when I fell in love with the simplicity and egalitarian nature of our faith."

"I am so proud of you, azizam."

138

"Thank you, Granny. I am sorry for auntie's untimely death. Unfortunately she never was one of my favourites; nevertheless I hope God will forgive her sins. She had a very cutting tongue."

"Do not talk about the dead that way, my dear. It will not please God."

Instead of responding Khanum, bent and gave her a hug tighter than when she was a little child.

Khanum started work at the psychology department of a famous hospital. Her job was satisfying as it made her feel useful. The days, months and years that followed, besides work, and according to season, were spent in playing tennis after work, skiing during weekends, and partying almost every night. All these occasions provided opportunities for meeting marriage prospects from all walks of life, business men, government officials and young graduates from good families one of which was meant for her. His name was Sassan and he came from the respected house of Zand. He was a handsome young graduate from Harvard University with a doctorate degree in political science. His mother was a friend of a friend of Aziz Bano who, having seen a picture and having made enough enquiries about Khanum and her background, had decided that she and only she deserved her son. To this end several occasions were arranged the purpose of which was cunningly hidden from the major players. Had it been known to them neither would have participated. It was during the fifth dinner party and, after a long meaningful conversation, when Sassan recognized that beyond the visual beauty of Khanum laid a deeper more stunning beauty – that of integrity. Highly intelligent, Sassan was not looking for a doll but a companion for life. He was a man with a naughty past, and seasoned enough to choose for the right reasons.

Khanum, in turn, was surprised by the ease with which she could relate to him. His light touch did not make her shiver nor did his smell nauseate her. There was something in his eyes and in his soft tone that revived her dead spirit and made her smile with real pleasure. She found herself blushing when he looked at her. These sensations were new to her and they made her scared – terribly scared.

And one day Sassan asked her out to a tête-a-tête dinner without any chaperons. At first she refused but then, faced with her mother's threat of disownment, she accepted only if they were going to go to the Darband hotel's outdoor restaurant, the garden of which spread on the foothill of mount Alborz, sloping down to the high walls of the Imperial Palace compound. The restaurant was famous for its Italian band, French food and super-rich clients. Socialites frequented the venue. There, amongst acquaintances, Khanum would feel safe – any other place would have been too frightening for the first date. Sassan, utterly smitten, would have climbed mountains for her let alone abide by her choice of a venue. She was different from the cunning and calculating women who had crossed his path. It was not her extraordinary beauty or her sexy legs that had attracted him. It was her purity, grace, dignity and aloofness. He wanted her so much that even the thought of her induced the pain of desire in his loins. Every night he made love to her in his dreams and the next morning the maid had to change his sheets. He saw her face on the moon, on the waters that ran through the narrow roadside streams and on the pages of his lecture notes. His female students at the University of Teheran wondered why he had grown so thin, pale and without any further interest in them. In the past, some had shared his bed at the nearby Intercontinental Hotel.

The moments of the day of rendezvous dragged like empty years until he found himself ringing the intercom. A few minutes later the gate opened and she appeared in a silk dress of emerald green embroidered with gold threads and fresh water pearls, low cut at the neck and short in length revealing her slender, shapely legs. She looked stunning. They shook hands and politely he led her to his top down, white convertible Jaguar E type, opening the door for her. She gently slid in and made herself as comfortable as her pounding heart allowed. He sat by her and threw her a tender glance. It melted her heart. She smiled at him and he at her. The weather was perfect and there was no wind to mess up her long wavy hair. Cheerful, they drove away, passed Tajrish and drove uphill; passed the waterfall that noisily thrashed at whatever lay in its path before taming into a gorge. Children stood near the waterfall to be sprayed by its splashes. The air was much cooler up on the mountains. The sky was clear mauve and the moon and the stars were shining brilliantly. Somehow the usual air pollution had dissolved into a sweet love elixir. The couple giddy with happiness left the car and hand-in-hand floated uphill. To reach the restaurant, they crossed the narrow bridge that vaulted over the rivulet, climbed the steps and came face-to-face with the very polite maître de hotel who led them to their reserved table close to the dance floor. As they took their seats all eyes turned towards the handsome couple, being recognized by many whose tongues immediately began to waggle promising an active tomorrow for the gossip mongers.

Browsing through the menu, they discovered they shared the same taste for food. The band began playing Cha-Cha-Cha and Khanum's shoulders and feet captured the rhythm. The two rose and, waving their bodies rhythmically, moved to the floor and danced to the beat of the music that gradually melowed until they found themselves tightly entwined, breathing each other's scent and feeling the flame of desire ignite in their loins. He whispered into her ears of his love and longing and she reciprocated by pressing herself to his enflamed body without repulsion. The dance and the dinner finished with a marriage proposal that received neither a yes nor a no.

Three dragging days passed with Sassan's telephone messages hanging in the air. On the fourth day which was a Friday she talked to him and invited him to join her mountain climbing. Excited, he hurried to her house, collected her and together they walked to the nearby park that led to the mountain track.

Hand-in-hand on a narrow dusty and, at times, stony trail they ascended Mount Alborz passing by noisy waterfalls, tamed creeks and busy refreshment kiosks until they reached the zenith of their route from where they could view the ugly city sprawling aimlessly in all directions particularly the west. In spite of the blazing sun, up close to heaven, the air was cool and fresh. They found a solitary wild fig tree under which they sat holding hands, he relaxed, and she tense. He guessed she had a secret to tell so he respected her pensiveness until he saw tears gather in her eyes.

"What is it, my darling?"

He asked in such a tender tone that broke her resilience.

"I cannot marry you, my love," she whispered, turning her gaze at the broken thorn that was being tumbled by the breeze. His heart sank. Gently he lifted her chin up, kissed her tear drop, kissed her lips and then asked why?

"I am dirty."

"You are dirty?" he asked, astounded.

"Yes I am," she whispered before pouring out the tale she had guarded with debilitating shame – for so long. She found herself recounting – without tears but with a vigour that was cleansing her inside of the disgust that had kept her awake at nights, turned into anger over minor issues and at times had incapacitated her power of perception.

Patiently he listened. Only the change in his facial expressions from shock to disgust and then to compassion and empathy revealed his inner turmoil. Khanum noticed all and loved him more.

She stopped. He pulled her to himself, kissed her face, her eyes, her lips and then pressed her head to his chest and kept kissing it.

Free from the dreadful burden that had battered her self-respect for so long, she suddenly felt light. The confession had the effect of cleansing her mind of the unbearable self-doubts that had made her hate herself and all men. She let her head rest on his welcoming shoulders for a while and then gently pulled back, gazed deep into his kind accepting eyes and asked, "Will you still have me as your wife?"

"I will be honoured to have you as my wife." He whispered giving her a look that vouched for his sincerity. Then, smiling, he bent and said, "Let me kiss the mouth from which only truth spills out."

He pulled her to himself and they kissed and kissed until the desire became too improper. They rose, held hands and giggling like children, descended the steep hill.

Two months later Aziz Bano's wish for her daughter was granted. She married a decent man from a good family with a bright future. No mother could have asked for more.

The wedding took place at Darband Hotel. Delkesh, now a very famous singer, was amongst the guests. She sat next to her old beau, Farhad Mirza, and flirted with him all through the night. To everyone's surprise and delight he had committed himself to a clinic and succeeded to rehabilitate himself – at his age it was a miracle.

Chapter 10

Teheran – the last years of the Pahlavi reign.

The shah of Iran was rejoicing the elevation of his status on the international arena with unprecedented pride. He had caused a huge rise in the price of oil and was vociferously asserting his aim to enable Iran to become an advanced industrial state. The Western powers openly saluted his international and domestic successes while planning his demise. His support for Egypt in its conflict with Israel had estranged Iran's ancient amicable relation with the Jewish state and his arrogance had alienated his close neighbours and the United States.

Prime Minister Hoveyda, proud of his Majesty's domestic policies, was busy proclaiming full employment while disregarding the high inflation brought about by the pouring of oil money into an economy without sufficient infra-structural support. The ports were suffused with imported merchandize without enough means of delivery. At times perishable goods rotted and had to be discarded in the waters of the Persian Gulf. Construction was booming and the construction workers had abandoned their usual bread and cheese lunch for hamburger and Coca Cola. Airplanes were full of foreign investors coming to invest in the land of opportunities. Five-star hotels operated to full capacity with their restaurants and night clubs offering pleasure seekers exciting venues to spend their time and money. This economic prosperity created an unprecedented social neurosis particularly amongst the ever-expanding Middle Class. Palatial homes were mushrooming up in Shemiran which had become the Capital's most expensive and exclusive residential area, while new suburbs were sprawling on all sides of the city like malignant cancer cells.

The roads suffered from heavy traffic jams and the air from car fumes. The sky was never again pure azure and Damavand Peak forever snow-capped was hardly ever visible from behind a veil of pollution. The shah's unmeasured modernizing steps, together with people's overseas visits for business, pleasure or shopping brought about a change in social values. Western values competed with the old cherished ones. To be westernized became fashionable and to remain traditional an affront to progress. The gap grew wider and wider but those partying and prospering paid no attention to the schism that, as yet, had not surfaced.

Sassan's university career was replaced by a ministerial position with a handsome salary, a chauffeur-driven Mercedes Benz and entrée to royal palaces in which Khanum's elegance and beauty, at times, outshone that of the royals. In spite of her education and intellectual aptitudes, Khanum had no aspirations for herself except making Sassan a proud husband and being herself a useful member of society. God had given her everything except the ability to bear children. She had asked her husband to take a Sieghe, a temporary wife with whom he could sire a child she could call her own. But Sassan had refused. He not only idolized her but he also respected her beyond measure and a Sieghe, would be an insult he would rather die than inflict upon her. He loved her so much that he glutted in the fact that she could bear no children. He wanted her for himself and no one else. A child would be competition – and that he could not tolerate. So he came up with a noble suggestion. Why not establish an orphanage? The Empress was a kind lady and had an earnest ear for any suggestion that ameliorated social mêlées. He was sure that she would help with any orphanage that they would set up and aid with its financing. So, one cool evening when they were having dinner by the pool, he asked his wife if she would mind having several children. Khanum's eyes flared with joy.

"Yes, yes, yes my darling."

"What about an orphanage?"

Instantly her enthusiasm faded and her small jaw dropped. She thought for a while then raising a brow and in a matter of fact tone said, "Why not? One for the children of abused mothers?"

"Why only limit it to bastards?" he asked thoughtlessly.

She went pale.

"Please don't use that word to describe innocent souls. It is more accurate to call them "children of bastards". If we establish such an institution I would want to help the child and the mother."

Sassan, stunned by her desire, exclaimed, "The mother?"

"Yes the mother – a social outcast! Do you think if a woman has not been discarded by her family, or reached the end of her endurance, she would want to place her child in an orphanage particularly in Iran where family ties are so strong?" Khanum stated in an emphatic, irate tone and then stopped, raised her questioning eyes to him to gage the level of his comprehension and empathy. Dumbfounded he remained silent regretting his hasty response. Staring at him intently, she saw in his kind, attentive eyes a timid request for pardon. Content, she relaxed her tense shoulders, softened her tone and added, "That mother, my love, would only be doing it out of desperation."

Embarrassed by his own tactlessness on an issue that he knew his wife was so sensitive about, Sassan lowered his eyes and bit his lip. Again her mind had worked more rationally than his, he thought, and instead of feeling resentment, he felt admiration for her deep sense of human understanding. His heart warmed to her even more than ever. Slowly he threw her a loving glance. She felt its warmth and smiled. He gave her a wink, smiled back and in a tone laced with honey said, "Yes, Khanum joon, as usual you are right. It makes sense to offer the mother some sort of involvement in the running of the establishment; she can earn a bit of money, be near her child and perhaps regain her lost self respect."

"Bravo, your Excellency!" She clapped and then stretched over the narrow table, stole a quick kiss from his lips, returned to her seat and continued, "And the child won't feel totally abandoned. We shall offer willing mothers priority in positions for which we need staff."

"Perfect my love! I shall ask the Empress on Wednesday when the Minister and I have a meeting with her."

Khanum was staring at him with affection. It was always a pleasure to look at him, so elegant and handsome in his usual white shirt and grey pants. Hearing the name of the Empress she frowned and asked: "Why do you need to take the case to the Empress, Sassan?"

"Obviously out of respect, and for financial assistance!"

"We don't need her assistance. Any royal involvement will come with a string attached to it. I want to run my institution according to my own program. I have enough to fund it and I have enough friends who are as generous as the Empress and willing to help, out of the goodness of their hearts, and not because they have been complimented."

"Azizam, in my position I have to be diplomatic. The Empress will expect to know in advance of such an undertaking by my wife. After all I am a government official and as such her servant."

"First you are not her servant. You are the servant of your country. Besides, this is my project and not yours. If I am paying for my venture I do not need the Empress's approval. And, if she really is interested in the welfare of her nation – as you so gallantly emphasize – she will admire our project, give her unconditional support, particularly in dealing with the bureaucratic side of the affairs, and honour us by coming to its inauguration. She can also encourage those of her family members who are using her name to win business contracts left right and centre, to contribute to this fine cause."

He acknowledged her logic and sensed a tinge of jealousy in her tone. It pleased him. It gave him confidence in her love for him. Men around her were like flies around a jam jar!

He closed his eyes and started tapping his knee with his right-hand fingers, a habit to calm his nerves and direct his thoughts. He knew his Empress and he knew his wife. Both expected respect, both were proud but fortunately not arrogant and he loved them both – in a very different way. He opened his eyes and met those of his wife's that were blazing with expectation.

"My love, I am sure her Majesty will admire your project even more if out of respect I mention it to her."

Khanum, comprehending his reason, pinched her shapely nose and gave him a reluctant shake of her shoulders. "Ok, now let's see who will benefit from our venture: less abused girls will find their ways to Shahre-No (the red district of Teheran) and less innocent lives will be stigmatized. And for this worthy deed of yours, the almighty will forgive all your numerous carnal sins and take you to heaven instead of the hell you would otherwise deserve!" she teased him, laughing and blowing him a kiss.

Happy, he gave her a big smile and exclaimed a loud 'enshallah'. They had often amused each other with naughty stories of his past and thus she had become privy to all his secrets.

At that moment, for them, the world seemed perfect. The air was balmy, the mild breeze soothing, the sky filled with twinkling stars and life with comfort and security. Khanum's only worry was to see Anna the maid's face drawn and dark – that meant domestic trouble which disturbed her peace. Everything for her had to run smoothly and nothing left for later, or unresolved.

Blacky, the poodle, that so far had remained relaxed under her chair heard a noise; reluctantly he unwound his slender trimmed torso, rose and wiggling his tail moved towards the sound. Sassan finished the last drops of his Shiraz wine, put the glass down and said, "So tomorrow morning I will have my secretary follow up the necessary steps to procure the required legal permissions and you will look for suitable premises."

"Javadieh is the poorest area. I shall look there."

Sassan rose, took a deep breath, glided to the Jasmine bush that was dressed in white, picked a handful of flowers, whistling a happy tune, returned and dropped them inside the low cut collar of his wife's cotton shirt. She took his hand, pressed it to her palpitating heart and kissed it and then rose to her feet. Hand-in-hand they left for their bedroom. On their way up they saw Anna, followed by Blacky, come down to clear the table.

Happily, she had a smile on.

Prime Minister Hoveyda was right in his boasting of no unemployment. Native domestics had become a novelty of the past. Now domestic labour was imported from the Philippines and Bangladesh.

Khanum never walked – she always ran. The permit was obtained very quickly and the news was passed on to the Empress whose charming smile assured Sassan of a verbal endorsement – without any financial commitment. Soon a house in Javadieh, south of Teheran was purchased, renovated for the purpose, comfortably furnished and a large black and white placard over the gate announced the birth of Lucky Mother's Orphanage. Within a month, the establishment was full and half of the mothers in employment.

A sophisticated luminary and a good sales woman, Khanum organized various lucrative charity events in her lovely home at Niavaran during which donated pieces from family, friends and benevolent merchants were auctioned – even Fatimeh Sadat contributed ten of her famous quince jam jars for one of the Tombola tables. The funds went to the orphanage in which Khanum herself taught English to some of the enthusiastic mothers and the elder children who, under supervision, were daily delivered to and collected from the nearby public school. She also made it compulsory for the mothers to take a one-hour course in Women's Hygiene and Birth Control she taught herself.

Motherhood, even though it was surrogate, went well with Khanum and she found herself less exacting and more tolerant. Every night she went on her knees and thanked God for her life and the good people involved in it.

Their social life was extremely busy; almost every night they were invited to dinner or to a new show at the renovated Roodaky Hall where famous international entertainers and musicians like Frank Sinatra, Henry Mancini and Charles Aznavour performed. Sassan's gentleness, good looks, elegance and professional success had endeared him to everyone particularly young unmarried girls. Khanum was not as popular as her husband – that is among the snobs of the high society. She was meticulously picky and under no circumstances tolerated fools. Her tongue was sharp but never stinging. Her straightforwardness and lack of tact at times cost her popularity but she believed a handful of sincere friends were more valuable than a thousand superficial acquaintances. She attended the parties just to please Sassan whose position was climbing higher and higher. Now he had become a Deputy Prime Minister whom the shah liked very much and that was why they were often invited to the Palace of Niavaran to watch movies at the Palace's private movie salon or play Charades and other party games favoured by the royal couple. Khanum loved the shah but was not a fan of the Empress. Yet she admired her love of everything Iranian. By her order most historical monuments and sites were refurbished, artists were patronized and craftsmanship encouraged. At first people took the good with the bad and lived comfortably. Women could walk the streets at nights without fear and entrepreneurs invested and reinvested as though even the sky was not the limit. So long as one did not criticize the regime, one was as free as a bird and that was wonderful for those apolitical. Of course nothing wonderful lasts forever. Perhaps this is because often blessings are taken for granted. Judging in retrospect this is what politically happened during the last prosperous years of the Pahlavi era.

Change happened too fast and led to rising expectations which were at times intangible. In its haste to enact the shah's impulsive plans, the government made mistake after mistake. The shah himself, made one wrong decision after another until he lost the trust of his people. Whispers of criticism turned into complaints which were eventually put down in letters published in daily newspapers. Religious sermons at the mosques turned political and vociferous mullahs became staunch critics of the Pahlavi regime. People started to meet, exchange grievances and demand reform and political freedom, albeit, from an autocrat reluctant to relinquish absolute power. At that point in time the call was for reform and no one dreamt of a revolution. Protesting masses took to the streets; Prime Minister after Prime Minster was appointed and dismissed and the monarch to exonerate himself, sent faithful servants of his regime including Prime Minister Hovaida to jail. Money and the rich began to leave the country. The shah kept wavering in his decisions – one day he was a benevolent dictator the next he was an unbending autocrat. Rumours had it that the Empress surrounded by leftists and traitors, was interfering in decision-making that could save the monarchy from fall. As the central government weakened, the opposition strengthened until the streets flooded with demonstrators shouting anti-regime slogans. The shah once again fled the country handing his throne on a silver platter to Khomeini the agitator whom he had exiled decades back.

Only God knows what impelled him to do so. Instead of gathering a handful of Iranian soil and taking it with him as a relic, had he remained in Iran, obliged his nation's demand for democracy, died and been buried under that same soil that he valued so much, history would have remembered him as a patriot. But, on the other hand, perhaps, indeed he was a patriot – and thought, perhaps, by giving up his throne he would save his country from further bloodshed. The true answer to all these 'perhaps' will unfortunately remain a mystery – for he took them with him to his grave in a land not his own. The question "why" Khanum kept asking herself, still remains without a viable answer – some believe it was because the West forced him and others think it was his wife who decided for him, either because he was under the influence of heavy medication or she had her own agenda to safeguard.

At that time, the nation did not have a clue that he was terminally ill.

The Idol-Breaker Khomeini entered Iran to a welcome fit for the Prophet himself. Instead of offering a national amnesty, like the Prophet upon his conquest of Mecca, he let revolution take its eccentric course. Blood of the guilty as well as the innocent was shed staining the conscience of those who lived to regret the unjustifiable executions which turned a revolution that could have been bloodless to a holocaust.

Innocent men and women, together with the guilty, were whimsically arrested, jailed and, in some cases, summarily executed without a fair trial. A shameless vengeance fever surfaced and no one felt safe anymore.

The imported labour from overseas began to leave Iran for safer and more lucrative shores – like their employers who had already left. The queues for petrol had vanished, food provision was still low and meals were simple and tasteless. Bottles of alcoholic beverages were thrown out of the shops creating mounts of broken glass on the pavements and roads. In private houses they were hidden in safer places than those of the occupants' cash and valuables.

A fatal car accident saved Aziz Bano and Ali Khan from a future they could not have been able to bear. Their death was not revealed to Shokat Bano. She was told they had left for the United States to visit their daughters. Their departure without a farewell had surprised her but, under the circumstances; she was prepared to believe anything that spared anxiety. The shock of the loss gave Khanum a nervous break-down for which she was hospitalized for weeks and when she returned home she found their chauffeur driven car together with their domestic from the Philippines vanished. She was so mentally exhausted that she did not care at all.

A month later, warned by a well-wisher of an impending arrest, Sassan, disguised under a long beard and long hair in a Dervish's garb went into hiding at the villa by the Caspian – his only solace a long solitary walk at dawn and one at dusk on the sandy shore, during which, if lucky, he would find an illegal fisherman with a fresh catch that he would buy for Shahri to fry for lunch or dinner even though her cooking was rudimentary. She was just fifteen and untrained. Robot-like he went through the days reading the daily newspapers, their front page exhibiting the corpses of the executed politicians, most his friends. At nights he listened to the Persian Language BBC hoping for good news which seemed non-existent. What had happened to the support of the Western governments, particularly the United States that the shah had been enjoying throughout his reign? And why the shah had not allowed his brave and dedicated generals to fight to save Iran from this mess? He kept wondering and wondering. At the end he realized the entire shah's devotees, including himself had been blind to the true nature of the events – so many hands must have been at work – so many foreign interests must have been served by the change of the regime. Then, frightened, he would hear Khanum's voice, "Sassan do not touch politics. It will burn you." She was right – she had always been right. How he missed her – how!

Thus days turned into sleepless nights for this fugitive.

Khanum, against her will and inclination had stayed behind to provide a protective normal façade to their daily life. An intuitive person, she had sensed being watched so she was very careful. Her only moment of happiness was the nightly call from the street telephone booth to her husband. And one evening Mohammad answered, instead of his Master. In a whisper he reported that Agha had been taken in a pasdar's jeep to the Pasdaran's Headquarter and, as yet, had not returned. Khanum's worst fear was realized. She rushed back home, hastily found the cash she was hiding under her matress, shoved the notes in her hand bag, tied her scarf around her head, grabbed her bag, ran down the stairs to the garage, opened the gate, jumped into her old Mercedes, drove it out, closed and locked the gate behind her and then sped out of Teheran on the dangerous road that wiggled around the mountains to the villa by the sea. Fortunately on her way out of the city she was not detained by any of the pasdars who at junctions stopped the cars to search for arms or alcohol. Four hours later she arrived by the gate of the villa hooting furiously for the gardener to open the gate. After several hoots and Khanum's obscene words the gate slid open and Mohammad's head protruded out. He immediately unbolted the gate and opened it wide. She drove in, stopped by the servant's quarters, opened the car door, jumped out and inundated Mohammad who looked terribly embarrassed to have been caught in his pyjamas, with rapid and at times incoherent questions to which she received no satisfactory answers.

Woken by the sounds, Shahri jumped out of bed and bare-footed ran out to see who it was. She recognized the car, whispered an Allah Akbar, and politely saluted her mistress with a 'salam'. The night was chilly. To keep warm she hugged herself tight and remained silent thinking God forbid, what would she do if her Mohammad had been taken away.

Exhausted with exasperation, Khanum, cursing fate, limped to the small villa. She opened its door, stepped in and felt Sassan's aura encapsulated inside. She smelled his scent. It burnt her heart. She dropped on his bed and cried and cried until Shahri, her face dark with sorrow, entered carrying Khanum's bag and a tray of tea, bread and cheese. Khanum lifted her head up, waved the tray away, rose from the bed, walked to the bathroom and took a long hot shower. The maid, thinking that she might change her mind, placed the tray on the top of the oak chest of drawer, slid the arm of the bag from her shoulder and placed it on the bed. Then, ghost like, she walked out and disappeared into the darkness.

Back from the bathroom, trembling from nervousness Khanum dropped her towel from around her waist, picked up Sassan's pyjamas top that neatly folded laid on the bed, took it to her nose, closed her eyes, inhaled its familiar scent feeling goose pimples flame up on her arms. She kissed the garment as if it was her Koran and then fitted it on. It was far too big for her, yet it touched her skin and gave her comfort. Hugging herself tightly she dropped on the bed her face pushing down his pillow, tears saturating the fabric till exhaustion overwhelmed her.

She rose at dawn with an excruciating headache; drank a glass of the tea brought for her by Shahri and then drove to the local committee where a queue of sad, silent souls, tickets in hand, stood waiting for their number to be called out. They all seemed dazed by the speed of change in their lives. Inside of each and every affected individual dwelt a stabbing unbearable dolour that could not go away until he or she could learn what had happened to the missing loved one.

Khanum's heart was beating so fast that at times she felt she would vomit. A pasdar handed her a ticket and she joined the creeping line which eventually reached a large crowded room. There she collapsed on a flimsy grey metal chair that disintegrated beneath her weight with a thud. Hurt, she remained sprawled on the ground. A few rushed to help. She refused. She had no energy for standing. The earth beneath her felt solid and safe. Slowly she crossed her legs and sat rigid.

The humid air in the room was stuffy with sweat and nicotine odour. No one spoke. The only noise heard was of physical movement and the intermittent call of a number. Pasdars entered and left in haste and to guard their secrets they spoke in whispers.

Two hours flew away in a fretful anxiety. Eventually Khanum's number was called by a youth of no more than sixteen. She rose from the floor, tidied her attire and followed the boy to a large room full of armed youths acting as revolutionary vigilantes. A bearded one, in green parka jacket, sat behind a grey metal desk on a rusted metal chair that creaked as he moved. Confidence oozed out of his large black eyes that sparkled from behind the shade of his long lashes. Having worked at the bakery near Khanum's villa, he immediately recognized the slender woman in a long sleeve T-shirt, jeans and a blue scarf. Automatically he rose out of respect then he remembered he now was more important than her so he dropped back on his seat. To gage their reaction to his silly folly he swept a quick glance at his colleagues. To his delight, mouth open, they were all leering at his beautiful applicant whose graceful demeanour was so unlike others. Relieved that they had not noticed his idiocy, he released a short sigh and with his hand gestured Khanum to sit on the empty stool. Then he placed his long index finger on his nose which was eaten up by a large Aleppo boil and hushed the word that was forming on her lips. If the other's heard her questions, he would have to reply with harshness. He did not want to do that. He had always liked the woman. She was the only one of the inhabitants of the area whose gardener had brought him 'aidy' (new year present) on her behalf, every New Year day the family had spent here in their villa. He believed one must never forget kindness. Now it was his turn to do something for her – and the only thing he could do was to be polite and honest. He already knew why she was there. It was him who had taken her husband from the villa to the Komiteh and then driven him to the prison at Evin.

Eyes clouded with sympathy, he straightened his narrow shoulders, immolated a friendly air, and in a tone tinted with regret told her that one of the fishermen had recognized Agha Zand and, to ingratiate himself, had reported his whereabouts to the local komiteh. Immediately a message had been wired to the Dadsetani Enghelab (the office of the Revolutionary Prosecutor General) asking for direction. The next day an official order for his arrest had arrived via fax. He assured her that he himself had delivered her husband to Evin where he was safe and sound waiting questioning about his political activities which, enshallah, would amount to nothing and he would be released soon.

Amazed at his naivity, shaking her head she gave him a long penetrating yet kind glare and whispered, "Son, safe and sound are the corpses that come out of Evin, not those who are kept there."

Then, slowly she rose to leave. Filled with respect for the woman's grace, forgetting his colleagues' reaction, the boy stood up. She nodded her thanks and, in a haze, limped out of the room. Once inside her car, she put her head on the steering wheel and began to cry and cry until her tears dried out. Then she lifted her head up, wiped her eyes with the edge of her sleeve and sped to the villa where she halted the car by the gate hooting for Mohammad to open which he did immediately.

She parked the car by the servant's quarters, got out, rushed in, sat on the carpet and asked Shahri for a cup of tea. Then, facing Mohammad who had followed her inside said, "Agha has been taken to Evin prison. Soon the Revolutionary Guards will come to confiscate this house. You already have a copy of the deed which is under my parents' name. Make more copies and when they come give them a copy. That might stop them confiscating the property until they find out that they are dead. If they confiscate this house, the first thing they will do is throw you out; so it is in your best interest to endeavour to preserve it for us all."

A devastated Mohammad whose lips were quivering shook his head in understanding and then began to weep.

Khanum swallowed the lump in her throat and said, "Mohammad, one never knows what happens next these days but rest assured that I will look after you even if I leave the country. I will leave enough money for your salary and the expenditure of the garden with one of my friends or my grandmother. If worse comes to worse, use the money from the sale of our citrus fruit, enlarge the size of the vegetable garden so that it will feed you and your wife. You are both young and healthy – work as hard as you can and try to remain childless until certainty returns to our country. Prosperous times are behind us, at least for a long while, so be wise and make the most of this fertile land as if it was your own. Now I must speed away and see what I can do for my husband. When you pray please remember us and hopefully we will be all alive once this hurricane passes over." Shahri, pale and tearful handed Khanum a glass of tea too hot for her to drink in a hurry.

"Please pour some cold water in this."

The maid took the glass, emptied it a bit and then topped it with cold water from the tap. Khanum tea-glass in hand, walked to the villa, collected her bag, stepped on to the veranda and stood still. The sea was unusually calm for the time of the year and a fisherman's boat floated yonder. Perhaps it was there to spy on her? She thought with apprehension. She threw the remainder of her tea over a bush, took a crisp walk around the lawn, picked an untimely wilted rose and threw it away, picked a rose bud to preserve between the pages of her Koran as a souvenir of this beloved place; closed her eyes, swallowed her grief lump and then hurried to the domestic quarters where she put the tea glass on the kitchen counter, embraced Shahri, shook Mohammad's hand, jumped into her car and sped away to brave the unknown.

At home, she took a long hot shower, habitually moisturized her skin and then naked, as though defying Hejab, ran down to her basement's storage room where she had hidden her last bottle of vodka in a sack of rice. Cuddling the bottle she went to the dining room where the crystal crockery was neatly displayed in a mahogany chest. She opened the door, took out a vodka receptacle, filled it and then walked to the sitting room, pushed in Delkashe's last tape, sat on the armchair that faced the marble fireplace above which hung her smiling portrait. Smiling! She carefully placed the bottle on the table, and began caressing her glass and occasionally sipping from it. Delkesh sang a jolly song. Time reverted back and she was at Golestan

159

surrounded by family and friends. No one had yet died. No one had yet been executed and no one knew the meaning of fear – except her – but that was a different kind of fear.

Delkash sang on, the bottle emptied and the portrait on the wall began to swing. She rose, took the bottle that shook in her hand to the kitchen where with difficulty she opened the window and threw it out. With a crushing noise it hit the asphalt, shattered into shards that sparkled like diamond pieces under the rays of the shining moon. "Splendid." She exclaimed lingering by the window so that someone could see her nakedness. The street was deserted. Most of the neighbours had left in search of safer shores. Shaking her head, she closed the window and zigzagged to her bedroom where her anguish broke into interminable tears. She dropped on her bed and cried herself to a deep dreamless sleep. When she woke up, it was three in the afternoon. Her head ached, her breath and the room stank of alcohol and reality slapped her on the face. She opened the windows, took several deep breaths oblivious to the beauty that lay in her view. The tea roses were everywhere – creeping on the walls and around tree trunks. The weeping willow that shaded the manicured lawn had already turned pistachio green and the two flower beds surrounding the swimming pool were crowded by violets in purple and white hues. She left the window open and faltered to the bathroom, bent over the toilet and threw up her anxiety and the acid that was burning her inside. She wiped the toilet seat from her mess, threw the soiled toilet paper into the toilet and flushed it down. Stretching her back she took several deep breaths again and then stepped into the bath tub, turned the cold tap on and took a long shower. The chill calmed her. She dressed and went to the kitchen, brewed herself a strong coffee and then, cup in hand, returned to her bedroom, sat on the armchair next to the telephone table and dialled the numbers of all she knew who might be able to help. Only two answered their phones. Conversations were curt and hopeless. Dejected and listless she banged the phone on its cradle, changed into proper Islamic gear which as yet had not become compulsory, rushed to her bureau, withdrew her birth certificate from a drawer, tucked it into her pocket, and called a telephone taxi for Evin prison. She was not going to drive her car to that place – if noticed its possession would rob her of a fair treatment.

The dreaded prison lay on the foot of barren hills that dominated the old village in which are many large luscious gardens – still with owners – but not for long. From the car window she spotted a make-shift shed in front of which stretched a long queue of the hopefuls without any prospect, again waiting to visit or receive news of missing loved ones. She ordered the driver to park the car under the shade of a tree and asked him to wait for her return. He wished her luck, turned on his radio and relaxed behind his steering wheel. She stepped out of the car, tidied her chador so it fully covered her scarf and joined the queue. The silence in the street was deep, only broken by the whiz of a fly or the sigh of a mother whose search, like Khanum, had brought her to this morbid place. Suddenly the shattering sound of machine guns broke the tranquillity of the area and made those waiting tremble with apprehension. No one dared to speculate for who the bullets had been.

'How many?' Khanum asked herself in a fit of terror. Then she began to whisper a prayer Fatimeh Sadat had taught her to recite when fearful. She heard something hit the asphalt. A cry for help made her jump out of her skin and the line curved into a circle. A few minutes later the circle slit open and a man carrying an old woman over his shoulder, rushed towards a parked Paykan. The Paykan's driver recognized him. Rocking his head back and forth in distress he opened the car door, jumped out, whispered something, opened the back door and helped fit the fainted woman inside the car. The door slammed shut, the driver returned behind his steering wheel and a few minutes later the car sped away. The line became straight again. Stillness returned. A fly buzzed around Khanum's head and face. Furious she slapped her face to kill it but it escaped. All living entities crave for freedom, she thought, happy that she had missed the fly. A voice from the loud speaker announced that the office would close in five minutes. The line disintegrated and she walked back to the taxi and returned home. That night she could not sleep at all. There was no more vodka to help her. She heard the Moaz call the faithful to prayer. She also heard some shooting by the armed boy pasdars – now having fun. She got out of bed, showered, drank tea instead of her usual French coffee which was finished and couldn't be found at the supermarkets anymore. She heard the door bell and knew it was the same driver that had driven her to Evin yesterday. Looking austere in her black chador, she hurried out and they arrived by the make-shift office sharp at seven. The queue was short. As she stepped inside she saw a long counter above which wobbled several notice boards. She stood in the queue towards the sign that read 'Sisters'. Her turn arrived. Politely she asked to see her husband. She was curtly asked for her birth certificate in which her marriage was recorded. Calmly she withdrew it from her bag and handed it to the hostile recipient. He scrutinised every page hoping to find a fault. Disappointed he threw her a harsh glance, irately tore a receipt out of the nozzle of a machine and distaste oozing out of his entity ordered, "Show this to the guard at the gate when giving him your birth certificate and upon your return – if you are allowed to return – he will hand you back the document." She gave him a scornful look, grabbed the number and dashed out without any thanks. The guard at the gate was friendlier. He took her birth certificate and quickly instructed her as what to do once inside. Trying to remember what she had to do, and after being physically searched by a woman guard, she entered the compound. Here again make-shift buildings were scattered around. Pasdars guarded every corner. The actual prison building was beyond the visitors' sight. The temporary offices housed the dossiers from the old regime's secret service. She entered a large one-storey building with a long passageway. On each side of the cold corridor there were closed doors with a number plaque. She had to wait by door 13 until her name was called. Half an hour into a dreadful wait she heard her name called out.

Hand trembling, heart pounding, she grabbed the handle and opened the door. Ghost like she stepped inside and found him standing behind a glass barrier subdued and aged. He seemed as though he had lost his soul. So drawn was the face that had always radiated with hope and ambition. Their eyes met; their hearts melted and time stopped clicking away. They yearned for a touch, a word of love – a single moment of privacy. None was to be. Fortunately they still had their eyes through which they communicated their love and longings, their anguish and their fears. She whispered, "I love you." And he whispered back the same. They kissed through the glass. It felt ice cold. The shape of her lips smudged the glass. She took out a tissue from her bag and wiped the mark clean. They talked through the phone about their health and the weather – it was just to hear each other's voice – nothing of importance they could exchange through a bugged phone.

Their donated moments passed brutally fast, yet they took pleasure in just devouring each other with their eyes, breathing the air that smelt familiar and being immersed in the eternal energy of pure unselfish love that had joined their souls together forever under a lonely fig tree in another life – centuries ago – as it seemed . In that love they also saw God and realized how lucky they had been to have found each other from amongst the strange horde of human beings that occupy the earth. The realisation momentarily illuminated their faces and made the left moments strangely gratifying.

"Time is up," announced an excruciating bell-sound. They blew each other a kiss. She defied the order and stood still. He gave her a long loving stare and then walked out of the enclosure's door disappearing from her hungry sight.

Their carefree life had suddenly become cruel and unfair. The man was not allowed a moment of repose. The pasdar who had led him to the visitor's section now led him to the torture chamber – a frightful room that conveyed suffering, pain and betrayal of any sense of decency. Various loathsome instruments and a bunk filled the room. Two giants stood ready to inflict pain. An empty chair awaited the prisoner.

"Sit down, your Excellency," the man sitting in the middle of the other two ordered, mockingly.

Sassan sat down and looked at the covered faces with contempt. The disdain in his eyes encouraged further animosity in the judge and the jury. The inquisition lasted an hour and when the inquisitors failed to obtain the desired information, mostly pertaining to the whereabouts of comrades and hidden wealth of the Pahlavis, the giants commenced their task first by forcefully unclothing the struggling victim so that they could have an easy access to the sensitive areas and pressure points of his body. Then they stretched him on the bunk and cuffed his feet and hands to the metal bars attached to the edges of the bunk. Smiling, the elder of the two commenced inflicting pain. To his chagrin the victim bore his dolour with dignity of the innocent. Then the other ogre, sneering at the brave man, applied a few electrical shocks to the tip of his penis and sides of his testicles. Sassan screamed and screamed like a mad hyena before losing consciousness. Further daily inquisition and torture failed to make him betray his friends. Angered by and surprised at the man's fidelity, his inquisitors gave up and chose to let the Hanging Judge, Ayatollah Karimi, decide his fate.

Two weeks before his last torture, during the morning's fresh air break, Sassan made friends with a sympathetic man named Mohsen who was the prison's chief cook. From the way inmates and the guards greeted this man it became apparent he was well liked and respected. Where there were so many evils around it was a breath of fresh air to meet a respectable man. Then, to his own surprise, he found himself the subject of preferential treatment at meal times and occasional evening visits by the cook during which they talked about life outside the jail and laughed at Mohsen's funny anecdotes. The man had a great sense of humour and managed to make even dire situations seem funny. Sassan began to look forward to their meetings that broke the monotony of his existence. Besides Khanum, who could say nothing during her weekly visits, Mohsen was his only reliable link to the outside world even though he only divulged selective news. This he had realized when last night, after Mohsen's departure, he had heard two guards whisper about the national unrest caused by Mojahedin's anti-regime activities and that Ayatollah Karimi had been called upon to act. Mohsen must have known this and had not told him about it. But that didn't matter much. He was a kind man and he was lucky to have him as a friend.

Known only to a selected few, early in the morning, Karimi had come to the prison to select his victims. Often his choices were whimsical – but no one cared – the executions were to impress upon the opposition the power of the regime. A food lover, he had demanded shami-pook (a delicious meat patty) for lunch.

At around 5 pm Mohsen put the remaining shami-pooks in a large dish he decorated with plenty of radishes, fresh mint and tarragon leaves. He covered the patties with slices of lavash bread, put the dish and two plates on a metal tray and carried the tray to the Zand's cell where they could dine together.

Sounds of foot-steps often bear bad news for prisoners. However through time, the inmates find themselves able to differentiate between a friendly and a hostile echo. Sassan almost immediately learned to recognize his friend's. Tonight from all nights he felt a miserable tang in the bottom of his heart and longed for a friendly company. He was so depressed that he couldn't even occupy himself with reading. He just lay on his bunk staring at the ceiling and praying for Mohsen's footsteps. And when he heard them he jumped off the bunk and ran to the iron bars of his cell. He saw him come, tray in hand, smiling. The warden accompanying him unlocked the cell door and let him enter. He put the key on the cook's tray to lock up when leaving.

The two sat on the bunk and over their shami-pook and lavash wraps delved into a long talk about the carefree time of their youth, their family and friends. Suddenly Mohsen realized Sassan was married to the little girl everyone called 'Khanum'. Memories of the Mistress's kindness returned and surged in him the feeling of fidelity he harboured for the family – their picture framed in silver still sat on the top of his television set. After his father's death he had sold their home at Fumen, and together with his wife and son returned to Teheran. He had found a job at the Hilton Hotel as the chef's aid. Once the hotel was taken over by the Revolutionaries he had found himself transferred to the kitchen of the prison as its chief cook – with a huge salary increase and good standing among the important pasdaran.

A sensible man, he said nothing to Sassan except that he had heard of his wife's family. He knew any reference to her made him miserable.

It was around eight in the evening when Mohsen left

Sassan's cell. Instead of heading home he went to the office where the prisoners' files are kept. He found Sassan's file, read it and wrote down his address and phone number on a page of his pocket diary. Then he went in search of Agha Afzali, the Prison Supervisor and a friend, who knew of all the executions planned. He found him stepping out of his office. To his enquiry Mohsen was told that Sassan in fact had spent his last evening talking to him. He was one of the ten on Karimi's list. "But he is not a Mojahed!" Mohsen exclaimed deeply disturbed.

Afzali gave him a meaningful stare scratched his bolding head and said, "He probably did not have ten Mojaheds to execute and his eyes fell on Zand's name." Mohsen shook his head in despair and angrily said, "It seems he thinks people are the same as the cats he used to hang while under treatment at Chehrazie's mental institution."

"Hush Mohsen, there are rats in the walls with sharp ears. If you are not careful with what you say you might end up on his list."

Deeply distraught, Mohsen shrugged his shoulders, glanced at his wrist watch and whispered, "Let us do something good for a change – after all we do have a conscience?"

"Like what?"

"Let's call Zand's wife and allow her a last farewell with her husband." Afzali, himself shocked by what was happening under his nose, blinked and said, "Why not. We can get her number from his file."

Mohsen produced his pocket diary and shaking it said, "I have it in here." The two rushed into Afzali's office where Mohsen grabbed the phone and dialled the digits Afzali read from his diary.

In bed Khanum was unsuccessfully trying to concentrate on the contents of the page she was attempting to read when the phone sounded. Surprised, she picked up the receiver and instantly recognized the voice asking for her.

"Salam Mohsen and what a great surprise after all these years?" Aghast as how quickly the woman had recognized his voice he said, "Khanum Joon I am calling from Evin prison. Could you please get yourself here as soon as possible?"

Utterly confused she asked why.

"Please Khanum do not ask any questions. Just come." Mohsen begged.

"What are you doing at Evin Mohsen?" she demanded, her voice shaking with terror.

"I am a cook here. By chance I met Sassan Khan and discovered he is your husband – a fine gentleman Khanum."

'He is! Thank God he is alive,' she thought feeling at ease a bit.

"Please hurry Khanum joon."

The phone went dead. She thought she was having a nightmare. Or perhaps this was a bad joke? But it was Mohsen's unforgettable voice on the phone and he never joked with her.

She knew the prison's number by heart. She dialled. Afzali picked up the phone. She asked for Mr. Bagheri. Mohsen came on the line and wondered why they were cut off. He reiterated his request and when he told her the reason the receiver fell from her trembling hand.

Half an hour later she halted her car by the gate of the prison where a stocky bearded man with peppery hair in a crisp white shirt and well pressed black trousers was standing. He hastily opened her car door and politely bowed. She stepped out in such a hurry that she almost fell down. He gripped her arm. Shaking with wretchedness, she managed to steady herself.

"Please Agha take me to Agha Bagheri," she politely

requested her teeth clattering by the turmoil inside her.

"Lalleh Khanum, I am Mohsen Bagheri," he whispered reverently.

She gave him a long, indolent look and a sad smile – he had changed beyond recognition – the lanky boy to a dignified gentleman. In urbane words he expressed his profound sorrow while hastily leading her inside and to a shed in which Sassan was counting the minutes. He left the door half open and respecting the couple's last private moments stood at a distance.

They embraced, kissed and kissed and she cried in his arms and he kissed her head and inhaled the smell of Jasmine that had become her natural odour. He imprisoned that scent in his lung, to become the elixir that would give him courage to bear the pain of death with dignity. He took off his watch and his wedding band and asked her to wear them forever. She took his hand and put it on her heart and said, "Without you my love, this will stop beating."

"No love. You must live for both of us. Just think how kind God has been to us. He meant you for me and me for you – what better luck. Nothing lasts forever. We have had our share of happiness. I am grateful for every moment I have spent with you and consider myself a very lucky man. Please promise you will not mourn me and live to be happy."

"My love, you have been the light of my eyes, the warmth of my heart and the pillars of my strength. How can I live without you?"

He bent down and kissed her tears. "Do not think of me as dead – just think that I have escaped to freedom."

"Agha Zand we must go now," Mohsen called in a voice heavy with grief.

They embraced one more time. They kissed one more time and then he turned and walked away.

She stood gazing at him until his silhouette melted into

darkness – leaving behind a trail of familiar aroma for her to inhale with greed. She stood transfixed to the earth oblivious to her surroundings in a haze of sadness. A night guard pitied her. He came close and said, "Sister you had better leave now." She didn't hear him. He gently took her arm and led her to her car. Absent minded, she thanked him, opened her car door, got behind the wheel and then her eyes widened in fright as she heard the shattering sound of machine guns – running three separate times, followed by ten single gun shots. She let out a loud scream and dropped forward hitting her head on the steering wheel. The guard closed the car door, whispered an Allah Akbar and briskly walked inside to find the chief cook.

At the execution site, ten bodies crumbled face down on the ground soaking in their own blood. Later they would be taken in a truck to the morgue to be buried – without Islamic rites – in a mass grave dug for the 'corrupters on earth'.

She opened her eyes to a call of her name. Focusing with difficulty she saw a blurred quivering image squatting at the foot of the open car door, gently shaking her leg. Slowly she became conscious of the freshness of the dawn breeze fanning her burning face. She shook her head to retrieve her orientation and blinked several times before she could figure out Mohsen's puffed up face and swollen red eyes. Realization hit her heart. She moaned a cry and closed her eyes again.

He whispered: "Allow me to drive you home. You cannot stay here any longer."

She tried to move but her muscles were locked in tension. Mohsen noticed her state. He opened the back door and gently pulled her out from behind the wheel and placed her on the back seat. She put her head against the back of the front seat and began to cry – a dry soundless cry.

He sat behind the wheel and drove her home. In the

house, holding her arm he followed her up the curved staircase to the kitchen that was light and immaculately clean.

As though in a dream she filled the electric kettle and switched it on. From the kitchen cabinet she took two large tea glasses and from the tea container two tea bags. Her hand was quivering so hard that she missed the tea glass and the bag fell on the kitchen top.

"Let me do it, Khanum. You sit there."

Thankful for the offer she walked to and dropped on one of the two kitchen chairs. When the kettle switched itself off he made tea, placed a glass on the table in front of her and holding his own sat on the other chair. Their seats faced the window through which they could see the snow-capped mountains. The sun had risen and the street cleaners were at work. She opened the window. A cool breeze, tinged with a pleasing fragrance of honeysuckle rushed in. She took a deep breath and smiled.

"Mohsen can you smell the honeysuckle?"

"Yes Khanum. It is lovely."

"Sassan loved it. That is why I had the gardener plant it by the gate so that every evening, upon his return home he would be greeted by their scent." She murmured and then added, "Who could ever think of you from all people in this world, as the one who could do what you did for me?"

"Khanum joon, to be honest I did it for the Mistress and not you. How is she and how are your respected parents?"

"My grandmother is well but my parents died in a car crash not long ago. I believe God loved them too much to allow them to live through this hell."

"I am so sorry to hear this. They were such fine people."

Khanum, shaking her head, whispered a 'yes' and then added, "They were so lucky to die when they did – so lucky."

Mohsen put his glass on the table and asked,

"Will you take me to the Mistress one day?"

"Of course I will. Tell me about Bagher Khan. Is he well?"

Mohsen fixed his eyes on her, contemplating whether he should reveal the truth to her or not. In her aura he read such sincerity that words began to pour out of his mouth.

"Khanum joon, years ago when I was too young to understand, I participated in sodomy with a man from your family. The tragedy is that I was a willing partner!"

"That bastard Abbass Mirza?"

Face flushed and fingers nervously scratching the surface of the table, Mohsen whispered, "Yes".

They both fell into a poignant silence, staring at the far away mountain range. Mohsen turned to Khanum, dropped his head and said, "Somehow my father found out."

Mohsen paused.

Khanum staring at him with horrified eyes waited.

"He did not die of alcohol poisoning. It was rat poison that killed him."

"Rat poison?"

"Yes, rat poison. My father mixed it in his ghormeh-e-sabzie, the night of the Master's Kharji."

Suddenly Khanum began to laugh and laugh until Mohsen joined in her laughter.

The two street cleaners below heard them and turned their gaze up to the open window to see what madness had induced such hysteria – in such dire times.

"God bless your father's soul. I am sure he is in heaven now. He saved many lives from being ruined – the good man that he was. I loved him dearly."

Mohsen never knew Khanum had any relationships with his father, let alone love him. When they were working for the family she was just a kid. It deeply touched him to know that this noble lady had been close to a mere cook and remembered him with fondness. Why, he couldn't figure

172

out. Suddenly in her he found a friend he could trust. This was such a relief. He threw her an affectionate glance and decided it was the right time to unburden his heavy load.

"The good man that he was, Khanum joon, he could not live with the guilt. So when we returned to Fumen, he turned the deeds of the land the Master, God bless his soul, had given him to my name, helped me build a house and then one Thursday evening he put some of the same poison in his meal, went through the same pains and died."

Mohsen took a deep breath, fixed his wet eyes on the ground and murmured: "I killed him."

Sad and sorrowful, for a moment she was lost for words and then nodding her head she said, "Your father was one of the finest men I have known in my life – he did what he thought was right. But he was too noble to be able to ethically justify his action. Hence, to find peace, he had to do what he did and you must not blame yourself for his decision."

"I cannot forgive myself – ever."

"Do not do that to yourself. You are making your father's soul restless. He wanted you to be happy and, if you really love him, fulfil his wish by accepting your destiny, and make the best of it. Look at what you have done for me – out of the blue you gave Sassan and me the gift of a few extra moments of togetherness! I believe for this act alone, you have gained absolution for all your sins, if any. Rest assured that tonight you have made both God and your father very proud of you."

She stopped, took Mohsen's cold hands in hers, and squeezed them with as much strength as was left in her.

He looked at her with eyes that expressed a thousand thanks and remained speechless. She gave him a serene smile and said, "When we go to the Mistress, don't tell her about the suicide. She loved him very much. It will upset her greatly."

"I know Khanum joon, and I think she knew of his act and yet let him go free."

'So it was that knowledge for which Granny was feeling so guilty', thought Khanum before saying, "Probably you are right. My grandmother is an amazing lady and she was very fond of your father. You, my friend, have inherited his nobility. Thank you Mohsen, thank you for being the brother I never had."

"Khanum joon, I am so lucky to have found you – it is wonderful to have someone who shares your past – particularly these days when one feels so lonely – with no one to trust – with no one to rely on, one feels like a fish out of water."

Khanum began to rock in her chair, shaking her head here and there. Then she stopped, put her hand on Mohsen's and said: "I need you to do something that will please God more than what you have done for me."

"I will do whatever you ask of me, Khanum."

"I own an orphanage which might be confiscated soon because it is registered under Sassan's name. I have a total power of attorney from him. I want to turn the deed of the building to your name and will double your present salary under the condition you leave your job and look after the welfare of the children for me. We only took in children from abused mothers."

'What a lady,' Mohsen thought with admiration – and then a thought crossed his mind that widened his eyes. Khanum noticed that and shook her head. "No" she heard him exclaim. "Yes," she whispered.

The time was not right for asking questions. So he said, "Khanum you will be doing me a great favour. I hate my job. I hate the jail and what is going on there. I feel so guilty to earn my living from that hell. But I am scared to resign – not for myself but for my family. God bless you for giving me the opportunity to do so. They cannot stop me from

174

running an orphanage can they?"

"I do not think so. That will be the first thing we will do tomorrow – no today."

"No Khanum joon; today I will have to find Agha's body and bury him in a decent grave."

Khanum's mouth fell open. She had forgotten that proper burial was forbidden those executed. Again she took Mohsen's hand resting on the table, and this time, kissed it. Blushed crimson he gently withdrew it from her grip, rose and said, "Khanum joon, please don't embarrass me any further. I am still your servant. You go and rest until I return. I know the morgue-keeper; he is for sale and will give us Sassan Khan. Jafar my son has a Paykan. We will take the body to Fumen and I will bury him in the cemetery where my father is resting. No one will ever find him there."

"I will come with you."

"No Khanum. They will be watching you. Please just stay at home until I return."

Chapter 11

The same day at the Morgue

Traffic in the air-polluted south of Teheran is bumper to bumper, its noise excruciating. On the crowded pavements unkempt men, women in black chadors and load-bearing donkeys intermingle with ease. Some are hurrying to do their errands, some loafing around and many busy dealing and arguing over the right price with street vendors. In this kaleidoscopic atmosphere hardly anyone paid attention to the white Paykan parked by the gate of the city's morgue, its engine running and its young driver anxiously monitoring a closed ominous looking black steel gate. A middle-aged man sitting next to the driver was deep in thought.

The youth, thinking black thoughts, was unconsciously tapping the steering wheel. Eventually, unable to restrain himself, he turned to the elder man and said, "Father, please say something. I cannot bear this wait."

The man turned and looked at him with affection. "What do you want me to say, son?"

"I do not know – anything, anything that can make time pass faster."

"Are you scared?"

"Yes, very."

"Fear is worse than death itself. One must never be afraid of doing a good deed – that is what we are here to do."

"I am not as courageous as you are, father. I am even scared to look at a dead body let alone handle it."

"Dead bodies are just like live bodies except they are void of spirit. Ours will be such one day and some Good Samaritans will handle them with respect, as we are going

176

to handle Agha Zand's."

"Did you know him well, father?"

"Well enough to like and respect him, but I know his wife better. We owe everything we have to her grandparents – they were great people. Royals! I never told you that I grew up in a garden called Golestan, did I?"

"No father, you have never told me anything about your youth."

"Perhaps one day I will." There was sadness in Mohsen's tone when he uttered this last sentence. His son's sensitive antenna detected it and the forming word froze on his lips.

Jafar was a pleasant looking, intelligent youngster with a soft heart. He had finished university and was looking for a job which seemed impossible to find. His unemployment was causing him and his parents' great distress. These days, in the absence of any constructive activities for the youth, most of those unemployed were turning to opium. Neither Zahra nor Mohsen wished that to happen to their only son. And last night when Mohsen informed them about the Orphanage and suggested to his son that they should jointly run it, the gloom that had clouded the atmosphere of their cosy home turned into a bright light infusing their hearts with abundant joy. Elated, Jafar embraced the idea with enthusiasm and grateful to the lady his parents called Khanum rose at dawn to get the car started. His Paykan was second-hand and very problematic. He kept praying to God and pressing his foot on the gas pedal to make the car start and eventually when it did he drove it to the nearest gas station and filled it up. Upon his return home he stopped by the bakery and bought fresh sangak bread for his mother's breakfast. It pleased him to make her happy – she was such an undemanding person and so dedicated to her family that nothing they could do for her seemed enough. He simply adored her and wished for a wife just like her – simple, honest, dedicated and a good ironer. Like his father, he was pedantic about his outfits' tidiness.

Suddenly, from the minaret of the nearby mosque the Moaz's Allah Akbar rippled through the air and returned both Mohsen and Jafar's attention to the task at hand. They began to fidget while fixing their gazes at the gate. It was twelve noon and time for prayer. Inside the morgue employees, believers or not, were busy rolling up their sleeves as they rushed to the garden's small pond for ablution. The small prayer room was getting gradually packed.

Mohsen kept glancing at his watch, while Jafar kept his gaze fixed on the gate. To his relief he saw it slide open and a head protruded out, moving to the right and then the left where he spotted the parked white Paykan. His head disappeared and the gate slowly slid open. Jafar pressed his foot on the speed pedal and drove in. A grim looking youth of about eighteen, swimming in his shabby oversized shirt and pants, nodded towards a discrete parking space facing a side door. There Jafar parked. The two hurried out of the car and followed the youth into a large, semi-lit hall with a foul stench and a grotesque mount of bullet ridden corpses stored in various forms, like discarded statues. The sight was unbearable for anyone with the slightest sense of decency. Mohsen and Jafar each whispered an Allah Akbar and sent a curse to those responsible. Suddenly a surge of nausea hit Jafar. Holding his mouth with his hand he ran out and threw up the disgust that had spurted the bile into his mouth. He was shivering so hard that at first he could not open his car's door and once he managed he collapsed on the driver's seat and fainted.

Time was running out. The boy hurriedly led Mohsen to an anti-chamber where he found Sassan, stretched on the floor in his white shirt and grey pants, perforated by bullets and smudged by blood. A tag with his name was attached to his toe. Mohsen's lips began to quiver and tears streamed down his grey cheek. He looked at the peaceful face and believed he had accepted death with the grace that had been his forté in life – otherwise an expression of fright would have frozen on it – like the ones in the other room. Shaking his head, Mohsen knelt on the floor, bent and kissed the hardened forehead smudged with blood and dust, detached the tag from his toe, tucked it in his own pants' pocket and gently lifted the corpse, dropped it over his right shoulder, slowly rose, stepped through the half open door through which he could see the Paykan. The car door had been opened by the boy now holding a shabby blanket. Jafar, pale and stinking had returned to life. Yet mute he was glued to his seat not daring to turn his eyes to what was being laid on the back seat. Now he closed them praying for forgiveness. Mohsen took the blanket from the boy and spread it on the body hiding it from sight. Then he closed the door, returned to the front of the car, opened the glove compartment and withdrew a wrapped bundle of rial notes and handed it to the boy.

"Son, thank Sayed Ali from me and tell him he has bought heaven for himself." The boy put his hand on his heart, nodding his head closed and opened his eyes. Mohsen realized he was dumb. He withdrew a handful of notes from his pants pocket, counted ten, and gave them to him to keep for himself. The boy put the notes on his heart, nodded his thanks with a serene smile and ran to open the gate.

"Jafar, open your eyes and let's get the hell out of here." Annoyed by his son's cowardice Mohsen commanded while fastening his seat belt.

"Father, please forgive me. I should have pulled myself together – but I just couldn't. Please father, I am so sorry."

Mortified himself, Mohsen murmured, "Nevermind son."

Fifteen hours later, having been washed by the kind

mullah of the village and shrouded in white, Sassan was buried beside Bagher Khan at Fumen's cemetery near a wild honeysuckle bush. The task completed, Mohsen felt an untimely surge of pride – at last he had done something to make his father proud of him. This act was his absolution from the sins of his youth and he hoped God would forgive him and let him live with a clear conscience – without any more nightmares.

From the cemetery they drove to Mohsen's old aunt. He gave her another pack of cash for the Kharji of rice and ghormeh-e-sabzie to be cooked by herself and taken to the local Mosque on Thursday evening, which would be the seventh night of Sassan Khan's death.

In Teheran, Khanum had managed to locate the Mahzari (notary), in whose office all their previous legal transactions had been undertaken and who was a close family friend. Not willing to talk on the phone, she had invited him to her house and now over an insipid tea, had told him of Sassan's execution which as yet had not been publicized and what she intended to do with the orphanage before it fell into the wrong hands.

Her guest so far had listened patiently, going through three cigarettes and the whole pot of tea, even though it was flavourless. At times he had exclaimed an Allah Akbar and or a sad Astakhfar (God forbid).

Khanum lifted the tea pot and finding it empty rose to go inside to bring more tea.

"Khanum joon, please make it a bit stronger and more tasty. My mouth is as dry as dust."

"You shouldn't smoke so many cigarettes," she commented disappearing from his line of vision. The mullah fell into a deep contemplative silence – his mind racing to find legal ways to do what was demanded of him. Throughout his career he had been an honest man without ever participating in any act that lay outside of legal boundary – even when offered a fortune. But now the situation had changed. One had to please God rather than the devils incarnate.

Khanum was getting used to domestic chores now that the only servant serving her was the gardener, who in the spirit of Islamic brotherhood had become lax and too familiar. She detested his impertinence and, prudent enough, had given him this afternoon off. She had cleaned the garden and the veranda herself and to her own surprise had found the chore relaxing and easy – after all it was only Blacky and the wind that messed up the outdoor area.

Flirting with his cigarette, the Mahzari, his countenance grimacing, was gauging the gravity of what he had heard. At that moment he felt he did not want to belong to the rank of the clergy any more. The few evil ones had stolen its dignity and made its name synonymous with dirt. When nervous, he always perspired and now he withdrew a handkerchief from his pocket and wiped off the gathered sweat beads from his wide forehead and upper lip. Then he adjusted his white turban that felt terribly uncomfortable.

The flip flop of Khanum's sandals on the tiles broke his concentration. He rose for her. She put the tray on the table.

"I think this will taste better, I have infused it with few pods of cardamom and a tinge of cinnamon."

"You never had a claim to be a good cook, my girl. I drink whatever is hot to wash away the taste of nicotine from my mouth. Naturally if it is strong and tasty I will also enjoy it."

"That is beside the point. I really mean it – you should not smoke. It will kill you."

"Something will kill me eventually! So let me enjoy the only luxury left to me."

Nodding in unison, they both acknowledged the temporariness of it all. She poured the tea. "Is this better?" she asked. "Yes it is the right colour and I can smell its

181

aroma!"

Khanum returned to her seat, lost a breath and began to heave.

"Do you suffer from asthma, child?"

"No – it is nervous breathing – I do not want to take tranquilizers, they make me drowsy and I do not like the feeling – so I try to live with the abnormality until it suffocates me which I hope will be soon."

"Nonsense girl, and where have your high spirits gone to – ha?"

"My spirit died with my husband. I have no one to live for. I have nothing to hope for – how I am still breathing is beyond my own comprehension."

A haze of disappointment veiled the olive complexion of the Mahzari. His white beard began to quiver. He knitted his thick peppery eyebrows, fixed his reproachful eyes on her and said, "You live because God has given you life – an amazing gift. You were born to travel through a journey with a beginning and an end. During this journey you are to experience the challenges meant for you. By honourably overcoming these challenges, you will reach the core of your essence and thus become worthy of being a human being." He stopped, took a sip of his tea, the glass of which had remained in his grip. He put the glass down and then shaking his index finger in the air said, "There lies the difference between us and Allah's other creatures."

Khanum fixed her perplexed eyes on him and asked, "Do you know how hard it is to have no one in this wide world?"

"Yes I do. I have lost a wife and a son. To me the world is a passageway, my child, and we are simple passengers passing through it. Those loved ones we leave behind will desperately miss us. But, fortunately, time is healer of all emotional maladies. You are alive. Sassan is dead and I am here for you. I am your friend. You have your grandmother still alive and now you have found this Mohsen guy who so far has been very loyal, so you really are not alone at all."

She thought a bit and then waving her head in agreement smiled serenely.

Practical as ever, he returned to the business at hand. "You should also turn the deed of this house to Mohsen's name. I am sure one of these days they will come for it."

"No, no, no. They cannot. The land of this property was my mother's inheritance from her father. My father built on it and when I married they gave it to me as my dowry. I am not on their dammed black list."

Losing his patience, the Mahzari extinguished his cigarette with anger, fixed his irritated eyes on her drawn face and shaking his hands in desperation said, "But your husband was. Listen to my advice child. Soon they will confiscate everything you own for one Foundation or another; they will close all your bank accounts and prohibit you from leaving the country. You will join the rank of the deprived for whom they have dispossessed you. Islam respects the right of ownership and these people, in their heated revolutionary zeal seem to have forgotten that. You, my dear girl, will have to fight their justice system before anything could be salvaged and that will take years. So let me have the deed for the house as well and tell Mohsen to bring his birth certificate with him when we next meet here. I will need yours too. I will have to do the registrations myself when my clerks leave the office. Also tomorrow go and withdraw all the cash you can from your account, give a cheque to Mohsen for the rest and prepare to leave the country."

Khanum could not bear what she was hearing – was she losing control of everything in her wretched life? That cannot be. The thought was so agonizing that the muscles of her face began to twitch, a deep frown spread over her forehead and heaving she began tapping her leg, a habit she had inherited from Sassan.

The notary lit another cigarette and helped himself to more tea.

"My passport is valid and thank God I still have an unexpired Multiple British Visa but why should I leave my country? I love Iran," she said with illusory confidence.

The seasoned Mahzari realized that trauma had corroded her power of rationality. He coughed, spat the phlegm into his white handkerchief, tucked the cloth into his robe pocket, shook his head and said, "The new Iran doesn't love you, my dear and your kind – at least until the vengeance fever subsides. You have a flat in London, go there and bide your time. Perhaps one day, God willing, all will be calm again and you can return. From what you say Mohsen is an honourable man. He will transfer the house back to you."

"If he is still alive by then?" she retorted wistfully.

"My daughter, God gives and God takes. What is meant for you will always be yours. What God wills no man can take away and what God wants to take no man can keep. Have faith and remain the marvellous individual you have been so far."

The man's soothing words mellowed her resentment and within the recesses of her muddled mind she began to glimpse at the reality she was trying to deny. It was unbearable. Her tears began to run. He allowed her the liberty of feeling sorry for herself. She had the right, he thought.

Sniffing her running nose and wiping her eyes with the edge of her sleeve, she rose and left to bring him the deeds and her birth-certificate. In her bedroom, while she was searching her file folder the phone rang and a woman's soft voice asked for her. She recognized the voice.

"Zahra joon, salam."

"Khanum joon, salam must come from me. I am so

sorry about what has happened. Please accept my condolences."

"Thank you. My father was a sick man and now he has found peace. Do you have any news for me, Zahra joon?" Suspicious that the phone might be tapped Khanum spoke in code.

She was right. Her phone had been bugged ever since Sassan's name had appeared on the wanted list.

"Yes, Khanum joon. I just received a call from my husband and he asked me to let you know that Bagher khan has already welcomed his guest and he will cook him ghormeh-e-sabzie which they will share with their friends at the mosque on this coming Thursday evening."

Khanum released a sigh of relief, turned her eyes to heaven and silently thanked God.

"Thank you for letting me know. By the way, Zahra joon, when will I see your husband?"

"Either tonight or tomorrow morning, they have already left for Teheran."

"Could you please ask him to bring his birth certificate with him?"

"Chashm Khanum. Do you wish him to do anything else?"

"Yes. Bring you too."

"I would love that, Khanum joon."

The next morning, at half past eleven both Agha Mahzari and Mohsen arrived, each carrying a leather brief-case and wearing a black mourning arm band on their shirt sleeves – a sign of respect for the widow. She guided her guests to the veranda by the pool and went upstairs to the kitchen to bring the tea tray down. Today Agha was without his turban and black robe. He looked smart and neat in a Pierre Cardin suit although without a tie.

It was a pleasantly cool and bright morning. A few chirping birds were having great fun in the midst of colourful blossoms. Blacky the poodle, curled in a circle beside his owner's cushioned chair, was fast sleep. The poor dog had not been washed nor trimmed ever since the fall of the shah when all vets and dog-trimming salons were forced to close down. His long curly hair was mud-smitten and he smelled foul. Iranians in general are not animal lovers and dogs are considered unclean by praying Moslems. Agha, who was worried that his trousers would become dirtied by brushing against the dog, pinched his nose and with the tip of his shoe gently kicked the dog awake. Groaning, Blacky opened his eyes, rose and swinging his fluffy tail moved to the farthest corner from the strangers; laid down, rested his pointed jaw on his paws while staring at the man who had disturbed his peace.

Mohsen distributed the tea from the tray that Khanum put on the glass table, then mechanically opened the packet of Mino cookies that sat next to the tea pot and offered one to the Agha. He pulled one out and put it on the side of his saucer. Mohsen returned the packet to the tray, sat next to the old man and in a voice condensed with grief described how he and his son had dealt with their undertaking. Khanum, her heart tight with grief, imbibed every word that fell out of Mohsen's mouth visualizing the scenes – wishing to have been there, to have had one last look at the face she had loved so much. And when he told her of his calm facial expression she smiled. 'An Agha to the end,' she thought with pride.

The Mahzari, his face veiled by agony, kept shaking his head, at first in shock, then regret and finally in appreciation of a sacred deed performed with perfection by a good man.

In the profound silence that followed, they drank their tea and inhaled the fresh, scented air that under any other circumstances would have been extremely pleasant.

The Mahzari put his tea glass on its saucer, picked up his brief case and took out three documents which he spread on the table. He straightened his narrow, thin shoulders, swept an assessing glance at Khanum and Mohsen whose eyes were fixed on the documents and asked if he had brought his birth certificate. Mohsen bent towards his bag, picked it up, unzipped it and took out his small green birth-certificate that still bore the Imperial insignia on its cover. Politely with both hands he presented it to the old gentleman. "Here it is, your Excellency." The Mahzari took it, swept a quick look over it and said, "They plan to change the cover of the birth- certificates – and the hassle it will cause our offices!"

No one made a comment.

He opened two of the documents and gently slid them towards Mohsen whose eyes were fixed on him.

"You, my son, were born under a lucky star. However you have just proved you deserve your good fortune. These are the deeds for the Lucky Mothers' Orphanage and this house that I have persuaded Khanum to transfer to your name for safekeeping. Do you realize how much this lady trusts you?" He asked looking straight into Mohsen's eyes.

Mohsen, not having been privy to the second plan, turned his questioning eyes to Khanum who said, "Mohsen joon, it is to protect my interest. If the house is under your name they cannot confiscate it – this is just a preventive measure."

Mohsen looked up at the sky, raised his hands in prayer and loudly declared, "Ya Allah, be my witness that I pledge to be worthy of this trust. Within the best of my ability I will guard all that belongs to this wonderful lady until it is safe for her to reclaim them."

"Thank you, Mohsen." Khanum whispered.

"Good. Now please sign on the lines next to which I have marked with a cross and then give them to Khanum to do the same."

Mohsen withdrew a blue biro from his shirt pocket and

187

went through the pages and signed them all. Then he politely placed the documents in front of Khanum.

"I shall take both your birth-certificates to my office; once I am done with them, my driver will return them to Khanum."

Khanum, having finished signing, pointed to the third document and asked, "What is this one for?"

The Mahzari extinguished his cigarette in the ashtray full to the brim, cleared his voice, avoided her inquisitive glance and turned to Mohsen and stated, "Without Khanum's permission which I hope she will grant I have prepared this I Owe You document for you to sign. This is a means of security that bounds you to her for the market value of this house and the orphanage. As a man of honour you must not betray her trust. Should Satan deceive you, Khanum will be entitled to the market value of both properties which you must pay her or else go to jail."

Frowning, Khanum voiced her objection which was promptly rejected by both men. Mohsen immediately signed the ticked places, closed off his biro and returned it into his pocket. He sat erect like a man full of responsibilities.

"The date on all these documents is 5th of the last month during which Sassan Khan was alive and free. No one can confiscate either of the properties because at the time he was still a free man."

"Thank you, Agha. You always think of everything. Bravo indeed."

Khanum proclaimed with a serene smile.

Agha, nonchalantly shrugged off the compliment, turned to Mohsen and said, "Son, you should move to this house as soon as possible and rent yours."

"Chashm Agha, whenever Khanum permits us." Mohsen replied looking at Khanum with questioning eyes.

"As soon as possible, I love company. By the way why did you not bring Zahra today?"

"Khanum she is a naïve woman, my wife. I did not want to expose her to things that God forbid she might repeat to wrong ears."

The Mahzari admired the man's foresight and asked, "Mohsen Khan, do you know anyone who can help Khanum leave Iran safely?"

Colour drained from Khanum's face.

"Yes I do. There is a gang of "drug smugglers" who also smuggle people out through the mountain paths to Turkey. I know a pasdar who knows the leader. According to him the guy is trustworthy."

"Excellent. First move to this house, then bring him to my home and not here. If he sees this house he will triple his price."

"Why do I have to leave my country? What have I done wrong?" she whispered into the air.

"Nothing, my lady," Mohsen responded respectfully.

The old man extinguished another cigarette, poured himself more tea and said, "Child you must accept that we are living in dangerous times. Values are changing; what was right yesterday is wrong today and, being among the aristocracy, is a crime in the eyes of those in power now. All revolutions cause anarchy at first and you, a single woman, without a husband cannot risk becoming a pawn in the wrong hands. Leave and thank your lucky stars that you have that option."

"I will not leave my country where my roots are. I would rather be jailed or executed like my husband than become a refugee in a land that does not belong to me. I refuse to become a "nobody". I refuse to become a second-class citizen in a foreign society. I want to be buried here near my husband." She stopped, cupped her face with her quivering palms and broke into a heart rendering sob, moving back and forth, whispering, "He is so alone in Fumen. I should be with him there. Where can I go without him? What can I do without him?"

"Khanum joon, permit me to make all the arrangements for your departure and then I will take you to Fumen which is almost on the way to the border. There, we can stay at my aunt's cottage and you can visit Sassan Khan every day?"

She paused, removed her hands from her wet swollen face, and looked at Mohsen with eyes that had an unusual glitter.

"That is exactly what we will do." She said thinking happily that once there no one could force her to leave.

Blacky sensed turmoil in the air. He rose and toddled to his mistress, crouched by her chair and began to lick her toes that were out of her casual sandals. For the first time in her life she did not object to the dog's saliva that najest (soiled) her skin.

Mohsen, sitting next to her discretely moved his legs away from the pet. Just like Agha Mahzari, he did not want to have to dry clean his pants because the dog had najest it with his saliva.

"Good. I will contact the pasdar tomorrow morning when he will be at his post at Evin. Khanum joon, I am not as educated or as wise as you, but for what my advice may be worth, I would like to ask you not to look at your departure as permanent. Nothing but death is permanent. Look at it as a long holiday. Iranians are resilient; they will fight against tyranny if not today, in the years to come. Let the revolutionary fever subside and the dust settle, then return home."

She smiled, nodded her consent and thanked him for his advice. Then she turned her eyes to the Mahzari who was fitting the documents back into his brief case. He was a meticulous man and that was one of the reasons for his success and popularity. Satisfied that he had not left anything to chance he turned to Mohsen and said, "I have to leave now. My driver will deliver the completed documents tomorrow. Khanum has my telephone numbers and knows where my office is. Should you need anything give me a call."

They all rose. Khanum approached him with open arms. The two hugged – a sulking child and a spoiling father. He kissed her forehead, whispered a safekeeping prayer in her ear and, briefcase in hand walked to the door followed by Mohsen and from afar Blacky.

Having closed the gate, Mohsen returned to the veranda cleared the table, took everything to the kitchen and then the two walked to Shokat Bano's house. The once busy street was empty and forlorn. Facing them on the north, Alborz stretched the width of the horizon, a gigantic wall protecting the Capital and its environs. The trees that Hussain Agha had planted had grown tall and leafy, their branches arching over the roadway. Plenty of water rushed through the streams carrying all sorts of discarded refuse.

"Mohsen, do you remember when all this was a huge garden full of fruit trees and how cross Hussain Agha used to get with you for picking Grandpa's pears when Huppy was unchained?"

Mohsen burst into laughter and then said, "Those were the carefree days of my life. Until last week I never dreamt I would pass this road again!"

"Such is life, Mohsen Khan, full of surprises – good and bad."

The forever open gate was shut. Khanum rang the bell and a few minutes later Fatimeh Sadat, bent by age, the edges of her crisp white scarf almost touching the ground opened the door. At first she did not recognize Mohsen and then, when he greeted her, she recognized his accent. An ecstatic smile brightened her wrinkled face as she opened her arms to hug him. He lifted her up like a child, kissed her face while words of endearment poured out from her toothless mouth. He gently put her down and held her bony hand.

"Fatimeh Sadat go and tell the Mistress who has come to see her."

Khanum ordered, wincing at Mohsen whose smile was getting broader and happier.

The two slowly walked a good few steps behind Fatimeh Sadat who was limping ahead. When she entered the room they halted their pace.

"Mistress, you would not believe who has come to visit us?"

"All my friends are either dead or overseas. I cannot think of anyone who would want to come and see me these days except Ezrael (the angel of death)."

"Mohsen, the son of Bagher Khan."

"Mohsen!" She exclaimed her eyes shining with delight.

The news brought back memories of happy times – how short and transient they had been. She sighed. Suddenly she became conscious of her looks. Her right hand went to tidy her white hair and then to the bottle of Jolie Madame perfume that sat on her bedside table. The door opened and Khanum entered while Mohsen stood outside waiting to be permitted in – just like old times when servants could not enter the Mistress's room without permission.

Shokat Bano now sitting upright in her bed with the satin quilt smooth on her legs called out, "come in son and give us the pleasure of looking at your handsome face again."

Her voice settled deep in his heart and warmed it with the sense of security he had always felt when in her presence. Feeling like the servant boy that he had been to her, he stepped in, bowed and came forward to take the thin shrivelled hand offered him to kiss.

Shokat Bano with eyes that twinkled with affection admired the dignified and elegant man that the lanky boy had become. He was not as handsome as his father but pleasant to look at, even with a beard, she thought with a smile. He kissed her hand. She pulled the hand away and opened up her arms.

"Now come and give me a hug, son."

Embarrassed, Mohsen paused. She read his mind. "Come now, I always acted as your mother and don't you ever forget it," she said in a loving but commanding tone. He raised his eyes to her, smiled and fell into her arms. She kissed his greying hair, patted his shoulders, pushed him away and turning to Khanum teased, "You still have an eye for handsome men, my dear. Tell me where did you find this one?"

"I did not find him Grandma. He found me!"

"Loyal to the end, just like his father – I miss Bagher so much. He was not only my cook but a friend. Ahmad was never as good a cook as his uncle."

She stopped. Out of respect no one spoke. She resumed.

"And not as faithful, but I bear no grudge against him. He left my service as soon as a better offer came his way – without even negotiating with me. I would have matched the offer, only because he was Bagher's nephew, but such is the way of the world. I cannot complain. Fatimeh Sadat is still with me and surprisingly she has turned out to be a good cook – as well as a good companion!"

Shokat Bano stopped and threw the old maid a loving glance that made her flush with pride.

"Son, sit and give me news of Bagher, and your family."

Mohsen sat on the arm chair that faced the Mistress and enlightened her with the pleasant things that had happened to him in life.

"And how did you find Khanum?" Shokat Bano asked enchanted by what she had heard.

Mohsen had vowed never to lie. He went mute. Khanum kept her worried eyes on him. He begged God's forgiveness and made up a story.

Remarkably perceptive the old lady could not be duped. She never tolerated being deceived. Yet she did not want to intimidate her visitor by doubting his honesty. So she turned to her pensive and gloomy granddaughter and asked,

"Azizam you know that no one has ever been able to hide anything from me, so tell me what has made you look like a ghost and what act of God has brought back this dear boy to us?"

A quick anxious glance exchanged between the two which did not escape the old lady's still perfect vision. The secrecy flamed her curiosity further more. She became insistent. Her insistence did not bother Khanum. In fact she welcomed it. Inside she was yearning to put her head on the old lady's chest, feel her warmth and let it balm her wounded heart and soul. Half of her craved to pour out her grief and cry on the only shoulder left to her. And the other half warned against doing so. The shock of the news might harm her fragile health or even give her a heart attack. This precious old lady was the only family and friend she had in this wide crowded world. Her sisters, two strangers now had cut off contact with her. Upon hearing of the execution they had celebrated her loss – so jealous they had been of her life. Not even a phone call had she received from them.

She left her seat and sat on the edge of her grandmother's bed, grabbed her warm hand in hers and calmly told her all that had happened to her husband. The old lady, stony face, listened without uttering a word. Only the throbbing of the veins in her sagging neck and random twitching of her lower lip gave her inner turmoil away. Then when Khanum stopped she opened her arms and the two embraced tightly. They sobbed together. A tearful Fatimeh Sadat ran out and few minutes later returned with a try of chamomile tea. She put the tray on the coffee table, gently tapped on Khanum's shoulder until she released her grandmother. Wiping her tears with the end of her scarf, Khanum returned to her chair and they all drank the hot concoction tinged with cardamom and a bit of honey.

Shokat Bano, put her empty tea glass on the side table, turned her face to Mohsen, looked at him with grateful admiration and said, "Son, God bless you for what you have done for my Lalleh. God bless you indeed. Indeed you are the son of my Bagher – just like him, a good man with a large heart. Thank you and thank you a thousand times, my son. Thank you."

"Thank you, my Mistress. I grew up under your shadow. What values I have I acquired from you. Thank you for everything you did for us, my dear, dear mother. I have not and shall not ever forget your kindness especially towards my father. You were his Goddess."

"Now enough of that, you, my dear, have not told me anything about your father? What is he doing now?"

"Your ladyship my father made me an orphan many years ago. God bless his soul, he died in Fumen."

He threw a quick glance at Khanum who remained silent. A dark shadow passed over the Mistress's face. She sighed and said, "Your father was a fine and honourable man. God will forgive his sins – if any – and take him to heaven."

"Enshallah Mistress." Mohsen exclaimed in a sad voice.

"How is Zahra and do you have any children, my son?"

"Yes Mistress. I have a son. His name is Jafar and he is twenty. Zahra will be very jealous to know that I have visited you without her. She would want to come and kiss your hand. She has been a good wife and I must thank you for her."

"Don't thank me. It was your father who chose her for you."

He accepted the fib graciously and then asked permission to leave to prepare dinner for the inmates.

"I think it was your father's spirit who willed you to be in my granddaughter's way so that you can find and look after me in my old age! God be with you and keep you safe for your family and us, my dear."

"I shall remain your servant forever."

"Don't talk like that anymore. My sons have left me for their foreign wives and are living in Europe. Now God has given me a third son. I shall never forget what you have done for us. Enshallah, you receive your reward in both worlds."

"My lady, what I have done is nothing compared to what you did for my father."

Mohsen, bowed, took the stretched hand, kissed it and cautiously stepped back until he reached the door. Then he turned and left the room followed by Fatimeh Sadat who wanted to know when Zahra was going to come and visit them.

"I think he knows everything?" the old lady whispered to herself.

"Yes, Grandma and I too, know it now. The two of you saved us all from that bastard. And you MUST not feel guilty about it – not for a minute."

"You too?"

"Yes Grandma."

"Did Mohsen tell you how Bagher died?"

"Yes, in his sleep."

"I hope I die like that. It is the best way."

Chapter 12

It was a fine morning when Mohsen, Zahra and Jafar moved into Khanum's house. To impress upon the neighbours that they were relocating, a van delivered their suitcases and several large cartoons filled with old newspapers, sacks of rice and dry provision. Their arrival surprised the curious gardener whose crooked mind was busy planning how to become the owner of the property, more than the remaining neighbours whose only aim was to conceal their real identity from strangers. He was watering the vegetable garden with his ears pricked up and his senses focused on the hustle and bustle racketing at the gate when Khanum walked into the garden, summoned him to her presence on the veranda. Surprised, he dropped the hose, rushed to where she was standing, greeted her with a curt salam, delved a hand in one pocket, leaned to his left and stood still. His eyes bore malice, his posture insolence. She noticed all without allowing any reaction settle on her countenance. Then in an exacting voice explained that the house had been sold to an old friend of the family before the Master's imprisonment and she would remain in it until she found a small apartment to rent. She gave him the choice to stay and work for the new owners or leave. Bewildered he was contemplating the option with a sarcastic smile tilting on his tanned unshaved face when Mohsen who had been listening to the conversation from behind the window of the upstairs' bedroom, arrived walkie-talkie in hand. He looked very intimidating in his Revolutionary garb of green parka and pants. Curtly he introduced himself as the new proprietor of the house, commented on the messy state of the lawn that had not been weeded neatly and tree branches that had not been trimmed for a long time and in a demanding tone, asked him why he had not been performing his job properly. The gardener surprised by the attack, was lost for words. Not daring to look at this hostile man in the eyes he kept his head down – trying to find the right excuses. Mohsen did not give him time to think. He placed his walkie-talkie on the table, put his hand into his pocket, withdrew his cheque book, turned to Khanum and asked, "Khanum how much do you pay this man per month?" Smiling at Mohsen's connivance she replied, "three hundred toomans."

"That is three thousand six hundred per year".

"Correct." Khanum responded with her smile intact.

Mohsen sat on the garden chair, put his cheque book on the table, wrote the sum of the annual wage, signed it, rose and handing it to the gardener said, "Take this, go and turn off the hose you have left running and then leave my property." Flabbergasted the man took the cheque, glimpsed at the sum and stuttered his objection.

Khanum so far silent threw him a resentful glance and said, "Asghar Agha, you better take the cheque and thank Mr. Bagheri for his generosity. He is a very important officer at Evin prison. You are a part-time worker here and the labour laws do not apply to you. So thank your lucky star and do not close all doors behind you with this very kind and important gentleman." Her stress on the words 'Evin prison' made Asghar apprehensive of the consequences of further negotiations. He put the cheque in his pocket, threw Khanum a contemptuous look, turned his pock-marked face to Mohsen and, in a subservient tone, wished him a long life and then added, he would be honoured if ever he was called upon to serve such an important brother.

In the parlance of the revolutionaries the word 'brother' had replaced 'agha'.

With Asghar gone the only problem to resolve was how to stop Blacky's incessant fretting. At first he moaned and groaned all night long and barked at whoever stepped out of the building. Then gradually Mohsen's generous leftovers, tastier than anything Khanum had ever fed him, won his allegiance. Zahra never went near the dog and he learned to make himself rare while she was in the garden picking herbs or trimming the creeping roses that had invaded the entire length of the surrounding walls. Zahra had green fingers and an everlasting passion for nature. Child of a peasant, she was born in a rice field where her mother's waters had broken bending to plant rice. Her first breath was of the field's scented air and her first mattress a heap of turf. She was daughter of nature and now God had made her the mistress of a paradise she never dreamed of inhabiting. She returned Providence's favour by taking loving care of this unexpected gift. Every morning she woke up to a new plan and within the first few months of her stay the garden became alive again – the same as it used to be when Khanum together with the gardener had the heart to give it love – after all what does not thrive on love?

One late afternoon when Zahra was watering the lawn and humming a happy tune she heard the door bell ring rapidly. Blacky's ears pricked up. He was relaxing by Khanum's empty chair. Zahra dropped the hose, turned its tap off and ran to the gate.

He followed her – albeit at a distance.

"Who is it?" she asked in a soft voice.

"Open the door Sister. We are from the local Komiteh and want to see the owner of the house."

Warned to expect such a call, she calmly asked them to wait until she could put on her chador. She ran to the entrance hall and grabbed her black polyester cover from the bronze hook that was originally installed to hold Mink coats; hastily she spread it over her head, ran back and opened the gate to four armed unshaved, parka-garbed pasdars, resembling Che Guevara's men more than soldiers of Islam. They were holding their guns as though threatened by the punitive figure of the female who politely invited them in.

They entered with heavy purposeful steps, smiling at their presumed newly acquired property. Their hungry eyes roamed around appraising every brick, every cracked pillar and the pair of antique Italian lion statues guarding the main entrance door, with greedy uncouth inquisitiveness of hungry marauders. The bearded leader, who seemed a bit older than the others, turned to Zahra, his face tight with a forged expression of righteousness and said, "We are here to confiscate this property for the Foundation of Emmam. Its owner was a Corrupter on Earth and was sent to hell. We know his wife lives here."

"You are wrong brother. Its owner is one of you and at the moment in a meeting at Evin prison. I have the prison's number, you can check for yourself. And yes Mrs Zand is our guest."

From a distance Blacky began to bark. One of the pasdar's raised his gun and aimed to shoot the dog. Zahra jumped in front of him yelling, "Blacky get lost."

The dog sensed danger, furiously wagging his tale increased the vehemence of his growl.

Jafar dealing with the Orphanage's accounts in the study heard Blacky's bark. He was in charge for a further two months until his father could be replaced by the new cook at the prison. He dropped his pen on the table, jumped off his chair, ran downstairs and out into the garden where, the sight of armed men nailed him to the ground. Malice oozed out of the strangers' countenance. His heart began to palpitate fast. Had they wised up to their theft from the morgue and come to take his father and him to jail? He thought for a moment and then giving himself an air of innocence asked, "Mother is there anything I can do for you or these gentlemen?"

"No son. Just calm Blacky. He is making our brothers nervous."

Jafar released a sigh of relief which went unnoticed, ran to Blacky, lifted him up and stroking him lovingly, carried him to the side of the building away from the sight of the intruders.

Huffing and puffing with disbelief, the leader in an acrimonious tone demanded to see the deed of the house. Too agitated to ask for their identity credentials, Zahra ran inside and returned with the booklet, its photocopy and her husband's birth-certificate which she politely handed to the senior pasdar. He examined every page of and every name on the document; opened the birth-certificate and compared the names. Assured that the name matched the one on the last page of the deed, he handed the documents back to Zahra, his grave face drawn with surprise.

"I am keeping the photocopy for our file sister. The Zands were lucky to have sold the house when they did." He whispered to the cool afternoon air and nodding to his comrades they left a devastated Zahra to pray for the safe-keeping of the foresighted Mahzari. She returned inside and collapsed on the nearest chair.

"If the house has been sold why the widow still lives there Kazem?" Davoud the youngest and most intelligent of the four asked his senior mate. They were descending Saltanat Abad Street to get some ice cream from the confectionery shop on their way to their Komiteh Building – a confiscated house allegedly to have been a SAVAK (the shah's security service) base.

"I am going to find that out. That is why I took the photocopy of the deed. I cannot believe they had sold the house just before he was taken and that to a friend. These people have an everlasting affinity to their ancestral seats.

They never sell unless compelled to. Zand was a rich man. So is his wife. Most of Niavaran belonged to her grandfather. My father used to dig wells for him."

"You know the family then?" Davoud asked excitedly. He was new to the neighbourhood and hardly knew the people into whose properties he was daily intruding. A sharp boy, he just wanted to know everything.

"Not personally, but I have heard stories about them. They were so rich that they had Delkesh sing for them in person. My father told me he heard her sing there himself. He was very proud of the experience."

"Who is Delkesh?" Davoud asked. Coming from a small village he had never heard of the singer.

"We were not born when she sang."

They all laughed before entering the shop. The vendor, familiar with their request, immediately took out four cups of strawberry ice cream from the freezer and placed them on the counter. The boys picked them up, thanked him and walked out without paying. The vendor did not mind – so long as they left his sight and his shop quickly. Besides, it was prudent to be on good terms with the pasdars – even such young ones.

It was late afternoon, when exhilarated by exercise and fresh air Khanum returned home to hear the news of the visit from a pale and distraught Zahra. That frightened her. Time to leave had arrived. The matter was discussed over dinner and Mohsen decided to take a few days off to drive her first to Fumen and then to his contact.

Early Wednesday morning Khanum together with Mohsen visited Shokat Bano. The old lady received them with open arms and a happy smile. Now completely bedridden, every morning she opened her eyes hoping to receive a visitor with whom she could exchange a few words and receive some exciting news of life outside her domain that was limited to her bedroom which was bright and had a large window through which she could see the garden, the sun, the moon, sometimes a few stars and of course Zahra in her bellowing chador come to entertain them. On Fridays it was Mohsen's turn – early in the morning he arrived, unloaded their needed provisions, drank a cup of tea, gave them a few black market video tapes to watch and dashed off leaving Sadat to sort things out.

Khanum often dropped in late afternoons on her way back from her walk. Shokat Bano found the early visit today strange but said nothing. Content, they made small talk, gossiped about the married men whose wives and children lived overseas leaving them free to indulge in various affairs of the heart. They joked and laughed at trivialities that make life pleasant. Khanum told her Mohsen was driving her to the villa by the Caspian on his way to visit his father's grave at Fumen from where he intended to bring her lots of Koluche, a small sweet loaf made of flour, ground walnut and saffron, a specialty of Fumen. The old lady's eyes glimmered with pleasure and she licked her lips several times as though tasting the remnants of Koluche crumbs on them. It had been such a long time since she had tasted a good Koluche.

"Mohsen bring me a dozen. Fatimeh Sadat likes them too."

"Shall do, my Mistress."

"Good, now before leaving both of you come close so that I can recite the safety-prayer in your ears."

They each obeyed and Khanum, her heart hammering hard, hugged her tight, feeling her warmth, inhaling her pleasant odour and being one with her – just for a short moment. She kissed her so many times that the old lady lost her breath and pushed her away.

"Stop it, Khanum, you are killing me."

"Granny I love you sooooo much."

"I love you too, but there is a limit to everything," the

old lady said as though advising a little girl.

Khanum kissed her one more time.

That was to be their last encounter.

In the car she blurted to Mohsen, "I did well, didn't I?" and then burst into tears. Nodding, Mohsen respected her grief and allowed her time to pour it out. So they drove in silence. The journey ahead was long but the highway to Rasht was empty, so he could drive fast.

Gilan is a prosperous and beautiful province. Driving through it is very pleasant. The highway passes first through lush greenery that lies along the foothills of Alborz range and then tight olive groves and vast rice and tea plantations.

They had lunch of bread and lamb kebab in a small restaurant. She did not eat much; she was saving her appetite for a loaf of warm Koluche.

When the highway ended and the car turned into a beautiful, tree-lined road Mohsen turned to Khanum and said, "This road was built by your aunt, Khanum Nosrat Aghdas. Fumen was her dowry!"

"Wonderful. I never knew that."

"The natives still remember her with respect and her son, Nasser Khan, has built a mosque and a school for the town." "My cousin is such a generous man and gives willingly. That is why he is so successful in life."

"It is the people's prayers that safeguard him."

"I tend to agree with you, Mohsen aziz." She responded looking out at the beautiful natural scenery that raced away from her vision. The car entered the town's main street; Mohsen parked it in front of the most famous Koluche maker and bought ten freshly baked aromatic loaves, just out of the oven. Even though the treat was very hot, they went through four of them on their way to the cemetery. Khanum was not really hungry – she was anguished and nervous. The pungent taste of the spicy loaf seemed to calm her nerves – she devoured them with zest and as he parked the car, the thumping of her heart increased and her lips began to quiver with emotion. The remnant of the last Koluche fell on her skirt. She brushed it off on to the pavement as she got out of the car.

At the graveyard, under an orange tree, near a honeysuckle bush, a small marble slab, only the death prayer carved on it in gold paint, stood in remembrance of a nameless man. Khanum knelt by the stone, kissed it, washed it with her tears, kissed it again, put her cheek to feel the cold stone and through it the warmth of her husband's soul. Aloof, Mohsen stood afar, whispering the death prayer and trying to overcome the disturbing memory of the day at the morgue.

Khanum rose and gently walked to Bagher's grave which was on the right-hand side. A large rectangular white marble slab marked his eternal residence. There she bent, put her hand on the stone, closed her eyes to visualize him and then whispered the same prayer. She opened her eyes to a white butterfly quivering over the honeysuckle bush. Her eyes widened with delight. She interpreted the coincidence as something holy – God's love for Sassan and Bagher – what else! She straightened her back and faced Mohsen. "I want to stay here with him until I find the strength to go away."

A frown appeared on his wide forehead. He had arranged to deliver her to the smuggler the next day. He pursed his lips, deepened his frown, thought for a moment or two and then turned his benevolent eyes to her and said "let me call them and see if we can change the arrangement."

"Tell them you will call them when I am ready to leave."

"Please let me see what can be done. We cannot play with these people. Besides, who knows they might get caught and then we will lose the money we have paid."

"Okay, talk to them. But I beg you to try to help me."

The plea in her voice could have broken the hardest heart, let alone Mohsen's.

They arrived at Zaynab Khanum's small and spotless cottage standing by a rice paddy. Aunt Zaynab, in spite of two missing front teeth, was a pleasant looking widow with a genuine smile, thick deeply-lined skin and a chador the edges of which were loosely tied around her neck, making field work in Hejab possible. Her home had two tiny rooms with cemented floors covered by frayed kilims. The tiny bedroom in which a neatly folded bundle of bedding served as a cushion to recline against was allocated to Khanum. Two huge nails protruding out of one of the white-washed walls served as clothes hangers. On one, a shabby raincoat hung aimlessly and on the other a black chador.

Zaynab and Mohsen were to share the other room in which everything else, including cooking was undertaken. The toilet was outside in a shed and there was no bathroom. People without means, used the town bath-house or a brook – all very simple and primitive.

Mohsen delivered Khanum's small travelling bag to her room and then returned to the front room where the two ladies were sitting on the floor chatting. He looked around and found an old telephone perched on the room's sole window sill, its wire hanging down across the wall like a black snake. He picked up the receiver and dialled a number. She became all ears. His conversation was in code and his voice occasionally fluttered. Every time it raised Khanum's heart beats quickened and when it fell a sigh escaped her tight mouth. Eventually the conversation ended with Mohsen nodding in accord. Yes Khanum could stay at Fumen till twentieth of Khordad (May), which gave her a month and twenty days. Overjoyed, she rose and gave him a big hug and a quick kiss on the forehead. Zaynab turned her eyes towards heaven and sent the Almighty a loud praise.

Then she turned her happy eyes to Khanum and said, "There is so much to do in the field, and with the pain in my back, I was wondering how I could ever manage. God has been merciful. With your help, Khanum joon, I can finish my tasks. Now I have to pray for good weather."

Her mood elevated, Khanum stretched her arms to heaven and loudly implored God to hear Zaynab Khanum's request and grant her good weather. Then, humming a happy tune, she went to her room to change into her jeans and T-shirt – the only outfit she had brought with her beside the peasant set she had to wear for her exodus. Upon her return, she found Aunt Zaynab squatting next to a gas burner on which she was preparing sabzie-polo, a rice dish with herbs to be eaten with Mahi doodi, a smoked dried fish. The smell of garlic in the rice was mouth-watering. Within an hour, the trio enjoyed a delicious dinner hearing about Aunt Zaynab's endeavours to procure Government provision-coupons that enabled her to manage to live without asking Mohsen for help. Everytime she mentioned money she blushed with embarrassment. Taken by the dignity of the poverty-stricken, hard-working aged woman who was sharing her meagre provision with her, Khanum found herself feeling as small as an ant.

On the same gas burner now sat a large hot water kettle on which was fitted a smaller tea kettle – the way tea is brewed in the absence of a samovar.

Khanum was so excited that she did not want the night to end. But Mohsen had to return to Teheran early the next morning. She helped Zaynab take the dishes out to wash in the cold water of the narrow brook running by the cottage. The water came from the mountain and was supposed to be clean. However, at times villagers did die of dysentery.

Just as dawn was breaking, Mohsen dropped Khanum by the cemetery and left for Teheran. It was near home and she could walk back.

Everyday, Khanum rose at dawn, went in search of wild flowers, which she made into two beautiful bouquets, one for Sassan and one for Bagher. She placed the flowers over their graves; talked to her husband, kissed his headstone, prayed for Bagher, trained the honeysuckle crawlers to creep over both graves and then returned just in time to give Zaynab a hand in the rice paddy. Neither the murky knee-high water of the paddy or the pains caused by a leech or two sucking her blood bothered her. She learnt to carry a lighter with which she could burn the leeches off her skin. She found being in the open relaxing and soothing. Colour returned to her face and her comb stopped being entangled by falling hair. The itchy rash on her stomach vanished without a trace. Then one day when the two had squatted by the brook washing their clothes, Zaynab turned to her and said, "Khanum joon, I have no education and I have not travelled the world like you. In fact I have not set foot outside of Fumen, but one thing I know, and that is life is God's gift, to be valued by being lived well. You have abandoned it. This will make God turn his face from you. It was written that your husband died the way he did. Destiny is Providence's plan for us. Don't frown on it. Accept it with grace and make the best of it. Begin to live again – don't waste your days in remorse. Death will come to us all – in its own good time – don't go chasing it. Chase life – it is beautiful."

Zaynab stopped when she saw tears streaming down Khanum's sun-burnt face.

"Khanum joon, you are like my daughter. Crying will not solve any problems. Pull yourself together, smile and let the world smile back at you."

Khanum put her washing in the tray sitting between the two of them, washed her face, hugged and kissed the wrinkled, weather-beaten face of the woman whose life had offered her nothing but back bending work – and yet she had found beauty in it. Suddenly she felt ashamed for having been so ungrateful for her own.

A soft breeze teased her hair away. She sniffed it. It smelled yummy. She turned her eyes to the sky; it was spotless blue – quite beautiful she thought. Her heart filled with joy. She rose and went inside. There she picked up the telephone and called Mohsen. He answered. Whispering she asked him to sell two of her Tabriz carpets and give the money to Aunt Zaynab as a gift from her. Mohsen asked no questions. The tone of Khanum's voice revealed to him the reason behind the request. – she had returned to the world of the living. That made him happy and eternally grateful to his dear old aunt.

On the 20th Khordad, Khanum, disguised in a long and loose peasant's outfit, sat in a minibus heading for Tabriz and then the border of Bazargan. On her lap was a light travelling bag in the lining of which was sewn her passport, birth certificate, university degrees and two hundred, hundred dollar bills. In the visible part of the bag were ordinary travelling necessities a peasant woman would carry, including a set of keys. Inside her padded brow were sown her diamond wedding ring and some other precious stones dismounted from their settings. On one of her fingers was Sassan's wedding band and on her wrist his watch.

The man next to her, a Kurd was her guide but they were to act as strangers. The minibus driver seemed to be in a hurry. He sped through the highway relentlessly as though driving a Ferrari in a race at Monte Carlo. No one objected. They all were in a hurry. The passengers, hugging tight to whatever they were carrying, looked at the green scenery running away from them, thinking of what they had left behind and what lay ahead. None dared to talk to his or her neighbour – such was the extent of their phobia.

Every now and then the mini bus was stopped at a search point for a document and suitcase check. The driver

209

seemed to be persuasive enough not to allow any gendarme inside his vehicle. In silence they drove through Tabriz where the driver stopped for refuelling and toilet service.

Khanum and her guide left the bus two stops before the border where a distinguished looking man in Kurdish attire acknowledged them with a quick shake of his turbaned head. Khanum's heart missed a bit and she became transfixed to the ground. The tall, well-built man was the image of Sassan with a moustache. She kept her amazed gaze on him thinking perhaps it was a ghost she was seeing. No it was not. The man was alive, active and commandeering. Her gaze still fixed on his face she noticed his skin was tanned and as thick as leather. Sassan's had been pale and soft. His eyes had the same shape but were blue. Suddenly she felt a strange feeling squeeze her heart. Pained she released a heavy sigh. Catching her hum of grief, he threw an evaluating glance at her. She caught it and kept it for just a bit too long for a woman in her situation. He smiled and in fluent Farsi without a tinge of any provincial accent ordered her and the guide to follow him to the parked black Range Rover. The man had the deportment of an authoritarian tribal chieftain. His wide brown pants and white shirt were not of coarse cotton but of the finest quality and his brown belt had a Gucci buckle. He was no ordinary smuggler. Khanum surmised that from his ensemble, the words he used and the Cartier watch she saw him nervously glance at. She couldn't stop herself from throwing him quick glances – his resemblance to her beloved was extraordinary. She felt the welling up of tears in her eyes. She turned them towards the darkening sky; there she saw a canopy of stars twinkling at her; smiling she took it as a good omen.

"Sister, please sit in front and Reza you in the back."

He ordered directing his gaze at Khanum's hand that held the handle of her bag.

"Good you are wearing a wedding band. By the way my name is Khodadad Mohammadi and you are supposedly my wife Kiana."

Offended by the man's manner, in a sarcastic tone she asked, "Isn't Kiana too classy a name for a peasant?"

"No. It is an old Kurdish name. Remember it and answer to it."

No one had ever talked to her in such impertinent manner – not even her father.

"Is your real name Khodadad Mohammadi Agha?"

"My real name should not concern you," he replied surprised at her audacity.

"Where are we going now, Khan?" Reza asked with reverence.

Khan was a nomenclature referring to a tribal leader.

"To Abol Farm. We shall spend the night there. Tomorrow morning you return to Teheran in the mini- bus with the goods and I shall take this lady and the children across the border. "Children?" Khanum asked astonished.

"My children will accompany us. It is easier to cross the border as a family than man and wife."

"I thought we were to ride through the mountains to Turkey."

"Yes, but after meeting you I have changed my plan."

Khanum fell into a pensive silence. Night was upon them, a single woman with two strangers. Yet she was not scared. The worse had already happened to her. Fear attacks when there is something to lose. She had nothing to lose except her life – which at that moment seemed worthless – to her and the other two in the car.

They drove for an hour through strange terrains, off the highway on to a narrow bumpy country road till the silhouette of tall trees became visible under the moon-lit sky dotted with an array of sparkling stars. Gradually a high mud wall began to reveal itself stretching as far as the eyes could perceive.

"Where are we, Agha Mohammadi?"

"You are in no man's land or better said a land claimed by many and owned by no one – in which my ancestors built a caravanserai that in the bygone days accommodated travellers until it's well dried out. Unused the building and the garden died until I decided to renovate the property and turn the wasted land into a polo ground – the sport being the passion of our lives – that is mine and my late wife's."

Surprised at his change of tone she asked, "You have lost a loved one too, Agha?"

"Yes Khanum. My wife died in a car crash going to Noshahr."

"May I ask what your real profession is or was?"

"I am or was an orthopaedic surgeon."

An orthopaedic surgeon turned into smuggler! It did not make sense. The man's life story was indeed intriguing – Khanum wondered, deeply curious.

The car halted by a huge green metal gate that contrasted with the ancient mud wall capped with red gable. Reza jumped out of the car and opened the gate, then quickly returned to the vehicle. They drove in. The lit gravel pathway stretched beyond sight passing an impressive two-storey domed house of the Safavid period in front of which a long water canal descended into a large swimming pool and then found its way out sloping down and beyond. The car parked in front of the back entrance, the door of which opened and a Philippine servant in white overall stepped out.

As though accustomed to receiving visitors, the woman greeted her master and his guests in good Farsi.

"Are my children asleep?"

"Yes Sir. It is past midnight now."

"We are hungry. Have you anything to feed us with?"

"Yes sir. Shall I serve you in the kitchen or the main

dining room?"

The Khan threw a questioning glance at Khanum's tired face.

"Kitchen will be fine with me."

"Reza, go and close the gate and then to your room, Fe will bring your supper there." The Khan ordered while ushering Khanum inside. Then he turned to the maid and said, "Guide the lady to the guest room. She might wish to freshen up."

Suddenly Khanum became conscious of her painful bladder. She had not relieved herself for almost twelve hours. Quickly she followed the maid along the cool corridor passing several closed doors. The maid stopped by the last door, opened it and stood aside. Thanking her, Khanum stepped into an elegant double bedroom with a large window. She dropped her bag on the large bed and went to look out. Under the moonlit sky she saw an oasis in the midst of a no-man's land. Her face lit with admiration. She turned around and saw the door closed and the maid vanished. She headed for the en-suite the door of which was open.

When she returned to the room she found laid on the bed a white embroidered bath robe and a pair of towel slippers, just as was done in five-star hotels overseas. The enigma was becoming more tantalizing.

Dinner was Eshkeneh, an Iranian version of the French onion soup mixed with dried fenugreek and eggs instead of cheese – a delicious aromatic meal by itself. Khanum was so hungry that she forgot her usual immaculate table manners and gulped down her food like a hungry beggar. The sight brought a gratifying smile to the thin lips of the host who merely played with his soup.

"Please don't look at me like that. I have not eaten properly for almost two days." Khanum said smiling back at the twinkling eyes that were sending strange messages. She ignored his eyes, wiped her mouth with her crisp white napkin and asked, "At what time you want me up tomorrow morning Agha?"

"Shall we have coffee in the sitting room?"

"I don't drink coffee at nights but a cup of hot water would be nice."

"We have home-grown chamomile and mint infusions if you wish?"

"Thank you but hot water will do."

Fe, sitting on her chair by the kitchen door, rose to serve.

The host led the way to a large room with stone floor and white-washed walls. Its furniture was not elegant but seemed comfortable. The chairs were upholstered in Kilim and other local hand woven textiles harmonizing with the rustic style of the interior. Wide solid cushions were scattered around a huge fireplace framed by a masterfully plastered surround. On the centre of the mantelpiece a huge copper vase held yellow and red roses exuding their mild fragrance; competing in beauty with the picture of a blond lady with large green eyes and long curly hair spread over her bare shoulders.

"That is the picture of my wife, Delbar."

"She was beautiful."

Khanum remarked sitting on the sofa that faced the mantelpiece. He sat by her stretching his arm on the back of the sofa above her shoulders – as though a close friend. "Yes she was beautiful in looks and in personality." Eyes still fixed on the picture he whispered in such a touching tone that barred further inquisitiveness.

"My husband was also beautiful," Khanum murmured her eyes wandering over the patterns of the huge Tabriz carpet that covered almost the entire area of the room.

"Mrs. Zand I apologize for my curtness earlier on. I had to play my role in front of Reza. I know you well. I am

214

related to your husband and, by pure chance, we went to the same university and at the same time."

Khanum's mouth fell open unable to believe her ears. She straightened her posture, turned her head to the so-called smuggler, smiled with joy and said, "Khodadad Khan, am I calling you by your real name?"

"My real name is Khodayar and my family name is also Zand. Sassan and I were third cousins removed from our father's side but our great grandfathers never saw eye-to-eye – hence the family rift that was fortunately bridged at Harvard where we discovered our kinship. Then, during the shah's reign we took different paths and that is why you never met me. When Mohsen was brought to me by my contact at Evin and told me who he wanted me to smuggle out I immediately accepted the task in spite of the fact that I never do this for women."

He stopped, lit the elegant pipe he had picked up from the table and was caressing; took couple of puffs in, blew circled fumes out and then continued, "I only smuggle out politicians and military men on the run. I am not in this just for profit. The money goes into the purchase of medicine and surgical equipments barred from being imported to Iran by the sanctions. I save lives while making money. Therefore I have no qualms about my business."

"Bravo Agha." Khanum interrupted, throwing him a glance glowing with esteem. 'So they were cousins – that explains the likeness', she thought thanking her lucky stars.

"People are dying at the hospitals and at homes, even from simple untreated flu that turns into pneumonia and minor injuries into gangrenes. Our hospitals are in great need of medical practitioners and supplies. Since I cannot offer my services as a surgeon, I provide the middle man with medicine – not those with expired due dates sold in the bazaars but with up-to-date ones."

He stopped to poke at his pipe.

"Incredible cousin; I wish there were more men like you in this world. Thank you and thank you for what you are doing for Iran and me," she exclaimed, clapped her hands, then she stretched across and stole a quick kiss from his wide forehead.

The touch of her lips sparkled a delicious feeling inside his numbed heart. He blushed.

"Khanum joon, do not thank me. Thank Providence."

"Indeed I have to thank Providence. Now please tell me how I can help you – if at all possible?"

"Of course it is possible. Become part of my team. I need all the influence and funds I can get my hands on."

A sullen faced Fe, tray in had arrived, offered Khanum her cup of hot water and her Master his chamomile tea. Khodayar thanked and dismissed her for the night.

"Count me in, handsome smuggler," cup in hand, she said with a wink and a broad smile. He winked back and like children they began to laugh.

He finished his tea, put the cup down, smiled and asked, "Would you like to stay here a few days before we leave for Turkey?"

"That would be wonderful. I hate the thought of leaving Iran. I hope I die on the way out so that you can bury me next to my husband."

"Please do not talk nonsense."

Outside, the moon had retired behind grey pregnant clouds and hungry wolves were howling for food. They both rose and indolently ambled to their respective bedrooms.

He could not sleep. Life was stirring inside him again and the excitement of it was unsettling.

Outside the clouds burst into a heavy rain, and a vicious storm, wheezing insanely, lashed at whatever lay in its path. Frightened horses and dogs began to holler and Khodayar heard Fe run to close the open windows that were furiously colliding against one another and the adjoining walls.

That night, in spite of the storm's savageness Khanum fell into a deep sleep – sleep of someone secure – without any frightening nightmares. Early in the morning she woke up refreshed, without any debilitating sense of anxiety. She showered, enjoying the sense of every droplet on her skin. Then she dressed in her peasant's garments and dashed down the corridor to the kitchen where she found her host seated between a pair of deformed twins eating their breakfast of bread, feta cheese and cucumber wrap. She hid her surprise with a smile and said, "Good morning". The girls looked up at her with lethargic eyes and then resumed their consumption.

"My daughters, Mehr and Mehri – unfortunately they are dumb but not deaf."

Khanum nodded her understanding and occupied the chair facing Khodayar. He looked smart in his tribal riding gear. Fe, with a cold greeting poured tea in her cup. She sensed the maid's resentment. It amused her. Probably she was in love with her handsome master and thought of her as a rival! All maids fall in love with their masters. Her own maid, Anna was in love with Sassan – his shirts were always immaculately ironed while a few creases remained on her dresses and skirts. With empathy, she smiled at the dull-faced maid and thanked her for the tea.

As soon as the girls started fiddling with breadcrumbs Fe took them to the garden's playground. Shortly after, Khodayar took Khanum for a walk. They passed by a kitchen garden, a large poultry den and a modern stable grounds. Their walk was tranquil – each immersed in thought, listening to the whistle of the wind, the chirping of the birds and the occasional bark of a dog. The peace and the security of the surroundings were too precious to break with base talk. They walked on until Khodayar stopped and turned to her.

"The twins are adopted. I found them abandoned by the gate of the village clinic where I help the doctor – when time permits." He said as though there was a need for explanation.

"What a wonderful thing to do, Khan."

"Stop calling me Khan. My wife called me Khodi, please address me as such. By the way do you know how to ride a horse?" he asked grabbing her hand and pulling her towards the stables. His touch electrified her – the way Sassan's used to do. What was happening to her? Was she going mad? She pondered. Ashamed she tried to withdraw her hand but his grip was too tight and too determined. She relented, thinking she would never castrate his name by calling him Khodi – he was too much of a gentleman for a nick name!

The stable was of red brick, lodging thirty gracious Arabian horses busy munching their hay or protruding their handsome heads out of their individual holes in the wall that Khanum did not know what to call – perhaps 'horse-window'.

"These are beautiful! You did not tell me you breed horses!"

"There are many things I have not told you yet," he teased. She smiled.

Two Afghan stable boys appeared from behind one of the stable walls and bowed to their master. The elder of the two asked if any horse was to be saddled.

"I do know how to ride a horse, but not in this gear." Khanum replied pointing to her long skirt that covered a wide black cotton pantaloon.

"If you take your skirt off you can."

She thought for a while, then, giggling unfastened the rope that tied the skirt to her waist, and stepped out of its midst – looking like a slave girl out of Sinbad's story. One of the Afghan boys bent and picked the skirt up, folded it neatly and hung it over his arm.

"Which horses shall I saddle, Master?"

The other Afghan asked politely.

"Shahzadeh (the princess) for Khanum and Malek (the sovereign) for me."

Ten minutes later Khanum was seated on a gracious white stallion and her host on a jet black one trotted out of the stable yard into a vast green terrain that stretched to the foothills of the Zagros Mountains. They rode smiling at the day's beauty, galloping past the gorges and the waterfalls that revealed themselves and then quickly disappeared – their beauty breathtaking.

Days passed in a pleasant atmosphere of relaxed innocent comradeship until the Gods became envious.

Iran was invaded by Saddam Hussain's army.

The plan was to fly Khanum in a helicopter over the mountains to the nearest Turkish village with a bus service to Ankara. However, with the bombardments, even though they were happening mostly in the south of the country, that plan became too dangerous to implement. Now they had to take the long mule route on horseback. Khodayar was well-known to the gendarmes who patrolled the routes. Most were on his pay roll. Having once caught him red handed, they realized what he was doing, admired his undertaking, took his pay-off and let him operate freely. Their responsibility was to catch the runaways and drug smugglers. The Khan was neither. They had never caught him smuggling people out. Most of the live cargo had flown over their heads below or above the air force's radar range.

The sky was not yet milky when three riders, galloped out of the stable towards the mountains, past familiar gorges and waterfalls and beyond where the path became too narrow and the abyss too deep. Here they had to halt for the Afghan to blindfold the beasts. Three hours into their ride they commenced the descent towards an oasis with mud huts engulfed by trees visible from behind a veil of translucent mist arising from the surface of a small lake.

They dismounted, their horses, panting and heaving with exhaustion. At first Khanum's legs refused to move – her muscles unaccustomed to such long and strenuous exertion. Mindful of her discomfort, he gently lent her his arm; smiling she took it with dignity and limped to the weather-beaten wooden gate that had been left open. The Afghan stayed lingering with the mounts. Inside they found an old woman, her grey hair covered by a long white muslin scarf, busy drawing water from her well. Swiftly she detached the heavy container from its rope, placed it on the ground then raised her face to the entrants and warmly saluted the Khan and his companion with the wave of her hand. The Khan hugged the old woman, kissed her weather-beaten, deeply lined tanned face and asked after her health. Complaining of the plight of old age she took the Khan's offered hand, rose, brushed away the creases of her long colourful cotton skirt and guided them to a large white-washed room with an open window and a stone sink the tap of which was leaking, and its droplets splashing on the grey stone in a rhythmic thud. The brick floor was covered by a withered Turcoman Kilim. Two neatly wrapped beddings tucked at a corner served as bolsters to recline against. At a far corner a tea pot on a samovar was steaming. Next to the samovar a clean white cloth was wrapped around a collection of lavash bread. A small rusted fridge sporadically burped its malfunction. On the top of the fridge sat a few tea glasses and a couple of plastic plates hosting some metal cutlery. Having ushered in the guests, the hostess kicked off her sandals before stepping in. Out of respect she had not asked the Khan and his companion to take off their shoes – city folks never did.

"Please sit down and make yourselves comfortable. Omar will be here soon," the woman said in a thick Kurdish accent before busying herself with breakfast preparation.

The room in its simplicity was cosy and welcoming. Khanum dropped on the floor, relaxed her aching back against the makeshift bolster, closed her eyes and fell into a deep sleep. Khodayar edged closer to her and gradually her head tilted to the left and rested on his shoulder. The warmth of her breath suffused through the tissue of his linen shirt and lay on his skin making his heart palpitate with joy.

He loved her so much.

Soon the Afghan accompanied by an old tall pleasant-looking man in tribal clothes, carrying a large clay jar of fresh milk, appeared at the door kicking their shoes off. The Khan's finger went to his nose and hushed them to whispering.

They crossed the threshold and stood still. Omar threw a quick glance at the sleeping lady, bowed to the Khan and then the two tiptoed across the room. Omar handed the milk to his wife and then from above the bedding bundle took a plastic cover which he spread on the floor. Hastily between the three of them a meal of milk, aromatic tea, bread, honey and curd was laid on the Sofreh. Once everyone sat down, Khan gently shook Khanum out of her sleep. She opened her eyes completely disoriented. It took her a few seconds before realising where she was and then she hastily collected herself, sat upright, greeted her host and joint them in taking breakfast,

"Omar what time is the bus to Ankara?" Khan asked sipping at his tea.

"In half an hour, Khan, I have already paid the driver to borrow an immigration stamp from his brother, who is a real immigration officer, with which he will stamp Khanum's passport."

"Excellent, and when are you going to get the new consignment from Ankara?"

"God willing today; the mules and my sons are ready to

carry them through. We have had to change route because the gendarmes have changed and I don't want to take any unnecessary risks."

"You are a jewel Omar Khan – always cautious and prudent. God will reward you with a secure place in paradise," Khodayar exclaimed, affectionately patting the old man on the back. Then he rose and asked Khanum to follow him out. She thanked her hostess for the breakfast and followed him out where the sun was shining benevolently and the mountain breeze was pleasantly cool. Suddenly she found herself shivering. To keep warm she hugged herself tight.

Ahead of her he walked to where the mounts were busy nicking the fodder heaped for them. He went to his horse and from his saddle bag withdrew a large encased volume of the Koran which he handed to her. She respectfully took it and brought it to her lips to kiss when its heavy weight surprised her.

"Are you hiding something in the cover?" she asked bemused.

"Yes – the dollars you paid for your freedom," he responded bemusedly.

She went crimson.

"That was not part of the deal."

"What deal?"

Lost for words she went purple.

"Will you keep your promise?" he asked in a tender voice.

"Yes – so long as you phone me once a week."

The hooting of a car diverted their attention. Omar, his wife and the Afghan carrying Khanum's travelling bag stepped out of the room. The Afghan ran to Khanum. Before taking the bag from him, she held the Koran up to Khodayar to kiss and then unconsciously she kissed the spot on which his lips had laid. He saw that and his heart's throbbing accelerated to an unbearable momentum. Hastily she took her bag, fitted the Koran into it and hung it on her thin shoulder which slightly bent under the weight. With a heavy heart she embraced the old lady, shook the hands of the two men and then hugged the Khan. He kept her tight whispering all kinds of prayers.

The bus took in its passenger and wobbling on the bumpy road drove away. Khodayar kept waving until the bus became a speck suffused in a plume of dust and gasoline fumes.

Five hours later the Khan took dinner with the girls and went to Khanum's bedroom and lay on her bed inhaling her jasmine scent still lingering on the sheets. He kissed the pillow on which her head had rested, then folded his arms behind his head and fixed his eyes on the red roses he had given her the day before.

Thirty-six hours later Khanum passed through the visa section of Heathrow Airport without any hassle. Once settled in her flat, she called all the pharmaceutical companies on his list – alas, to no avail. She did not give up. The telephone book became her bible. Then one day her luck changed. One of the product managers turned out to be Funny Sarah, her roommate at boarding school. Sarah was the daughter of an English knight with a great sense of humour, hence the nick name. Sarah shared a dormitory with her and another friend called Shirin. The girls were referred to as the three musketeers at school – so intimate was their relationship.

Sarah and Khanum met for lunch at St. Lorenzo in Beauchamp Place, a happy reunion during which reminiscences brought laughter to their lips and a few occasional frowns to their foreheads. Unfortunately neither had heard from Shirin for a long time now. Sarah listened intently to what Khanum told her about her friend's activities in Iran. The prudent girl advised her to establish a company in Dubai through which she could purchase whatever she needed. Due to international sanctions, no European company was able to deal direct with Iran. The idea was excellent and practical. The friends parted with a plan to lunch once a month.

At home Khanum phoned Khodayar and gave him the result of her finding.

Time passed swiftly. The war became a disaster for both countries. The United States supported Saddam and provided him with otherwise inaccessible strategic information. Iranian cities were bombed repeatedly. The Iraqis managed to advance but the Iranians united in their love of their country and regardless of their political views fought ferociously. The war became a stalemate and smugglers and middle men became rich – one among them Khodayar. The government officials wised up to his activities but, as it suited them, they closed their eyes and let him bring in the needed medicine and medical equipment procured through Khanum's company in Dubai.

Two years passed in futile fighting. Due to a shortage of medical practitioners Khodayar was invited back to practice at a government hospital. His dossier closed and in ownership of a valid passport he went to London and married Khanum at Chelsea Town Hall, and had the marriage certificate verified and stamped at the Iranian Consulate. They spent their honeymoon at an ancient inn on the shore of Ulswater Lake, in Cumberland, walking around the lake, dining at English pubs and uniting in love's intimacy at night. Life, for both, became beautiful again.

The war went on. Khodayar returned without ever asking her to accompany him. He loved her too much and understood her more than she understood herself. He knew that he would never be able to erase her devotion to Sassan's memory and he did not want to do that because she had never ever shown the slightest inclination to compete with Delbar's memories. Her love for him was a strange one. Nevertheless, content with having what he had of her, he left the decision to come and live in Iran to her. It seemed to him that she had divided her world into two zones. Iran always belonged to Sassan and the rest of the world to Khodayar. In fact he was right in his assumption. Khanum could never live with Khodayar in Iran – there were too many ghosts to haunt her there; nevertheless she hoped one day he would join her in London where they could live the rest of their lives in peace and contentment.

The war continued its destructiveness – on both sides. Khodayar, in company with many other surgeons, was sent to the front. One day when he was operating in a medical tent on the outskirts of Ahvaz a bomb blast wiped off the whole camp. News reached Khanum. She cried for three days and then walked to the nearest church to her house and thanked God for having given her two extraordinary men of whom she was proud. She called Mohsen who had power of attorney from Dr. Zand, and asked him to send Mehr, Mehri and Fe to London. It was difficult but Mohsen had carte blanche to spend. While practising in Teheran, Khodayar had called on Mohsen at Niavaran, first to meet the man his wife trusted so much and second, to see the house she had lived in with Sassan. The two men had become good friends and every Friday the doctor had lunched at Mohsen's Kebab restaurant. Finding the food excellent, he had recommended the eatery to all his friends and caused its great success. Impressed by his manners and wisdom, Mohsen was never able to address Khodayar by his first name. He bore him too much respect to do that. To him he was 'the respectable Doctor.' Mohsen had wanted to take his respectable Doctor to meet Shokat Bano but Khanum had not given him her permission. She did not want anyone in Iran to know of her marriage to him. Both men had respected her wish.

A few months later the girls together with Fe arrived in

225

London and were lodged in Khanum's old apartment. Gradually Fe learned to love her mistress and value her generosity; particularly now that she had her Portuguese lady to manage the apartment while she dedicated her entire time to the girls.

The war eventually ended. One million Iranians lost their lives and probably as many Iraqis, for nothing. Neither Saddam nor Khomeini could claim victory.

Widowed again and very wealthy, Khanum led a tranquil life in the mansion Khodayar had bought her at Princess Gate in Knightsbridge. The house was very close to Hyde Park where she took frequent solitary long walks and, weather permitting, bicycle rides. In the afternoons she played bridge and during the evenings she enjoyed the company of her friends. Her weekends belonged to the girls.

She had many suitors, some deeply in love with her and some captivated by her wealth and largess. None got close enough to even kiss her.

She spent freely particularly on the victims of the Iranian Revolution. There were so many refugees without means of sustenance, let alone a dignified life and to them she gave of herself and of her money. She never forgot Aunt Zaynab whose heart had failed while washing dishes by her brook. She had left the carpet money for Jafar.

Giving had become the sedative for her restless soul. She missed Sassan's smile and Khodayar's adoration; she missed her orphanage and above all she missed Iran. She read all the articles about Iran and listened to the BBC both in Farsi and English waiting to hear good news.

Ayatollah Rafsanjani became the new president and he promised amnesty and progress. A fresh breeze of freedom began to fan the Iranian ladies and the Sisters of Zahra, fundamentalist vigilantes responsible for throwing acid at the faces of women with the slightest make-up disappeared, and there were fewer pasdar knocks at private doors. So it seemed Iran was recovering from its own holocaust. Khanum was in daily contact with Mohsen. The orphanage was confiscated and was being run by the Foundation of the Emmam. Fortunately Mohsen was still living in the house at Niavaran thanks to the foresighted Mahzari, himself in Paris now, without a robe and a turban.

Success and wealth had not affected Mohsen. He had remained his faithful self. It was his meticulous investigation that had found Khanum on the list of the wanted as the wife of Sassan Zand. But as the wife of Shahid or Martyr Dr Khodayar Zand, whose name was given to the street where he was born, she was highly respected and entitled to several benefits. Mohsen had warned her that as the wife of a Martyr she could get herself out of the first list – but she should be prepared to stay in Iran as long as it took. He also informed her of the peaceful death of Shokat Bano – in bed when asleep. He had organized the ceremonies befitting her ladyship's rank and buried her side-by-side the Master and Mashhadi Mosayeb. The news was very sad. Nevertheless she had learnt to cope with losses that are part and parcel of life – besides, she had promised her beloved grandmother not to mourn her and hoped she was right in believing that in death she would reunite with her Agha.

Instead of letting her tears loose, Khanum sent a cheque for one thousand pounds to the Oxfam charity organization. And then one sunny day she summoned all her courage and went to the Islamic Republic's consulate, handed in her old Imperial passport and applied for a new one. Cooperation had replaced hostility in the consulate. Within a few months Khanum, in a long skirt suit with her hair covered by a long scarf from Marks & Spencer was welcomed by a grey-haired Mohsen at Mehrabad airport. She was driven home in her own old Mercedes Benz now almost a vintage car. On the way she noticed the new highways criss-crossing the city, itself inundated by new high-rises. She could not believe her eyes. Teheran did not look as though it had put behind a revolution and a devastating eight-year war. The city seemed extraordinarily alive and green. She could not recognize one single street through which Mohsen drove to Niavaran and eventually her house which now had an automatic gate. As soon as she climbed out of the car, the familiar waft of honeysuckle greeted her nostrils and suddenly she imagined seeing Sassan's smiling face standing by the pool, opening his arms to welcome her. She blinked away the phantom and in its stead saw Jafar, tall and clean shaven, smiling at her. He looked healthy and handsome, just like his father centuries ago! Suddenly Blacky, fat and trimmed, appeared from behind him wagging his tail and barking. For a moment the dog halted, sniffed deeply and then ran towards Khanum. Laughing, she opened her arms and he ran into its folds and began to lick her face and her neck. Zahra, now prosperously stocky, hurried down the stairs and breathless rushed to embrace Khanum. For a second, time stood still. Khanum felt as though those stolen eleven years had just been a dream. The lions still guarded the main entrance door looking at her with their hostile, daring eyes. She embraced Zahra tight. They kissed and wooed each other for a long time, tears of happiness wetting the edges of their scarves. Then Jafar came to kiss Khanum's hand. She hugged and kissed his forehead. She appraised him with her shining eyes and complimented him on his looks and smart shirt. Her compliments made the young man her fan forever.

The time to enter the house came. She had been dreading it ever since she had stepped out of the airplane. She was scared of how she would feel in a home she had shared with Sassan. She had often wondered whether his spirit would be waiting there to reprimand her. Her heart began to palpitate fast. She felt cold sweat gather between her breasts and under her arms. Hesitatingly she crossed the threshold and instantly sensed the house's changed aura. She felt relieved. This was not the home she had shared with Sassan. It was the home of the dear people who had been so faithful to her and she was merely their guest. She sent up a silent prayer.

That night she lay awake in her own bed that smelled of Zahra and Mohsen. She thought for a long while, thinking and yet not thinking – agitated by the sensations that were blazing inside her heart. Tired, she had forgotten to draw the curtains through which light was penetrating in. It was good to be able to see the star-filled sky and listen to the noise of the night. Everything has a noise, even a still night. She listened hard and detected the call of a frog and then Blacky's footsteps searching for the noise. She listened for the wind but she only heard the whiz of the early morning breeze that became her lullaby. She opened her eyes to the sun's rays that poured over the bedspread not matching the curtains. Zahra had replaced the pistachio green satin curtains with red velvet. Automatically her hand went for the bell above her bedstead then she withdrew it. Zahra was not her maid. She rose, pulled her dressing gown out of the open unpacked suitcase, put it on and went out towards the kitchen. Zahra, busy there, saw her.

"Khanum I was waiting for you to ring for your breakfast. I have prepared toast, quince jam and coffee. Is that sufficient?"

"That is plenty, Zahra joon. I'll take it with you."

"We have already eaten Khanum joon. It is almost eleven." Zahra said lifting the breakfast tray. Khanum took the tray from her, humming a happy tune descended down the stairs and out into the garden, thinking how little Zahra's behaviour had changed.

She put the tray on the old coffee table and sat on her old chair facing the pool. Blacky ran to her and lay by her

229

feet occasionally with his wet nose tickling her toes that were sticking out of her pink silk slippers.

After breakfast, Khanum in her Islamic coat and sneekers headed out of the house in search of the places she had loved and remembered so vividly. She walked to Saltanat Abad, and then turned right up the hill to the Niavaran palace now a museum. There, from the familiar confectionary shop she bought a Persian ice cream and, licking it, walked to Tajrish and its bazaar. The fruit section had remained the same. She toured it without venturing into the huge multi-level modern mall that had spoilt the ancient ambiance of the bazaar and returned towards home. Occasionally she lost her way crossing new roads and old ones with new names. By the time she reached home it was late afternoon and Mohsen was waiting for her. She asked him to drive her to Fumen. He promised to do so on the coming Thursday and then he gave her the good news about finding a way to get her off the black list.

For the next seven months together they went from one office to another completing questionnaires about past activities, signing various forms and profusely thanking those who did their job without asking for reward. Khanum became recognized as the wife of a Martyr, beneficiary to several provision coupons and other advantages that would have been plenty had she had children. The system valued and respected its Martyrs. What came to Khanum, she gave to Mohsen who in turn gave to the needy.

A respected citizen again, she aimed to release the confiscated properties she and her sisters had inherited from their parents – not for their financial values but out of respect for her parents. That took another three years and the only property she could salvage was the villa by the Caspian.

One day when they had returned from Fumen and were sitting outside to dine, Khanum went to her room and brought the promissory note that bound Mohsen to her for the value of the house at Niavaran. She withdrew the document from its envelope, gave it to Mohsen and asked him to tear it up. The house was to be his home as long as it was meant for him.

The generosity was overwhelming. Zahra began to thank her between sobs and Mohsen, his accent accentuated by emotion said, "Khanum jahn, how can I thank you for this?"

"Mohsen, you and Zahra are my closest and dearest friends. In fact I consider you as my family – the only family I have. God has given me enough. You, my dear, deserve more than this house. I remember you always resented my cousin Parviz because he was called Parviz Khan and you were a mere Mohsen, the cook's son. At the time you were too young to realize that being an 'agha' takes more than dressing well or having a Khan hanging after your name. You have proved you are more of an 'agha' than Parviz ever was. God bless his soul, he was too agha to work after he left Iran. He married an older Italian Countess for her wealth and when he realized he could not tolerate her demands, he drank himself to death. Look at what you, a mere Mohsen, have achieved for yourself and your family! All I can say is that I think of you as my brother. I really am very proud of you, Mohsen Khan."

She stopped, bent close and with her soft fingers wiped the tears that were rolling down his clean shaved face. Then she gave him a big hug and whispered, "You have made Bagher a very proud father, azizam. Not only because of your deeds but because you have discarded that awful beard!"

He smiled and looked at her with eyes that expressed a thousand thanks and an eternal devotion. A marvellous feeling squeezed his large heart and illuminated his face with a bright smile.

"One request I have of you, Mohsen Khan."

"I remain your servant Khanum."

"I want you to invite me to the wedding of your son, hopefully celebrated in this house."

"Enshallah Khanum, he finds a woman who will make him as happy as Zahra has made me."

"You did not find Zahra. It was Grandma who chose Zahra for you which means I should find a wife for Jafar."

"Jafar will be honoured if you find his wife for him."

"Wonderful!" Khanum exclaimed. Then shaking her head she said, "But you know Mohsen – nowadays the youngsters find their own mates. Let's hope he will find a woman you, Zahra and I will approve of."

"Enshallah Khanum."

Chapter 13

June 2009

The office of the town's Municipality, once someone's home, was crowded by applicants waiting to resolve a problem amongst myriads of problems created by constantly changing regulations, or to submit an application for building or object to a suddenly tripled council tax. A few bureaucrats were behind their desks dealing with petitioners or on the phone arguing. Janitors floated around, tea tray in hand, waiting for tips or a possible whispered plea for a photocopy of an otherwise inaccessible document or a service that would cost more if the ordinary channel was to be pursued.

In the last three years, most agricultural land in the area had been bought by Teheran developers, hiking land prices. Indeed it had become more pragmatic for farmers to sell their land than farm and compete with cheaper prices of imported food. Consequently the peasants of the past, rich and fat, playing with their prayer beads, floated around with ease, knowing whose hand they had to grease to have their application for an illicit building approved, or the route of a new highway diverted from their shop-front or home. Everything could be fixed if one was able to pay the price. But there were also those whose dark, drawn faces expressed inability to bribe for legitimate requests – they had to wait until their hair turned white (there are many seemingly middle-aged but under forty men in Iran) or die of anxiety and its side effects, bequeathing their problems to their equally powerless inheritors.

Corruption had become a norm in spite of President Ahmadi Nejad's tireless efforts to end it.

At the beginning of the attack on corruption, dishonest

bureaucrats were sacked and some imprisoned until their replacements, equally crooked, wised up to the system's catch-ups and became more cautious in their dealings. Thus life went on as before, problems compounded for the poor who were the direct target of the President's election campaign policy. The brilliantly swift distribution of the Shares-of-Justice, the doubling of salaries of civil servants, the police force, and pensioners were outcomes of his populist fiscal policy. His rival, Mir Hussein Mousavi was an advocate of privatization and free economy with a tight monetary policy. This naturally appealed to the middle class and the wealthy.

By the Caspian coast, those who were the beneficiaries of the building boom secretly favoured the reformist candidate and to, save their skin, openly praised the President and his achievements particularly in front of bureaucrats like the Mayor whose signature was required for all the local government's enactments. Our Mayor, nodding his head to all praises of the President, had not as yet made up his mind. He never could make up his mind without someone's aid. All in all, he was an ineffective individual whose only aspiration was to maintain his position. Therefore, all sorts of activities took place under his shapely nose without his awareness or, if conscious, he simply turned a blind eye and accepted the occasional gifts that found their way in his wife's accepting palms. Nevertheless, in spite of his incompetence, he did pursue his promise to Khanum. His discreet investigations, proved interesting and amazing. The cleric in question seemed to be an imposter. The reports on the man were contradictory but it was possible that he had been a SAVAK informer during the shah's reign, who, with the change of the regime had found it more prudent to hide under a mullah's robe than become an informer for the regime, as most of the SAVAK members had. Under the cover of his respected gear he could get all he desired – prestige, money and more. A few months after the collapse of the monarchy it seemed, he had fled Teheran and found refuge in the house of an intimate friend who was a respected local merchant until the search for SAVAK members cooled down. Then finding the pure air of the North healthier than Teheran's smog and the provincial secret police less efficient than those working in the Capital, he managed to fabricate the necessary resumé, apply and be granted his present position at the school in which Nargess and the Mayor's daughter were studying. Within his locality, he became respected and popular enough to be invited to perform at the religious ceremonies current in society and lucrative for the clergy.

Nazr or a religious vow is made in times of need. It is asking God for a cure, a wish or forgiveness in lieu of which the vow maker will undertake a charitable action like feeding the poor in the mosque or at home, over which a cleric presides. The fee for a cleric's home performance is as high as that of a medical practitioner. In small towns and villages the service is monopolized by the resident mullah. The monopoly makes the profession extremely rewarding. Agha Abolfazl's weekly income from home visits was equal to his monthly government salary at school. For him the salary was the caviar on his toast.

Mayor loved his daughter and the thought of her ever being abused made him frantic. He had to do something about this creep before he had a chance to do something to her – something unbearable? Nevertheless any action coming from him against a cleric would jeopardize his position. Their rank was beyond reproach. He thought and thought. It was a matter of conscience. However, in this case, being ethical and at the same time efficient seemed to be impossible. In a society where the clergy reigned supreme, what effectiveness would a testimony of a mere Mayor could have? Who would take his side against a seemingly respected Agha, (as they all are referred to) even if evidence pointed to a dubious background? The accused would become the beneficiary of the protection given to the holy profession. Even solid evidence could not hold against their sacred rank – some holy miracle would descend from heaven to prove the evidence fabricated and the criminal unfairly accused. Exonerated, his grace would find position elsewhere – and the victim punished for false accusation or conspiracy against the regime.

Befuddled, the Mayor contemplated in vain. Unable to resolve his town's most serious problem, he lost his appetite and sleep until his wife Kobra noticed the pallor of his skin and thinness of his stature.

Kobra was a pragmatic woman. Her marriage to the Mayor at the age of fourteen was arranged. As was expected, she respected him for being an efficient breadwinner, a good father and nothing else. She kept her house in good order, taught her children how to cook, iron and clean the house immaculately and saw that her husband's shirts were always crisp white. Her sole pleasure was day dreaming – to be Shirin (Iranian Juliet) to the invisible Farhad (Iranian Romeo) of her dream. When her husband was elected the town's Mayor, she became ecstatic – not for herself but for her daughters who with an important father could catch good husbands – or perhaps marry for love! Kobra, with a limited education, was fairly alert, foresighted and wise. She often helped her husband in his decision making. Her mother believed the Mayor owed his position to the wisdom and cooking expertise of his wife. Kobra had no inhibitions. What came to her mind she verbalized and that was why her only true friend was her husband. He respected her candour. She valued his camaraderie and was always perceptive to his moods. Recently she had noticed a change in his carefree behaviour. At first she was suspicious that he might be having an affair with one of the women at work and then, when he stopped touching his food, she began to worry about his health. She cooked his favourite dishes to no avail. Terrified of becoming a widow, one afternoon when he had risen from his siesta and was waiting for his tea, her face tight with concern she sat by him on the floor and caringly asked, "Agha what is bothering you? Have the members of the Town Council been nasty again?"

"There is nothing wrong with me, wife," the Mayor responded brusquely.

"Don't lie and don't think of me as a fool. We have been married for twenty years and if you think I don't know you, you are a bigger fool than I think you are!"

He raised his lacklustre eyes to her, smiled at the way she had expressed her concern and replied, "I know you are no fool dear. But some things are not fit for the ears of respectable women. So don't hassle me any further and let me sort this one out by myself."

She furrowed her shapely eyebrows, pursed her round lips and retorted, "You have never been able to sort anything out by yourself, what makes you think you can sort this one out?"

"I don't know yet but I am not going to involve you in this."

Kobra threw him a reproachful and at the same time tender glance. She knew he was a simple-minded person, naïve enough to think of himself as clever – the worst character flaw in anyone.

"By being your wife I am involved in everything you do so let me know the cause of your anxiety, my dear husband. Perhaps I can help – just a little."

Hesitant, he fixed his tired eyes on her concerned face and then asked her to make him a cup of chamomile tea instead of the usual Darjeeling.

She rose, stretched her aching back, walked to the

counter of her open pine wood kitchen on which a huge electrical samovar sizzled. She fingered her tea jar, found a chamomile tea bag, dropped it in a long glass and then filled the glass with hot water from the samovar, dropped in two sugar cubes, hastily stirred the concoction with a tea spoon; put the glass on its saucer and the saucer on a colourful plastic tray made in China. She extracted a box of fresh dates from her fridge, put it on the tray and carried it to him.

"Eat the dates. They will give you energy. Your face resembles a death mask," she said in an emphatic tone tinged with care, while crossing her legs and reclining on the large bolster that was against the wall – arthritis was crippling her, yet she bore the pain with the dignity of a Mayor's wife and never complained. Men did not like complaining wives. There were always younger girls to marry and she did not want to share her husband with another woman, like Mehri Khanum, her next door neighbour. The poor woman was forced to diet, bleach her hair blond and have a nose job done in order to compete with the new wife who had monopolized her husband's bed and pocket.

Kobra had not told Mehri Khanum that, in spite of the fact that her husband shared her bed, hardly ever anything exciting happened.

The Mayor, placed his empty tea glass on the tray, looked deep into her large black eyes and said, "Swear on the Koran that you will not repeat what I will tell you to anyone, even your mother."

Kobra rose, hurried to their bedroom, took the thick volume of the Koran that lay on her bedside table, kissed it twice, brought it to her husband, placed her hand on it and swore not to divulge what she was about to hear to a single soul. Sure that the information would remain locked within their four walls, the Mayor poured out his heart. Kobra listened intently, her eyes popping out of their sockets –

such was her bewilderment. The incident petrified her. Shocked, she rose, hurried to the kitchen, grabbed a large glass, filled it with hot water from the Samovar, returned, crossed her legs, bent over, took her husband's tea spoon, lifted his tea bag, dropped it into her own glass and pressed the spoon on it hard enough to extract what elixir was left in it. Satisfied with the colour of the end result, she began sipping the concoction while contemplating. The Mayor, his eyes fixed on her, rapidly turned his prayer beads around, occasionally releasing a sigh, till his wife's soft voice broke the pregnant silence. Slowly and meticulously she presented him with a practical plan. Delighted he stretched across the tea tray and stole a quick kiss from her forehead. Giving him a triumphant smile she patted his back and urged him to return to his office – there were always those waiting for an excuse to have him sacked.

The next morning, the Mayor called Agha Abolfazl, praised his charitable deeds and invited him to dinner.

Agha, in his impeccable cream coloured aba and white turban arrived to a warm and courteous reception – due to his respected rank. In their narrow corridor, the Mayor introduced him to his wife gracefully clad in a black Islamic garment and white scarf. Then, formal and polite, he ushered Agha to the sitting room where they sat around a small glass coffee table on which a large tray of fruit, a bowl of pistachio nuts and a dish of cream puff pastries were displayed. Ordinary guests were never shown to the armchairs in case they dirty the upholstery. They had to sit on the carpeted floor and rest their backs against the bolsters. Formal furniture was only for important visitors. Surprisingly enough Kobra had decorated the open space of her home tastefully, using pastel colours instead of red or chocolate prevalent at homes of her rank and real flowers rather than plastic false ones. In its simplicity the area was cosy, smart and fragranced by the steam rising from the rice

239

pot. At first words were exchanged cautiously and politely. Kobra Khanum served a strong and tasty tea. The Mayor offered pastry to Agha who politely thanked him away and turned his eyes to the nuts bowl craving for a glass of whisky. The Mayor helped himself to two pieces of the pastry and then filled a small plate with spoonfuls of nuts for his guest. Kobra, tea glass in hand, joined the two and engaged them in her entertaining local gossip.

Initially Agha was on guard, but gradually, listening to the woman's soft voice telling simple tales, he relaxed to the point of enjoying himself, albeit for once. He found the sensation strange. Nevertheless, for a few hours he let himself be his old self – the self he missed so much – that had forsaken him. To his own surprise he found his tongue loosened and Kobra Khanum, her eyes twinkling with joy, managed to extract from him much useful information about his daily routine, likes and dislikes. It delighted her to hear he preferred to work in a larger town than theirs which had not developed since the shah's days. Sharply perceptive, she realized he had allured the girls by his magnetism and eloquence. The man seemed able to charm a snake out of its den, let alone naïve girls. Her own heart palpitated fast every time he looked at her – rushing blood to her cheek – a sensation she had never felt before.

Kobra, figure slim, features delicate and aura relaxed appeared much younger than her age of thirty four. Femininity glowed from her entity and when she laughed two small dimples appeared on her rosy cheeks. The white scarf she wore over her auburn hair accentuated the charm of her face from which Agha could not remove his eyes. The Mayor noticed this and was petrified. Awful images began to parade in his mind, sweeping away his timid smile.

Tall and well-built Abolfazl was a handsome man with fine features overcast by a trimmed black beard. His deportment was graceful and his poise such that one could not but respect. Kobra found herself captivated by his penetrating eyes, his interesting character and strong hands that she imagined could impart many pleasures – the ones her body ached for.

The evening passed swiftly and Agha, full of gratitude, departed well after midnight.

The meeting not only did not enlighten the Mayor but furthered his confusion and apprehensions. In a dire mood he left his wife to clean up and retired to bed. Kobra, humming a joyous tune finished her chores, entered their bedroom and found him, tucked under the eiderdown snoring heavily. Languidly she stripped naked, like the women she had seen on a satellite's porno channel, (when the Mayor was at work and the girls out). She switched the light off and quietly crept under the cover close enough to feel his warmth. He did not stir. She closed her eyes, grabbed her large bosoms, played with her erect nipples and gradually let her right hand slip down and down, caressing her erogenous zones, becoming active at first delicately and then heatedly until the delightful contractions made her moan with pleasure. Satisfied she opened her eyes and Abolfazl's image melted away. She heard a fart – its stench sickening. She covered her nose with her hand and vowed to stop the use of garlic in her cooking.

For a few weeks running the mullah found himself dining at the Mayor's house, with his wife pampering him just a bit too much.

As perceptive as a fox Abolfazl, a survivor who wore an appropriate mask for each occasion suspected that the hospitalities he had been enjoying were not totally altruistic; so he sharpened his receptive antenna. Trained at Saint Cyr and by Mossad, he trusted his intuition and began to watch every word that came out of his mouth and analyse those he heard. He started carrying his revolver again, hidden in the pocket of his wide pants over which hung the pleats of his robe. At dawn he went to the nearby forest and practised shooting birds which took care of his dinner. He loved game kebab – simple to make for a man used to a cook's services.

Life continued its course. With each setting of the sun national exuberance increased. Involved in heated discussions and colourful speculations young and old, poor and rich, waited for the Election Day.

It was past noon when Khanum and Nargess returned from Teheran with the tongue-tied girl a virgin again. Shahri not quite comprehending what had happened to her daughter trusted Khanum's promise that she could marry without bringing shame to the family. Taghi nosed around for interesting information he could relay to the head Basiji for a pat on his shoulder. Mohammad, still in his dire mood relentlessly kept trimming the bushes and the trees. The plant amputation gave him great satisfaction for in his mind each clack of the secateurs was cutting off a body part of that Satan incarnate. Thus busy he expressed no interest whatsoever in what had been done to his daughter.

Within a fortnight of absence, Khanum found her garden thriving with delicious offerings. Iranian herbs are strongly aromatic and they are eaten fresh with meals often instead of salads. Plenty had grown in the herb corner. One of Shahri's tasks was to pick a handful each day for Khanum's meals and make beautiful bouquets for visitors from Teheran who admired their freshness and pungent taste. Tomatoes, egg plants and okras had become ripe and luminous. The fig trees were bent under their heavy green burden not yet ripe; plums, apricots and peaches were almost ready for consumption. Everywhere cucumbers had crept up their supports and hung down like green bananas. The flower beds were colourful and the bees busy buzzing over them. The lawn was green and over-grown. Mohammad had not found the energy to use the heavy lawn mower and Khanum did not have the heart to reprimand him. She knew that, once the evil man was brought to justice, all would become normal again – or at least she hoped.

The bell sounded and Khanum rose from her mat on which she was sunbathing; wrapped her towel around her waist and bare-foot ran to the door. To her surprise it was Mrs. Babazadeh, her neighbour whose husband, an opium addict had just died of lung collapse. It seemed everybody along the coast had an addict relative.

The Iranian anti-narcotic force was efficient, diligent and surprisingly incorruptible yet the drug found its way into the country from Afghanistan and affected mostly the youth who loafed around aimlessly, unemployed and without any outlet in which to have innocent fun. Most people blamed the drug problem on unemployment and wondered why the Vice Police cadre who endeavoured to enforce strict social behaviour, especially amongst the youths failed to win its battle against drug dealers.

Mrs Babazadeh, a bleached blond, was fat, jolly, and gossipy. The joy of her life was eating and taking care of her husband who had made millions from buying the confiscated properties, including their home, from various foundations cheap, and later, selling them with huge profits. They had three children their ages ranging from ten to twenty one. None of them ever played in their beautiful huge garden, nor swam in their swimming pool nor took part in any visible social activity. Khanum often wondered what they did beside eating, watching TV and playing games on the computer. While Mr. Babazadeh was alive, the smell of his opium revealed his existence around mid-morning, mid-afternoon and then late at night.

Their lifestyle suited Khanum, because her guests could swim in the sea in bathing suits without anyone reporting them to the pasdaran. Thus she maintained an amicable relationship with Mrs. Babazadeh whose visits had increased in frequency since her widowhood.

Khanum welcomed her with a salam and a smile. Mrs. Babazadeh, her perspiring plump face red from exhaustion of having walked the short distance between the two houses, entered murmuring an incoherent 'Ya Allah'. Huffing and puffing she took her chador off, tidied her unkempt fizzy hair with her fat hands, excused herself for intruding and then asked for a glass of iced water. Smiling her welcome Khanum politely took her chador and hanging it on the guest dresser noticed she was kicking off her flip flops.

"You do not have to do that here," Khanum said walking to the open kitchen area. There she took a large glass from the crockery shelf, extracted ice water from the fridge nozzle and presented the glass to her still puffing guest. She grabbed the glass, drank the entire content, put the glass down on the kitchen counter and murmured her thanks. "I was just sunbathing. It is lovely outside; shall we sit on the veranda?"

"No, no. I hate the sun."

"You won't be in the sun."

"I prefer inside." Mrs. Babazadeh said walking towards the sofa on which she usually sat. Khanum followed her. The woman dropped on the couch with a sigh of relief, flipped open her inseparable Spanish fan made in China and began to aerate herself complaining of the heat, the rising prices and laziness of all servants. The room was actually pleasantly cool yet, out of jealousy, she pretended it was hot. It mattered not to Khanum who was patiently waiting to know the reason for the visit. The woman sweeping her gaze around turned her surprised eyes to her and asked, "How come there are no flies here?"

"Because we spray the plants four times a year and Mohammad keeps the garden clean of any refuse."

"Why do you not sit next to me, my dear," she asked with her fat hand tapping on the empty space next to her.

Khanum obeyed and then put her hand on her head and feigned a headache.

"My dear, it is because you are always in the sun, either gardening, or having your legs in the air like Indian gurus or baking your skin black like Negros. Honestly what kind of a life is that?" Khanum knew of her spying on her from the window of her second floor bedroom. In order to shut her up, she asked if she wanted another glass of water. Shaking her head, the woman said no and then contrived an air of sadness, wobbled in her seat, sniffed her nose as though crying and in a tone heavy with sorrow said, "Tonight is the Cheleh of my beloved husband. In his remembrance I have invited Agha Abolfazl to come and conduct the ceremony. Babazadeh always spoke well of you. Will you come to pray for him with us?" Quite insulted for the late invitation Khanum thought a bit,; attributed her bad manners to ignorance, and then considered the advantage of meeting the rapist in person. The opportunity was great. She forged an appropriate expression of sympathy and accepted the invitation.

Rising to leave, the widow asked Khanum if she could also invite Mohammad and his family to the Cheleh. Fully aware of a catch to her altruistic generosity towards the lower ranks, she nodded her consent and walked her to the door. There the woman pulled her chador from the peg almost tearing it, spread it over her head, pinched and held its two edges below her neck and, swearing at the heat, stepped out. The two, strolled to the gate next to which Mohammad stood spade in hand. Mrs. Babazadeh turned to the gardener, gave herself a sad expression, and patronizingly extended to him her invitation and then adroitly asked if he could possibly help in the kitchen. Mohammad threw a questioning glance at his mistress. She lowered her eyes. Not knowing what was expected of him he thanked the lady and expressed his willingness to be of assistance in the kitchen.

Secure of a free hand in the kitchen, Mrs. Babazadeh turned her attention back to Khanum and asked, "by the way who are you going to vote for?"

"I have not made up my mind yet."

"We all are for Mousavi – you should vote for him. He is our only hope for change," she said walking out of the gate and banging its door hard.

"She is full of frustration. I really feel sorry for her. Anyway none of you can go to the Cheleh."

"Why, Khanum, it won't please God to refuse our neighbour's request of assistance in a time like this?"

"I know that, but the devil incarnate will be performing at the ceremony. Will you be able to face him calmly? No. So I will offer to help her in your stead." Mohammad's countenance darkened, his purple lips began to quiver and his eyes clouded with despair. He pushed his spade deep into the ground as though dipping it into the heart of the rapist.

Khanum read his mind and felt for him.

He whispered an Allah Akbar.

She looked at him with sympathising eyes and said, "all of you take the day off and I will tell her you had to go to Noor to visit your sick father. Send your young nephew, Hashem to help her in the kitchen and I will offer my help with the guests."

"Allah Akbar," he whispered again.

"What has Allah got to do with this?" Khanum asked irritated.

"He has brought this criminal within my reach without giving me the power to kill him!"

"Koran says it is better to leave vengeance to God."

"I will never find peace until I have made this ungodly creature pay for his crime!"

"Mohammad, once I knew a better man than you, who

decided to become the sword of justice. He killed the man who had brought dishonour to his family. Later his conscience failed to cope with the guilt – peace lost to him forever, he took his own life and left many to mourn his loss. Do you want this for your children – make them orphans?"

Leaning on his spade, Mohammad pondered in silence and then looked at his mistress and wistfully whispered,

"Chashm Khanum. I will do as you command."

"You know Mohammad everything happens for a purpose. I am glad he is coming to the ceremony. It will give me a chance to meet him and gauge how we can deal with him," she said, her kind eyes fixed on his tense face, her tone so compassionate that it dissolved his wrath. He whispered an 'enshallah' and left to lock the gate when through the space between the decorative bars he saw the Mayor crossing the road to the villa. He turned to his mistress and alerted her of the coming guest. Khanum, her stomach rumbling with hunger swallowed her disappointment at yet another intruder. The Mayor briskly nodded to Mohammad who had opened the gate for him and stepped inside. Khanum welcomed him with a smile, ordered Mohammad to tell Shahri to bring them some pomegranate juice and then led the way to the villa. As they entered the hall a pleasant whiff of cold air greeted them.

"Khanum you must be paying a fortune for electricity to keep this house so agreeably cool."

"I turn the chillers on from eleven to three in the afternoon. At nights the villa is cool. So the cost is minimized."

They sat on the same sofa, facing each other. From his body language she sensed good news. Shahri arrived with two glasses of pomegranate juice. She put her tray on the coffee table and before disappearing asked at what time she should bring the lunch tray. Khanum admiring her foresightedness turned to the Mayor and asked him if he would take lunch with her. He nodded his refusal, apologized for his intrusion at lunch hour, his only available time for private visits. Khanum smiled at his lie, and gazed at her watch. It was half past twelve. She picked up her glass and tasted the juice.

"This is very good, Shahri Khanum, and I'll take lunch at one."

The Mayor, drank his juice in a hurry, wiped his mouth with the tissue he extracted from its box, expressed his delight in the taste and quickly told Khanum of his finding and the plan that had come to his mind to get rid of the criminal.

Impressed by the simplicity of the plot, she smiled her appreciation.

"This is a great plan and, should you need any assistance with its implementation I know a very important person at the Ministry of Education."

Scared out of his wits, he shook his head in refusal and in a firm tone said, "Khanum Aziz no one must know of my involvement in this. Otherwise I won't help you. God forbid if anyone here finds out that I have been manipulative, I will lose my job."

"As you wish Agha Mayor – this is your project, I just wanted to help." Khanum said gently patting him on the shoulder.

"That is right. This is my project – after all I am the Mayor of this town."

"And a good one too," Khanum added her eyes glowing with affection.

He rose, and the two walked to the gate where Shahri was waiting to give the Mayor a bunch of fresh rocket. He looked at the vegetable with curious eyes and asked, "What is this Shahri Khanum?"

"I do not know its name. Khanum brought the seeds

from London. It is a bit bitter but Khanum says it is full of vitamin C." He turned his questioning eyes to Khanum. "It is called rocket. In Europe they use it in salad like lettuce. I hope you will like it. You cannot find it in Iran yet."

Impressed by Khanum's last sentence; thrilled that Kobra would have something to boast about with the neighbours; he gratefully accepted the bunch and said, "I am sure my wife will know what to do with this – she is an excellent cook."

The setting sun had spread its crimson wings over the Caspian turning the waves copper. A cool breeze was blowing from the west and on the clear sky a pale, thin crescent of the moon was smiling its appearance. Standing on her bedroom terrace Khanum, for the first time in years saw commotion in Babazadeh's garden. Chairs were being put in straight rows, a black table cloth was being spread over the never-used table tennis that had rotted by climatic effects and someone was actually weeding the garden in haste and another trimming the hedges that had become over-grown. She smiled a melancholy smile – it seemed death had awakened zest in the inhabitants – what tragedy to have allowed so much beauty hide beneath neglect, the sight of which could have brought to the consciousness of the dead man the blessings he had never had the sense to enjoy. Perhaps had his mind been appreciative of these gifts it would not have let itself be numbed by opium. Khanum wondered with a deep sigh. Pensive she left the terrace to dress appropriately for the wake. All she needed was already laid on her bed ready to wear. She just had to put some make up on.

Ten minutes later groomed in a black Armani linen pants suit and silk scarf, about to take her Hermes black crocodile clutch when she heard the sound of light footsteps climbing the steps. Surprised, she called to find out who it was. Nargess' soft voice surprised her.

"What are you doing here Nargess? I thought you had gone to Noor with your parents."

"Khanum I have been sick for two days now. Nothing stays in my stomach. That is why I had to stay home. Hashem just left for the other house and I have come to see if you need me for anything."

"Have you been eating unwashed fruit or vegetable from the garden?"

"No Khanum joon. I have no appetite for anything."

"Come here and let me see you in the light."

Nargess moved close to her. Under the ceiling light Khanum saw that the girl's skin was pale and her eyes weary and sunken. She took her wrist and searched for her pulse. It seemed a bit on the fast side.

"Have you had your monthly period yet?"

"I am two days late Khanum, but that is normal. I am often late."

Panicked Khanum prayed for her assumption to be wrong. She could not take her to the town's obstetrician. They had to go to Teheran again. She hated the idea.

"Child go home to rest, eat little, drink plenty of liquid until we go to the doctor in Teheran. Try not to worry your father with your condition. If he asks, tell him you have diarrhoea or something."

"Chashm Khanum. Shall I make salad for your dinner?"

"No, I am sure Mrs. Babazadeh will feed us a feast."

"I know but she will be feeding you Halva, dates and Sholehzard (an aromatic rice pudding with Saffron) – all Nazri stuff which you don't like."

"Like it or not I have to taste them, otherwise she will be offended, stop talking to me, and throw her slugs and snails into your mother's herb garden."

"That she will – the silly woman loves doing that." Nargess said a serene smile parting her dry thin lips.

"Yah – she is so childish in her behaviour! Nevertheless

she is our neighbour and should be respectfully tolerated."

The Babazadeh residence was built right in the middle of the garden. The paved area on the south side of the building was prepared for the men, the north for the women. Khanum discreetly passed the male zone and entered the ladies'. There she was greeted by the seated hostess whose eyes were red from crying and her daughter Mitra, the only two people she knew. Mitra politely rose and guided her to a place of prominence, where a pleasant looking lady clad in a heavy black chador sat alone, her eyes roaming around with curiosity – comparing the lifestyle of the wealthy with her own – envious of their power of purchasing paradises like this house.

As Khanum took up her seat next to her, their eyes met and the woman immediately recognized her. She had often spied on her through the open gate of Golestan busy gardening in shorts and T-shirt with a colourful gardening apron around her waist.

Khanum politely introduced herself. Kobra gave her a charming smile and in a deep accented voice said, "Khanum Zand I am Kobra Khanum, Agha Mayor's wife. You know my husband."

"Of course I do and I have a deep respect for him. I know we are neighbours. Unfortunately I have never had the pleasure of making your acquaintance and now that we have met we must visit each other often. "

"I should like that very much and my daughters; they would love to come and pay their respects to you. There is so much they can learn from you Khanum."

"Do send them over – but let me know in advance so that I stay home," Khanum said, safeguarding herself against visits at ungodly hours.

Kobra, elated by the coincidence, went on talking about her daughters, their scholastic achievements and the several marriage proposals for each that the Mayor had rejected.

This Khanum knew was an utter lie yet she kept on smiling and making appropriate comments.

Soon trays of tea, soft drinks and Halva began to circulate and whispers mixed with the sound of the sea made the evening cheerfully alive – instead of mournful and dull – that is until a soft cultivated voice, amplified by a microphone politely demanded silence. It took a few minutes before all was quiet. Then the mullah's pleasant voice rose in praise of the dead man and his good deeds. Mrs. Babazadeh's wail at each mention of her husband's name was so loud that the mullah wisely terminated his speech and broke into a beautiful song of Koranic verses, that more than a thousand years ago had opened the hearts of the infidels to the worship of one true God – a forgiving God – a compassionate God.

Khanum noticed Kobra crying hard. Surprised, she assumed the woman was afflicted by a deep inner turmoil that was producing such sadness in her. She certainly was not weeping for the deceased. She had never met him in person – she had already communicated that to her.

Kobra withdrew a tissue from the black bag she was holding on her lap. Blew her nose in it, then with the same dried her tears, threw the tissue on the lawn, turned to Khanum, took a deep breath and said, "It is Agha Abolfazl's beautiful voice that affects me so much. God forgive Babazadeh, from what I have heard, he was not such a good man and his wife is well rid of him. Enshallah she will marry a good man who will pay her attention and make her happy. You know he was much older than her."

"I know that. I heard she was his maid and that he had been married before."

"Yes he married her because he made her pregnant. The news gave his poor wife a heart attack from which she died. The respectable woman that she was, she couldn't tolerate having a servant as her Havoo (a second wife). He inherited all her wealth."

"That I did not know. By the way Kobra Khanum, do you know Agha Abolfazl?" Khanum asked testing her discretion.

Kobra's face instantly lit with a broad smile.

"Of course, who doesn't know him? He is such a fine gentleman and so educated. He knows about everything and, unlike other Aghas who only want your money, he goes out of his way to help and..." suddenly she caught herself and stopped. Khanum noticed the sparkle of panic that flashed out of her eyes, and became perplexed.

The Mayor had told her his wife was privy to their secret. Perhaps Kobra did not know that Khanum was aware of her knowledge of the incident? None-the-less she became apprehensive of her enthusiasm for this criminal – even if it was in pretext.

The praying stopped. The waves kept roaring. Black clouds spread their wings over the clear sky and an untimely howling gust began lashing at whatever lay in its path. Table clothes began to fly throwing off whatever was sitting on them. Mrs. Babazadeh quickly abandoned her lamentation and began praying for the winds to hasten the clouds away before they burst and ruined her expensive ceremony.

The guests hurried to the sheltered alley-way where they had already seen the table on which numerous offerings – some sweet and some savoury were piled up in plastic dishes. Khanum, already there and standing alone, picked up a plate, helped herself to a Halva piece and a Shami, her favourite meat patty and slowly manoeuvred towards the graceful mullah who was surrounded by a group of chatty elders. Suddenly the heaven burst and shafts of lightening zigzagged across the lit sky stabbing at the heart of the horizon that kept changing colour from silver to blue and then black again. The storm was so violent that rain drops kept bouncing back like jetting fountains. The covered space was not large enough to accommodate all, many rushed inside the building. This furthered the hostess's devastation. Sure valuable things would be missing the next morning she spread herself on the second step of the staircase barring intruders.

It took a long busy, boisterous ten minutes for heaven to shed its tears for Mr. Babazadeh. Then the sky cleared allowing the moon to smile and the stars sparkle again oblivious to the mess left below.

Khanum had finished eating and was loitering near the mullah waiting for the opportunity to talk to him alone when she spotted Hashem come out of the side door tea tray in hand. She waited until he came to her. She refused his offer and whispering asked him where he was going to take the tray to. "To the ping-pong table, Khanum."

"No. Go to where the Agha is standing and tell the men talking to him, that Khanum Babazadeh wants everyone to go to the table and eat something. Stand there until they move."

"Chashm Khanum." Hashem enjoying the sense of conspiracy in the chore approached the group and did precisely as told. The men bade the mullah farewell and headed for the table. The circle broken, Khanum became visible to her target and her serene smile caught his shrewd eyes. Suddenly a feeling of sadness squeezed his heart. The aura and resemblance to his wife was striking. He quickly closed his eyes; buried the thought in the recesses of his mind, waited for a second or two before smiling back at her. Slowly she moved towards him and politely introduced herself. He recognized the name and for a split second became perplexed. Then in control again, he threw her an appraising glance which was returned with a testing glare. He sensed danger and regret at the same time. Perhaps he shouldn't have done what he did to her servant girl – after all this woman was on his side. He started feeling uncomfortable and his left eye began to twitch.

Khanum noticed his nervousness. Assured that somehow she had intimidated him, smiled and said, "Agha, I have heard so much about you and your kindness to our community that I felt I must come and express my gratitude to you."

"It is very kind of you, Khanum. I have heard much about your generosity to our community too. I am sure God will take you to heaven when your time comes."

He stopped, gave her a challenging stare. Khanum perceived the drag on the word 'time'.

He fixed his forceful eyes on her face. The stare fazed her. To regain her calm she looked up at the moon and said, 'we are so lucky that the clouds have cleared away.' 'Yes we are indeed.' He responded politely. There was something in her aura that made him realize he could not treat her like an enemy – perhaps it was the resemblance. A quick sad sigh escaped his mouth, but his trained will-power managed to subdue the sentiment that had flared up inside him. In his new life there was no room for sentimentality – he had already cried enough. He resumed the identity he deplored – alas, this time, with difficulty and said, "enshallah you will live to enjoy a long life during which you follow the straight path you have taken so far and won't step into any 'muddy waters'."

She detected the emphasis on the word 'live'.

The insinuation did not daunt her at all – in fact it made her more determined to pursue her objective.

"What does 'muddy water' mean Agha?" Khanum asked, in a tone tinted by scoffing.

"It means making a gross mistake."

"Dear Agha, I really don't understand what you are trying to tell me. Clerics are very colloquial in expressing their intentions! Why are you not?"

She certainly is obstinate – just like her. He surmised with a wave of anguish hitting his heart again. Something strange was happening to him. It made him extra cautious and yet agitated.

"Khanum Aziz, a 'gross mistake' often refers to decisions badly made," he said looking her with eyes that exuded cutting shards. Unhurt, she smiled. He froze. She sensed she had cornered him, so she continued.

"Expressing an opinion on people's decisions is often subjective. People are free to choose sir – of course that is when the society allows freedom of choice."

Abolfazl did not like the twist the clever woman had introduced into the course of their conversation. How could he argue against his own convictions? But under this circumstance he was impelled to do so.

"Khanum we are living in an Islamic society in which the dictates of the Koran and the Hadith (the Islamic dogma) are to be followed without question. Therefore social choices fall within the folds of Islamic mores. That by itself curtails certain freedom."

She could not abstain from smiling at the poignant words so colloquially flowing out of the mouth of an impostor.

"My dear Agha, I am sure you agree with me that the worst oppression is despotic treatment of people in the name of Islam. Islam did not come to enslave people. It came to free them from the bondage of ignorance that had chained them to the worship of idols and socially restrictive and at times tyrannical behaviour – like burying live infant girls. From the Prophet's teachings we learn that man has a will and that will allows him to choose. Koran sets out rules and regulations that, if interpreted correctly and applied properly, are conducive to appropriate behaviour and the formation of a just society. The practice of Ijtehad allows our clergy to interpret the teachings of the Koran in such a way as to meet new social demands caused by progress. This by itself, if used for the betterment of society, can curtail fundamentalism that inhibits freedom of choice. I hope sir, you also know that the Koran sets out exact punishments for pathological behaviour referred to as sin – one among these punishments is the stoning of adulterers – a hard one, no?" She asked raising a brow.

He felt cold in spite of the warmth and humidity of the air.

"Madam, you seem to know your religion well."

"Yes I do. I am a student of religious philosophies."

"Therefore you must know that for any accusations to stand in a court of law, especially an Islamic court of law, eye-witnesses are required – particularly in the case of adultery."

"Yes sir, I am not only aware of that but also aware of how false witnesses can be produced and how people's rights are abused through evidence fabrications. Even judgements are for sale nowadays! Did you know that?" she asked narrowing her eyes. Then, without expecting any response to her question, looking him straight in the eyes she added, "I hope decent people like you will aid the authorities to clean our society from drug dealers, lechers, rapists and other criminals."

"Enshallah Khanum, when you get to know me better you will find me a servant of our society," Abolfazl said in a strangely sad voice then nervously adjusted his robe that had slipped down from over one shoulder, pinched its edges, straightened its folds, bowed his farewell, turned and left the house without a word to anyone.

Driving, he found himself crying as though something strange had cracked inside him. The oncoming car lights became blurred in his wet vision; he turned off the highway towards the forest and parked the car in his usual place, stepped out, threw his turban and robe on the back seat, drew his revolver out of his pants pocket and began shooting at the air – the noise frightened a bunch of birds out of their nests, flapping their wings they flew away.

That same night from a warehouse on the periphery of Karaj a huge sealed truck drove out of a gate, turned right and then left into the highway towards the west. Five minutes later a green Samand, with two armed men, drove out of the same gate way and followed the truck on the back window of which was written in large white letters, 'boro be omid-e-khoda', go putting your hope in God. The driver, an innocent looking man in his mid twenties was brought up to believe that Emmam Mehdi, the Shiite's last Emmam, (who had disappeared and his reappearance would mean the end of the world), was always present and sitting next to him on the passenger seat, as he was always sitting next to the President during his meetings. He had seen the chair allocated to the Emmam with his own eyes. That had made him proud to have been christened Mehdi. He had also been to the well in which the Emmam is believed to have disappeared. He had dropped into it his sealed envelope in which he had placed his letter of request for a Samand from the Emmam, plus his ten, one thousand rial notes as his Nazri. During his last visit he had noticed there were two wells now, one for women and one for men – in which had the Emmam disappeared became an enigma his simple mind could not figure out. He had made a mental note that next time, he would make two donations one into the male-well and the other into the female-well – that would ensure that the Emmam would receive his Nazri and grant his request. With a new Samand he could earn a lot of money carrying passengers – like his cousin Akbar. But he did not want to think about Akbar who was not a true believer. He had tried to show him the right path but to no avail. So he had to let it be – it was all in the hands of God. It seemed that he was the only one in the entire Bagheri family from Fumen who was a real Moslem. Nevertheless he liked his relatives and always remembered them in his prayers, especially his cousin Mohsen, an important restaurateur in Teheran who after his father's death, during the war, had helped him with his education.

It was a long drive to the Bazargan border. His orders were to halt only to refuel. Occasionally he glanced at his mirror to check if the Samand was following him. He had taken cargos many times to Turkey and beyond without an escort and he found it strange that this time his commander had found it necessary to have him escorted. Before starting his voyage the commander had asked him to perform the ablution necessary before dangerous missions – for if killed one had to be clean to enter heaven.

The two in the Samand were his mates. They had trained together. He had found their evening religious courses fascinating but hated the day combat classes. He could never kill even if ordered by the Prophet himself. He was taught that anyone who opposed the Emmam was a Mohareb, a fighter against God, and his blood could be spilt without hesitation. But he had no stomach for bloodshed.

One hour after his last refuel at Tabriz he felt the urge to relieve himself. On the first road-shoulder he pulled off the highway, jumped off, unzipped his trousers and was about to start when the ringing of his mobile made him jump out of his skin. Quickly he emptied his bladder, zipped up, ran to his truck and picked up the mobile only to hear a reprimand for wasting time. He apologized, disconnected the line, swore at the caller's unreasonableness, put his foot on the speed pedal and drove away as fast as he could – the highway was deserted.

As they approached the border the Samand decreased its speed widening the gap between the car and the truck.

It was close to dawn when the truck slowed down and stopped for the custom check. The Iranian officer approached the vehicle and asked the driver for his passport and other documentations. All was in order.

The Samand arrived and parked at a distance. Both men stepped out, went to the officer talking to the driver and gave him a letter to read immediately. The young uniformed official took the letter, walked towards a lamp post, stopped where the light was brightest, unfolded the letter and read the content. He returned to the driver and waved him away without inspecting any of his cargo boxes.

The truck crossed the border and halted. The driver's friends kept the custom officer engaged in petty talk while discreetly watching what was going on across the border.

At first everything went as normal and then they heard loud angry exchanges between the Turkish officers and their mate. One of the two took out his mobile and dialled. Mehdi, his mobile within his tight grip, took the call.

"What is wrong?"

"They insist on opening the boxes of our fresh fruit."

"Are they not the ones we paid off last week?"

"No."

"Ok. Have you got your revolver on you?"

"No. It is in the car."

"You stupid ass."

"I never thought I had to kill anyone."

"You imbecile, why do you think the boss armed you?"

The mobile went dead.

The older of the two men fuming with anger whispered to his partner, "We should have never allowed this imbecile to drive the truck."

"No, but we cannot leave him there. We either have to kill him or get him out of Turkey; otherwise it will be us paying for his stupidity. Give me the mobile."

On the other side the heated argument had acquired a sharper pitch.

Mehdi's mobile buzzed again. Nervously he took the

260

call. One of the angry Turks aimed to grab it from his hand but his friend stopped him.

"What am I to do?" the driver asked in a frightened hushed voice.

"Stop arguing with them. Tell them you have an urgent need to use the toilet, and upon return you will let them inspect the cargo. Inside the toilet you will find a window. Get out through it and cross back to Iran. They won't be able to see you. We wait for you in the car. Don't get caught. God forbid, if you do, take the tablet – remember heaven is waiting for you."

The phone went dead. The driver now saturated in cold sweat, whispered an Allah Akbar, forced an innocent smile, apologized for his silly insistence and meekly asked if he could use the toilet before unloading his cargo for them to inspect. One of the officers threw him a contemptible glance and with his hand pointed to the left of the customhouse. Full of thanks he turned and ran towards the building. The custom officials, their suspicions heightened kept pacing up and down speculating about what they might discover.

Mehdi, turned his head back, found the officers immersed in discussion, did not go to the toilet, instead turned south and disappeared into the night.

Three days later, through the internet people learned that the Turkish officials had informed the government of Iran of their finding in an Iranian cargo truck left at their custom zone, twenty tons of gold bullion and six and half billion dollars in one hundred dollar notes.

The newspaper Omidvar made the incident public knowledge.

Immediately rumour began to circulate that the money was to arm the Hezbollah in Lebanon and a rival prominent Ayatollah had got wind of the plan and had informed the Turkish custom officials.

The Central Bank of Iran denied any knowledge of a

transaction to this value.

The Iranian government denied the whole affair.

A few weeks later, the office of Omidvar was ransacked and the newspaper banned from being published.

The death of this popular paper bitterly disappointed Khanum who had found its content surprisingly illuminating.

This led to a new run of rumours: Omidvar's editor had been fed with false information so that it could be closed down. It seemed to Khanum these days one could not even believe one's own ears.

She was wondering about the rumours when she received a call from Mohsen wanting to know if any of her friends needed a good cook.

"Who are you recommending Agha?"

"Mehdi, a young cousin of mine."

"Why are you not employing him yourself, Famous Restaurateur?"

"Because he wants to work near home."

"Where is his home?"

"Fumen."

"I shall tell my cousin Nasser, he will find him a job at Fumen"

"I do not think it will be a good idea. Never mind, Khanum joon. I shall think of something else."

"Are you keeping a secret from me now?"

Silence.

"He told me he used to work for the government. Now he wants to work for himself, save money and marry one day."

"Government ha?"

"Yes government with capital G."

"Do you trust him?"

"Yes otherwise I wouldn't have involved you in it."

"OK. Send him over; he can live at the domestic

quarters until I think of something for him."

Two days later Mehdi arrived at Golestan in an ancient Samand. Khanum instantly gravitated to the boy's simplicity, naivety and honesty.

A week later Khanum discovered that the Anti Drug Force had wised up to the Afghan's activities and had arrested him and his employer was looking for a caretaker. She found his telephone number through a mutual friend and called him in Isfehan. A few days later, Mehdi moved to his new home where he could take care of the house, cook for his employer while in residence and in his free time, make some extra money driving passengers around in his second hand Samand – all the time thanking the Emmam for having read his letter of request.

Chapter 14

The end

It was five minutes passed eight in the morning when Khanum dialled the Mayor's number praying to catch him before his habitual swift departure from office. She knew, early each morning, he showed up, signed a few of the documents piled up on his desk and then to attend to his private affairs, left under some plausible pretext. Like most of the locals he was involved in real estate, of course without their municipality headaches.

He had just arrived to an unusually crowded room where everyone having heard his footsteps had risen in respect and was in the midst of exchanging greetings when his phone rang. He quickly picked up the receiver, gracefully fitted himself on his chair before saying, "The Mayor at your service."

All eyes became fixed on him.

As he recognized Khanum's voice a broad smile bloomed on his unshaved face and then, after a minute or two, vanished. His jaw nervously twitching, he put the receiver down, released a heavy sigh, threw his hands up uttering, "even at this early hour of the day I am called upon to do a favour."

An elderly man, to ingratiate himself, shook his head in sympathy, wounded his prayer beads around his thick fingers and commented "your Excellency, people have problems and in you have found a saviour."

"Brother, who am I to be a saviour, I am just servant of my constituents." The closed door squeaked open and a janitor appeared tea tray in hand. The Mayor waved him away from his desk towards the applicants. A few dull minutes passed before the janitor left with his empty tray.

The Mayor asked who had arrived first. Heads pointed to a young clean-shaved man in clean jeans and a white Ralph Lauren T-shirt. The man took a large folded document from his lap, stretched over to the Mayor's desk and put it there. "Your Excellency here is the plan for Mr. Ghaderi's building."

"What do you want me to do with this plan?"

"They told me downstairs that you have to sign it before they can issue me the permit."

"I have to sign the permit and not the plan, Agha. You take this to Mr. Molavi who deals with these matters; he will arrange for someone to come and inspect the site and the deed of your land and if they find no discrepancy between the actual dimensions and what is registered on your deed, they will study the plan and based on its size they will tell you how much you have to pay for the permit. Once you settle your account they will issue the permit which then you have to bring here for me to sign." Realising that he had been duped and misled, the frustrated man rose, and picking up his plan asked in a troubled tone, "How long will all take sir."

"If you are lucky a month."

"One month?"

Instead of honouring the question with an answer, the Mayor glanced at his wrist watch and forged a frown. "Gentlemen you have to excuse me as I have to leave now to get to my meeting with the Governor on time."

The men's earlier euphoria turned into bitter disappointment. Sighing their discontent, they exchanged meaningful glances while the Mayor rose, picked up his black leather brief case, straightened up to give his punitive stature extra height and walked to the door – grumbling beneath his breath, about the responsibilities weighing on his shoulders. The thwarted folks, shaking their heads in wonderment followed him out. Some had been waiting for his decision or signature for months.

By the time the Mayor arrived home to interrogate Kobra, Khanum and Nargess were on their way to Teheran passing through the majestic mountains sheltered by a colourful spread of wild flowers and haunted by a plume of milky mist rising to escape the enclosure and find freedom. There was no breeze yet the air was cool and fresh. The Chalous road to Teheran is winding and dangerously narrow but spectacular in beauty. The deep valley between the mountains is steep and deep. It has swallowed so many vehicles that it is called the 'valley of death'. Only just recently the Ministry of Roads and Structure had installed safety barriers on the road rims. But accidents keep occurring.

Depending on the season, vendors selling native produce squat by their make-shift stalls erected where there is a permissible opening. They demand exuberant prices. People coming from Teheran are mostly on vacation, and bargain only for fun. They make an enjoyable day of the four-hour trip by having a meal or refreshment in one of the cafes built along the river that rushes to Karaj Dam and beyond. They take pleasure in stopping by the vendors or filling their containers with pure water from the waterfalls that appear here and there. Plenty camp for the night where there is running water and shade.

The taxi in which Khanum and Nargess were travelling had already stopped four times for the poor girl to throw up. Now her head on Khanum's lap, her eyes closed she was trying to hold off another spasm. In spite of the open windows the car stank of her breath and Khanum herself was beginning to feel nauseated. She gently tapped Firooz on the back and in an apologetic tone asked him to stop the car at the next cafe'. Khanum liked Firooz. He was a cautious driver and a well informed gossiper. But today due to the girl's condition only a few words had been exchanged.

For a mid-week day the road was busy and a green ribbon or handkerchief was either tied around the radio antennas of the passing cars or was being waved out of their windows. Even truck drivers were exhibiting their Green unity. The euphoria about the coming election was extraordinary and infectious. It seemed people had united behind Mousavi and his vociferous wife believing them capable of ameliorating the existing social and economical mêlées. These active, socially conscious young people, highly technical particularly in the area of Information Technology were determined to bring about the desired change by their votes – unarmed, trusting the reliability of the electoral system and the honesty with which the votes were to be counted.

Ahmadi Nejad's focus was on the strict enforcement of Islamic social behaviour with a Vice Police guarding against abuse of that behaviour. So hopefully, with such a conscientious Vice Police force, this time the names that went into the ballet boxes would come out the same – the nation hoped. Iranians have a great sense of humour – after each rigged election they amuse themselves laughing at the way planted potato bulbs produce poppies!

During the day youngsters engaged in friendly political discussions, often praising the merits of their candidates. In the evenings young and old glued to their television sets watching the debates between various candidates which were proving surprisingly informative. The debates were accusative in nature. To the audience's surprise they were revealing the rift within the ruling class. The youth perceived this as a good omen. From 476 men and women who had applied to seek the presidency, the Guardian Council had selected only four individuals – all from within the system – two conservative and two liberal. People had accepted this limitation and hoped at least one of the two liberals would win and endeavour to bring about the desired change – a change for a better life within a democratic system.

So the green waving cars passed while a cleaned up Nargess was enjoying the fresh air, Firooz Khan having a breakfast of fresh Barbari bread, curd whey and honey, and Khanum talking to Mohsen on her mobile.

They were, as usual, to lodge at Niavaran for the duration of their stay in Teheran.

Two hours later the taxi parked by the house and beeped for someone to open the gate.

Jafar, his jet black oiled hair shining under the rays of the relentless sun opened the gate and rushed to open the car door for Khanum when his glance fell on the pale and frail Nargess who was looking at him with lifeless eyes. A strange feeling erupted inside him. He felt blood rush to his cheeks and his heart open up with delight. He had never seen Nargess before. Last time she was in Teheran he was in Fumen. Once Khanum was out of the car he dashed to open the door for the girl. He arrived too late; she was already out breathing deeply the air that was helping to overcome her dizziness.

Khanum paid Firooz Khan his due plus a generous tip. Jafar took out the luggage from the car boot and carried it inside. Khanum picked a long stem of honeysuckle and taking it to her nose guided Nargess in.

Now she had become accustomed to staying in this house without any feelings of remorse. Blissfully bad memories had receded in her mind.

By her request the guest bedroom downstairs was allocated to her. In its wardrobe she kept a few pieces of elegant clothing suitable for Teheran.

Zahra, her serene smile intact, welcomed her with a tight embrace, kissed Nargess and ushered them inside Khanum's room which she had filled with Tea roses from the garden. She knew Khanum would want to rest a bit, take a shower and change before rushing the girl to the obstetrician. So she took Nargess's hand and led her upstairs to the kitchen and asked her to sit down. Nargess felt so miserable that she couldn't even lift her head up to look at the kind lady who was now making her cumin tea believed to be a good remedy for nausea. Zahra poured the tea and placed the large cup in front of the girl. "Azizam drink this, it will settle your stomach."

"Thank you, Zahra Khanum," Nargess murmured. A cumin scented steam was arising from the tea cup. To cool it, the girl took the teaspoon from the saucer and began stirring the concoction. When the steam died down she began sipping at it until only cumin remnants were left at the bottom of the cup. Zahra sat next to her and watching her with sympathetic eyes said, "You must eat the seeds too." The girl threw her a tender glance, lifted her teaspoon again and with it brought out most of the soaked seeds and emptied them in her mouth. Their pungent taste brought a quick frown to her arched eyebrows and then vanished as she swallowed them with relief. Zahra smiled and gently took her arm and whispered, "Now I think you should take a bath." The two rose and walked to the bathroom next to Nargess's allocated bedroom. There, within the privacy of four green tiled walls the girl, immersed herself under a hot shower till a semblance of tranquillity returned to her. She took her time to dress and then smelling of Colgate soap and cheeks red from the water's heat returned to the kitchen where Jafar was talking to Khanum. He threw her a quick glance, felt a delicious sensation and then as though scared to remain under the same roof as her, dashed out to start the car. It was already five in the afternoon and they had to leave almost immediately for the clinic which was in the middle of the town. Jafar, drove his new car, a white Samand out of the gate, got out, opened the right hand door of the back seat for Khanum and the front seat for Nargess.

Caught in the rush hour bumper-to-bumper traffic their drive was slow. This gave Jafar ample time to inform Khanum of all the gossip regarding the election. It seemed the current events were not only transmitted through mass media but also the internet's Facebook and something Khanum had never heard of called Twitter. According to Jafar whose friend worked at the Ministry of the Interior, responsible for running the election, this campaign was the most expensive in the Islamic Republic's history. Funds were spent on, among other things, a mass distribution of computerized propaganda means, such as CDs and DVDs. This had caused a rise in the number of text messages sent by the cell phone subscribers, from 60 million messages a day to some 110 millions. Such was the involvement of people, all hopeful that the most popular candidate would win.

Khanum listened with interest but Nargess did not hear one word. Her mind was bursting with muddled black thoughts. She could not connect to anyone without feeling like dirt. Her only wish was to die so that her polluted body could turn into dust. Even that frightened her – to go to hell was not a step one willingly took – Agha – God curse his soul, had taught them adultery was an unforgiveable sin. So even in hell she would not be rid of him – he would be there to torment her further.

Inside her there was so much anger that she felt she would choke. Slowly she rolled the window down. A whiff of hot polluted air hit her and upset her sensitive stomach. She pulled the window up, swallowed the acid that had rushed into her mouth burning her throat and loosened the tie of her scarf.

"Are you ill, Nargess Khanum?" Jafar, as though aware of her every move, asked in a concerned tone.

"I need a bit of air please."

He turned his head back and asked Khanum if it was alright to turn the air conditioning on – he knew she was never comfortable with cold air in the car. Khanum nodded her consent glad that the boy had taken some interest in the girl. Suddenly a thought tickled her mind and she smiled. Jafar and Nargess! One never knew what lay ahead. Recalling the saying 'each dark night leads to a bright morning' she shook her head in acceptance of the proverb's truth and turned her attention to the traffic officer who was arguing with a motor cyclist riding on the wrong side of the road.

Jafar, to everyone's delight, found a parking space quite close to the doctor's surgery.

Appointment times are never precise at clinics. They are even worse in Iran where life's non-ending problems have made people neurotic or hypochondriac. It took an hour of waiting, few minutes of amicable chat, a thorough physical examination and an immediate urine test to confirm Khanum's worst fear. An abortion was suggested and agreed upon.

Three days later Nargess, pale and pathetic became a virgin again.

She had never been a talkative person but now hardly a word escaped her narrow lips. Without a will to live, she lost her appetite and wouldn't leave her bed. Nothing anyone did brought a spark of life into her eyes that she kept closed. Light seemed to bother her. One day Jafar, worried sick about the girl's condition, suggested perhaps they should call the doctor for advice. Khanum agreed and immediately picked up the phone. Five minutes later he drove to town to collect a new prescription from the doctor's surgery and buy her the prescribed tranquilizer and vitamins. His attentiveness was not missed by either Khanum or Mohsen who liked the girl and felt very sorry for her. Every evening, from his restaurant he brought her filet kebab and forced the girl to eat at least a piece or two. Gradually the effect of tranquilizers mixed with loving care began to manifest itself in her countenance and appetite. She left her bed, tidied her appearance and made herself available for domestic chores – particularly ironing at which she excelled. This was noticed by Jafar whose shirts never suffered from the tiniest fold of a crease. Zahra, having detected the chemistry between the two youngsters, gave her all Jafar's shirts to iron. Delighted, Nargess outperformed her skill. It pleased Zahra to see them so peacefully content together. In spite of their newly acquired wealth neither Mohsen nor she had forgotten their origins. This made them more grateful for their fate and accepting of Nargess.

Khanum to break the monotony of their lives took them to Golestan Palace, told them why she had named her garden Golestan and fed them rice and kebabs at the heart of the Bazaar that was nearby. At home, Jafar, exercising great patience, taught the recuperating patient how to play backgammon which soon became their evening pastime.

Khanum lingered on in Teheran much longer than necessary to give the relationship time to mature.

Mohammad was not told of the abortion. He was under the impression that Nargess was taking care of Khanum's domestic chores while in Teheran – after all they were guests at the Bagheri residence and Khanum needed someone to make her bed and iron her garments. During all the years he had been in the family's employment, he had never set foot in their Teheran residence. So he was never privy to the ownership of the house at Niavaran.

Sometimes Khanum took the family to dinner at one or another of the many restaurants at Darband. The old hotel was shut down. The locality had expanded deep into and across the breast of the mountain. However, the old waterfall was still rushing down to and through the palace now a museum.

Even during summer's hottest days the air at Darband is cool. So it has become a popular venue amongst the wealthy and the restaurants there are usually packed for lunch and dinner. Even tap water has a price at these lucrative establishments.

Under the current focus on sinful behaviour, many youngsters have taken to mountain climbing and Darband has a wiggling path that goes up and up beyond the vision of the vigilantes. There, lovers can forget themselves in the ecstasy of being together – alone – under the blue sky – free from suffocating political contraptions that squeeze the joy out of life.

Darband had remained Khanum's favourite venue. Nowadays she found herself able to visit the places that reminded her of Sassan without remorse. "Life is God's gift, to be valued by being lived well, otherwise God would become angry and turn his face away," a sage had told her years ago – the wise woman was dead now but her words still echoed in her ears.

A day before the election, a rumour began to circulate that the pens at the polls were specially made in China to be rubbed off and that electorates should use their own pens. When Jafar told this to Khanum she whispered a heavy Allah Akabr, wondering at the originality of the ploy – or the rumour.

At the crack of dawn on Friday 12th of June, all over the world, old and young queued at voting posts. The International TV news channels were focused on Iran showing the long lines that stretched for kilometres. Khanum heard a foreign television commentator say: "India had its Ghandi. Iran has its youths."

Noon had not yet arrived when mobiles became busy, reporting voting posts in areas sympathetic to the liberal candidates were being closed under the pretext of running

273

out of ballot papers. Rumours of different natures spread across the country increasing tension in the palpitating heart of the nation.

Eventually the last rays of the sun gave up their struggle and disappeared behind a veil of darkness – the doors of the election posts closed. People excited by the exuberance they had witnessed retired to their nests – sat in front of their TV screens, their mobiles, and telephones within reach – waiting for the outcome of the election.

Those watching BBC saw Mousavi declare success, CNN viewers saw a long line of voters by the consulate in Washington waiting to cast their votes and Iran's news channels showed a victorious Ahmadi Nejad announcing that out of 42.2 million eligible voters 85% had voted and 62.63% of these votes were for him.

Shocked, people poured out of their homes shouting, "Where is my vote?"

Khanum watching poppies bloom out of potato bulbs sat with her mouth wide open wondering how that could have happened.

Angered by the outcome Mohsen, Jafar and Nargess were already out lost in the crowd.

Khanum nervously changed the channels hoping for something that might suggest otherwise – no, Ahmadi Nejad was re-elected and with an unbelievable majority. Well, she thought, the donations of the Shares-of-Justice, the doubling of the salaries and the New Year food hampers had brought him millions of votes and added to those were the votes of his devoted Revolutionary Guards and Basijis. Questions began to manoeuvre in her mind and she wondered perhaps he and his supporters had become frightened by the ferment into which the country had fallen and in order to maintain stability had quickly hijacked the election. Or perhaps the special erasable ball points imported from China had been used to change the names on ballot papers; or the ballot boxes themselves had been swapped during delivery? How otherwise could the greatly supported Green Movement count for naught?

Exhausted by all the 'perhaps' that presented themselves to her boggled mind she felt utterly defeated. She closed her eyes to think clearly; suddenly in her inner vision began to dance the power of a nation united in its demand for basic human and civil rights. An untimely smile appeared on her face. She shrugged off defeatism and opened her eyes with hope.

"Khanum Jahn shall I make you a cup of chamomile tea?" Zahra asked quietly, her Gilaki accent accentuated by disappointment.

Khanum threw her a hazy glance, rose and said, "No Zahra joon, let's go and see if we can get some sleep. Tomorrow will be a very important day and we must not be tired for it."

By the coast things were calmer and to the Mayor's delight Kobra's plan had worked. His clever manoeuvring with the Town's Council had succeeded in having Agha Abolfazl transfer to the boy's secondary school at Babolsar which was a sort of promotion as it was in a larger town. The cleric had welcomed the change and in the meanwhile had asked for a short leave to go to Teheran on an urgent family matter.

The matter was indeed urgent.

Abolfazl was an agent provocateur of the Opposition based in the United States, financed by the CIA. His employer, a CIA operative stationed in Iran ever since the Revolution, was an old friend privy to his life story. They had worked together during the problematic era of Prime Minister Amini decades ago and Abolfazl owed him his life. It was in his house that he had hidden when the revolutionaries were searching for him. Nowadays they did not meet face-to-face. They communicated through mobile phones and street telephones. Two days after the election he was summoned to Teheran to participate in the daily demonstrations.

Abolfazl had his last dinner at the Mayor's house where Kobra's red puffed eyes played on his nerves and made him happy to leave the dreadful town.

In Teheran he reported to their headquarters, an old house in avenue Ferdowsi very near Bank Meli's huge headquarters. There he was instructed through a tape recorded message, to participate in the organized demonstrations fully armed with a revolver, a knife and several razor blades. His orders were to sniff out Basijis who would be mixing with the crowd in plain clothes intending to injure the demonstrators.

He was to shoot at those in helmets, wielding electrical clubs. He was told these people, mostly Lebanese mercenaries would be appearing on their motor bikes from nowhere, to hit or kill the demonstrators and disappear to nowhere again. He was warned that the situation could become ballistic and it was his duty to protect the demonstrators as best he could. He was told that he was not alone in this mission but for security purposes the identities of all those involved had to remain secret.

For the duration of his stay, because of his senior rank he was to lodge at the basement of the building – others were reserved rooms in different three star hotels around the Azadi square.

Tired from the long bus drive in his cumbersome attire of the clergy he longed for a few minutes of rest. When his briefing was terminated he thanked the colleague who ran the tape recorder for him and asked to be taken to his room. The young man threw him a respectful glance and said in perfect English with a broad American accent "please follow me General."

"Were you born in the States son?" "No sir; my mother

276

took the mountain path, soon after my father's execution. I was almost one." "Had my son been allowed to live, he would have been your age now." Abolfazl said in a voice almost trembling with emotion. "I know all about the awful things that happened to your wife and baby – senseless and cruel indeed." The General shook his head and with his hand pointed to the door. The young man said a polite "After you, Sir," and once they were both out of the room he briskly walked to the end of a long and dark corridor and then descended a set of stone steps to a room which must have been a domestic quarter. But it was clean and blissfully cool. "General, this is the best we can offer you sir. On the left of the corridor there is a small toilet and wash basin but unfortunately no shower. Hopefully this will be your last assignment. I have an Egyptian passport and an Emirate's business class ticket to New York via Dubai, for you in my safe."

"Thank you son. Let's see if I outlive this mission."

"Enshallah you will. General, God be with you sir," the young man said shaking Abolfazl's hand.

Left alone, he shed off his aba which he had hated all these years. Before his luck changed he had been a smart man, wearing French designer suits and silk or pure cotton shirts.

He unpacked his small suitcase and took out and kissed the single photograph that he carried with him in his wallet. The picture was of his young wife and baby son who had been taken by the revolutionary guards to Evin prison. Shirin, even under torture, had not revealed his whereabouts. They had sexually violated her before shooting her and his son. When he heard the story from a released female friend, he drove to Darband, ran like a goat to the peak of the mountain and burst out his fury at a God whose soldiers were capable of such atrocities. There, at the top, from where he could visualize the cruelties that were being inflicted by brother on brother something cracked inside his mind. Hate replaced compassion and revenge became the motivating power to continue with his miserable, lonely existence. Straight thinking lost to him, he chose to do to others what had been done to his wife. Along the way down the slope, he saw his CIA friend almost breathless from exertion. They embraced, expressed their pleasure at the coincidence and commenced their slippery descend until fatigue forced them stop at a kiosk for a cup of tea. The American, happy his friend was still alive and devastated to hear what had happened to his family, invited him to stay at his house. The General accepted the offer with a grateful smile. He was living at the house of his ex-driver. They drove there, collected his suitcase and headed for the American's rented home. There he was put in touch with Dr. Nejati one of the most active members of the Opposition operating from California. His involvement gave him a cause to live for – that was almost thirty years back.

He kissed the worn-out picture several times, put it on his heart, talked with his wife and son as though alive, kissed their images again and then lovingly fitted his treasure into his ancient wallet and secured the wallet in his trousers pocket. Filled with sadness, regrets and guilt, his knees gave in and he dropped face down on his bed imploring God for death. The business of living had become too cumbersome and he did not want to leave Iran – he wanted to be buried in his own country near his wife and son – who most probably were in a mass grave at Behesht Zahra. He had no sympathy for the American Government and those they backed – in fact he hated them for he believed it was them who helped Khomeini to topple the shah. Somehow he felt good that Ahmadi Nejad had been re-elected – a thorn in their eyes. "Please God take me to the hell I deserve – it will be better there than here. I cannot go on anymore – please hear me. Please!"

He heard himself cry out loud.

Evening was upon him and he felt famished – he had not eaten for almost ten hours. He rose, tidied up his creased trousers, took several deep breaths, climbed the few steps to the toilet where there was a sink, washed his face, emptied his bladder, washed his hands, combed his peppery hair with a small comb he extracted from his pants' pocket and slowly walked out of the premises to Istanbul Avenue. There, from a kiosk, he bought a sandwich and a bottle of mineral water and then hailed a taxi to drive him to Avenue Fereshteh at Elahieh, then to Niavaran Palace and back. The taxi driver negotiated an excellent fee out of the crazy man and put his foot on the speed pedal until he hit the traffic jam and the drive became a creep. Half an hour later they arrived at the leafy Avenue Fereshteh where his home once was. In its place he found a modern elegant high-rise. Tears welled up in his eyes. He closed them and let memory take him back to when he was a respected citizen and a happy man.

"Agha we are passing the Palace now," he heard the driver say. He opened his eyes and said more to himself than the driver, "I used to visit his Majesty every Thursday afternoon. We rode horses together."

"Agha you better watch what you say. I liked the shah myself but there are many who hate him."

"Yes I know. There is more hate in people than love." He closed his eyes again and found himself standing erect amongst the international luminaries come to celebrate the 2500 years of Iranian monarchy, intent to hear the shah, at the zenith of his power, in all his splendour standing by Cyrus the Great's tomb, pomp and pompous, saying to the greatest Emperor in the history of mankind, "Cyrus, sleep in peace as we are awake to preserve your Empire."

A burst of mad laughter broke the silence in the taxi.

This man has clearly lost his mind, thought the driver before saying, "Agha are you all right?"

"Yes – I am all right. Do you remember the celebrations of the 2500 years of our Monarchy?"

"How can I forget it sir. At the time I owned a hotel in Shiraz and made good money out of the event. Now look at me, a taxi driver!"

"I was a general then and look at me know – a howling dog! And where is our King of Kings, Shadow of God on earth and the defender of the land of the Arians?"

"He is dead and buried somewhere in Egypt – while his nation is still paying for his mistakes." The driver replied in a wistful tone.

The following day people headed towards Azadi Square to ask for their alleged stolen votes and express their support for their legitimate President Mousavi.

Khanum persuaded Zahra to join them in the demonstrations.

Jafar brought the car out and everyone except Mohsen who had to be at his restaurant climbed in.

Half an hour later Jafar parked the car in a street away from the Square but leading to it. Nargess had not only recovered her health but her looks as well. In love, she had become self conscious. Every morning she combed her long straight brown hair habitually parting it on the right side and clipping it away from her forehead with the fancy gold hairpin Khanum had given her, making sure it was visible from under her white linen scarf. In position of only two garments, she wore them alternately and made sure they were spotless. To smell like a lady she dabbed a little of the sample scent Khanum had given her behind her ears and on her wrists.

She could never be considered beautiful with a thin, long and pointed face but she had a pleasing aura about her that was attractive.

Khanum liked her and hoped to become instrumental in the girl's happiness. She had not forgotten Mohsen's promise to allow her to choose a wife for his son. Toying with the idea she could not but acknowledge that Nargess's past could not be accepted by an ordinary Iranian man with ease. Nevertheless, the two youngsters' attachment had not escaped her sharp senses.

Khanum also liked Jafar. She could never forget what he and his father had done for Sassan. In her heart she believed he deserved someone more resourceful than Nargess – a bit classier, more educated and certainly older. However more than anything else she believed in destiny. So she decided to leave the matter in the hands of the Almighty and wish for the best.

The day was as bright as a late spring day could be. Holding hands, the group joined the crowd that was becoming denser and livelier by the minute. On each side of the long road on which the demonstrators were walking stood revolutionary guards, and a hitherto unknown force, men in helmets with electrical clubs, some on foot and some on motor bikes. Their faces were covered behind black helmets and their arms mobile and swift. Suddenly in the midst of the moving crowd Khanum's eyes caught that of Abolfazl's. He went white – she grey. There was something about this man she could not figure out. A part of her was partial to him and the other detested him. There was a sadness hidden behind the shrewd sparkle of his eyes that she had detected even at the Cheleh and again now. His deportment was of a gentleman, his voice soft and his sentences cultured yet he had behaved like a beast. Why? And today he was not in his aba! Why? Her mind became confused by all these new 'whys'. Why – why – why! So many whys without any justifiable reasons! Was she going mad or the world had gone mad? She shivered and felt a sharp pain inside her head. She squeezed Nargess's hand just to feel that she was not alone in the midst of the mystery surrounding them all.

The crowd was flowing peacefully towards Freedom Square, chanting "we want our votes back,", "Where is my vote?", "Ahmadi-e-Pinochet, Iran Chile nemishe!" (Ahmadi you are a Pinochet but Iran is not Chile!) They protested with tight fists waving in the air, green bands worn around raised arms or foreheads. A few demonstrators carried green banners, others placards on which their motto was written. Then suddenly a gun was shot, a scream heard and the hell's inferno broke loose. Khanum holding to Nargess's hand looked to the left from where the gun shot was heard. On the pavement she noticed two club wielders beating a woman and besides him a fight was in progress. Khanum saw Abolfazl, withdraw a knife from his pocket, approach one of the club wielders and push it into the side of his waist. The man, his hand in the air for his next hit, swung around and fell back with the knife deep inside him. Two women helped the beaten girl up; a man lifted her, threw her almost paralyzed body over his shoulder and ran towards an opening. Several people surrounded the injured and one dared to lift his helmet up. The black eyes that gazed at him were filled with imploring plea and pain. The man's skin was too dark to be Iranian.

"You bastard, how can you try to kill your brothers and sisters? How? You traitor," the demonstrator yelled, kicking him on the side. "Allah Akbar," recited the foreigner in a thick Arabic accent.

An old woman spat on his face and cried, "This bastard is not Iranian." Then she knelt down, and began slapping him with as much hatred as she could muster. Two other women collaborating in compassion, managed to stop her and cry for a doctor. Their scream was stifled by a second gunshot and Khanum saw a man bend on his stomach before hitting the ground. Suddenly a handful of

Revolutionary Guards appeared swinging their clubs, aiming to disperse the crowd. In panic Khanum realized they had been separated from Zahra and Jafar. She held tight to Nargess's hand and tried to move away from the crowd when a man lifted the shot victim up. It was Abolfazl.

"Stop Agha. I know this man," Khanum found herself shouting. Bewildered, dragging Nargess behind her, she negotiated her way to the man holding Abolfazl. The Basiji stood still. She reached him. "Is he dead Agha?"

"Yes; he is in hell."

Nargess saw the face and began to scream.

"Control yourself girl. He is already dead," Khanum screamed in a voice thick with exasperation.

The girl trembling hard cupped her mouth with her free hand to stifle her cries. The bystanders took her state as sign of grief for the dead. One kind woman came near and expressed her sympathy, another asked for their relationship. Nargess heard them not. She was elsewhere – in the woods by the creak sprawled on the earth pain expounding in her head. Khanum now holding the girl's arm fibbed without knowing why. "Agha this man is uncle to this young girl. Let us come with you so that you can give us his corpse for a proper burial."

"He is a murdering Mohareb. He just killed my friend with a knife."

"No, he did it in self defence. I saw it all," she shouted her biggest lie.

"He just killed my friend, woman. Go before I take you too."

The Basiji said while adjusting the body on his shoulder. Something fell from the pocket of the dead man. Khanum hastily stepped on it. The Basiji gave her a filthy look and with his side knocked her away from his path. She jolted but kept her foot on her find, and her sad eyes on the

Basiji who headed for the parked windowless truck deemed for such incidences leaving behind a crooked line of blood stain on the road surface.

When the crowd dispersed, Khanum removed her foot from over the object, bent and lifted what turned out to be a worn out Gucci wallet. She opened it. In one of the pockets she found a photo. She pulled it out. It was of a smiling beautiful young woman lovingly holding a baby. She knew the face. It was Shirin, her old room-mate at school in England. Her hand shaking she turned the photo and on its back read "Shirin and Ali at Noshahr, summer of 1978." She grabbed hold of Nargess's freezing hand and pulling her behind herself ran to a quiet corner, let her hand go, squatted on the pavement and began going through the contents of the wallet more carefully. She found nothing except a piece of paper on which a telephone number was written, a laundry receipt and some toomans.

She rose, took the speechless girl's hand and negotiated their way through a labyrinth of empty side streets until she found a taxi. Inside she let go of her control and began to shiver from shock.

"Khanum joon are you sick," the girl asked.

"Hush girl. Let me be," Khanum whispered while resting her head on the back of her seat.

At home she went straight to the telephone in the family room and dialled the number on the paper she was holding while Nargess sought the emptiness of the kitchen as her sanctuary.

An old woman answered the call.

"May I speak to Shirin Khanum."

No response – just heavy breathing.

"Khanum are you there?"

"Yes. Who are you?"

"I am Mrs Zand, an old friend."

The old woman did not recognize the name.

"Do you not know what has happened to my daughter?"

"No Khanum joon, I hope nothing bad has happened to my dear friend – we were at school together in England."

"Are you Lalleh?"

"Yes Khanum, I am Lalleh. Shirin joon may not have told you my married name."

"No, I only know you by your maiden name. Lalleh joon my Shirin is not with us anymore. They came here for her husband, General Azizi and when they did not find him they took her and Ali, her infant son, to Evin. They tortured and raped her and when they could not extract any information from her they shot her and the baby too. "

For an instant the world became totally black and Khanum felt her head about to explode. A few seconds passed in silence then she collected herself and was about to express her condolences when the phone clicked dead. In a way glad, she dropped on the nearest chair her entire body convulsing – her mind perplexed, her soul burning with fury. So this man too had decided to become the sword of justice. The rapes were his means of vengeance! What is happening to us all? She kept whispering while rocking back and forth on the flimsy chair that was cracking under her weight. Suddenly she found herself sprawled over the carpet her legs in the air. She moved to rise when she heard Mohsen's car enter through the gate. A few minutes later he stepped inside and saw her sitting on the sofa massaging her hurt knee. She turned her gloomy face up, stared at him with eyes that reflected deep torment, ignored his greeting and in a lamentable tone said, "Mohsen, Mohsen you wouldn't believe what I have to tell you – you just wouldn't." Uncontrollable tears poured down her grim face leaving behind long traces of black mascara.

At that moment, they heard Zahra's voice calling if anyone was home.

"Khanum and I are here come up – all of you," Mohsen

yelled concerned by what he read in Khanum's countenance.

"Is Nargess up there too?"

"Yes, she is in the kitchen."

Nargess heard Jafar's voice, came out and joined him in the landing. From her puffed eyes he gathered something must have gone wrong but didn't dare to ask what. They entered the TV room and froze to stillness by the deep grief painted on Khanum's smudged face.

"Come in and sit down." Mohsen commanded in a stern low voice.

Deeply concerned, they all sat facing Khanum who was nervously scratching her arms and shaking her head back and forth. She swept her tearful gaze over their faces as though judging their ability to comprehend the depth of the drama she was about to reveal; then she focused her eyes on Zahra. "Do you remember me talking to you about my friend Shirin whose address I was trying to find?"

"Yes Khanum joon."

"I know where she is now – buried in a mass grave at Behesht-e-Zahra."

None could connect Shirin to the recent events.

Khanum wiped her eyes and face with the tissue she was holding, blew her nose, and slowly told them what had happened to her friend, her baby and her husband General Azizi – known to them as Abolfazl.

"Ya Allah!", 'Oh my God' was almost unanimously exclaimed by all except Nargess. Zahra noticed from the corner of her eyes that for a second Jafar stroked Nargess's back and then stopped.

No one knew how to interpret the news – so they sat in silence until Mohsen, the most practical person in the room rose from his seat, sent a loud Allah Akbar, went to the kitchen and returned with a tray on which he had put three glasses of homemade arak with ice and a slice of lemon,

286

two glasses of mineral water and a dish filled with an assortment of nuts.

"I think a drink and some fresh air will do all of us good."

Zahra helped Khanum up and together they descended the steps and went to the garden where they hoped the serenity of nature would sooth their nerves and enable them to make sense out of the current events.

As soon as Blacky heard Mohsen's voice he ran to him and began licking his shoes. Khanum smiled at the dog's change of allegiance.

Mohsen read the meaning in the smile and said, "The kiss is not for me. It is for the smell of kebab on my clothes."

"I am not a jealous type Mohsen."

"I know, but Zahra is!"

"You should be flattered. That shows how much she loves you." Khanum responded without a smile.

Mohsen perceived the depth of her sadness and respecting it remained silent. He carefully placed the tray on the table, lifted one of the arak glasses up and put it in front of Nargess, "Azizam, drink this. I know how upset you are. This will calm your nerves. Please try to put the past behind you. I know it is hard. But try. You are young, pretty and very intelligent. You will make a very good wife for a lucky man."

The girl serenely looked at Mohsen, expressed her thanks and took the glass to her mouth. After the first sip her face grimaced in revulsion. She put the glass down and very politely said, "Mohsen Khan please forgive me if I don't drink this. I do not like the taste and besides, it will not please my father to know I have touched alcohol."

Mohsen threw her an approving glance which made her blush.

Khanum saw the glance, read his mind and smiled. He

returned her smile with a wink.

Here were two adults who in a way, had gone through the same traumatic experience as this girl. And they each knew that they had escaped the abyss into which they could have fallen only because of the love shown to them by those who mattered. Now it was their turn to return the favour to Providence by saving this unfortunate girl.

Khanum borrowed Mohsen's mobile phone; called Golestan and relayed to Mohammad the end his subject of hate had met and asked him to let the Mayor know too. After a loud 'thanks be to God', Mohammad asked Khanum's permission to take a pilgrimage to the shrine of Emmam Reza at Mashhad. Khanum not only granted him the permission but invited him to come and stay with them in Teheran on his way to the holy city.

That evening Mohammad took Shahri and Taghi to the nearby kebab café to celebrate God's justice, and later he passionately satisfied his wife's longing for love.

The next evening when Khanum and Mohsen were enjoying their arak by the pool Mohsen opened his heart to her about his past, his regrets and hopes and then he asked her if she thought Nargess would make a good wife for Jafar. Khanum fell into a contemplative silence. It dawned on her that she might have been selfish in being manipulative. Her silence surprised Mohsen, who thought the question would have made her happy. Khanum threw him a benevolent glance furrowed her brows and said, "Mohsen, your question is putting me in a morally awkward position. I love your son as if he was mine; hence I have high aspirations for him. I also love Nargess but in a different way. She is my charge and somehow I feel responsible for her future. With all the surgeries, a stranger may never find out what has happened to her but Jafar knows everything. She would be the luckiest girl in the world to marry a man like him and enter your family. But are you sure he loves her enough to never use her past against her?"

"If he does I will cut his tongue out."

"Mohsen joon you may never know?"

"Khanum I know Jafar well. He has a heart of gold and the mind of a sage. He is incapable of hurting a fly let alone someone he loves."

"Have you discussed this with Zahra yet?'

"Yes, and she loves the girl. You know, in spite of our prosperity we are still country folks, with country values, Khanum joon."

"Wonderful – your values are far deeper than city folks'. I think I might go to Mashhad with Mohammad myself!" Khanum exclaimed smiling, and then added, "It is good he is arriving this evening. You can ask his permission."

"That was on my mind."

An hour later the door bell rang. Jafar went to open it. Khanum heard Mohammad's voice. Nargess ran down the stairs to his father and, sack in hand, brought him to the veranda. Over a cup of tea Mohammad – astonished at his good luck – accepted the marriage proposal put forward for his permission. No one had bothered to ask Nargess's opinion – but that had not seemed necessary. Love for Jafar glowed from her serene eyes.

Mohsen's mobile began to ring.

Blacky, now fat and lazy, opened his eyes and moved to rise. Khanum gently patted his head. He sniffed her with delight, licked her toe and decided to remain put.

Mohsen swore at the disturbance and took the call.

Eyes fixed on him, Khanum noticed a heavy cloud darken his complexion and a nerve begin to thump on his wrinkled temple. Bad news she thought.

"Okay Agha Afzali, I will be there in thirty minutes."

He clicked the mobile off and fell into a profound

silence. Khanum noticed the welling up of tears in his eyes.

"What is it Mohsen?" She asked concerned.

"They have taken Ahmad's son to Evin. It was Agha Afzali, the prison's warden – my old friend."

Khanum remembered Ahmad well and also Afzali who had allowed her to see Sassan before his execution.

"Why?"

"He was caught setting fire to a Basiji office."

"God help him." Khanum exclaimed devastated.

At Evin, Afzali aged, pale and remorseful guided Mohsen to the prison's infirmary over-crowded by wounded demonstrators, in need of urgent medical attention.

The door of the infirmary was wide open and the wail and cry of those in pain loud and distressing. It seemed as though the bodies were sown together – such was the state of the hall.

"Akbar Bagheri." Afzali cried out.

Mohsen noticed a crouched body stir slightly. He carefully negotiated his way to it.

"Akbar, it is me, Mohsen."

A head soggy with blood tried to lift itself without success. Mohsen squatted down, lifted the head up and saw the boy's swollen purple face; his lower lip slit open, blood oozing out from in between clots – his eyes beseeching help. Mohsen tucked his arms in between his limp ones, lifted him up, dropped him over his broad shoulder and negotiated his way back to Afzali. They had not stepped out of the hall when the width of a rifle barred Mohsen's way.

"Where are you taking this Mohareb?' a man in plain clothes asked.

Afzali answered, "Your Excellency he is my nephew and we are taking him to hospital."

"I know who you are but that won't make any difference. This man stays here and will be treated like the rest of the bastards."

"Agha please forgive him! We will make sure he will never again be diverted from the right path," Mohsen pleaded almost in tears.

"Go and leave him where you found him or else you will be sorry for your disobedience."

Afzali begged again and this time his answer was a spat on the face.

An ogre standing nearby grabbed Akbar's torso from Mohsen's folds and like a piece of garbage dropped him on the floor. Akbar landed on a dying or an already dead individual with a thump. Mohsen cried out his protest attacking the ogre with all his might. Two men grabbed his arms; almost lifted him up and threw him out of the clinic. Afzali, caught him in time, steadied him on his legs and then walked him to his car.

"I do not know who these people are. They cannot be Iranians!" Afzali murmured while opening the door for his friend.

Devastated, Mohsen drove home like a drunken lunatic. His tale astonished all. No one could find the right words to console the man who was crying like a baby.

Later, that same night Afzali telephoned again; this time with the news that many at the infirmary had died including Akbar and their corpses had been taken to Behesht-e-Zahra cemetery – for burial in a mass grave early in the morning.

Mohsen, his voice as though coming from the bottom of an abyss asked if he knew anyone at the cemetery who could let them in during the night. Afzali's affirmative answer stopped the throbbing of his neck's veins. He thanked his friend, banged the receiver down and yelled for Jafar who was talking to Mohammad in the driveway. Surprised, the two stopped their conversation, turned their heads to Mohsen who seemed deeply distressed. As they hurried to the veranda they heard him telling Khanum he had to go to Behesht-e-Zahra to collect Akbar's body before day break. Her mouth open and her eyes wet she kept nodding her head back and forth – thinking of another corpse!

Jafar, in a trembling voice told Mohammad who Akbar was. Then he walked to his father and hugged him tight. Mohsen kissed his forehead and hastily pushed him away. "We have to speed to the cemetery right now."

Behesht-e-Zahra is about eighty kilometres from Teheran, near Emmam Khomeini airport. It is a very clean, well managed cemetery with tree lined wide avenues and colourful flower beds. On one side are private family mausoleums and on the other sides are various marked zones for outdoor graves. There are several unmarked mass graves the existence of which is known only to the authorities. However Zone X was recently prepared to swallow the Moharebs.

At nights the gate of the cemetery is locked and guarded. However Afzali's cousin was a night guard and had agreed to let them in.

Once inside Jafar parked the car in the darkest spot. The three jumped out, quickly shook hands with Agha Reza who without losing time started walking ahead.

Above, the clear sky was illuminated by a full moon.

They reached a large open grave lit by moon shafts. The men stared down at a site that made the bravest of them tremble with horror. Mohsen, collected himself, whispered a prayer and jumped down, furiously lifting several corpses until he found Akbar. He picked him up, embraced him tight and kissed his cold bruised forehead several times before lifting him up for others to pull up.

Eighteen hours later, Akbar was buried in a cemetery in Karadj.

The arms of the government swiftly made sure that all the elements of meddlesome foreigners were expelled from Iran. Thus was terminated the international coverage of the events. But the IT experts kept transmitting their reports of occurrences. The demonstrations continued. The schism had so widened that even Mohsen and Mohammad participated to voice their objections, this time, in front of the parliament, where the crowd went mad and set fire to cars and newspaper kiosks. Shots were heard. Neda an innocent passerby fell. Her fall was captured by a lens and transmitted across an astonished world. Government increased its efforts to re-establish calm. Jails became full and within weeks almost a thousand souls went missing. One amongst them was Jafar. He was spotted using his mobile to take photos of someone beating up a young pregnant woman when a baton fell on his arm sending the mobile flying in the air and breaking his bones. Another stroke of the baton sent him to the ground from where he was dragged away and dumped into a windowless van containing twenty other bruised and beaten individuals – male and female. They were driven to a building ninety minutes away – an unofficial detention centre known as Kahrizak. There the new arrivals were first segregated and then the males were ordered to strip to their underwear and stand in lines. Two militias began rubbing their genital areas with their batons and calling them 'scum' and exclaiming: "Ah, yes, the balls of the foot soldiers of the heretic Mousavi". Then they began to laugh. "In no time you would be confessing to trying to overthrow the divine regime with or without these balls."

Jafar and others were trembling with fear. Some were crying and one threw up.

Jafar, in company of five others was thrown into a cell too small for them to sit in. So they stood up all night, without food, half naked, till dawn when the youngest, just nineteen was taken out. Later they heard him howl like an injured dog. Then the cry died down. A profound silence dawned. Half an hour later two guards grabbed Jafar's arms, dragged him to a room where the screaming boy, completely naked, was unconscious crumpled on a mat, his face in a pile of vomit with blood leaking from his rectum. A man named Asghar, pushed Jafar forward.

"Take a good look. That will happen to you if you resist, you faggot lover of foreigners."

Jafar deranged with fury gathered all the mucus in his mouth and spat on the face of the vernacular guard. The man slapped him on the face, kicked him on his testicles and threw him down on his back. The other guard put his foot on the curve of his back to hold him down while Asghar unzipped his trousers, took out his genital and urinated on him saying, "This will teach you not to dissent. You scum, realize that we have been sent to re-educate you, you spoilt Western piece of shit. We have permission to do, to such of you, what pleases us for you are a Mohareb."

Then he pulled Jafar's underpants down and pushed his baton down his rectum. A violent scream shook the room.

Two hours passed. Six other detains were beaten or raped by other guards. Jafar opened his eyes and moaned. This time three men attacked him until the bleeding from his wounds became so severe that he was dragged to a small room and left in the care of a male nurse. When he regained consciousness he found himself in a slightly bigger room. The drawn faces of those staring at him expressed pain and shame. No one uttered a word. They either looked through each other or at the peeling paint of the ceiling just wondering at the grotesqueness of it all.

Time crept away in utmost agony. Then one morning Jafar blindfolded was taken to meet the commander in a room above his cell. There his eye band was removed and he saw a stocky bearded man, full of his own importance extinguishing the butt of his Winston cigarette in a filled ashtray.

"Leave us now." He commanded in a Turkish accent.

The two guards left the room and closed the door behind them.

"Sit down Bagheri." He ordered without raising his eyes from the document laid open in his view.

"Jafar lurched forward and collapsed on the grey metal chair that faced the commander. The cold metal below him felt good.

The commander raised his head and with curious eyes that were crossed scrutinised the breathing corps whose head had tilted to one side. His sharp eyes detected the pain and the shame the man was feeling. Satisfied that the torture had been effective, he slowly pushed the open document towards him and in a patronizing tone said, "Son, I hope the experiences of the past few days have put some sense into your muddled head. Sign this document, repent and go out to serve your country."

Jafar straightened his head with difficulty then very slowly stretched it over the table and read the content of the document which was a confession to following traitors who are servants of the foreign powers. He lifted up his head, gave the commander a contemptuous glare and pushed the document away. He fixed his eyes on the commander's which were glowing with triumph and asked if he knew what his guards were doing to the detainees. The man, his face crinkled in thought, scratched his bold head, threw him a threatening glance and said, "Nothing illegal is taking place here. Everything that has happened to you and the others has been sanctioned by our superior in his battle against Moharebs. Now sign you scum."

Jafar leaned back on his chair, gave the man another contemptuous look and said, "First, you and your superior are scum. You are representatives of Satan on earth and not our Leader who is a man of God and a man of God will never sanction these acts. I will never believe that he has given your superior his sanction to sin so violently. No man of God, knowingly, would allow such atrocities even against enemies of Islam, let alone Moslem brothers." The huge man his face red with rage, stretched over the narrow table and punched Jafar on the mouth breaking his front tooth.

Jafar covered his bleeding mouth with his trembling hand and threw him a long disdainful look that conveyed all the hate in his heart.

Back in the cell he was subjected to further torture until his mental resistance gave way and he succumbed to signing the document.

At Niavaran, Zahra, ill in bed, was being nursed and consoled by a devastated Khanum and a totally mute Nargess. The girl had become a walking robot again.

Mohammad and Mohsen were out every day in search of Jafar. He had been lost to them for 18 days. Then one late morning Mohsen's mobile, laying on the dashboard began shaking and shrieking. He asked Mohammad to take the call. At first Mohammad couldn't clearly hear Jafar's inaudible voice. And then his face lit up, he turned to Mohsen and offering him the mobile cried loudly, "It is Jafar Khan, Jafar Khan, Aziz." Mohsen grabbed the mobile, swung the steering wheel towards the edge of the road where he put his foot on the brake so abruptly that both men almost collided with the front window.

At Kahrizak, they were taken to the commander's office where they were told of the sum required to bail Jafar out. It was huge. Mohsen called Khanum. One hour later she arrived with the deed of Mohsen's house and ten million toomans of her own money in cash.

At home they surprised Zahra out of her sick bed. The joy of finding Jafar alive was beyond description even though his enchanting smile had vanished together with his vivacious spirit and energy. His face resembled a concentration-camp inmate – so pale and haggard it seemed.

He too had become a broken urn.

Khanum, together with Mohsen, took him to a psychologist, a doctor and a dental surgeon. After several sessions the psychologist confirmed that he was suffering from severe depression with extreme feelings of self-hatred resulting from a sense that he will never be clean again. The doctor's physical examinations revealed severe anal damage and the dentist implanted a new front tooth.

The news of the atrocities performed at Kahrizak was revealed to the world and reached the Leader's ears and together with the President, they ordered its closure, transferred some of the inmates to Evin for questioning and punished those responsible for the rapes.

Khanum invited the whole family to stay at Golestan where they would be away from the hell in which they had been burning. Zahra asked one of her trusted friends to house-sit for them while away. Khanum called Firooz Khan to come and pick them up and Mohammad and Mohsen went shopping for the provisions the best of which could only be procured in Teheran.

Two days later they arrived at Golestan where the garden was as lush as ever, the calm sea aquamarine and Shahri floating in the air with happiness. She had given up the hope of Nargess ever marrying. Now she was engaged to marry a handsome man from above their station in life! What luck? To keep the evil eyes away she kept burning wild rue and whispering prayers. Often when she had been at the end of her wits Khanum had told her never lose sight of hope in a world that has a thousand faces. She had never believed her. What an idiot she had been – to lose hope – hope that is the light of life and the force behind survival.

Gradually peace, tranquility and warmth of love manifested their effects on Jafar – he began to eat and play backgammon with Nargess who now had become a champion but purposely lost to make him feel good.

One early morning when Khanum and Mohsen were mountain climbing at Kelardasht, where the air is pure and the ascend challenging, Khanum suggested that in order to help Jafar come out of his misery and regain his self-respect they should each tell him their secrets and how they had managed to come out of their dark abyss. Mohsen immediately saw the sense in her suggestion and admired her sagacity. For a woman to have the courage to confess to such happening in her life was indeed remarkable. But Khanum was a very special person with a special attitude towards people and life.

He gave her a long adoring glance and said, "thank you, Khanum joon for this brilliant idea. I will tell him my story and what my father did for me. That should shake him out of his dejection. I think one story will be enough."

"Whatever you think is best Mohsen. I just want to see him happy again. Enshallah we see light return to his lovely black eyes." Khanum wished and then raced Mohsen up the path and puffing heavily won. They had a light lunch on the way down and arrived home looking forward to a dip in the cold pool for Khanum and the sea for Mohsen.

In the afternoon, refreshed from her siesta, Khanum found Mohsen and Jafar sitting in the veranda, chatting about Zahra's worries regarding the wedding at Niavaran. Asking for her, she was told she is in the domestic quarters dealing with the dress-maker who is fitting Nargess's wedding gown.

Shahri, smiling as though owning the world arrived with her tea tray which she put on the table and quickly vanished. Now she wore the black pants Khanum had brought her from Teheran and a white shirt over which she had a nice pink apron. Her scarf was tied in a knot below her chin like Zahra Khanum's and not the Northern peasants!

"I do not think of any one happier than Shahri in this wide world," Khanum remarked lifting her cup.

Both men nodded their acknowledgement.

Ever since their retreat from Teheran, no one talked politics. The subject had become taboo. Cumulatively they had left the wellbeing of Iran in the hands of God. To preserve their sanity, they had looked at what had happened in Iraq and Afghanistan as the result of foreign invasions and decided that their beloved Iran was still an intact sovereign nation – that was all that mattered – for now. They also knew no dictatorship could last forever and any regime to survive had to liberalize – so they lived with hope

Mohsen took a sip of his tea, found it too hot, put the cup down, turned to Jafar, gave him an affectionate glance and said "son, once you told me I had never talked to you about my youth, now I want to tell you a bit about myself – in front of Khanum who knows me even better than your mother does!"

Jafar, taken by surprise, looked deep into his father's eyes caught a strange glimmer that penetrated his heart. Meekly he smiled and light heartedly asked, "What is there to know Baba?"

"Plenty Jafar khan. Plenty!" Khanum exclaimed with a meaningful nod that was a signal for him to keep quiet and listen."

In complete control of his nerves, Mohsen narrated the story of his youth, his mistakes and the cause of his father's death. Jafar, his body rigid as a rock, his mouth half open listened unable to believe a word. Only an occasional quiver of his lower lip and a nervous tick of his right eye lid exposed the depth of his astonishment.

By the time Mohsen finished Jafar was in tears – good tears – tears expressing gratitude for a father's unconditional love – a love which had compelled him to reveal such a dark secret, so that his son could feel less haunted, less dejected and less ashamed. Mohsen rose went to his rising son, held him tight, kissed his hair that was shiny even without the oil, and told him how proud he was of him and that nothing on earth could take that pride and love away. Jafar took his father's hand and kissed it several times. Then he lifted his face and met his father's eyes with a smile – the smile of a man who was willing to allow the light of hope penetrate into the dark recesses of his clouded mind.

Khanum watched them with delight.

"Jafar, look at that mulberry tree over there, by the wall." Khanum pointed to the tree Mohammad had trimmed umbrella like.

"Is that really a mulberry tree?" Jafar asked, fascinated.

"Yes that truly is a mulberry tree – an artistic topiary achieved by Mohammad's cunning cutting. Son, there is a story to tell about such a tree too."

"Khanum joon, one story a day is enough." Mohsen interrupted and then turning to his son said, "Shall we go and see what the dress-maker has done for your bride?"

Smiling with happiness, Jafar took his father's arm and together they descended the steps and turned towards the domestic quarters.

Remaining seated Khanum, her face shining with an unprecedented joy turned her eyes to the mulberry tree and to her surprise felt nothing – it seemed to her just a tree like all other trees – void of any significance.

She heard a car drive down the gravel path. She knew it was Ali come with the recent gossip and the bills to account for. Then a second car sounded its entrance. She knew that belonged to Mehdi come to offer his assistance and play badminton with them. She loved badminton. It kept her fit.

She turned her eyes towards the blue sky and whispered, "Khodaya Shokret. Thank you God."

A bird flapping its tiny wings flew over the fence, made couple of circles around the mulberry tree, found a notch amongst its neat and tight branches, settled in and began singing melodiously.

This is odd, Khanum thought. She adjusted her spectacles so that she could see well. Indeed, it was a nightingale – a rarity in the vicinity, yet here it was nesting within the branches of her mulberry tree singing for her.

She smiled remembering Sassan had told her once, if he had a choice, he would want to reincarnate as a nightingale – perhaps it was him come to be with her again? What joy!